PRAISE FOR ELLEN BYERRUM'S CRIME OF FASHION MYSTERIES

"Devilishly funny. Lacey is intelligent, insightful and spunky... thoroughly likable." (*The Sun*, Bremerton, WA)

"Laced with wicked wit." (*SouthCoastToday.com*)

"Fun and witty... with a great female sleuth." (*Fresh Fiction*)

"A load of stylish fun." (*Scripps Howard News Service*)

"Always well-written, entertaining, and stylish." (*More Than a Review*)

"Skewers Washington with style." (Agatha Award-winner Elaine Viets)

Killer Hair (also a movie)

"Girlfriends you'd love to have, romance you can't resist, and Beltway-insider insights you've got to read. Adds a crazy twist to the concept of capital murder." (Agatha Award-winner Sarah Strohmeyer)

Designer Knockoff

"Clever wordplay, snappy patter, and intriguing clues make this politics-meets-high-fashion whodunit a cut above the ordinary." (*Romantic Times*)

"A very talented writer with an offbeat sense of humor." (*The Best Reviews*)

Hostile Makeover (also a movie)

"Byerrum pulls another superlative Crime of Fashion out of her vintage cloche." (*Chick Lit Books*)

"As smooth as fine-grade cashmere." (*Publishers Weekly*)

"Totally delightful... a fun and witty read." (*Fresh Fiction*)

Raiders of the Lost Corset

"I love this series. Lacey is such a wonderful character... The plot has many twists and turns to keep you turning the pages to discover the truth. I highly recommend this book and series." (*Spinetingler Magazine*)

"Wow. I loved it! I could not put it down! I loved everything about the book, from the characters to the plot to the fast-paced and witty writing." (*Roundtable Reviews*)

Grave Apparel

"A truly intriguing mystery." (*Armchair Reader*)

"A likeable, sassy, and savvy heroine, and the Washington, D.C., setting is a plus." (*The Romance Readers Connection*)

Armed and Glamorous

"Whether readers are fashion divas or hopelessly fashion-challenged, there's a lot to like about being *Armed and Glamorous*." (*BookPleasures.com*)

Shot Through Velvet

"First-rate... a serious look at the decline of the U.S. textile and newspaper industries provides much food for thought." (*Publishers Weekly*, starred review)

"Great fun, with lots of interesting tidbits about the history of the U.S. fashion industry." (*Suspense Magazine*)

Death on Heels

"Terrific! A fabulous Crime of Fashion Mystery." (*Genre Go Round Reviews*)

"I loved the touch that Lacey was a reporter trying to track down a murderer, but could always be counted on for her fashion-forward thinking as well. If you haven't yet picked up a Lacey Smithsonian novel, I suggest you do!" (*Chick Lit+*)

"Lacey is a character that I instantly fell in love with." (*Turning the Pages*)

Veiled Revenge

"An intriguing plot, fun but never too insane characters, and a likable and admirable heroine all combine to create a charming and well-crafted mystery." (*Kings River Life Magazine*)

"Like fine wine that gets better with age, *Veiled Revenge* is the best book yet in this fabulous series." (*Dru's Book Musings*)

Lethal Black Dress

"Only a fashion reporter with a nose for vintage dresses could sniff out the clues in this brilliantly conceived murder mystery." (Nancy J. Cohen, author of the Bad Hair Day mysteries)

PRAISE FOR ELLEN BYERRUM'S
THE WOMAN IN THE DOLLHOUSE

"An ingeniously crafted psychological thriller that bewitches on page one and continues to mesmerize until its shocking conclusion... we can't imagine a better read. Byerrum has deftly structured a compelling narrative that never lets go. You won't either, by the way. This is one book you're practically guaranteed to finish in record time." (*Best Thrillers.com*)

"Reminiscent of the best of gothic suspense fiction, readers will be thoroughly entertained by Tennyson. Her strong will and even sharper wit ensure that readers will be cheering for Tennyson to break free and discover the truth. That the book starts with such a vulnerable beginning only makes the crafty conclusion all the more satisfying." (*Kings River Life Magazine*)

"Byerrum is a storytelling virtuoso! An expertly crafted, terrifying, tour de force psychological thriller that harkens back to the bloodcurdling, spine-tingling era of spellbinding Gothic novels, with Byerrum's genius. The setup is sharply executed, irresistibly designed, and the atmosphere eerily ominous. Twists are brilliantly layered and liberally piled on. The ending doesn't waver an ounce as it reaches its pulse-pounding climax... A theatrical chef-d'oeuvre... Byerrum's literary masterpiece." (*Examiner.com*)

The MASQUE of the RED DRESS

A CRIME OF FASHION MYSTERY

ELLEN BYERRUM

Lethal Black Dress Press

Published by Lethal Black Dress Press

ONE

"*G*ET YOUR TINY white hands off my red dress, BEE-YATCH!"

"It's NOT yours! It's not for sale!"

"It is TOO mine! I just bought it!"

At first, Lacey couldn't see what the two furious women were fighting over so fiercely. Then suddenly a spray of dark red burst over their hands and arms in the noonday sun. Each was trying to pull some sort of scarlet object away from the other, and neither was letting go. It was turning into a tug of war.

The crowd around them parted in apprehension, and Lacey got a glimpse of the prize. It was a dress, but what a dress. Rivers of blood-red ribbon, sequins, and beads flowed over the layers of crimson tulle, ruby taffeta, and scarlet silk and satin that flirted together in the long-trained skirt. As the women tussled over it, the garment unfolded into a full-length gown. The sleeves were sheer slashes of scarlet, and the heavily beaded bodice caught the light and glinted in the sunshine. Stiff with fabric, the thing could almost stand on its own, the mass of material resembling a blood-soaked figure.

This bloody spectacle didn't stop the two women struggling for this prize, a multitiered theatrical costume in a riot of red hues, supposedly worn by the actress who played the character of Death in a legendary musical production of *The Masque of the Red Death*.

Fashion reporter Lacey Smithsonian decided this garment was entirely suitable for death. *I hope it doesn't become an accessory to murder,* she thought.

This tug-of-war was taking place at the annual multi-theatre yard sale in Washington, D.C., where the many theatres of the Nation's Capital disposed of their leftover costumes, props, set pieces, posters, and miscellaneous theatre memorabilia. The crowd was full of theatre people, actors, designers, techies, set builders, costume collectors, and everyday theatre fans.

Drama and farce were bound to happen, but mostly in the attire of the motley-dressed crowd. Lacey had dropped by this Saturday in midsummer in search of random inspiration for her fashion column, but she hadn't expected *this* much drama.

This particular claret-colored gown of contention was caught between Lacey's fellow *Eye Street Observer* reporter LaToya Crawford and her smaller-yet-pugnacious opponent, a woman Lacey didn't know. The crimson garment threatened to wind up in bloodshed or layers of torn tulle, or both. Lacey considered the prize. She couldn't blame the contenders. This costume begged to be touched. *Now, that is the power of a spectacular dress.*

Lacey wasn't sure whether to pull out her reporter's notebook or stand ready to help LaToya, her compatriot at the paper. Or to try to separate the two, but she couldn't see a way to get between them and survive. And was the red dress strong enough?

LaToya seemed to be winning, inch by inch. The other woman was no match for LaToya, who at the moment resembled nothing so much as a fierce Amazonian warrior, tall, beautiful, and black. Her pale frizzy-haired blonde adversary was shorter by a good five inches and pudgily out of shape. Yet she held on, red-faced and sweating.

"They sold it to *me*," LaToya said through gritted teeth. "It's *mine*."

"It was a mistake!" The other woman huffed and puffed and pulled. "We'd never sell this dress! It wasn't supposed to be on that sale rack. You'll be sorry!"

Empty threats, Lacey thought. *Theatre people.*

"You'll be on that rack yourself if you don't let go of MY DRESS!" LaToya dug in her heels for one last hard yank, and the prize was hers. She emerged victorious, red gown in hand, shaking off her conquered rival. The smaller woman backed away defeated, grumbling under her breath, rubbing her chafed hands.

The stunning ruby ball gown at the center of the struggle was connected to a vague theatre world rumor. Lacey tried to remember: something about the leading lady supposedly dying. During the show? After the first performance? Wearing the red dress? Or was it a different show? She couldn't recall the details. *Anyway, that wasn't the dress's fault, was it?*

LaToya surprised Lacey, but not by fighting over the dress. LaToya was a determined reporter, capable of relentlessly running down any news source for a hot story. However, LaToya Crawford was the last person who would go to the mat over clothes that had been *worn by someone else*. She had told Lacey as much, just before the red garment reached out and mesmerized her.

Love happened that way, unexpectedly yet passionately. The fact that this was a dress and not a man didn't matter. LaToya had fallen and fallen hard. She was in love with the red dress. And now she had fought for it and won.

You just never know about love, Lacey thought.

ः

This Saturday morning in June had started off calmly enough. The annual multi-theatre "yard sale" of leftovers from the city's smaller playhouses was a treasure trove of oddities and eye candy, with rows of tables full of props, racks of costumes, piles of furniture and entire stage sets. There were custom-made props, such as giant kitchen spoons and forks from someone's avant-garde production of *Lysistrata*, a cut-in-half dining room table from a comedy of manners, and dilapidated thrones from various historical epics. Like a jam-packed antique store, it was hard to know where to look first.

Most in the District, even the tourists, knew about the big theatres, the Kennedy Center, the National, the Warner, Arena Stage, and Ford's, where President Lincoln was shot. However, there were many other lesser-known theatres in the Capital City, dozens of smaller playhouses and theatre troupes with a variety of approaches, from edgy political drama and new minority playwrights to improv and sketch comedy, from children's theatre to big musicals and intimate cabaret shows.

More than one theatre specialized in Shakespeare, another in George Bernard Shaw, and another in bilingual shows in Spanish and English. They offered new works and novel takes on classics, showcases for struggling actors, and even venues for emerging playwrights. Every year or two some of them cooperated on this yard sale, held in a parking lot just off Fourteenth Street Northwest, a central location for many of the theatres.

Lacey had come not to buy, but to *eye*, the costumes, the shoes, the one-of-a-kind hats and gowns and outfits made for imaginary characters and real-life actors. She wondered whether anything there could really be suitable for a modern woman's closet, or just for parties and events, such as masques and balls.

Lacey had a headline or two in mind for her "Crimes of Fashion" beat: EMPTYING THE COSTUME SHOP. SELLING A WORLD OF DREAMS. There might even be a "Fashion *BITE*" in it: ACTORS WILL WEAR ANYTHING! On stage, they certainly would. Or nothing at all, if the part or the director called for it. Lacey had seen enough of those sans-clothing shows on D.C. stages. She preferred shows with wonderful costumes to shows full of shapeless pasty naked bodies, no matter how dedicated to their art.

This June morning she feasted her eyes on glorious stage stuff. Bloody heads from Shakespearean productions nestled with angel wings and skulls, stage makeup, false noses and fake beards and wigs. Prop swords battled with magic wands.

All because Tamsin Kerr, *The Eye*'s theatre critic, had tipped Lacey off to the sale of what she called "woebegone fripperies," theatrical detritus no longer needed or filling up cramped storage spaces. This style scribe adored woebegone fripperies.

At last Tamsin herself arrived on the scene, yawning and hefting a large cup of coffee.

"Where did you get your brew?" Lacey inquired.

"Over by the swords and sorcerers. Somebody was smart enough to set up a snack bar."

"Maybe I'll get some coffee."

"Only if you like it dreadful. I do." Tamsin tilted her cup and swigged.

Tamsin might be sleepy at this early hour, not quite noon, but she was still intimidating. Actors who caught sight of her backed away and whispered to their friends about her latest reviews. The theatrical crowd parted for Tamsin, whose reputation exceeded even her height, which was nearly six feet.

"I can think of better things to do on a Saturday morning, Smithsonian," she said.

"Most Saturdays, yes," Lacey agreed. "But I wouldn't miss this. Thanks for the tip."

"There might even be the slightest chance of a story in it for me, but I doubt it. Nevertheless, Hansen will be toting a camera or two." Tamsin squinted at a gaudy display of Elizabethan caps and moved on, yawning. She enjoyed the occasional "transformative production spun from the minds of geniuses," she told Lacey, but there were also years of watching bad plays, puzzling direction, and egregious acting. Not to mention the playwrights. "Dear God, the playwrights."

Tamsin defied the June heat in black jeans and a severe long-sleeved black shirt. This theatre critic would never be seen in something as frivolous as cutoffs and a tank top. Tamsin's dark cloud of curls floated around her shoulders. Her blue eyes were discerning. Lacey admired Tamsin's dedication to her own interior style critic, but she could be an enigma.

She wasn't a regular fixture in the newsroom. Being on the theatre beat made Tamsin a bit of an outsider, and her late deadline for reviews meant she filed her stories after most of the staff went home. Actors and directors feared her. Reporters didn't understand her, and they assumed she had a "soft beat." Hard news reporters tended to be snobs about their own political, finance, and international news beats. For the most part, Tamsin ignored the other reporters as well, considering them lesser beings. Lacey was an exception.

"It's not easy being different," Tamsin once said to Lacey. "Yet when you get down to it, it's one of the few things that matter. The anonymous are not remembered."

Lacey's position at the newspaper rested somewhere between the two worlds. Fashion reporting was considered frivolous, and yet newsworthy mysteries and murders seemed to follow Lacey's beat like a lonely puppy. Reporters dismissed her daily work, but they were jealous of her scoops.

Like Tamsin, she had her own reputation to live up to, as the paper's fashion reporter, the "style queen." She could never simply toss on a pair of old shorts and a T-shirt and just *go*.

When the weather turned hot and humid in Washington, it was difficult to dress well. Linen was a favorite in D.C., but in the steamy heat linens collapsed into a puddle of wrinkles. Lacey favored vintage clothing from the 1940s, which suited her petite and curvy figure. Summer clothes from the period were rare and fragile, and she was reluctant to wear those cherished items except for special occasions.

Instead, she chose newer clothes with a strong retro vibe. Today, she settled for a crisp apple green cotton skirt and a patterned sleeveless blouse. A brimmed straw hat shaded her pale skin and blue-green eyes and protected the fresh blond highlights in her long honey-brown hair. For unexpected purchases she carried a tote, which contained a partially frozen bottle of water. It would eventually melt, but it would stay cold.

Todd "Long Lens" Hansen, *The Eye*'s head staff photographer, caught up with them, ready to work, with cameras and camera bags slung over his shoulders. The laid-back, sandy-haired, long-legged lensman wore his usual jeans and blue work shirt. He made his way to Lacey's side.

"Hey, Hansen."

"Hey, Lacey! I'm here at Tamsin's beck and call, but I'm here if you need me. What kind of pictures do you want?"

"Colorful, newsworthy, and anything that isn't me." There were too many old photos of Lacey in embarrassing situations in Hansen's files. "I do not want to be humiliated today."

"Ah, don't be a poor sport. We've gotten some great photos together." He grinned and lifted his camera. "Me with my zoom lens and you with your—

She blocked the lens with her hand. "I get it. Have a good time and remember I'm not the focus. There are lots of cool costumes and props to photograph. Like that tinfoil spaceship over there."

"No killers today?"

"Killers aren't everywhere," Lacey said.

"They *are* everywhere," Tamsin interjected. Her caffeine was kicking in. "You just don't know who they are. Yet. They are like spies. And you, Smithsonian, have known more than most people."

"Spies or killers? And I do not."

"Both. And the evidence is empirical."

Killers? Lacey had met a few, over the past year or two. As for spies, they were everywhere in the District of Columbia. The Spy Museum claimed that every sixth person in the city was working for one government or another. And since the contentious elections, with Russian interference tilting the electoral scales, people were tense. Distrustful. The media was under fire by the administration and vice versa, and it was a daily struggle to remain sane.

There were days when Lacey's fashion beat felt to her like a sanctuary.

"Like that crazy Russian friend of yours," Tamsin continued.

"Kepelov?" Lacey uncapped her semi-frozen water bottle. "You never know. He's ex-KGB or FSB or something, but he wears cowboy getups and wants to settle down on a ranch in Texas. He's totally pro-USA. I think."

"So, any spies here at the props and costume sale?" Hansen raised his camera hopefully.

"Refreshing their disguises among the costume shops, no doubt," Tamsin cracked.

"Ah, the critic speaks," he said.

"And must be obeyed."

"Spies in disguise would be a great story," Lacey said. "But how would we know?"

"Your department, not mine," Tamsin said.

"How about you, Tamsin? What are you looking for, picture-wise?" Hansen asked.

"Follow your muse," she said grandly.

"Will do. Suggestions, anyone?"

"I saw some stuff from an *Alice in Wonderland* over on the other side," Lacey said. "Huge hats from the Mad Hatter's tea party. Colorful. Practically hallucinogenic."

"Hallucinogenic hats. Got it."

Hansen strolled away into a sea of likely subjects. Lacey left Tamsin in the shade of an umbrella with her coffee and headed toward the costumes, which ranged from the awful to the sublime, some from theatres with bare cupboards and consignment-store rags, some from theatres with lavish budgets underwritten by major corporate sponsors.

A rack of tuxedos from elegant shows like *Private Lives* was being swarmed by impoverished actors, looking to score formal wear in the event they were ever nominated for a Helen Hayes award. And a tuxedo was a smart addition to any man's Washington wardrobe. There were so many formal events to attend, and for actors, the occasional restaurant or catering job that required the same look. Lacey personally believed that a tuxedo improved many a man.

She caught sight of Will Zephron, a young actor-slash-waiter, bearing a black shawl-collared number and a big grin.

Will saw her and waved his prize tuxedo in salute.

"Hey, Lacey! Look what I just bought! It's perfect, it's my size, and it was on stage in some Ayckbourn thing at Round House. Missing a button, but who isn't? Hey, what's up with you, anything bizarre happening today?" Will had once spilled a tray of champagne on a broadcast journalist at the White House Correspondents Dinner, and had feared he'd never work as a waiter—or an actor—again. No one wants a clumsy waiter.

"Nothing bizarre, except D.C. style in the summer," she responded.

"Don't I know it! Don't let me get in the way of your fashion vibe. I keep my drama on the stage."

As if. The actors she knew liked their drama all the time. "Good shopping?"

"Are you kidding? Snagged this great tuxedo, now I have to score some white tux shirts." He pawed through a long rack of tuxedo shirts and pulled out a likely candidate. "Waiting tables, you know. Can't have too many."

"Mind if I quote you?"

"For publication?"

"Maybe."

"As long as you identify me as an actor and not a waiter."

"You got it. Are you going to try that shirt on?" She didn't see a changing booth, but there were theatre curtains hung up for sale in the next aisle.

"Nah. It'll fit." Will measured the shirt against his body to show her, then charged back into the shopping fray, tuxedo tucked safely under his arm.

It'll fit. Just like a man.

She looked for Hansen at the *Alice in Wonderland* costumes, but he'd moved on. She hoped he'd gotten something *whimsical*. Lacey was in the mood for *whimsy*. She watched a petite dark-haired woman trying on one of the enormous Mad Hatter hats, three feet tall in eye-popping yellow, pink, and green. She was squatting down to check it out in a short mirror. The chapeau dwarfed her, but she and her friend laughed, and she bought the hat.

Lacey showed her press pass and asked them, Why that hat? The woman said her name was Micki and she was an actress.

"The big hat? It's just fun! And you know, Halloween."
Micki said it wasn't nearly as heavy as it looked, being made of
some kind of foam. She was concerned only with where to
store it. "I live in Adams Morgan. I'm really limited on closet
space."

"But it's like art. Pop art," said her friend. "Don't store it!
Just display it. Hang it on the wall."

With such unassailable logic, they decided it was *perfect*.
Micki's friend bought one like it in red, blue, and purple.

Lacey wandered on. Shakespeare was well represented by
props and costumes, likewise the witty George Bernard Shaw
and the dreary Arthur Miller, and of course Tennessee
Williams, with a trove of broken glass animals from *The Glass
Menagerie* and a box of faux-dirty T-shirts from *Streetcar*.

The yard sale was awash in color and dazzle and local
theatre history. Some offerings were threadbare, having
already been lent out or rented to local colleges and high
schools and returned in less-than-pristine shape.

There's always Halloween.

But down the aisle, Lacey found some intricate Elizabethan
costumes from an old production of *Romeo and Juliet* at the
Landsburgh. This smart theatre, one of the District's best,
included a typed history of the show, a description of the
outfits, and the visiting celebrity actors who had worn them,
many seasons ago. A big-name wearer seemed to raise the
price considerably. Lacey looked at the tags. *Not on my salary.*

She was keeping her eye out for costumes from a long-ago
production of *The Women,* by Clare Boothe Luce, and around
one corner, there they were. The stage production was set in
the late 1930s and the costumes had been a triumph. The
famous 1939 film version had featured a wardrobe by the
legendary designer Adrian, who exulted in very broad
shoulders, very high hats, and a glossy Technicolor fashion
show set in the middle of the black-and-white film. The stage
costumes for the D.C. production were even more outrageous,
with even more wildly exaggerated shapes and oversize
shoulders in a spectrum of Crayola colors. And the price tags
were exaggerated too.

While Lacey admired the imagination that went into them,
they were definitely costumes, not clothes she could imagine
wearing on the street, outside of Hollywood or Broadway.

It was the difference between life and the theatre.

"Hey, Smithsonian," a voice called.

LaToya was heading her way. Ready for a hot summer day in black cropped pants and a crisp white shirt, she wore large silver hoops in her ears and her shiny black hair was pulled back in a sleek French twist. LaToya had her own sort of style magic. She was statuesque and wore her clothes well, one of the few reporters at the paper who was not a fashion disaster.

"You're up early," Lacey said.

"Disappointing date last night. Got home early."

"And I didn't think a yard sale was your thing."

"Never say never. I'm open to new experiences and I'm curious to see how you do that thing you do. Broadway says it's your fashion voodoo."

"Broadway" was Broadway Lamont, the homicide detective she had in her sights, but not her possession, not yet. Detective Lamont was a large and muscular black hunk of a man. His main talent seemed to be intimidating suspects, but LaToya intimidated him. Lacey could see the fear in his eyes whenever LaToya was on the hunt.

"It's not voodoo," Lacey said.

"ExtraFashionary Perception then. I hear that's your specialty," LaToya teased.

Lacey smiled. "How do these rumors get started?"

"No rumor. The message is in the clothes and you are the receiver."

"Well, my EFP isn't helping today. The things I love, I can't afford, and the things I can afford, I don't love. But maybe you'll get lucky."

"Moi?" LaToya fluttered her perfect red nails. "I have no intention of handling any old clothes worn by sweaty strangers under hot lights. Let alone wearing them." She shuddered, surveying a rack of black dresses. She almost touched one, then daintily wiped her fingers on the air.

"But that's where the magic lies," Lacey answered. "Think of all the people who may have shared a bit of their soul with these things."

"Their soul too? Now you're just being creepy." LaToya rolled her eyes. But then her gaze fell on a rack of formal gowns. "OMG. What is *that*?" She pointed a perfect red nail at one particular red dress.

Lacey pulled it down off the rack and read the attached tag. "Ahem. This stunning ball gown was worn by the Red Death in Kinetic Theatre's production of Edgar Allan Poe's *The Masque of the Red Death.*"

Neither one noticed that Tamsin had circled back to join them. She leaned over Lacey's shoulder to peer at the dress.

"Oh *that!* Let me think. That show was years ago. Before I was a theatre critic. Officially, anyway. Something is gnawing at my memory." Tamsin tapped an index finger on the side of her face as if drawing out the semi-forgotten file. "Red dress. Red mess. Aha. That is, I believe, a famous costume. Or should I say *infamous*. Is there a mask with it? There should be a mask."

"Don't think so. No." Lacey riffled through the gown and shook her head. She imagined a jeweled red mask gracing a mirror in a dressing room somewhere. *Purloined by some theatre person.*

"Probably lost over the years." Tamsin smiled. "That's it, though."

"That's what?" LaToya asked. "Look at all these reds! These are *so* my color." She took the long red dress from Lacey and hauled it over to a mirror at the end of the rack. LaToya held it in front of her and gazed at her reflection.

"It's really just a rumor," Tamsin told her. "I wouldn't worry about it."

"What are you telling us?" Lacey asked. "Or rather, not telling us?"

"Didn't I say?"

"No!" LaToya and Lacey said together.

"D.C. theatre lore. The actress who wore this gown supposedly died during the last show. Or right after it. Closing night. In this dress. Or maybe not *in* the dress? I don't know, actually. But I can tell you, this dress has a *reputation*."

"How did she die?" Lacey asked.

"Oh, she fell. Stumbled, fell from the stage, or a scaffold or a riser or something. I think it was an elaborate medieval castle sort of set, rising, falling, staircases, towers, moving platforms, that sort of thing. I'm so over those things."

"What sort of thing?"

"Effects. Theatres love big effects. Half the time they do it just because they can, not because it's necessary or serves the play. Simply because they have the money, or a sponsor to pay for it. A pool in the middle of the stage. A fountain that sprays the front row. A revolving castle. Why not? If the play is dull, throw in a turntable, a helicopter, a rocket ship, and maybe no one will notice the hole in the second act."

LaToya was dancing with the red dress and her reflection in the mirror. Lacey wondered what had gotten into Miss No Icky Old Clothes!

"Tamsin, what are you talking about vis-à-vis this red dress?"

"Merely this, Smithsonian. The 'Red Dress of Doom' over there sometimes comes up in conversation when grim theatre tales are told. I didn't write the story. It happened a couple years before I even started writing for *The Eye*. And *that* was a dark day, believe me." She tipped her coffee back with gusto.

"Freaky, I grant you that," LaToya said over her shoulder. "But it's not the dress's fault. People die. Life goes on. And will you just *look* at this amazing dress? This thing was made for me!"

"Actors will tell you they want to die on stage doing what they love," Tamsin added. "They're lying. Now I remember. Her name was Saige. Saige Russell. The actress who died."

"Could be just a story." Lacey knew every story gained some embellishment in the telling. "If there's anything to it, there should be clippings in *The Eye*'s archives." She mentally filed away the name Saige Russell.

"And you'll be checking it out for me, right?" LaToya's hands trembled ever so slightly as she clutched the red dress. But she held on tight. "And then you're reporting back to me, right? Just out of curiosity, I mean."

"Now that I think about it, I've seen that dress in action," Tamsin said. "Not the original production, of course. On actresses, wearing it to things like the Helen Hayes. It's become sort of a good luck thing, or a spit-in-the-eye-of-bad-luck thing." She snorted. "Actors."

"A good luck, bad luck thing?" Lacey asked.

"Sure. By wearing it, you stare death in the face. And you survive, of course. What are the odds? So you win. At least that's what I gather."

"So this Saige Russell. First she plays Death. And then she meets her own death?"

"Ah, the stuff of theatre myth," Tamsin said. "Or at least legend."

"Do we know for sure that the actress died?" Lacey asked.

"I have no idea," Tamsin said. "In the theatre, it's all about the story. The emotional effect. The dramatic weight of the thing."

"Just like journalism," Lacey said with a laugh. "Except for those— Oh what do they call those things? Oh yeah! *Facts*."

"Hey, this is Washington, guys," LaToya said. "Death comes in many ways. This just sounds like some weird-ass accident to me. And she wasn't wearing it at the time, right? And it's probably all just a rumor. On the other hand—" LaToya hung it back on the rack and stared at it. Lacey and Tamsin watched as LaToya wavered, but the red dress won. "Okay. I'm going with the *good luck* angle. This dress has found a new home. Mine!"

LaToya and the Red Dress of Doom went in search of the cash register. Together.

TWO

"HOLY COSTUME HEAVEN, Lacey! This is fabulous. So where are the wigs? There have to be wigs, right?" Stella asked. "Like, you know, the woman in that play thing who killed herself with the snake, or the queen who was guillotined?"

"No idea, Stella," Lacey said.

Even at a theatre yard sale full of actors who were prone to wearing gold lamé with high-top sneakers—*bless their hearts*—Lacey could have picked out Stella Lake Griffin. As much for her sheer presence as for her style. And then there was her distinctive New Jersey accent.

"I mean wigs would be terrific to use to decorate the salon. Elaborate wigs. Sort of like: Don't Lose Your Head, Just Your Old Hairstyle." Stella had a gleam in her eye. Lacey had seen it before.

"I thought you had to work today, Stel."

"Schedules can be adjusted, especially when I'm the manager. And when I read about this theatre sale thing in *The Eye*—it wasn't even *your* story—how could I resist. I mean, look at this stuff!"

Lacey's BFF, hairstylist, and personal critic, Stella, was not wearing her signature short, tight dress. Instead, each black-and-gold-legging-clad thigh featured the face and headpiece of Tutankhamun. Her King Tut leggings were paired with a daring gold bustier, showing off her recently acquired honeymoon tan. A long black-and-gold scarf dotted with pyramids graced her neck. On her feet were gravity-defying yellow high-heeled tennis shoes, which she claimed were "super comfortable." Lacey had her doubts. In the same shoes, she would have been flat on her face. But Stella liked her clothes with a dangerous edge.

"Nice leggings." Lacey indicated one skin-tight King Tut.

"So comfortable, you wouldn't believe. You should pick up a pair, though these babies are sold out. Limited edition."

"A shame. But I can't really see me in them."

"You never know till you try, Lace. Maybe the Van Gogh irises are more your style." Though Stella had changed her look numerous times throughout the past year, she was always in tune with her inner spirit and her outer stylist. At the moment, her hair was parted in the middle with two bright pink streaks on either side. It reached her shoulders. "What do think of my hair? I'm trying to grow it out. It's killing me."

"And yet, no one's really ever been murdered by their hair," Lacey said.

"Good thing, huh? Now, murdered *for* their hair, that's another story, right, Lace?"

Lacey nodded. They had shared parts of that particular story. But Stella wasn't dwelling on the past, she was back from her honeymoon and she had her very English mother-in-law, Lady Gwendolyn Griffin, in tow. Much to everyone's surprise, and her son Nigel's utter bafflement, "Lady G" and Stella adored each other.

"When Stella suggested we both come today, well, it was just the thing, don't you know," Lady Gwendolyn said to Lacey. "We'll take tea later, after we peruse the theatrical goods. You'll join us, won't you?"

The heat that morning had led Lady G to abandon her beloved tweeds. She opted instead for a pale linen dress, no doubt picked out by her new daughter-in-law. It was part of an evolutionary makeover Stella had undertaken.

"I knew Lady G would totally dig this," Stella said.

"Quite. I love the theatre. Almost as much as Agatha Christie. And when the play's a mystery, well, that's the very thing you want, isn't it?"

"The play's the thing in which I'll catch the conscience of the king," another voice quoted. "But which king, I wonder? Now that was a conspiracy. Shakespeare knew his stuff."

They all turned to see Brooke Barton, Esquire, their fourth member. Only the young blond lawyer could pull off this strapless gray pinstripe dress, an outfit that was both whimsical and preposterous. And yet somehow formal. Brooke wore oversize sunglasses and a pink bag slung over her shoulder. Her long blond hair was collected in a single braid down her back.

"I know I shouldn't have told you about that dress," Lacey teased her.

"Are you kidding? What else would I wear on a fine summer day off."

"And what are those?" Lacey was momentarily stumped by the pink suede wingtip athletic shoes on Brooke's feet.

"Aren't they great?"

"Do those come in high heels?" Stella chimed in. "I could really rock a pair of those."

Lacey kept her mouth shut. She actually didn't know how she felt about Brooke's absurd shoes. They certainly were conversation starters.

"I bought two pair," Brooke said. "In the pink. I also got a pair in blue."

Wingtip tennis shoes. Casual wear that wasn't really casual, Lacey thought, such an obvious choice for the athletic Washington professional, particularly rising young lawyers. Perhaps someone should design pinstripe jogging outfits? *No, on second thought, definitely no. Brooke would buy them all.*

"And I can run in these, too," Brooke continued. "So what do you recommend seeing here, O Fashion Maven?"

"It's a motley assortment," Lacey said. "Stella wants wigs."

"Totally," Stella said. "For the salon."

"And you, Lacey? What are you shopping for here?"

"Just looking." Lacey knew she wouldn't be buying anything. She preferred to go on the hunt alone, where she could trust her own instincts and not the crowd's. There were way too many people here for her to decide on anything. "Some people come for clothes, some for costumes for Halloween, and I'm told, some for disguises."

A look of interest crossed Brooke's face. "Disguises?"

"Here we go." Stella nudged Gwendolyn in the ribs.

"But that's perfect," Brooke said. "What better place for spies to refresh their covert wardrobes?"

"The Spy Store?" Lacey suggested.

"And did you see the news?" Brooke tapped her phone. "About that Russian billionaire who *allegedly* died of a heart attack in that Dupont Circle hotel?"

"I sense a correction coming," Lacey said.

"It was no heart attack. Blunt force trauma to the back of the head." She handed her phone over so Lacey could see the latest development. "Murder. And how many Russians does that make? A lot, let me tell you. Dozens."

Lacey skimmed the story. DeadFed dot com, the Conspiracy Clearinghouse web site run by Brooke's boyfriend, reported that autopsy results were in. The victim was another in a long line of Russians with connections to Vladimir Putin.

"Why did it take so long?" Lacey wondered. "He died months ago."

"Exactly," Brooke said. "And why did his family insist it was a heart attack?"

"They were afraid it was catching?"

"Exactly. They're terrified."

Conspiracy theories churned Brooke's blood and gave her a reason to get up in the morning. The fact that the attorney had fallen for Damon Newhouse, the only man who could match her in this fever of intrigue, was just the icing on her tort. And now, months after the fact, there was a fresh report on a dead Russian oligarch, crudely dispatched in a D.C. hotel, supposedly fast friends with the intrusive and evil Russian president. *Not anymore.*

"Intriguing," Lacey admitted.

"Ask Gregor Kepelov about this guy."

"You still think Kepelov's a Russian spy? As in currently?"

"If the trench coat fits. They say nobody is ever really *ex*-KGB. Unless they're dead."

"What's going on?" Gwendolyn asked.

"Brooke's on a spy hunt," Stella said. "I can tell by the look on her face."

"Just because he was once with the old Russian spy agency doesn't mean he's a spy now," Lacey said.

"Doesn't mean he isn't," Brooke countered. "You can't swing an umbrella without hitting a spy here."

True enough. And Lacey still had the occasional twinge of doubt about Kepelov. "This Russian's murder seems a little sloppy, doesn't it? Blunt force trauma? Why not something more clever?"

"You were expecting polonium or ricin?"

"Something like that."

"I agree. Sloppy." Gwendolyn said. "Very sloppy."

"Just what they want you to expect," Brooke said. "That's why this is more clever than you think."

"You go pick up some spooky disguise, Brooke," Stella said. "We'll recon later. I got places to go and stuff to see. Keep in mind HonFest, Lace. I want something awesome. You need something awesome too."

"HonFest?" Lacey had a sinking feeling she'd forgotten something.

"Tomorrow! Baltimore! Beehive hairdos and all that stuff. It's epic. You're coming, remember?"

"It's this weekend?"

"You promised!" Stella leveled a look at her. "You're coming to HonFest with me."

"As am I. I can't wait to see myself in a beehive," Lady Gwendolyn said.

"Beehive hairdos?" Lacey blinked. Lady G was the least likely candidate for that style.

"You'll be so cute with your hair up, Lace. Trust me. It'll be fun."

Lacey hadn't seen much of Stella since the honeymoon, so a little together time was important. She had even refrained from wearing her engagement ring from Vic Donovan on those few occasions they had seen each other. Lacey told herself she didn't want to take away from Stella's big moments and her rapturous descriptions of the islands she'd seen, and the food she'd eaten, and of course the wonderfulness of her new husband Nigel Griffin.

The truth was that Lacey was reluctant to share everything with the world at large. She wanted to keep the engagement, and Vic to herself. But the diamond suddenly glinted in the sunlight and Stella saw it.

"Oh my God, Lace, you're engaged!" Stella squealed. "Wow! It's gorgeous, Lacey. What a ring! Filigree? A little froufrou for my taste, but it's so perfect for you."

Lacey grinned. *As if Stella ever eschewed froufrou!*

"So when's the big day?"

"One thing at a time, Stella. I believe in long engagements." *Years. Maybe decades.*

"You're the only one! I promise you, marriage is wonderful. With the right person, of course."

"We're not here to talk about marriage," Lacey said, sensing an escape from engagement chatter. "While we waste time, someone else is grabbing all the good stuff."

"Yikes! This isn't over, Lace," Stella said. "I need all the facts. Every detail."

"Later. You go ahead. The wigs await you."

Stella was off, with Lady G at her side. *Saved by the wigs.*

"Hey, isn't that LaToya Crawford? From *The Eye*?"

Lacey followed Brooke's gaze. "That is definitely LaToya. But what on earth—"

There was some kind of disturbance at the cash register. At first Lacey couldn't tell what was going on. One woman was chasing another, knocking over a table full of props. Then the two women were fighting over something. Something red. Then the crowd parted around them and it was the red dress, the costume LaToya had fallen in love with. There was more shouting, and LaToya waved a receipt with one hand.

Lacey was willing to bet the more someone wanted something LaToya had, the more she was ready to fight for it. The tug of war was vicious but brief. LaToya seized the prize triumphantly from her frazzled combatant, who finally backed down in defeat.

"LaToya is one tough interviewer," Brooke said.

Lacey whistled. "I had no idea she was that tough."

LaToya paused to catch her breath, then she shook the dress out and stared at it. She seemed to be checking for damage. Satisfied, she looked up as Lacey and Brooke arrived at her side.

"A little misunderstanding there, LaToya?"

"You could say that! That crazy woman tried to steal this dress right out of my hands. She said it wasn't for sale, but they just sold it to me! I got a bill of sale for this dress. Possession is nine-tenths of the law, and I've got a receipt. I've got one hundred percent possession." She wiped a drop of sweat from her brow.

"Are you all right?" Lacey asked her.

"You kidding me? I'm good. I won!" It was clear that the dress was even more valuable to LaToya in the moment of victory.

But then LaToya's expression changed. She looked down at the red dress and frowned, and then back at Lacey. She suddenly thrust the bright compelling costume at the fashion reporter, piling its voluminous folds into Lacey's arms.

"Smithsonian, I've got an itty-bitty favor to ask."

∝

Lacey locked the red dress in the trunk of her vintage BMW. It filled the entire trunk. LaToya accompanied her to make certain it was secure. Brooke stood by to oversee the operation, a specialty of Brooke's.

"This is silly, you know." Lacey turned and faced LaToya.

"You're the one with the EFP," La Toya said. "What's it telling you?"

"She's right," Brooke said. "ExtraFashionary Perception."

"Would everyone stop saying that? You know that stuff is ridiculous." The dress was fast becoming a nuisance, but Lacey didn't need any EFP to tell her that.

"What is it about the dress?" Brooke asked LaToya. "Why did that other woman want it so badly?"

"I have no freaking idea! She wouldn't even fit in that dress. I just want Smithsonian to keep it for a couple of days, till it's, you know—cleansed."

"Cleansed?" Lacey stared at LaToya, checking for irony. There wasn't any. "I assume you're not talking dry cleaning?"

"Course not. I mean psychic cleansing. I'm not the one with the EFP. And I don't have a psychic friend. Like you do."

"Ah, this is a job for Marie Largesse," Brooke said.

"Yeah, Marie. The hoodoo queen of Old Town. If you can't do it, Smithsonian, maybe your psychic can do it. You got to vet and cleanse this dress for me. I'll take it back in a couple of days, when it's safe. I mean— Please."

Lacey didn't know what to say. She had the feeling her mouth was hanging open. "LaToya—"

"Thanks, Smithsonian. What are friends for?" She trotted off on her high heels, her burden lifted.

"So what's the story?" Brooke nudged Lacey, her eyes full of delight. "This big old red dress really came from Kinetic? Isn't that a Russian theatre?"

THREE

"*I* THOUGHT YOU weren't going to buy anything." Vic greeted her at her apartment door when she got home. He looked bemused. Handsome and dashing, as usual, but definitely bemused, one dark eyebrow arched over deep green eyes. He was handsome even when he was mocking her, she decided.

"I didn't buy anything."

Lacey arms were overflowing with the red dress. The thing was even heavier than it looked.

"Did you steal it?" Vic took it off her hands and lifted it up to look at it. "This is a lot of dress, Lacey. It's red. Really red. Must have been hard to steal."

"Tell me about it. I'm storing it for LaToya Crawford. Temporarily."

Lacey spread the costume out on her blue velvet sofa, its skirts reaching from arm to arm. It was a crazy confection of a dress, a deliciously mad swirl of blood red with multiple layers in various fabrics, shades, and textures. It was hard to even take in all at once, without someone inside it.

"You're not generally so generous with your closet space."

"And I'm not feeling generous. My closets are so small I can barely hang up what I have."

"How did this happen, then?" He was a little too amused.

Lacey pulled up a chair opposite the dress occupying her sofa. "Thumbnail version. LaToya bought it and was walking off with it when a woman from the theatre came running up and said it wasn't for sale."

"And yet, here it is."

"There were words. I couldn't hear all of them. 'Bee-yatch' was one of them. LaToya Crawford wasn't about to part with it. You've never really seen her in action."

"Formidable, I'd guess."

"She sets a high bar. And she was bigger that the other woman. But after that scene, LaToya decided she didn't want it at her place for a while."

"And why is that?" Vic moved the dress over and sat down in his accustomed place on the sofa. He stretched out and placed his hands behind his head, his mouth turning up at the corners.

He thinks this is funny? He should have been there.

"Um, it might have a history. She thinks we should, um, research the dress." Lacey cast a nervous glance at the gown.

"Research? Lacey, what aren't you telling me?"

"There is the slightest possibility this ruby-red gown here might be connected to a dead actress named, I'm told, Saige Russell. She allegedly wore it onstage for one last performance before she died. She played Death. That's the story. What I know of it."

"Here we go again."

"What do you mean by that?"

"Come here."

Vic stood and pulled Lacey into a hug. "Let me see if I've got this. You have a friend with a dress she's afraid to have in her own home? So she handed it off to you? And you took it?"

Lacey avoided his eye by snuggling under his chin. He was warm and comfortable and strong and she was exhausted.

"When you put it like that, it sounds funny. Anyway, it's only because Broadway Lamont's got her all excited about my alleged 'fashion voodoo.' As if."

"As if it really exists, which it seems to, sweetheart. Your infamous ExtraFashionary Perception."

"Not you too."

"Me too."

"Can we find something different to call it?"

Something about the dress made her pause. There was a mystique about it. While Lacey admired the effort and imagination that went into the gown, it was a costume, not clothing she could imagine herself, or anyone, actually wearing. It was the difference between life and the theatre, again. And the difference between daily life and, say, the annual Helen Hayes Awards, where many actresses had worn it.

She turned in Vic's arms to look at it. The red dress almost seemed to have a life of its own. The waning evening light hit the dress and it seemed to glow from within. As if it knew it was the topic of conversation.

"What else do you know about it?"

"Not much, and this is hearsay. It was made for a production of *The Masque of the Red Death* at the Kinetic Theatre in the District. A dozen years ago."

"The Poe story?"

"Adapted for the stage. According to our friend Tamsin, the leading lady took a header off the scaffold or the set after the last show. Something like that."

"She died at the theatre?"

She peeked up at him. "Supposedly. I can't verify it, darling. I don't know, in fact, whether Saige Russell was wearing the dress at the time. Or whether she really is dead. I don't know what the real story is. It's the *theatre*. Tamsin says it might be just—a story. A theatre legend."

"But it spooked LaToya and you want to find out why, don't you?"

"I might have a slight curiosity. Maybe if I wasn't on the fashion beat—"

"God only knows what disaster would befall you on another beat."

"I wonder myself. This is probably nothing. A theatrical tall tale. Smoke and mirrors."

"And someone died."

"Just a rumor."

"So far."

Lacey recounted Tamsin's hearsay about theatre people and their belief the dress could bring good luck or bad luck. And they lined up for the opportunity to dare to wear it.

"Is there no end to these fashion conundrums?" Vic smirked. "And you brought that bad-luck dress home with you?"

She picked up the dress up and shook out its complicated folds and layers. It looked unscathed by its adventure at the theatre yard sale.

"You don't believe in bad luck, Vic."

"I didn't use to." He stared at the dress as she hung it in a protective garment bag and zipped it up. "I think it's mocking us."

"Now you're playing with me." She hung it in the front closet and closed the door. "Don't worry, it won't be here long. I promise."

"You're still running off to Baltimore for HonFest tomorrow?"

"I promised Stella. I forgot all about it, but she's all abuzz."

"You don't seem too excited."

"You're not coming. And she's threatening me with a beehive hairdo."

He laughed and teased her with a kiss. "Take photos."

"Not on your life."

"At least a beehive wouldn't go with a killer dress straight out of Edgar Allan Poe."

"Thank goodness for small favors." Lacey held on to him, trying to forget all about the red dress.

"I can think of more fun things to do than talk about costumes or dresses or beehive hairdos." He drew her closer to him.

"So can I. Let's compare notes."

FOUR

*I*N WHAT MAD UNIVERSE *were cat-eye glasses and beehive hairdos ever* really *popular?* Lacey found herself wondering. *In the past, did Baltimore women* really *wear housedresses on the street with pink feather boas and call each other "Hon"? Or is this HonFest thing all just pretend?*

The world was full of Renaissance Festivals and street fairs and neighborhood block parties, but Lacey doubted there was anything else quite like HonFest. A street festival with a twist, Baltimore's HonFest was a fantasia of retro fashion from the Baltimore of the 1950s and 1960s, and possibly from some even more garish imaginary past. Certainly from the hallucinatory Baltimore celebrated in John Waters's *Hairspray.*

Lacey was happy she'd worn sunglasses so she could stare with impunity at this garish costume parade.

This annual festival in Baltimore's Hampden neighborhood was a glimpse into another world, both fun and a little frightening. It was a world where beehive hairdos reached the sky, cat-eye glasses were the cat's meow, and spandex pants were as skin-tight as the tattoos they barely covered.

"Listen, hon, my husband won't come *near* this thing with me," Lacey heard one woman tell another. "He says I'm embarrassing. Can you *believe* that?"

The woman wore fuzzy bedroom flip-flops, shocking pink skintight pants, and a skintight bandage top that exposed her ample stomach. She topped off her look with cat-eye glasses and sponge rollers in her dark brown hair, wrapped with a pink scarf. The woman's companion also wore sponge rollers, a pink housecoat, and purple bedroom slippers that slapped the ground when she walked. The two women burst into laughter, as if their clueless husbands had any business at this event anyway.

Lacey had to agree with the absent husband. She could only imagine what this women's hair would look like when the rollers came out. But they seemed to be having a wonderful time. While Lacey appreciated the merrymaking of HonFest, she could never get on board with wearing curlers in public.

What would Aunt Mimi say?

There were enough faux leopard prints and other faux animal skins to fill a faux jungle. Lacey's eyes were dizzy with all the leopard spots and tiger stripes. Women in strapless animal print smocks and mile-high hairdos were somehow managing to look like hip Wilma Flintstones and Betty Rubbles, though perhaps a little more generously padded. Tattoos were out in full force, but did they really go with 1950s vintage dresses? All that inked skin was fighting with the retro dresses, and Lacey decided the ink was winning.

In comparison, Lacey's look was very "cream cheese," according to Stella. Her light blue sleeveless-though-collared shirt was tied at the waist over a vintage white cotton skirt that flared at the hem. She hoped it would be retro enough for HonFest. Besides, it was comfortable as the temperature soared and the humidity spiked. To please Stella, Lacey wore a blue headband to hold her hair back. Her comfy white wedge sandals showed off bright red toenails from a new pedicure.

Lacey had driven to HonFest rather than catch a ride with Stella, so she could make a quick exit if circumstances warranted. She was beginning to feel out of place and was reaching for her keys when Stella caught up with her.

"Hi, Hon!" The queen of leopard and rhinestones herself, in a leopard-print bustier that cantilevered The Girls. Stella's outfit was in the spirit of HonFest and also in the spirit of Stella.

"Stel. I see you're dressing the part."

"I totally scored yesterday at that theatre sale you tipped me off to." Stella posed for effect. "Fabulous or what? You gotta see all the wigs I scored. And whaddaya think of my new gold lamé pants?"

"Positively atomic," Lacey admitted.

"Totally." She peered at Lacey over her rhinestone-embellished cat-eye sunglasses. "So fab. And can you believe my hair is finally long enough for a beehive?"

Stella's at-the-moment black hair with blond and pink highlights was beehived with the best of them, in black and blond stripes. Around her monumental 'do Stella had wound a leopard-print scarf accented with rhinestones. Her nails were long and dagger red.

"You're breathtaking, Stella."

"But you know what? I totally coulda gotten away with that Marie Antoinette wig I bought there. It's like two feet tall!"

"Next year," Lacey said. "For sure."

"This is such fun, what," Lady Gwendolyn said, making a threesome.

Lacey spun around to witness more makeover magic. Happily, Gwendolyn's HonFest look was not quite as startling. She was manicured and pedicured and once again, tweedless. In fact, with her restrained beehive and long fake lashes and simple pink sleeveless dress, Lacey had never seen Nigel Griffin's mother looking more glamorous.

"You look wonderful," Lacey said.

"You're welcome," Stella said, taking all the credit for this look.

"I love getting to 'go native,' don't you know?" Lady G said.

God help us, Gwendolyn, if this is representative of the natives.

"You didn't bring the ambassador?" Lacey asked. He was retired from Her Majesty's Diplomatic Service, but everyone still used the title.

Gwendolyn laughed. "Oh dear. He's a little stiff for this sort of event, you know. He simply wouldn't appreciate this festive atmosphere."

Lacey had only met him at the wedding. The ambassador's upper lip was stiff and the rest of him was ramrod straight. He seemed to have no sense of humor at all.

"She left him alone with his stamp collection," Stella said. "Fun times at Griffin Manor. But check out my Nigel."

Stella's new trophy husband Nigel Griffin, whose everyday uniform consisted of anonymous khakis, plain blue oxford cloth shirts, and noncommittal blazers, was unexpectedly sporting a retro Fifties bad-boy look, tight black jeans with a big comb in the back pocket and high-top Converse tennis shoes. A pack of cigarettes was rolled up in his white T-shirt sleeves, which revealed skinny arms and a "tattoo" applied with mascara: MOM. His brown hair had been combed back on the sides and the top piled high with one big curl, like a young Elvis Presley, all courtesy of Stella.

"Hello, Nigel," Lacey said. "Nice curl."

"At your service, Smithsonian."

"Greasier than *Grease*. Don't you love it?" Stella beamed at Nigel and he beamed back.

"You look like something out of *Rebel Without a Cause*," Lacey said.

"Oh I have a cause, Smithsonian. Stella is my cause." Lacey and Stella both laughed. "And what's this I hear? Victor Donovan finally popped the question? Good God! Never thought that would happen. You can tell me, did he do it up right?" He grabbed her left hand to study her engagement ring.

"You could say that." Vic had proposed to her with bullets flying all around them, in a remote cabin in the middle of nowhere. It was certainly memorable.

"I bet it was romantic," Stella said.

"We think so," Lacey said. At the moment Vic had said the words, it was exhilarating to be alive, let alone in love.

"Interesting stone, Smithsonian. Family heirloom?" Nigel was studying her ring intently. Though he was a *reformed* jewel thief, shiny baubles attracted him like a magpie. Lacey yanked her hand away.

"Leave her alone! Enough about the ring, Nigel," Stella said. "We gotta discuss your look, Lacey. Come with me, Miss Suzy Cream Cheese. The Glamour Tent awaits."

If you hadn't come to HonFest with your hair already in a beehive, you could get beehived on the spot at the pink Glamour Tent. Stella and the other stylists stood ready to tease those tresses sky-high. Lacey was opposed to all that back-combing, which could tear the hair and create a mountain of split ends. But if a Baltimore gal was a true Hon at heart, a little thing like split ends wouldn't stop her. The Glamour Tent was already full of fresh-faced young festivalgoers who looked adorable sporting updos wrapped in Rosie-the-Riveter-style kerchiefs.

"I'm really not up for a beehive, Stella," Lacey said. "A French twist is my limit."

"This is HonFest, hon, not the Grace Kelly Fest. But okay, maybe we'll settle for a twist and revving up your makeup. You need to make a *statement*, you know!" Stella pulled Lacey deep into the tent and squeezed her into a tiny makeup station between two stylists busy building beehives.

"What kind of a statement, Stel?"

"A statement like, 'I owe it all to Stella and I love it!' Like that." Stella began rimming Lacey's eyes with kohl, while her assistant worked on Lacey's hair. The makeup station was out of false eyelashes, so Stella rummaged through her corset-shaped purse.

"You keep extra eyelashes in your purse?" Lacey asked.

"Emergencies happen, you know." Stella's own lashes resembled two caterpillars that had landed on her eyelids. They were thick and long and black.

"Aren't we lucky Stella is here to save us," Gwendolyn said, reappearing at their side.

"Not over the top, Stella," Lacey pleaded. "I want to recognize myself when you're done. Please."

"Me? Over the top? What, are you kidding? My touch is as light as a feather." Stella cocked her head, put away her makeup brushes, and handed her a mirror.

"Stella! I look like a diva in an Italian film! A bad Italian film." Lacey's eyes were drawn into ferocious cat eyes, making her look like a feral panther woman, and her hair was pulled back and up into a very tall French twist, just a few bees short of a full hive. Lacey could hardly keep her eyes open under the weight of the false lashes and glue. She barely recognized herself, and she hoped no one else would either.

"I know! Isn't it great?"

"Smashing. Very *La Dolce Vita*," Lady Gwendolyn added. *More like Fellini's Satyricon*, Lacey thought.

"Not so prim and proper now, hey, Smithsonian?" Nigel said as they emerged from the Glamour Tent. "Donovan's going to flip for you."

Or laugh himself sick. At least among the HonFest crowd, Lacey didn't look as outrageous as she felt. She hoped to blend into the mob until she could escape.

But someone had noticed her.

Dodging behind a vendor's booth was the woman Lacey had seen the day before at the theatre sale, tussling with LaToya. She peered out from behind the booth, dripping a green snow cone down her black Kinetic-logoed T-shirt, the same outfit Lacey last saw her in. Theatre people, at least the ones Lacey knew in the District, loved their black clothing. They lived in it.

Stella tapped her on the shoulder. "Hey, Lace, isn't that the pudgy woman who was— You know, yesterday with the red dress—"

"With LaToya? I think so."

"She's following us! I saw her at the salon tent, and the hat booth, and then with the snow cones. She practically slopped one on Lady G."

"Oh, that one again," Lady G said, poking her nose in. "Bit messy, what?"

"Trying not to be obvious," Lacey said. "In a very theatrical way."

"What does she want?" Stella said. "There's no way she's getting that dress back from LaToya, right?"

"I'm going to find out," Lacey said. Her own snow cone was cherry, and she held it carefully so it wouldn't spill down her blouse.

Stella grabbed her arm. "Seriously? You gonna just ask her? Just like that?"

"I'm a reporter, Stel. It's what I do."

"Do report back to us, forthwith," Lady Gwendolyn commanded.

"Don't worry, Lacey, you can take her," Stella said. "She's out of shape."

Lacey walked straight at the woman, slowly, and she hoped non-threateningly. "Excuse me, are you following me?" Lacey asked loudly. "Do you want to talk to me?"

The woman dropped her snow cone and backed away. She looked stricken. She was perspiring and her face seemed permanently red. She didn't look healthy or well cared for. *With half a chance, Stella would take her scissors to that unruly mop.*

"No. Yes. Uh, I just—"

"Yesterday, you fought with my friend. Over that costume from *The Masque of the Red Death.* You remember the red dress."

The woman backed up against a tent pole and stopped. "You're Lacey Smithsonian, aren't you? And she's a friend of yours?"

"Why are you stalking me?" Could this woman have known she would be here in Baltimore? Did she follow her here? *That would be crazy.*

"I'm not stalking you, I'm helping out with the costumes here, and I— I recognized you from your column, and when I saw you here, I thought maybe—"

"Maybe what?" The woman just shook her head, at a loss for words. "You apparently know who I am. Who are you?"

"Amy Keaton. I work at Kinetic. I'm sort of the stage manager."

Sort of? "That's a start. Why did you try to get the dress back?"

"Because it was a mistake! It wasn't supposed to be on sale." Her face got even redder. "It's just a terrible mistake!"

"It was on the sale rack. They sold it to her, LaToya bought it. Fair's fair."

"I know, but there was a mix-up. I don't know what happened. It was some intern's fault."

"Oh, I see. The intern did it," Lacey said.

The intern did it! One of the most popular excuses in Washington. An *intern* was responsible for a multimillion-dollar mistake in the budget. A congressional intern released the wrong information. A theatre intern put the wrong dress on the sale rack.

It must be nice to have an intern to blame every time something goes wrong.

"Yes, it was an intern," she insisted. "Can't you talk to that LaToya person? That dress is part of our history at Kinetic. It really belongs with the theatre."

"Why don't you talk to her yourself?"

"I tried. She wouldn't listen. And she's kind of scary."

Well, that's true enough. LaToya could be intimidating. Even Homicide Detective Broadway Lamont was afraid of her. *Especially Broadway.*

"I know. That's a problem. Here's the thing. You don't want to back LaToya up against the wall. Now she wants that dress more than ever. What can you tell me about it? Is it true that an actress died after the last performance? Do you know whether she was wearing the dress at the time?"

"Well, I can't really— I don't know, I— I wasn't with Kinetic back then. I don't know the whole story." The woman looked away evasively, and Lacey concluded she was lying. About something. But which part? "I've only been with the theatre a couple of years, but I love working there— But if I don't— If I can't get it back— See, they are very serious people. They don't like mistakes. They *really* don't like them."

Sounded like a hostile work environment to Lacey. But she wasn't about to tell Amy Keaton she had the dress in her custody. *It's not mine to give away.*

"Why is *this* dress so special?"

"I don't know! Really. But it was an important production. Their first big hit show. And there's this tradition, they loan it out every year. Lots of actresses wear it to the Helen Hayes, and all that. People start lobbying to wear it years in advance. It's a *thing*. Please, please, please, this was just a stupid mistake and we need it back! I'll pay your friend whatever she paid for it. I'll pay her double, or triple—"

"Listen, Amy, I know mistakes happen, but I don't think there's anything you or I could say or do that would make LaToya Crawford part with that dress now."

Keaton covered her face with her hands. "That's it, then. I'm going to get blamed for this."

Lacey was sure now that Keaton was responsible for the sales rack slip-up. *She's probably already gotten chewed out for the mythical intern's mistake.*

"It's just a *dress*. It's not life or death." Even as Lacey said that, she remembered the dead actress who wore the dress on stage. *If the story is true.* "They'll understand."

Amy Keaton shook her head. "I'm going to have to find a new job."

The woman was clearly devastated. She turned and walked away into the HonFest crowd, her shoulders slumped in defeat.

Stella was instantly at Lacey's side. "What's the dish?"

"Her name is Amy Keaton. Works at the theatre. Claims the dress was sold by mistake. An intern did it."

"An intern? Yeah, right. So this Amy Keaton screwed up big-time." Stella's tongue was purple from her snow cone. "Screw-ups happen."

"Looks like it."

"She looks pretty bummed. Hey, I could offer to do her makeup for her. Maybe get some more dirt out of her for you? Get my fingers on that haystack on her head? What do you think? I'll go run her down and drag her into the Glamour Tent, if you think it'll help, Lace."

The image of Amy Keaton in a beehive made Lacey laugh. "I don't think that's going to help. Come on, we have beehives to ogle."

"And don't forget 'Baltimore's Best Hon' contest. It's coming right up!" Stella took Lacey's arm, and Lady G took the other. "Over there on the big stage. I love this stuff, Lace. And you know what their motto is here at HonFest? 'The higher the hair, the closer to God!' "

Lacey let herself be pulled along. "Isn't that your motto too, Stel?"

FIVE

*E*XHAUSTED AND OVER-STIMULATED from the sights and sounds of HonFest, all Lacey wanted was to plunge into her apartment building's pool. She needed to swim away the day and the sour memory of her encounter with Amy Keaton. The pool overlooked the banks of the Potomac River and was the saving grace of many a summer day. Lacey loved to lounge by the pool, watching the egrets pose like lovely ladies and the eagles and osprey soar and dive into the river. And after dark, millions of fireflies would come out to play.

But when she opened her apartment door, Lacey smelled charcoal wafting from the grill out on her balcony. That aroma could mean only one thing: Victor Donovan was practicing the manly art of barbequing.

I can swim some other time.

"Hello? Vic?" Lacey inquired from the open door.

"Out here. Hope you're hungry for steak." Vic grinned at her through the screen door of the balcony.

"Always."

"Charcoal's almost ready."

"I can smell it! What a surprise. There in a minute."

Lacey was suddenly even more glad to be home. Vic and steaks and *home!* The apartment building might have been a little shabby, but her million-dollar balcony view of the Potomac River could not be denied. And it was always cooler by the river, especially after a blisteringly hot HonFest day.

She threw her tote bag on the sofa and checked the closet where the red dress was hanging in its borrowed garment bag. She unzipped it: It looked innocent enough, in all its crimson glory. She zipped it back up. Kicking off her shoes, she padded through the living room and the French doors and onto the balcony to greet Vic with a kiss. He held her at arm's length and peered at her quizzically.

"Whoa, who's this mystery woman? Very exotic! But listen, I have a fiancée, lady. She'll be here any minute."

Lacey laughed. She had completely forgotten about her HonFest look.

"Sorry. Stella insisted. It was either let her do this or a beehive hairdo. Or this *and* a beehive. What do you think?"

"I feel like I'm talking to a whole different woman."

"Shall I scrub it off?"

"No, no. You look great. Like Gina Lollobrigida or something." *Great, another Italian movie diva.* He wound one arm around her waist. "I'm always discovering a new side of you, darling."

She admired the small café table that he had set. He'd prepared salad from a bag and added avocado, tomatoes, and onion. Corn on the cob was ready for the grill, along with a couple of beautiful steaks.

"This is fabulous. What's the occasion?"

"You. I thought you might have a long hot day in Baltimore. I'm surprised you didn't emerge from the time warp in a poodle skirt and cat-eye glasses."

"If Stella had her way, I would have. You should have seen poor Nigel."

"He was there? Shame I missed that." Vic had a low opinion of the Brit, having known him for years through Nigel's jewel-thief days.

"In tight jeans and a cigarettes-rolled-up T-shirt, his hair all poufed up. Early Elvis."

"Did you take a photo?" She showed him the pics on her phone and Vic laughed. "Nice. We'll use it for blackmail."

"No use. Nigel has no shame."

"You're right. He was born without."

"Handy for him. Also, no tact. He practically took my arm off gawking at my engagement ring."

"Uh oh. You sure he didn't switch it out, with some jewel-thief sleight of hand? Replace it with a gumball machine ring?" Vic took her hand and kissed it. She noticed he also made sure the ring was still there.

"He offered to appraise it for me."

"Of course he did. Which reminds me. When are you going to tell your family we're engaged?"

"Please! One thing at a time." Lacey didn't want to have that particular conversation with her mother and sister.

"They'll want to know. Sometime before the wedding."

"I'll send them an invitation. I just don't want to hear any crazy suggestions on how to do everything. They'll want us to get married back in Denver, you know."

"Would that be so bad?"

"Yes! They'll want to help! Meaning they'll want to run everything! And *ruin* everything! Let's not even talk about my family."

"You got it. So how was HonFest?

"Fun, but weird. I have no idea what to write about it. I love vintage, but not all vintage. I'm iffy about the Fifties, and wearing pink sponge rollers in your hair with cat-eye glasses in a cartoon of a house dress? And I'm pretty sure full-sleeve tattoos were rare on Fifties housewives."

"Nah, those gals were tough. Like Rosie the Riveter but with an anchor tattoo. We'll get you one that says 'Born to Rivet, Hon.' "

"That better not be another smirk, Vic Donovan."

He drew her into a hug. "I like you just the way you are. But you'd be cute in a beehive. Poodle skirt. Saddle shoes." He laughed and patted her hair. "Maybe for the wedding."

"In your dreams, buddy. How about those steaks?"

She took the pins out of her hair and shook it free, combing her fingers through the matted tangles from Stella's back-combing. Vic tossed the steaks and corn on the grill. Lacey enjoyed the sizzle. He moved behind her, putting his arms around her and resting his chin on her head. They stayed there a moment admiring the end of the day from her balcony above the river. The heat had moderated, and now it was pleasantly warm. The sky was soft, the river full of boats with white sails, bright against the water as the sun set. Gulls gathered on wooden posts at the river's edge where the green trees grew thick. Lacey spied an osprey aloft, fishing, and shaded her eyes. Vic handed her his binoculars for a better look. *Like a Boy Scout, always prepared.* The shadows deepened and the twilight advanced. The steaks were ready. Lacey and Vic settled down to eat just as the moon rose, a bright gold disc over the river. She never tired of it.

Leaning back in her white patio chair after dinner, Lacey felt full of steak and contentment. "I should go to Baltimore more often, if this is what happens when I get home."

"Don't have to go to Baltimore for that."

He made her smile. "I'll pencil you in."

"So, Nigel drooling over your ring was the highlight of HonFest?"

"Oh, there were other highlights." Unhappy Amy Keaton and her unhealthy red face came to mind. Lacey summarized the encounter for Vic.

"Hold on!" He frowned. "You saw this woman yesterday and she turns up again today?"

"Coincidence. You know what a small world D.C. is."

"You know I don't like coincidences. I'm glad she's LaToya's problem. She is LaToya's problem, right?"

"Definitely. I'll contact LaToya tomorrow and see when she can pick up the calamitous costume. I'm sure I can't convince her to just give it back, but I'll try that too."

"You could take it to work with you. Give it back to here there."

"It's a lot to haul around on the Metro."

"You could drive."

"I could, but driving into D.C. on a Monday morning seems like an unnecessarily frantic way to start the week." Besides, Lacey enjoyed walking to the King Street Station and reading on the ride to work.

"Just get rid of the thing," Vic said.

"Making you nervous?"

"Not me. I merely remember the last old dress you got involved with."

Oh yes. The "lethal black dress." The fact that the black dress had dispatched a broadcast reporter to the Great Beyond was beside the point.

"That one was black, not red. It was a beautiful dress, and I wasn't dating it, Vic. I was simply the first one to realize what really happened. Are you staying over tonight? You want to keep me from getting too involved with the Red Dress?" She winked at him.

"I'd love to, but I can't. Duty calls. However, I can stay for a while."

"I'll settle for a while. For now."

The setting sun threw a crimson glow over the Potomac River beneath the moon, but there was no one watching it from Lacey's balcony.

SIX

"*L*ACEY SMITHSONIAN! Are you there?"

Lacey decided six a.m. on Monday morning was way too early to have a buzzing phone in her hand. It took her a moment to recognize the insistent voice and the attitude to match.

"LaToya?" She sat up in bed and glanced at the illuminated numbers on her clock radio: robbed of at least another hour of sleep.

"Who else would be calling you at this time of day?"

Lacey could think of a variety of answers. Crawford wasn't even on the list. "Nobody, I hope."

There should be a saying, Lacey thought. *Like red sky at morning, sailors take warning? How about, Phone call at dawn, sleep be gone!* She rubbed her eyes and peered into the gloom. Light was peeking around the perimeter of her dark drapes.

"Someone broke into my place last night!"

"What? You had a break-in?"

"Yes, a break-in. A burglar. A thief. A thief in the night. In my home, my condominium, my personal space." LaToya paused in her outrage to catch her breath. "I waited until you were up."

"I'm not up. But I guess I am now." Lacey lurched into the kitchen and with one hand hit the power button on her coffee maker, filled with grounds and water the night before, while holding her phone to her ear with the other. "Are you okay? What did they take?"

"Nothing, so far as I can tell."

"Nothing? How do you know? Did you call the police? And why are you calling me?"

"Why do you think, Miss Fashion Reporter? I buy that *Red Death* dress and the next thing someone invades my privacy and rifles through my closet, desecrates my home. Broadway says whoever it was—"

"Broadway Lamont is there?" *Interesting.* Lacey wondered if LaToya had finally gotten something going on with the big detective.

"Who do you think I'd call first?"

Of course she'd call Broadway. "But he's homicide. Is someone dead?"

"Not yet, but if I find the creep who did this there WILL be homicide! Broadway is just doing a favor for a friend."

The aroma of fresh coffee distracted her. Lacey retrieved one of her promotional Fashion *BITES* mugs and poured herself some liquid energy. Sunshine was already flooding her kitchen. The day would be hot, but the early morning was pleasant. Lacey's weekend had had too much going on and not enough Victor Donovan to suit her. It was a shame she had to go to work today, she thought, and now there was LaToya on the phone with a Big Problem.

"Are you listening to me?" LaToya demanded. "Who the hell would break into my place? Does this *unsub* have anything to do with the dress I bought?"

"The what?" *Unsub? Someone's watching way too much television.* "How would I know? Besides, your red dress isn't even there, it's—"

The dress. Lacey's apartment was quiet and empty, apparently untouched. Vic had left a jacket on a chair. *But what about the dress?* Lacey raced to the front hall closet. The good-luck/bad-luck dress was still there, hanging in its zipper bag.

"Your dress is fine, LaToya."

"Well, of course it is! I'm the one who got burgled! But what does your EFP tell you?"

Run and hide, that's what.

"It doesn't work that way, LaToya. I'm not psychic. The EFP thing is just, you know, one of those things people say. Besides, you live in D.C. Things happen."

"Not to me, they don't. Besides, I live off Logan Circle. It's safe here."

"No place is safe all the time. Is Broadway there now?"

There was a pause, as if LaToya had to make sure. "Yes. He's calming me down."

Not doing a great job of it, is he?

"What does he say?"

"That I need better locks on my door. And a better building security system. And not to buy crazy red dresses from some crazy-ass theatre."

That sounds like Broadway Lamont. Lacey heard grumbling in the background. "No valuables taken?"

"No. And that's what makes it even creepier. Nothing taken at all. And whoever it was, they were here while I was *sleeping*. In my bedroom. Watching me sleep!" LaToya's voice started rising again.

"Nothing taken? Then how do you know someone was there?"

"All my damn doors were wide open! And—" LaToya's voice quavered. "They did things with my clothes—"

Lacey felt a sudden chill in her sunny kitchen. "Did things? What kind of things? Let me talk to Broadway—"

"We can't talk about this on the phone. You have to come over here. You have to see this for yourself. Even Broadway says you got to see this. *Now.*"

"Right now? Your place? Before work?"

"You got to see this." LaToya's voice broke. "This is all kinds of stone crazy wacko voodoo. Please."

"Okay, I'll be there soon." *Now that you said please.*

Lacey hung up and wondered what to wear. Between the summer heat, LaToya's meltdown, and Broadway Lamont, of all people, looking for a fashion clue, she would need to keep her cool. Maybe a retro sleeveless summer dress in a breezy mint-green polished cotton? The skirt was flared for coolness and movability. She paired it with straw wedge sandals in case she had to run from a cranky editor.

Or a big bear of a homicide detective.

Ↄ

LaToya lived in a one-bedroom condo in a glorious Beaux Arts building a block and a half from Logan Circle, seven stories tall and apparently unimpregnable. LaToya was waiting for her in the lobby by the concierge's desk, an enormous coffee in her hand. Not her usual put-together fashion plate self, she wore a pair of dark blue shorts, a white tank top, and athletic shoes. Without her makeup and all the eye-candy she usually wore, she looked younger, smaller, and less self-assured.

"You look like you're going running," Lacey said.

"I ran all the way to Starbucks after Broadway left. I didn't feel like being alone."

"No coffee for me?"

"I'm not the welcome wagon."

"Apparently not."

"Sorry. I'm just jangled, Smithsonian. I wasn't thinking. I have a splitting headache. I never order an extra-mega-grande caramel macchiato frappuccino or whatever this is, and yet here it is in my hands." She paused to consider it and took a long sip. "Good though. Want some?"

"If I'm going to see your apartment, you better lead the way."

They rode the elevator in silence and stopped on the fifth floor. Her manicured hand shaking slightly, LaToya unlocked the door and opened it wide. She stood aside for Lacey.

The pretty one-bedroom condo had been renovated and was sleekly decorated in black and white furniture, accented with blue pillows and blue rugs. One wall was cobalt blue, creating a striking contrast, and a white marble mantled fireplace made an elegant counterpoint. The windows looked out over a canopy of green trees. It was as smart and stylish as its owner. Lacey wondered how LaToya could afford this place in a grand old building with a concierge on a reporter's salary. It was nothing like her own cozy little slum in the sky.

As if LaToya read her mind, she said, "I had a little help from my parents. They hate the idea of throwing money away on rent. But that's not the important thing." Lacey tore her attention away from the décor and followed LaToya's pointing finger. She gasped.

"Oh my God."

On the phone, LaToya had said someone "did things" to her clothes. Lacey envisioned piles of clothes dumped on the floor, furniture overturned, pillows scattered, pictures smashed, lamps broken, the usual aftermath of a messy break-in. This was nothing like that.

The scene was eerily neat and composed. LaToya's clothes had been taken from her closet and placed carefully all around the room, on the sofa and chairs, and even at the petite dining room table, arranged in coordinated outfits. Everything was accessorized with scarves, belts, hats, purses. Matching shoes were ready for feet to slip into them. That was strange enough. But someone had also taken the time to neatly stuff each of LaToya's dresses with wrapping paper or other clothes so that they took on a semi-lifelike appearance, as if they were being worn by invisible women. The outfits at the table sat before a tea set, cups and saucers ready for the clothes' invisible occupants. LaToya's wardrobe seemed to be having an improbable tea party without her.

Lacey drew a deep breath.

"Wow. Broadway was here?"

LaToya nodded and sipped her coffee.

"Took my report, had some cops take photos, checked for prints. Said it was weird. Said *you* should see it. I was going to call you anyway."

"Thanks. It is weird."

"Weirder than weird. Scares me to death."

"LaToya, not to pry, but are you a sleep-walker by any chance?" LaToya shook her head firmly. "Okay. Heavy sleeper?" Another shake.

"Not me. I'm up and down all night. Not last night though."

"And you didn't hear anything?"

"Not a sound."

LaToya was still trembling. Lacey wondered if she was in shock. Anyone might be if some intruder had breached her security and played with her garments like they were a doll's dresses. It was hard to take it in.

"Do you mind if I take photos?" She didn't think she would forget this strange scenario, but she might want proof. She took her phone out of her purse.

"Be my guest. You won't be the first." Either the grande caramel macchiato thingy was kicking in, or LaToya was getting her spirit back. "Unbelievable! Some freak places my clothes all around my apartment. In my chairs! On the sofa! Round the table! My dresses, coordinated with my shoes, my belts, my scarves, my hats. Like some ghosts or something were gonna float around the room in them. And what's with all my wrapping paper stuffed inside of them? Somebody playing dolls with my clothes, in my house? If this was supposed to freak me out, it's sure as hell working! This is an invasion of my privacy. An invasion of my soul. I should never have gone to that costume sale."

"This may have nothing to do with the red dress." Lacey didn't believe it even as she said it. She took more pictures of the table set for tea with its invisible guests.

"Or everything to do with it! Fashion voodoo. I'd ask you to sit down, but all the seats are taken. It's that damned red dress. I know it is. That's what they were after. All this is 'cause they didn't find it here, I bet."

She slumped against a windowsill and Lacey joined her. She had to credit LaToya with tenacity. Once she got hold of an idea, she wouldn't let go. It made her a good reporter. And a pigheaded one at that. *She's a lot like me.*

"It's a theory. And your suspect?" Lacey asked.

"Who do you think? Who else but that pasty-faced woman who said the red dress wasn't for sale. After I already bought it, I might add."

"What's the intended message?" Lacey wondered aloud.

"The message?" LaToya was quiet for a moment.

"Was this person saying, 'I know how you wear your things'? Or maybe, 'This is how you *ought* to wear them'?"

"You mean like my yellow dress, sitting on the sofa with my yellow wedges and the yellow and red belt? Maybe. Anybody would put those together though. Wouldn't they?"

Maybe someone was just getting a picture of LaToya through her clothes. Why? To learn something about her? Simply to freak her out? To teach her a lesson? But what's the lesson?

"You didn't wake up at all?"

"No. And that is extremely weird, Smithsonian, because I am a very light sleeper. Practically lighter than air. I wake up when my neighbor down the hall snores. How did that woman get in my bedroom without me hearing it?"

"You don't know that it was that woman."

"She is the most likely suspect. That theatre woman got up in my face."

"You got in her face."

"She grabbed my dress! A defense was required. That, that woman—"

"Her name is Amy Keaton."

"How do you know that?!"

"I encountered her at HonFest yesterday."

"Hon *what?* What is that?"

"This street festival in Baltimore. Stella made me go. Hard to explain in ten seconds."

"She followed you up to Baltimore? What the hell?"

"Probably just a coincidence. She claimed she was helping out in the costume booths. She asked me to ask *you* to please reconsider giving the dress back. She said selling it was a big mistake, she would get the blame, her job was on the line. She went on and on."

"She blamed an intern, didn't she?"

"You've been in D.C. too long. Yes, she blamed an intern."

"Ha. I knew it. Better she follows you, the Clothes Whisperer, than *me*. I'm not sure I'd even recognize her, all pasty-faced, ratty-haired, dressed like a homeless—" LaToya paused for breath. She had a pretty detailed image of this woman she wouldn't recognize, Lacey thought.

"But why would she place your outfits around a room?" Lacey said. "Like set dressing, or a wardrobe test for a show? She said she's a stage manager. She doesn't seem the type to even know what goes with which dress."

"No." LaToya pondered that. "She's a hot mess."

"As far as I can tell, this Amy Keaton only wears black. You live your life in Technicolor."

"You got that right. But who else would do this? If the Keaton woman didn't do this, she's got a co-conspirator. Maybe the intern. And what about my red dress? You still got it?"

"It is safely in my temporary custody. Underline temporary."

"Is it dancing around the room by itself? Stuffed with paper and sitting down to breakfast at your table?"

"Perfectly calm, last time I saw it. In my front closet. I don't actually communicate psychically with clothes and fabrics, you know."

"Can't prove it by me, Miss Clothes Whisperer. The question is: What are you going to do about this, Smithsonian?"

"Me? I'm going to give that dress back to you as soon as possible."

"Oh no you're not, not with this closet freak on my ass. You promised to keep it till it's psychically cleansed."

"I promised no such thing." The last thing Lacey wanted was to play a game of hot potato with the ruffled red gown. She squirmed on the windowsill. Five little birds gathered on LaToya's window ledge behind them, sunning themselves. Lacey watched them fluff their wings.

She was easily distracted this morning, she decided. At least she *wanted* to be distracted.

"You've got the fashion voodoo, not me." It sounded like an accusation.

"I don't have any voodoo, LaToya. Don't jump to conclusions."

"So what's the plan, Smithsonian?"

Lacey wanted to sun herself like the birds on the windowsill and be free of all this craziness.

"If there is a connection, the first step for *anyone*—not necessarily *me*—would be finding out why Amy Keaton was so upset about the dress being sold. It's not world peace. It's just a costume. Clearly someone meant to sell it. It had a price tag."

"Apparently it is *not* just a costume. It is a very *special* costume. To *someone*."

True enough. "Besides the rogue intern theory, there must be some other reason the dress was at the sale in the first place."

LaToya pressed her macchiato to her forehead and thought. "Maybe someone did it to antagonize that bee-yatch. Or blame her for it. Make her lose that job. I'd buy that reason."

"Also, what do the police think about it? What did Lamont say? Have there been any other strange break-ins like this?" *Was there a strange game of playing dress-up going on?*

"He didn't say much. I'll have to tête-á-tête with Broadway later."

"Didn't he say anything?"

"He says at least no one's dead. *Yet*." She glanced at her watch. "Oh, damn, look at the time. I've got to get ready. If there's anything left in my closet that didn't get stuffed and mounted. I ain't touching these things. But what about that woman and my dress?"

"LaToya, if your break-in has anything to do with the dress, and I am not saying it does, you should find out more about it and the actress who wore it. Why it's so valuable. Such a theatre legend."

"Me? I'm not the fashion reporter! This is not a LaToya-gotta-figure-out-how-to-do-it thing, this is a Smithsonian-already-*knows*-how-to-do-it thing. There is a dead actress involved. I don't do theatre. Or death. Not my beat."

"It's not my beat either. Besides, I'm not sure the actress even died. Maybe the story never happened. Maybe the dress has nothing to do with anything. Maybe it's the kind of story that starts in a glass of beer, then grows into a myth. For all we know, the actress might be alive and well. She might have tripped onstage, the dress got blamed, and the story grew into a long, tall tale."

"You think so?" LaToya sounded hopeful.

"We need facts, not fiction. You're a reporter, you know what useful things facts can be."

"Then what about this freaky break-in?"

"I honestly don't know. Get better locks on your doors, like Broadway said." Lacey picked up her tote. "I have to get to work. You do too."

They agreed to meet later at *The Eye* and compare notes, but Lacey wasn't optimistic. Questions were always more plentiful than answers. *And what about the dress?* LaToya's break-in would only embellish the dress's notorious reputation, whether there was a connection or not. One thing was clear: That ruby-red confection would have to find a new hiding place. A place that was not Lacey's apartment.

Outside in the green and leafy Logan Circle, she grabbed a bench near the statue of Civil War General John A. Logan forever sitting on a horse. She gave Vic a call.

"Sweetheart. What's up?" His voice was deep and warm, like honey down her spine.

"I am, and a little too early. And I have a mission for you, should you choose to accept it."

"As long as it's not impossible. Is this mission fun or dangerous? Or both?"

"You are so suspicious. Remember that dress of LaToya's I brought home?"

"Aha. A dress. Dangerous, then."

"I wouldn't say that. I just think it needs to take up residence in another closet somewhere, for the time being. A closet in a galaxy far away."

"And why would that be?"

"LaToya's place was broken into last night." Lacey heard Vic groan.

"And you think they were looking for the dress?"

"Maybe. I really need to take a closer look at it at a safe place and—"

"Share an intimate moment with the red dress?"

"You know me so well." She gazed at people cutting across the Circle. They had cups of coffee, reminding her she was thirsty.

"The burglar was looking for that specific dress?"

"I don't know what the burglar was looking for. But anything is possible."

"Experienced Lacey Smithsonian viewers always suspect every possibility."

"That's a small possibility. The disturbing part—"

"There's a disturbing part? God, I'd be so disappointed if there wasn't one." She could hear him tapping on a keyboard. Perhaps taking notes.

"LaToya was asleep while persons unknown were rifling through her things."

"But the dress wasn't there. So what did they take?"

"Nothing. They—he, she, whoever—removed outfits from her closet and set them up around her apartment."

"Set them up? Like, strewn around?"

"No, not strewn. Placed with care, with the proper accessories, shoes, belts, that sort of thing, and stuffed with wrapping paper to give them shape. Sitting at the table. Lounging on the sofa. Like the Invisible Woman's costume parade."

"You're right. That is disturbing. You have pictures?

"On my phone."

"Send me some, when you have a chance. Sounds like bad performance art. Maybe the guy, because statistically it's a guy, is obsessed with LaToya and not the dress, which is still currently in your possession. Does she have a stalker?"

"Eww. That would be worse. For LaToya. I wouldn't want any stranger looking at me while I'm asleep."

"Don't worry, darling. That's my job."

 timeout

Lacey had taken an Uber to LaToya's apartment, but the office was just half an hour away, adding a stop for an iced coffee. In

Farragut Square, birds perched on the head and shoulders of Admiral Farragut. Men and women lingered outside with cups of coffee, hot and iced, resisting the race to their daily grind. Flower sellers' carts on the street corners were in full bloom. In an effort to ward off any more bad news, Lacey bought a bunch of blossoms. She wasn't sure they would help, but they were pretty.

It wasn't something she did every day, but today Lacey hoped that Felicity Pickles, *The Eye Street Observer* food editor, had something tasty on hand. Felicity was obsessive about tempting the staff with her recipes. She called it work. Lacey called it something else. *More like coercion.*

But Felicity's food was a big draw for Broadway Lamont. He was sweet on Felicity and her food and he wasn't nearly as intimidating when he was oohing and ahhing over something jam-packed with calories.

If I'm going to have Broadway Lamont involved in this mess, I want him sinking his teeth into one of Felicity's sticky buns. Not me.

SEVEN

*D*ETECTIVE BROADWAY LAMONT made it to *The Eye*'s offices before Lacey did. He'd had a head start. Luckily, the smell of sizzling bacon and cheese was in the air as she arrived. Lacey spotted Lamont with a plateful of something that looked like quiche, deep in conversation with her editor.

"Smithsonian. My office. Now."

Douglas MacArthur Jones beckoned her with a finger. His dark balding head was shiny with humidity or possibly sweat. Lacey popped her small bouquet into an empty coffee mug, dropped her tote bag at her desk, and picked up a notebook and pen, just in case.

She tried not to sigh, because Monday morning was too early in the week to start sighing.

Mac's office was in its usual state of chaos. Papers covered every surface, though she noticed a space had been cleared on his desk for a new framed photograph of Mac's blended family. Mac was African-American, his wife Kim Japanese-American, and their soon-to-be adopted daughters Jasmine and Lily Rose were a blend of African-American and Chinese. All wore implausibly big grins, including Mac. Mac's was a smile rarely on display in the newsroom, but he had changed since the girls had come into his life. He was a big teddy bear when it came to them. With reporters he was still just a bear, at least on the outside.

His new daughters were trying to make some stylish inroads into his wardrobe too, which was usually an explosive mix of colors and patterns. Today he looked almost coordinated, in khaki slacks with that unfortunate front pleating that did nothing good for his ample frame. His shirt was a bizarre plaid of orange, purple, and red, with just a sliver of khaki that almost looked like it was meant to go with the slacks. His psychedelic purple tie looked like an eleven-year-old picked it out. Lily Rose was eleven, Lacey remembered. Above the purple tie, Mac was balding and fierce, but not nearly as imposing as the big African-American police detective standing there eating quiche. Lacey nodded to them.

"Morning, Mac, Broadway. How's Felicity's new quiche?"

"What is it with you, Smithsonian?" Mac favored Lacey with his beetle-browed expression of puzzled concern. His eyebrows were the most expressive part of his face, and today they predicted storm clouds.

"And you would be referring to what specifically?"

"Some kind of crazy dress connected to some kind of a break-in at LaToya's place. Your specialty, I believe."

"I assume you mean dresses, not break-ins. I was just over there. I understand nothing was taken. Has a connection been proven, then?"

Is everybody suddenly seeing fashion clues now, where they may not be? On one hand, people taking fashion seriously might be a positive thing. On the other, Lacey didn't want anyone stepping on her beat. Or her process. Or her so-called ExtraFashionary Perception.

"Nothing that we know of," Lamont said. "She'll have to take a closer look at her closet, and right now she's pretty spooked."

"You're usually working homicide, Broadway. Why were you there?"

"Um—" He swallowed a piece of quiche. "Favor for a friend."

"LaToya called you? So she's got your private number?"

My, my! So she's 'a friend' now?

"I saw that look, Smithsonian. Don't get cute with me. Tell me about the fight LaToya had with that woman at the theatre sale."

"She already told you."

"I want your take on it. She's emotionally involved."

No kidding. "What I saw looked like a tug of war over the dress, between LaToya and a woman from the theatre. Short, blond, pudgy," Lacey said. "The theatre sold it to LaToya, but now this woman wanted it back. But you don't know if the two incidents are related, neither do I, and neither one has anything to do with me."

"I wouldn't rule anything out." Broadway glowered at her.

"Ditto." Mac's bushy eyebrows did a dance that Lacey interpreted as skeptical. *And probably hungry.*

"Felicity's quiche smelled pretty yummy, Mac," Lacey said. "Didn't you get any?"

The first lesson of the newsroom was to keep editors happy and well-fed. Especially Mac Jones. And that didn't seem to be happening today.

"Lamont got the last piece." He looked grumpy. Broadway grinned.

"Poor Mac. So what do you want me to do?" she asked. "It's not my story, you know, it's really LaToya's."

"It's fashion, so it's your beat. Do what you always do," Mac said. "Stay on the dress angle. Figure out what's happening. Dig up its past. See if it's cursed or something. Don't get killed in the process."

"You think the two are connected?" she asked Broadway.

"Normally, I wouldn't. But you're involved, so—"

"I'm not involved! I happened to be there when she bought the dress."

"Exactly," Mac put in. "Crawford buys some weird old dress, Smithsonian is on the scene, and the next thing you know Crawford's apartment gets, well, whatever it got. It's weird. It's never happened before. You're in the middle of it. So it's connected."

Lacey snorted. "She probably has some crazy stalker. Maybe the dress is innocent. Detective, you were at LaToya's, what did you think of the crime scene?"

"Bizarre." The big man rubbed his face. "I've seen all kinds of crazy-ass things. This wasn't messy, wasn't bloody, nobody got hurt, but it raised the hairs on the back of my neck. Course that could have been LaToya Crawford shrieking in my ear." He shook himself. "One thing, Smithsonian. I don't like perps who send a message, like this one did."

"And that message is?"

"How do I know? But it's some kind of message. Do I look like I speak fashion clues?"

"Perhaps not," Lacey said. He looked fierce, with his biceps straining the sleeves of his navy polo shirt and his black pistol peeking out of his shoulder holster. "But you do speak homicide. And the dress has a history. No recent deaths though, as far as I know."

"What do you mean 'no recent deaths'?" Mac thundered, his eyebrows arching in alarm. *Surely LaToya told Broadway about the actress's alleged death in the red dress?* Lamont didn't betray any sign of it. Neither did Mac.

"It's a rumor, Mac. And it was years ago. I'd have to research it."

"Research it," Mac ordered. "Where's the dress now?"

"I'm not sure. It was in my car trunk, then as of this morning it was in my closet." Lacey checked her watch. "Right now it may be in transit."

"In transit?"

"I asked Vic to move it. Just a precaution."

"So you're spooked too," Broadway said with a smirk.

"I wouldn't say spooked. But there is that story."

She recapped the tale of the red dress and the actress who had supposedly died onstage in it during Kinetic Theatre's *The Masque of the Red Death.*

"Great. A dead woman's dress. Now we're all spooked," Mac said. "Stay on it. And let me know what you're going to have for me this week."

The big detective pointed a finger at her. "And you get any hoodoo-voodoo fashion clues, you call me."

That almost sounded like an offer of help, but Lacey suspected Lamont just wanted to be done with the whole break-in and ease LaToya out of his life. If anyone here was spooked, it was him, and LaToya was the fear factor. Mac waved her away. Broadway Lamont balled up a napkin and tossed it in the trash. Lacey was dismissed.

She'd written a draft of her theatre yard sale piece, and jotted down a few notes for a "Fashion *BITE*" about HonFest, and now she was being ordered to explore the legend of the Crimson Dress of Doom. It looked like a busy week. She wondered whether she could wrangle some time off, because technically she'd worked all weekend too.

Could be worse. At least the fashion beat seems to be permanent job security.

Lacey returned to her cubicle and felt a chill suddenly racing down her neck. It had nothing to do with her chilling assignments. It was the air vent above her head. Another scorching day outside and the newsroom was freezing.

Typical. The newsroom's air conditioning, like most offices, was set for the comfort of men in suits and ties, not for women in their summer dresses. Like employees in offices everywhere, Lacey would have to surreptitiously crack open the window near her desk to let in some warm air. In fact, she considered it a small miracle that the windows in the building could still be opened. There was an edict that no one was to touch them, but it was roundly violated. Even editors were guilty of opening a window for some fresh air and a little warmth.

FROZEN OFFICES DEFY SUMMER FASHION! WOMEN SHIVER WHILE MEN SWELTER! Perhaps a headline for one of her "Crimes of Fashion" columns, she thought. Luckily, she was prepared. She grabbed her navy linen jacket and readjusted the scarf that went with her summer dress.

Another small surprise was waiting for her as she rubbed her chilled fingers. In the middle of her desk was an envelope and a note from *The Eye*'s photographer, Todd Hansen.

"With my compliments," it read.

Inside was a photograph from HonFest, capturing Lacey in her serious cat-eye makeup and caterpillar-thick lashes, courtesy of Stella. She was standing face-to-face with Amy Keaton, who looked frazzled, frizzled, and frumpy in the Baltimore heat. Both were gesturing dramatically, like an outtake from a bad movie. In the background, engrossed in the action, stood the impressively coiffed Stella, Lady Gwendolyn, and Nigel, leering like a bad boy in a Fifties biker flick. Surely a rumble was mere moments away.

Lacey put her head down on her desk. As long as this photo didn't make its way into the paper, *ever,* she'd survive. She placed the picture face down, then reconsidered and turned it face up, contemplating the other woman.

Amy Keaton was number one on her list of people to contact today. Lacey tried her number. No answer. It was early, probably too early for theatre folk. Lacey tapped the picture on her desk. What did Keaton's desire for this dress have to do with LaToya's break-in?

Not for one moment did Lacey think that Amy Keaton could pull off a completely silent breaking-and-entering operation, not to mention the weird silent wardrobe tableau someone had left for LaToya's edification. Nor did she seem the type to know someone who would or could commit that kind of crime. The theatre world was about the illusion of action, not actual action. Wasn't it?

On the other hand, Keaton did not act in the theatre, or even run the lights and sound, direct, design sets, or create costumes. She had said she was a stage manager, maybe with some vague additional duties. Lacey called again and this time left a message requesting a call back.

Lacey rubbed her still-chilled neck. Trouble was heading her way, she could feel it. She looked up. Harlan Wiedemeyer, *The Eye*'s death-and-dismemberment beat reporter, was bearing down on her. The stranger and more bizarre the story, the happier he would be. But this morning, he was far from happy.

"Smithsonian." His round face was pinched in misery. "We need to talk."

Lacey slipped Hansen's photo into her top desk drawer.

No sense in leaving potential blackmail material lying around.

EIGHT

*H*ARLAN WIEDEMEYER would normally be flirting with his fiancée, food editor Felicity Pickles, whose desk was across the aisle from Lacey's. But she was nowhere to be seen, and Wiedemeyer slumped over the divider of Lacey's cubicle.

"It's a bad news day today, Smithsonian. It's no good. Very bad. I feel it in my bones."

"This is a story you're working on, Harlan? This no good, very bad thing?" She waited for one of Wiedemeyer's usual news items, like a crazy murder or a worker ground up in a sausage factory.

"It's *my* story! Marriage, alleged connubial bliss. The truth is, I don't know about this marriage stuff, Smithsonian. Maybe it's not for me. I'm a jinx! Did you know? Bad things happen around me. How can I do this to my beloved Felicity?"

Wiedemeyer was in the midst of a panic attack about his impending marriage to Felicity, and the office A/C was freezing cold. Lacey could check those off her list of things to expect today.

"Did something happen, Harlan?" He nodded miserably.

"A tree. It fell on someone's car. Because of something I said. It was just a joke, but I said it, and a tree fell on his car. It's all my fault."

"Was anyone in the car?"

"No. Thank God."

"Did you chop down the tree, Harlan?"

He shook his head in sorrow. "It was dead. Wind blew it down."

"Did you make the storm happen, Harlan?"

"Maybe."

"Harlan. You are not a jinx. You don't conjure up tempests. You didn't make the tree fall on the car. These things just happen. Besides, even if, uh, certain things happen, the way they've happened in the past, they only happen that way that once. Right?"

She knew this logic was faulty even as she said it, but maybe Wiedemeyer would buy it.

"So you say." He wasn't buying it. "What about what I almost did to you?"

"It was lightning, Harlan. Not you. And it only happened once. Bad things happen every day to everybody. Lightning striking a giant neon Krispy Kreme doughnut sign could happen to, well, anyone." She paused. She knew they were both reliving the fateful moment.

The day she met Harlan Wiedemeyer, Lacey barely escaped death by doughnut sign. He had insisted on giving her a ride home from the office, because there was a downpour. He also insisted on detouring to the Krispy Kreme doughnut shop near her apartment building. Harlan loved doughnuts. As he and Lacey emerged from his Volvo, a lightning bolt hit the illuminated two-story doughnut sign and sent it crashing down onto his car, barely missing them.

"You told me that day you were *not* a jinx," Lacey pointed out.

"I know, I know. I didn't want to believe it." He cradled his head in his hands. "But what if I am? What if I'm some genetic anomaly of doom? A harbinger of disaster?"

He was clearly thinking of other incidents said to be jinx-related. When Wiedemeyer first came to *The Eye*, he had lit up at the sight of Felicity Pickles hoisting a tray of tarts. There were sparks between them, shy, awkward sparks, but sparks nonetheless. Shortly thereafter, her minivan was blown up by a bomb meant for Lacey. A former editor got into a tiff with Wiedemeyer and was later found dead with a bullet hole in his head. Wiedemeyer wasn't the killer, but he and Lacey found the cold dead body. There was more.

"What exactly are you worried about, Harlan?"

"Our children."

"Children?" *Oh my God. Are there children I don't know about?*

"The children we haven't had yet." He hung his head in remorse. "What if I jinx them? What if they hate me?"

"You're just borrowing trouble," Lacey said. "Children always hate their parents. They get over it."

Wiedemeyer looked up. He mopped his sweating brow and his eyes got misty.

"I wouldn't hurt Felicity Junior and Little Harlan for the world."

"Did you say Felicity Junior and Little Harlan?" Lacey tried to keep her face straight.

"They haven't been born yet, but we have plans. I can see them now."

So can I. Oh, the horror. "Harlan, chill. These are pre-wedding nerves. Everyone gets them." Lacey felt as if the Wiedemeyer-Pickles nuptials had been the topic of newsroom chatter forever. The wait was endless.

"I suppose. But how many poor bastards have nearly died, or actually died, because of me?"

"No one! No poor bastards have died because of you. You didn't cause the lightning that struck that sign. You didn't fire the gun that killed Walt Pojack."

"Maybe I've got some kind of force field or exotic chemistry that just, I don't know, makes bad things happen."

"You told me you were one lucky bastard."

"I did, didn't I?" Harlan plopped down in the infamous Death Chair decorated with skull graffiti, so named because the former fashion editor Mariah "the Pariah" Morgan had died in it. Lacey kept trying to ditch the stupid chair, but it always made its way home to her cubicle. "I am a lucky bastard. Felicity. *The Eye.* My friends. My band. I have a great life. But what about all those other poor bastards who come in contact with me? Those poor saps. They never saw me coming. Like that poor bastard with the car and the tree."

This isn't getting any better. "Hey, where's Felicity?" Lacey said brightly, hoping she could take this crisis off her hands.

"I don't know." His expression was tragic, yet comic.

Lacey's frenemy on the food beat was nowhere to be seen. Lacey found Felicity's relentless drive to overfeed everyone in the newsroom and make them her salivating slaves annoying— but *other* people adored her. *The Eye's* Pavlovian dogs panted with anticipation for her daily food fest, supposedly prepared for the weekly food section, and whenever Felicity's fattening food bombs went missing, there was sorrow in the land. Right now even Lacey would have been thrilled to see her hove into view. Harlan slumped down deep in the Death Chair. Lacey grabbed her coffee mug and stood up.

"I need some bad java. At least it's hot."

He looked up at her sadly. "That stuff will kill you. And it'll be my fault."

ભ

The newsroom kitchen was empty. Sometimes Felicity used the full kitchen on the sixth floor, where the executive offices were located and executives were rarely seen working. Lacey rode the elevator up and discovered the entire floor seemingly abandoned. Not even a receptionist in sight. The office where Walt Pojack had been found with a bullet hole in his head remained conspicuously unoccupied. Publisher Claudia Darnell hadn't arrived yet. Lacey realized she'd seldom been upstairs this early. Perhaps executives started their day at noon, she thought, instead of the plebian morning hours they kept down in the newsroom. It was warmer upstairs, too.

Lacey rode the elevator back down to the third floor and finally spotted Felicity, efficiently putting another quiche on a platter in the newsroom's small staff kitchen. The thirty-something food editor wore a shapeless pink dress and a matching pink sweater with embroidered pink roses, a sort of "grandma-chic" look. All that pink highlighted her chubby-cheeked, demented-doll look, as did her long chestnut hair, creamy skin, and round blue eyes. Felicity marched to a different fashion drummer than the rest of the reporting staff. Together, Pickles and Wiedemeyer looked like a pair of well-fed Kewpie dolls. Lacey thought they suited each other, in a weird way, and they obviously suited no one else. It was imperative, she decided, that they work out this bump in the road to the altar.

Lacey had introduced Felicity to Harlan, her true love. She had helped Felicity out of a jam in which she was the prime suspect in an assault on an editorial writer. She'd also helped Felicity shop for her wedding gown, a uniquely unpleasant experience. Felicity returned these favors by asking Lacey to be a bridesmaid at her wedding. Lacey suspected they were equally appalled at this prospect. Felicity didn't really like Lacey, the feeling was mutual, and Lacey shuddered at the thought of wearing some ghastly bridesmaid's get-up, which she had not yet even seen, to what was sure to be the tackiest wedding of the season.

No good deed goes unpunished.

The bride-to-be ordered the attendants' dresses online, and she said the wedding style was a Big Surprise and she didn't want to *spoil it prematurely*, so everyone would just have to wait. Lacey could only imagine the awfulness of such a dress. Right now, however, she couldn't be happier to see the resident cookie baker.

"Felicity! You're just in time. Harlan is looking for you. He's at my desk. He's feeling a little, well, blue. Why don't you go cheer him up?"

She turned to Lacey, her eyes brimming with tears.

"Oh Lacey! I don't know what's going on with Harlan. He's having cold feet, we had a big fight, and the wedding is next month!"

Naturally. A July wedding in Washington, D.C., so the entire wedding party will melt in the heat and humidity. But at least their feet will be warm.

"Why? What's going on with you two?"

"Nothing really. Just the tree thing."

"The tree thing?" Lacey filled her coffee cup and waited.

"Remember the big storm that went through D.C. late Friday night?"

"Sort of." Lacey didn't, she lived across the Potomac in Virginia, but she nodded.

"Harlan picked me up at my apartment. As we were leaving, he said something about my landlord, George, who lives upstairs. George is raising my rent again and Harlan said something about how maybe a tree should fall on him. He was just joking, of course, but just then the storm picked up and as we pulled away, this big oak tree fell on George's car."

"Your landlord's car?" *At least it wasn't a Krispy Kreme sign.* "Was lightning involved?"

"I don't know." Felicity wiped her eyes. "I think the tree was just dead. And the wind was awful. Did he tell you about that?"

"Listen, Felicity, these things happen." *Although they seem to happen more often around Harlan Wiedemeyer.*

"That's what I told him. Right? But what can I do?"

"What you always do, Felicity. What you do best. *Feed him.* Love him. Take good care of him. And please feed Mac while you're at it. Or else it's going to be a grueling week here."

"Oh Lacey. You're so right. It's my duty." Felicity squared her shoulders and picked up the plate of quiche. "I can do this. I'm on it."

"You go, girl. By the way, Detective Lamont enjoyed your quiche."

"What? Why didn't you tell me he was here? Are you in trouble again? What have you done now?"

"Nothing! I have done nothing." Lacey felt her hackles rise.

"Really?" Felicity had a wicked Resting Bitch Face. "Detective Lamont only comes around here when you're in trouble."

"Except when *you're* the suspect. Like last Christmas. Attempted murder, remember?"

Meow.

Felicity's eyes went wide. She opened her mouth to speak, decided against it, and flounced out with her quiche to save the world.

Lacey drained her cup and poured herself the dregs from the pot. It was going to be a long week at *The Eye.*

And she was still freezing.

LACEY SMITHSONIAN'S
FASHION *BITES*

SUMMER STYLE CHALLENGE:
SWELTERING OUTSIDE, SHIVERING INSIDE

Are these steamy summer days and nights playing havoc with your style? Of course they are. Washington's heat and humidity coat your skin with sweat, transform your clothes into a limp mess, and explode your hair into frizz. A summer rain soaks even the most carefully curated outfit. You lost your umbrella on the Metro. Fun times.

As if that's not bad enough, your workplace is ruining your attempt to enjoy sleeveless dresses and sandals and hot-day friendly hairdos. Not with their office dress code. No, they do it with that evil must-not-be-touched thermostat and A/C that would frost a polar bear.

The moment you step into the humidity outside, you melt into layers of wrinkles and soggy cotton. Then you return to the germ-infested icicle zone in your office, where you shiver in the air conditioning, which is blowing out of the vent above your head and whistling down the back of your neck. Hello, summer cold and flu.

Did you know that most offices' temperatures are set for the comfort of men wearing suits, not women in their summer dresses? You aren't surprised? Of course not. It is the eternal male-female struggle over climate control. The men who control the climate are comfortable and, if they aren't, they can at least take off their jackets. And the women? *Women suffer.*

This is the curse of the modern, environmentally controlled workplace under the thumb of some petty office despot wielding the power of the thermostat dial. Some companies call him "the building engineer." I call him "the devil." He laughs at your discomfort. He doesn't care about global warming. He just cranks up the cool another notch.

Does the same devil run *your* office's climate control? Here are some test questions.

- **Is your nose red from** the cold and freezing to the touch? Your hands too stiff to type?
- **Do you run to the** restroom just to run hot water over your frigid fingers?
- **Must you flee at lunchtime** to a sidewalk café just to warm up, despite the noise, the humidity, the diesel exhaust, and the UV rays?
- **Have you sneaked a small** portable heater under your desk, in flagrant violation of your office's draconian policies against Personal Warming Devices?

Then yes, your office is too frigid for women to work comfortably. No one wants to wear winter woolies when the outside temperature soars past ninety degrees and the humidity is ninety-nine percent. But you can't do anything about the weather outside, and your employer refuses to adjust the weather inside. What to do? Plan your strategy.

- **Have a light yet warm wrap** on hand, a jacket, a sweater, a shawl, or a large scarf. Keep one in the office in a color that will go with most of your summer clothes. I suggest black, white, navy or even red. Ditto for a cardigan sweater, if that's your style. My vote is for the easy-to-carry shawl or scarf, which can be folded up or even tied around your tote bag when you're outside. It's handy when you enter a chilly restaurant or shop on your lunch break in a frigid mall.
- **A pair of closed-toed shoes** under your desk for when your feet are freezing. Fleecy Ugg boots? Fluffy bunny slippers to slide those frozen toes into? Comfort vs. style? Your call.

- **Fingerless gloves, a la Bob Cratchit.** These are sometimes necessary in the frostier offices just to be able to type (or scrawl ledger entries with a quill pen, like Mr. Cratchit). Can't find them? Find your scissors and snip the fingers out of a pair of old cloth gloves, or find a pair of fingerless athletic gloves. Believe me, they work.
- **The cozy heater under the desk.** I'm sure those are allowed in your office, right? Oh, they're not? *Go rogue.* The choice may come down to policy or pleurisy. Your decision.
- **Hats! A little extreme to wear** in the office, but they do send a message that you are seriously *cold.* Even better, encourage all your female coworkers to wear hats and gloves to shame your management. (As if shaming them were even possible.)

And if nothing else works, coming to work in the summer heat looking like a homeless waif out of Charles Dickens in the dead of winter may embarrass your bosses. Maybe they'll finally give you a little heat.

The *good* kind.

NINE

HE EYE'S IN-HOUSE online archive contained brief summaries of three articles about that legendary production of *The Masque of the Red Death*. Long before current publisher Claudia Darnell bought the paper, it had begun as a slightly disreputable arts and entertainment weekly, and nothing had been too sensational for it to cover. A lurid death at a local theatre? *The Eye* had been all over it. But no one had scanned these old paper weeklies into the digital database.

Lacey headed up to the paper's library, where the hard copies resided in embossed leather binders and might have additional information that hadn't made it into the online archive. And it would get her out of the newsroom and the tension of the Pickles-Wiedemeyer pickle.

The library was on the fourth floor overlooking Farragut Square. Some decorator had been turned loose and ditched the newsroom's soothing green color scheme for stark gray and black. Through the glass doors the padded armchairs looked inviting, and most were occupied. But the space would have been nicer without the carpet's dizzying pattern of swirls in black on gray.

The serenity was punctuated by the occasional snore of reporters on break, hiding away in the magazine alcove. A sports reporter was slumped in his chair, head back, mouth open. Lacey saw a female production assistant asleep, head down, a magazine on her chest. *Obviously not a scintillating issue.* The library was so cold Lacey could practically see her breath, but the chill wasn't keeping these people awake.

If only the paper provided an adult nap room, we'd be so much more productive, she thought. *When we're not napping.*

The library wasn't large, but movable stacks maximized the floor space and slid apart at the press of a button. The volume she sought from twelve years before was easier to find than she expected, and Lacey lugged the big binder to a table by the window.

Nodding to the statue of Admiral Farragut and the birds perched on his hat, she settled down to read.

The newspaper's physical layout had changed over the past decade-plus. *The Eye* had matured from its weekly tabloid origins, but it was still the brash and bracing newcomer on the D.C. media scene. While the paper had vastly expanded its online coverage, the page count had begun to shrink in recent years, and Lacey was amazed at how thick these old issues were, stuffed with page after page of classifieds, personal ads, theatre and restaurant reviews. She flipped the dusty pages, trying not to be distracted by the ads.

The first article was a preview in the Arts section of the upcoming production of *The Masque of the Red Death*, describing the Kinetic Theatre's original design and unique production process. The show drew its inspiration from the Edgar Allan Poe text and the vintage Roger Corman and Vincent Price film, said the director, Yuri Volkov, but the Poe tale itself was so brief that they had needed to "flesh it out." That job fell to young local playwright Gareth Cameron. Dialogue would be kept to a minimum, however, and Kinetic was creating a musical interpretation of Poe's short story with the troupe's signature style of dance and movement. Nearly the entire troupe consisted of Russian émigrés who had trained in Russian theatres, according to *The Eye*.

Next came a review of the show's opening night. KINETIC THEATRE BRINGS RED DEATH TO LIFE was the headline. *The Eye*'s critic at the time (before Tamsin Kerr) described the movement style as "a cross between ballet, martial arts, and Cirque de Soleil" and the music as "heavy metal meets Russian folk songs way off-Broadway."

Nevertheless, she gave the show a rave, calling it "daring and visually exciting," and provided *The Eye*'s readers with a synopsis.

...The castle's seven rooms, described in the Poe story as being decorated in seven different colors, have been reinterpreted by the Kinetic Theatre as also embodying the seven deadly sins: Gluttony, Greed, Sloth, Envy, Lust, Pride, and Wrath. Set on interlocking mechanical platforms, the colors change and the rooms rise and fall and turn as dictated by the action.

True to Poe's tale, the plague of the Red Death is running riot through the land, the blood pouring from the bodies of its dying victims giving the disease its name. Fearful of this deadly plague, the cowardly tyrant Prince Prospero abandons his people and invites his nobles and favored subjects to his remote castle. They lock the gates and plan to party away the plague year, even as it ravages the common folk.

As an amusement, Prospero throws a grand masque, here staged as a play within the play, studded with nuggets from other Poe stories. His guests don elaborate costumes and masks of every color, the color red alone being forbidden. At the climax of the masque, Death crashes the party disguised as a beautiful woman, swathed in a glorious, flowing red gown, her face concealed by a jewel-encrusted red mask. Intrigued by this mysterious seductress, Prospero follows her, desperate to know her identity. They whirl and pirouette, up and down, around and through the castle's seven sin-themed rooms. The woman in red teases and beckons the prince further and further, until finally in the red room (for Lust) he catches and embraces her.

But she is the Red Death. The beautiful stranger opens her red gown to reveal the rotting corpse beneath. She removes her red mask to show her face, a gleaming jeweled skull. With shifting light and dazzling makeup, Kinetic's stagecraft sleight-of-hand transforms costumer Nikolai Sokolov's beautiful crimson dress from a lovely dream to a ghastly spectre of doom.

The Red Death spins exultantly across the ballroom floor as Prospero, realizing his fate, falls and dies. Death triumphs over all, laughing and dancing as the music swells. The rest of the cast join her for one last big production number as the revelers drop dead, one by one, leaving only Death to take the final bow...

Sounds like a hell of a show. At least our theatre critic was having fun.

Lacey turned back to the preview describing the costumes and the overall production design. This article was accompanied by several photographs. In the first, Saige

Russell, the young actress who played the Red Death, wore the jeweled red mask, only her eyes visible. In the second, she gazed seductively at the camera, wearing the red gown but sans mask. Saige Russell was lovely, with large green eyes and masses of wavy dark hair, and yet the only time in the show when she took off the red mask, she was made up to resemble a death's head.

A shame she had to play that part without ever showing her real face.

Lacey paged through the volume to find the issue immediately following the show's final performance. The news of the *Red Death* disaster had jumped from the Arts section to the front page of *The Eye.*

RED DEATH ACTRESS DIES IN TRAGIC CLOSING NIGHT ACCIDENT

Uh oh. So the rumors were true. Damn.

Lacey had convinced herself it couldn't possibly be true, that it was just a lurid local theatre legend, like Ford's Theatre's ghosts of Mary Todd Lincoln and John Wilkes Booth, and the spectral Hamlet in the National Theatre. Now she felt like the crimson gown was mocking her. Or maybe it was simply the world at large that mocked.

Saige Russell really was dead, it seemed, and had been dead for a dozen years.

The paper reported that Russell appeared to have fallen from the top of the highest mechanical platform on the stage in a freak accident, and she suffered a broken neck. Her body was not discovered until the next morning. A Kinetic Theatre spokesman said Russell failed to show up at the opening night party at a nightclub called the Black Cat. That was unusual, but everyone thought she was simply exhausted from the performance and went straight home. No one knew what Russell was doing on the stage after the final curtain, the paper said. The story neglected to mention whether or not she was found wearing her Red Death costume.

A Russian children's play, "The Nutcracker and the Mouse King," had been scheduled for the following afternoon, using the same elaborate castle set but with brighter set dressing. That show was canceled. *The Eye*'s story was short on facts, but long on sympathetic quotes from Russell's fellow theatre folk.

"Saige was on the cusp of great things," said one Maksym Pushkin, the actor who had played Prince Prospero. "A star in the making."

Of course. What else could anyone say?

"A beauty. A true professional," said Yuri Volkov, the play's director.

"She would have made it to the top," said Katya Pritchard, another Kinetic actress and Saige's understudy, apparently without irony.

It seems Saige did make it to the top, Lacey mused. *And then she fell off.*

More actors and theatre production people were quoted in several variations on what a terrible tragedy it was. There was nothing in the story that suggested to Lacey a connection to LaToya's break-in. After all, it happened so long ago.

Lacey jotted down all the names mentioned in the three articles and lugged the heavy binder over to the library's copier. It wasn't easy wrangling the oversized book, but she was sure Mac and LaToya would want their own copies. She noted that the last seat in the chilly library had been taken by yet another sleepy staffer. Fighting a yawn herself, Lacey re-shelved the volume and gathered her copies.

Back at her desk she left a voice-mail message for Tamsin Kerr, *The Eye*'s current theatre critic. Did Tamsin know of any actresses who had worn the red dress who might be willing to talk about it?

She checked her notes. Amy Keaton still hadn't returned her call. She tried her again: no answer, so she left another message. Why was this woman ducking Lacey's calls? *She begged me to intervene with LaToya, you'd think she'd want to hear from me.* Was Keaton feeling ashamed of her behavior, which might include that bizarre break-in? Lacey hoped that was the reason.

Because if Amy Keaton didn't do the break-in, my only other suspect is Saige Russell's ghost. Maybe she wants her red dress back.

TEN

*A*S PROMISED, LATOYA showed up at Lacey's desk in the late afternoon, wearing a sleek sleeveless linen paprika-colored dress and red heels. She was keeping warm with a patterned scarf twisted around her neck.

"Red, really?" Lacey asked. "I assumed you'd had enough of red dresses."

"Hell yes, red. I'm seriously jangled and red is my go-to color. Burgundy, crimson, claret, scarlet. Doesn't matter. This is my way of defying bad things. You want me, world? Bring it on, I am wearing a red dress! Besides, this one was still in my closet, untouched."

"Fair enough. Your go-to color might make a good Fashion Bite." Lacey filed the idea away for later.

"Bite on. I'm ready to bite the head off the wacko who burgled my place." LaToya took a breath. "So, what did you find out about my dress?"

"Only this." Lacey handed her the copies of the articles from the archive. "I haven't found any connection between that woman, the red dress, and your break-in."

"Not yet." LaToya's red fingernails separated the pages like small daggers.

"No, not yet." Lacey shifted in her chair. "I can't imagine who would dare tangle with you, LaToya."

"Makes two of us. I get that sucker, I'm gonna tear his, or her, lungs out."

LaToya almost sat down in the Death Chair but thought better of it. She kicked it out of the way and dragged another chair over and sat down.

"I'll take your word for it. If that Kinetic gown is going to cause such problems, are you sure you don't want to just take it back to the theatre? Get your money back? Get the Keaton woman off your case?"

"Smithsonian, this is no longer a matter of style. Now it's a matter of principle."

"Which principle is that?"

"The *nobody makes LaToya Crawford back down from anything* principle."

Lacey smiled. "No wonder Broadway Lamont is afraid of you."

"He is not afraid, he's just shy. He's gotta warm up to me." LaToya stared at the old photos of Saige Russell. "Okay, listen up. I'm too close to this story, I know that. I'm willing to let you take it and run with it, write the tale of the red dress, so I can tell it to my future children. All I want is a happy ending. And that red dress. After all, this may be the thing that brings Broadway and me together."

"So when are you going to take the dress off my hands? Soon, I hope."

"Are you crazy? I want it, but I don't want it till it's been cleaned," LaToya said. "Between you and me, Lacey, I'm not sure I really do want it anymore, but no one else is getting it."

"Cleaned? You mean dry cleaned?"

"Don't be coy. You know I'm talking about washing the weirdness out of that dress. That's what I want, a dress cleansed of all that bad juju. Psychically purified. Spiritually spotless."

"Not my specialty."

"So you say, Smithsonian."

"You just want it to have a *story*, LaToya. A great story to go with a great dress."

"We're reporters, Lacey. Everything is about the story. Who wouldn't want a notorious dress? Well, a certain amount of notorious." She read further and suddenly dropped the article on Lacey's desk. "Oh my god, she did die in that dress!"

Across the newsroom, reporters' heads popped up like prairie dogs.

"We don't know she died *in* the dress. And keep it down," Lacey whispered. "Don't forget, if that dress is related to her death and your break-in, the cops might want it for evidence. It will disappear into an evidence locker and that might as well be a black hole."

Mac materialized at Lacey's desk and loomed over the two reporters like a storm cloud.

"Someone yelling out here?"

"Not me." Lacey glanced over at LaToya.

"I wouldn't call that *yelling*," LaToya said, turning the articles over to Mac. "You've heard me yelling. That was more like a startled reaction. Mild surprise."

"I heard the words *dead* and *dress*. So there was a death associated with that crazy dress?" He raised his eyebrows at Smithsonian.

"Not necessarily," Lacey said. "The dress may have had nothing to do with the woman's death."

His eyebrows gathered together to form an impressive storm front and he pointed them at LaToya. "And what about the break-in?"

"I'm waiting for Smithsonian to find a connection," LaToya said.

"Come on, LaToya. There's no connection! Sometimes things just happen."

"Well, they don't just happen to me."

"These are a lot of articles for one show." Mac picked up LaToya's stack of copies and flipped through them.

"I got lucky," Lacey said. "And it seems *The Eye* had more than one theatre writer back then."

He snorted in reply.

"Unless it's murder, keep the noise level down out here. And keep me in the loop."

Lacey and LaToya watched him make an obligatory pass over Felicity's desk, checking for afternoon snacks. There were none. He walked away, grumbling.

"Okay, storm's over," LaToya said. "Did you talk to that frizzy-haired woman?"

"She hasn't returned my calls."

"She's the type, all right." LaToya glowered. "Makes you crazy, doesn't answer your calls, won't call you back."

"I'll try again. In the meantime, don't say anything to Harlan Wiedemeyer. He loves weird death stories, he'll want to steal this one."

"The jinx? I'd never tell Wiedemeyer anything. That man practices some strange upside-down magic."

"He's not a jinx. And he's heading this way."

"He is a jinx. My berry-red dress better not go up in flames." LaToya jumped up from the chair. "Gotta finish a story, I'm on deadline." She strutted away at top speed on her dangerous red heels.

There's got to be a name for that walk, Lacey thought. *Maybe the Reporter Quick Step.*

Lacey's desk phone rang, and it was Tamsin Kerr returning her call. Tamsin sounded like she was still in bed. *The life of a theatre critic.*

"Thanks, Tamsin, I need your special knowledge. Do you know any of the actresses who have worn the red dress from *Red Death?*"

A pause. "Ah, the famous dress. Possibly. Let me think. One curious thing, though. No one at Kinetic ever wears it, only actresses from outside the company. Their own people seem to think it's not a good idea, but they're happy to loan it out. I knew a few actresses at Woolly Mammoth who wore it years ago, and that one woman at Arena Stage, but they've all gone to New York, I don't even have numbers for them anymore. Oh, wait, I can think of at least two women at Source Theatre who have donned the deadly dress for special occasions. Susannah Kittredge and Noelle Pepper. One of them wore it this year to the Helen Hayes Awards and one last year, but don't ask me which was which. I'm good, but not that good."

"I appreciate your gift."

"Do get something dramatic out of this, won't you?" Tamsin yawned.

"I'll settle for newsworthy. You have their phone numbers?"

Lacey called Susannah Kittredge, who said she'd be happy to meet her for lunch the next day at Trio's Restaurant, and she would call Noelle Pepper, who was a friend. If that lunch, of course, was on *The Eye*? Lacey assured her it would be. Kittredge explained she had a daytime gig reading books for the blind through the Library of Congress, while Pepper worked in industrial films. Tomorrow though, she thought their lunchtime schedules might just possibly be free.

Of course they're free, if there's a free lunch. Actors!

ELEVEN

WHAT MAKES THIS gown so special?
Lacey loved good clothes, but she was always a little surprised when others got obsessed with a dress, especially when the obsession involved her coworkers. And her editor, of all people. It was a mystery.

Her only plan this afternoon was to go back to the beginning. She reread all the articles she had copied and found a name she'd overlooked before, the costume designer, Nikolai Sokolov. *The Eye* only mentioned him once, but he was also credited with the set and lighting design. He seemed to be a one-man wonder, but then the Kinetic Theatre was just starting out back then. The article credited one of the actors, Maksym Pushkin, as a wardrobe assistant. Lacey knew theatre people often worked double and triple duty, especially in struggling small theatres.

Sokolov was one place to start. In the archive she found a few more mentions of him in connection with Kinetic and other local theatre companies. He had won a couple of Helen Hayes Awards, Washington's equivalent of Broadway's Tony, but he had no other social media trails. She called Kinetic. Someone had to be at the theatre by now.

Someone was. However, Kinetic's artistic director, Yuri Volkov, made it clear he was sorry he'd picked up the phone. He reluctantly allowed that if she *really* had no intention of leaving him alone, she could come by the theatre, if she *really* wanted to waste her time. It would have been easier to just answer a few questions on the phone, Lacey thought, but no, he wanted her to jump through hoops.

Maybe it's a Russian thing. He makes Gregor Kepelov seem charming.

The sun was searing as she left *The Eye*'s cool lobby. The June heat wave had Washingtonians praying for rain. Lacey tried hailing a taxi, without luck. She strolled on in the heat, stopping at a café for an iced tea. When she reached the theatre both she and the tea were melting.

Kinetic occupied an old building just off Sixteenth Street NW near Dupont Circle, where it had resided for the past several years. *The Masque of the Red Death* had been produced in a different space, Lacey remembered from her clippings, one borrowed from another theatre.

The two-centuries-old red-brick building had clearly served many purposes. Once a church, later a warehouse and a nightclub, it had found its mission as a theatre for various troupes for at least the past half century. The edifice harmonized with the rest of the block's old-fashioned apartment buildings and townhouses. Miraculously, it had not been scooped up by developers, scraped, or turned into a jutting high rise of overpriced condominiums. Lacey opened the door and felt a welcome blast of chilled air. Though the building was old, the renovated lobby had the smell of fresh wood and paint.

Yuri Volkov greeted her at the door, but he was busy, very busy, he said in a pronounced Russian accent, with his new show about to premiere. He gripped a large mug of coffee in his hand, but he didn't offer her any.

Not my day for free coffee.

He had important things to do today, he complained, going over the score with the musicians, rethinking the choreography in the second act, overseeing the day-to-day business of the theatre, ensuring the water bill was paid and the electricity was working and the building inspector was happy. Unless she was there to write a positive story about the upcoming show, Volkov told her, he could only spare a few minutes. He left no doubt what a great concession he was making.

"I won't take up much of your time," she promised.

Volkov snorted. With a gesture and a dramatic sigh he allowed Lacey to follow him through the lobby and up the stairs to the light booth, where he checked the lighting plot, the placement of the stage lights, cue by cue. He sat at a long table in front of a laptop and a mass of cables and equipment, focusing intently. He clicked the mouse and the stage lit up, colored lights flashing on and off in sequence, casting shadows on his face. Bits and pieces of furniture and stage sets were spotlighted in turn as Volkov hit the keys. He worked in a fury. Taking a seat, Lacey studied him in silence.

The man was muscular and compactly built, and though he was still except for his hands and eyes, he seemed to vibrate with energy. His every controlled movement exuded passion for his work. His attention to each task was intense, yet he seemed weary. His dark hair was slicked straight back from his face, he had fine features and a straight nose, and his large round eyes were so dark they looked black in the dim light. He might almost be considered pretty, she thought, if not for his apparently permanent scowl and the deep vertical worry line between his eyes.

Lacey gazed down at the theatre below. The thrust stage was directly across from the booth, and the seats, laid out in a semicircle around it, were raked at a steep angle. The set was painted in shades of deep purple and moody blues. It featured multiple pieces that could fly in and out from above, including walls and windows and door frames and tables and chairs. White sheer curtains shifted with the lights into ghostly images.

Programs for the current show were scattered on the table, and Lacey picked one up. The upcoming Kinetic production was a song-and-dance extravaganza, a dark musical reimagining of *The Turn of the Screw*. Not quite the solemn Henry James original, she surmised.

They like their shows gothy and gloomy, don't they? And with singing and dancing.

As she read on, she realized this show seemed to be a reunion of sorts for some of the *Masque of the Red Death* crew. She recognized a few names. Volkov had directed the *Masque*, and both the playwright Gareth Cameron and the costume designer Nikolai Sokolov were credited in this new show. Some of the original dancers were on hand as well. Lacey began to hope she might get a story yet out of the red dress and this hot day's journey to the far side of Dupont Circle.

"So. You are here about that damn red dress?" Volkov finally turned around and stared at her.

"That 'damn dress' would be the one worn by Death in *The Masque of the Red Death*? Yes, I was at the big theatre garage sale on Saturday. You heard there was a conflict over the purchase?"

He shrugged elaborately in a way she assumed must be a theatrical specialty.

"Yes, a conflict. So?"

"I understand there was a mix-up, and the red dress from *The Masque* might have been sold by mistake."

"I'm not in charge of such things as selling old costumes! Let me tell you, one of the very few things here of which I am not in charge."

"You don't care that it was sold?"

"That stupid rag? Of course not." Yuri Volkov drained his coffee and slammed the mug down on the table. "Nothing but trouble. Every year some actress comes begging to wear that thing. You would think they are auditioning for a part, with the pleading and the wheedling, and the Please I must have it or I will die." He paused for breath. "Now it's been sold. It is gone. Good riddance."

"Why do you say that?"

"It is just a costume! A very clever one, it was good for the show, but people have romantic ideas. They think it means more. They think it means good luck. Or points for courage to dare such bad luck. Or whatever it is they think. Please. Actors! They give me a headache. Writers give me a headache too."

"My pleasure. Was it a mistake for it to be on the sale rack?"

"As I said, I was not in charge of the sale."

"Was Amy Keaton in charge?"

"Keaton? Maybe. Yes, I think so. I washed my hands of it. We needed to make space, get rid of clutter, all the old junk. We all decide to sell these things, but then *no*, the Keaton has to change her mind, start a big fight. So now there is one thing for which I am not personally responsible, *one thing,* and you see the problems I have when that happens?" He rubbed his head and smoothed his hair. "It never stops. And now I have a reporter asking me irrelevant questions. Not about my new show! No, about a show a dozen years ago that will not bring people into my theatre. I cannot sell tickets to a dead show. Thank you very much, Amy Keaton. Talk to *her* if you must. I will tell you this, that woman drives me crazy. A good stage manager, yes, but the complaining, the bitching, the moaning."

She's got nothing on you, Yuri Volkov. "I'd love to. Is she here?"

"Who knows. I haven't seen her today. As far as I know, she has not come in yet. I am here, I work my ass off, but I am alone. Do you see what I mean?"

"What can you tell me about Nikolai Sokolov?"

Volkov looked surprised. "Nicky? He is our resident costume designer. What do you want to know? Some people like him, some hate him. He is a perfectionist. Pain in the neck, but no one better at what he does. That is why I let him do this show. He is the best." Volkov didn't look very happy about it.

"Sokolov had a small part in your *Masque*. Is he an actor too?"

"Used to be. Technically perfect," Volkov said. "The movement, the action, the expressions, all perfect. You see this in some actors, they lead with their head, all brains. Not their guts. All head, that's Nicky. The best actors have both, brains and guts, but the very best? They lead with their heart."

"Can you be more specific?"

"Very smart man. At times it seems, maybe Nicky is too smart to be an actor, you know? Acting is a physical thing, especially our Kinetic acting. Big movement, big dancing, music never stops, very deep, very sexual, in your gut. Not Nicky. But in a pinch, Nikolai is your man. For small roles, cerebral roles."

"Would he care that the red dress was sold?"

Volkov finally laughed, his first. "Nicky? Why on earth would he care? He has designed hundreds and hundreds of costumes. The costume he cares about is the one he is working on right now. Like me. Always a new show. Opening night. Nothing else matters."

Lacey was getting nowhere fast. "Could you tell me about the production of *The Masque of the Red Death*?"

Volkov slapped his forehead. "*The Masque*. Always people think of Kinetic, they think *Masque*. Why? It was a million years ago." He turned away from her to tap on the laptop.

"What about the actor who played Prospero?"

Volkov wrinkled his nose. "Don't remember."

"Maksym Pushkin was the name in our archives."

"Pushkin. That's right. Good dancer. The ladies loved him. Hasn't worked onstage here in years. But he still teaches dance class now and then."

"Russian?"

"Many in our company are Russian. Most. Not all of course. We let others audition if they are able to dance our way. They must be in top shape, athletic, fearless, head, heart and guts. Perfect." He squinted at Lacey as if looking at her for the first time. "Smithsonian? Lacey Smithsonian? Not the museum. How do I know that name? Wait. Tamsin Kerr! She wrote a review about you. Yes?"

"It was supposed to be a news story. She just couldn't help herself."

"Ha. Once a critic, always a critic."

Tamsin was supposed to write a hard news story that happened to involve Lacey, a lethal black dress, a killer, and a confrontation to which Tamsin was an eyewitness. Instead, she had penned it as if it were a theatre review, and she featured Lacey prominently as the leading lady. Lacey tried to get the interview back on track.

"Right. Saige Russell. She died after the final curtain of *The Masque*. Tell me about her."

Volkov looked supremely irritated. "Idiot! Foolishly climbing all over the set after the show. In the dark. All alone. I have no idea why. There was nothing wrong with that set, let me tell you. We should have struck it after closing curtain, maybe she would be alive. But we didn't strike the set that night, because of a children's show the next day. Our children's theatre, very popular."

"So I've heard. Were you there when it happened?"

He stopped tapping on his laptop as if remembering. "No. We were all at the cast party. Wondering where Saige Russell was. Drinking. Dancing. Big party. I didn't hear about the accident till the next day."

"Was she wearing the costume when she died, the red dress?"

"The Red Death costume?" He shook his head furiously. "Of course not! Always that stupid rumor! No, she took it off. Costumes go back to wardrobe after the show, always, then later to the cleaners."

"Do you remember her? Saige Russell?"

He shrugged. "So many actresses. They come and go." Volkov lifted his hand in a dismissive gesture. "I remember she was beautiful, in a tragic way."

"Why do you say that?"

Another shrug. "Because she died so young. Maybe she wasn't really so pretty, but you say that because it is expected. Because it is sad."

Suddenly, he seemed to think of something, but it wasn't about the late actress, beautiful and tragic. He snapped his fingers. "You! Smithsonian! Now I remember! I read about you! You found the Romanov jewels! Diamonds and rubies, the lost corset!"

Lacey's turn to sigh. "Yeah. That has nothing to do with this story."

"Perhaps not. But every Russian knows about the Romanovs, wants to know more. It is a national curiosity." He narrowed her eyes at her. "Tell me. How did you do it?"

She had found the lost corset of one of the Romanov princesses and written about her adventure. How was she supposed to explain that ultimately it came down to a hunch, a feeling, a last possible resort? Lacey shook her head.

"I explained it all in my stories. In the newspaper."

"Bah. Trade secrets. I respect that. You are smart to keep secrets. A little theatrics, a little detective work, a little intuition. Perhaps you will tell me someday." He glanced at his watch. "You will find no jewels here. And the red costume is gone. I have work to do."

"I'm still interested in the story. Nikolai Sokolov created the costumes for this new show, *The Turn of the Screw*, as well as the *Masque*. Is he around right now?"

"He keeps his own hours. Geniuses make me insane. But the theatre is nothing without them. I am one too, so I know."

"Will you tell him I would like to speak with him?"

"Do I look like a secretary, Smithsonian? When I see him, *if* I see him, and there is no guarantee of that, I will tell him a reporter was asking about him. You want to see Nikolai, come see the show. You want to know about the long-ago production of *The Masque*, ask— Ah, who to ask? Ask Katya. She's a secretary now, paralegal, something like that." He named a law firm on K Street. "She was here back then. She has a long memory."

"Katya. Does she have a last name?"

"Pritchard. Katya Pritchard."

"Ah yes, Saige's understudy." Her name was in *The Eye*'s old articles.

"And you know what they say about understudies." She didn't, but he waved her away and turned back to his lighting plot. Yuri Volkov had had enough Smithsonian for one day.

Lacey showed herself out. She still had no idea what they said about understudies. *I'll ask Tamsin.*

Except of course for the cut-throat understudy in the movie *All About Eve,* an understudy of whom to beware. Was this Katya capable of pushing a leading lady off a platform to her death?

Should I watch my back around the understudy?

TWELVE

*A*S IT TURNED OUT, Katya Pritchard wasn't hard to find. Her law firm was well-known and well-placed on K Street and she was in the office and willing to talk. But puzzled.

"*The Masque?* That was ages ago! After all these years, you want to know about *The Masque?*" Pritchard said on the phone. "Why would anyone want to know about that ancient production?"

"Could I buy you coffee?" Lacey asked.

Coffee at Lacey's expense would be fine, according to Katya. *Of course it would.* At the Starbucks on K Street near her office, Katya ordered a complicated grande latte with about a thousand calories and a gooey caramel brownie to go with it. It looked wonderful. Despite her own deep desire for something chocolate, Lacey stuck with her plain black decaf coffee and a small package of mixed nuts. It didn't begin to fill the ache for something sweet.

The complex coffee ordering process gave Lacey a chance to observe this former actress and dancer. She would never have guessed the woman had been on stage: The day job had taken over. She was tall, but her dancer's body was now padded in fat, fed by Starbucks lattes and brownies. Katya wore all-black, fitting not merely for a former theatre person or a K Street grunt, but as a denizen of the Capital City. Clad in some sort of clingy stretchy fabric, she looked overheated. Her knit top had an unflattering round neckline and long sleeves that squeezed her ample arms. Pants in the same black stretchy fabric covered the woman's ample posterior.

Did Katya work in an office with a Felicity Pickles? Lacey wondered. *Or was she their Felicity Pickles?*

Katya was too young, Lacey thought, to wear pants with an elastic waistband. Stretch pants were a sign of *giving up,* in Lacey's opinion. Katya's face behind square black-framed glasses was soft and layered in plump folds, her skin pale and freckled and free of makeup. Her black hair was long and luxurious, obviously recently dyed, but she wore it in a severe and unflattering version of one of D.C.'s most popular hairstyles: pulled off the face and clipped up in back. She combed the bangs sideways to expose her ears, making her head look flat. Katya looked like a woman who had given up every vanity, except for her hair color. For that alone, Lacey silently applauded her.

"Thanks for the coffee." She settled into a chair opposite Lacey and set her drink and gooey brownie on the table. "Isn't this nice."

"Yes, it's beastly hot out there."

The sun's glare through the coffee shop window lit the disappointment that had settled into the lines of Katya's face. It was increasingly hard to believe that she was once in the cast of *The Masque of the Red Death*. Although her part was small, understudying the lead dance role must have been physically demanding.

"Katya is a pretty name."

"Thank you. It's Russian. Like my mother. My father was English. We wound up here."

"Yuri Volkov said it's not necessary to be Russian to dance for Kinetic."

"Maybe not, but it helps. That discipline is in the blood. I took dance classes since I was little. My mother insisted. So what are you writing about?" Katya apparently didn't know Lacey was a fashion reporter. "Something about that Kinetic production I was in?"

"I'm looking into the costume worn by the character of the Red Death in *The Masque*. The role you understudied? I saw it at the theatre yard sale on Saturday. Someone bought it."

Katya gasped. "They sold the red dress?" Her eyes were wide. "No!"

"Apparently it was sort of a mistake. But they did."

She surprised Lacey by laughing. "Oh my God. Generations of actresses will be denied their chance to wear that thing to the Helen Hayes. I was fitted for it myself, you know. I even wore it at dress rehearsal, for like five minutes. Saige and I were almost exactly the same size." She picked up her latte. "Yeah, I know it's hard to believe that now. Don't quote me."

She brushed crumbs off her top and looked away. *Ah yes. I was waiting for the obligatory 'don't quote me.'*

"Hey," Katya said suddenly, "do you want to see a picture of me in the red dress?"

Really? What are the odds of that?

"Do you have one with you?"

"Sure. On my phone." She dug it out of her purse. "I keep it on here to give me some inspiration for my diet." Katya looked ruefully at her brownie. "The spirit is willing, but you know."

"Wow." Lacey tried not to reveal the shock she felt looking at the picture. Young Katya in the tightly fitted crimson gown was beautiful and soulful-looking and very fit. "You look fabulous."

"Thanks. That was at dress rehearsal. I was actually a little thinner than Saige that day," she said with pride. "I wish I could have worn that dress in the show. It was a lovely creation. All those layers of reds, the mask, the headpiece. The colors just blended together like magic. It rustled when you walked, the way taffeta does, but it didn't make you feel fragile. It fell just right, and it had weight, a real swing to it. It made you feel strong and powerful, in control. That's the power of a great costume, you know. You sort of climb into it and just *drive* it. I didn't get to wear it for more than a few minutes at a time, because I never had a chance to take over the role. Saige never missed a performance. The gown, however, was amazing."

"I'm sorry you missed out on that. But at least you got to wear it for a fitting. So what was Saige Russell like?" Lacey sipped her coffee and took mental notes, not wanting to distract Katya with a notebook and pen.

"Saige? You wanted to talk about Saige?" Her face darkened. "I don't know, really. After all, time slips by. Memories fade."

Lacey doubted that. "You were friends?"

"Sure." Katya had a lovely smile, though it was lit with a hint of malice. "Theatre friends. You know. Hugging, cheek-kissing, hello-darling kind of friends. For a few shows. And then, well, she died."

"And you stopped doing theatre?"

"Life intrudes. You can't make a living if you're not Equity, and then sometimes you can't make it even if you are Equity. You forget about the theatre and dancing and you grow up, get a real job."

"Did you make Equity?"

Katya saw something in her memory. "Getting my Equity card was a peak moment. One of those moments you always remember. I was on my way." Katya's smile dimmed. "It didn't work out. A lot of the little theatres aren't Equity, so I lost those parts, and I couldn't get cast often enough to survive. I taught acting and dance for a while, but I didn't want to do that forever. You turn thirty, then thirty-five. Then—" She paused. "Being a paralegal for a big firm has its advantages, you know. Job security. Not to mention great health insurance."

"Insurance is good." Lacey hoped she would never look this sad to the world.

"It's a good job. I wouldn't trade my job for an early grave. I mean, Saige had her best role ever in *The Masque*. Great reviews, a hot show, she was on top of the world. She had Nikolai, and she was in love, and everything seemed to be going so brilliantly. And then she—fell off the platform. Fell off the stage. Fell off the edge of the world." Katya was looking at something in the distance, something in her past.

"You said 'she had Nikolai'? You mean Nikolai Sokolov?" Lacey asked. "The costume designer?"

"Nikolai." Katya took her time sipping her latte. "He broke the bank on that red dress for Saige." Something in her tone changed.

"So he was more than just her costume designer?'

"Oh yes. They had this big affair. I walked in on them a couple of times. Not quite *in flagrante delicto*. They 'frolicked' everywhere, in the dressing room, the costume shop, the theatre. The light booth." She laughed. Gossip with a soupçon of glee was perking Katya up. "It just proves that you can have it all, but the next minute you're dead. My life isn't that glamorous, but I'm not dead."

True. We're not dead.

"Do you still act?"

"No. I don't dance either. Not at this size. I could get parts, like comic parts, but..." The sentence trailed off and she looked away.

"Do you ever go to the theatre?"

"Once in a while. When I can get a comp. Who can afford theatre tickets?"

"What about Nikolai? Do you still see him around?"

"Around." She nodded. "His home base is Kinetic though. He's worked for a lot of theatres, the smaller ones. He's so talented, he can do anything. Costumes, sets, lights, sound. He's not a one-trick pony."

"He's making the costumes for Kinetic's latest show."

"Really." Katya was tearing her brownie into tiny pieces. "He would be. He's a great costumer. Nicky's not super handsome, he's good looking, but— Compelling. Dark hair. Intense. And those blue eyes. At least I think they're blue."

"You think?"

She made a face.

"They seem to change. Contact lenses, probably. His eyes were extra blue back then. No one has eyes that color. Gave him a very intense look. Brooding. Romantic."

"An actor too?"

"Isn't everyone?"

"All the world's a stage," Lacey agreed.

"Nicky did some small parts. Like me. But acting wasn't his main thing."

"Theatre tech people don't usually act, right?"

"Yeah, but he always said if he was on the stage with the other actors, he could get a better feel for the play, and what he wanted to do with the technical stuff."

"Did you date him?"

Katya's hand froze with a bit of brownie hovering near her mouth. "I wanted to, but Saige got there first. And afterward— Well, going after Nicky after she died seemed in bad taste." She popped the brownie in her mouth. "Besides, the show was over. When the show closes, that one little family kind of breaks up. Things cool off."

Lacey nodded. Or Nikolai might not have been interested in Katya, she thought, even though she'd been young and lovely. Chemistry was fickle and mysterious. Her black coffee was wretched and lukewarm to boot, but she wanted to keep Katya remembering.

"What about Yuri Volkov? Is he as intense as he seems?"

Katya grinned. "Intense? Yuri? More. He is a perfectionist. That's why he gets such strong performances. Geniuses are like that. He can make you cry."

"Did he make you cry?"

"A couple times. It felt like he wasn't satisfied until you broke down at least once. After that, you could be friends. Yuri is a little weird."

"Sounds like. Was he interested in Saige? Romantically?"

"That's the big mystery about Yuri. No one really knows if he's interested in men or women, or if he's even interested in sex at all. Not a clue. I think he just likes to keep that part of his life private. Really private. Whatever it is. Really, I think the theatre is his whole life."

"What can you tell me about the leading man? The one who played Prince Prospero?"

"Maksym. Oh yes. Good looking in a real traditional matinee-idol way. He had beautiful thick hair. Sexy eyes. Taller than Saige, and me. I think that's why he was cast. Not many of the male dancers were that tall. And Maksym was always in beautiful shape. Great dancer."

"Is he still around?"

"Yeah." Katya gazed at her drink again. "He went to law school, became a lawyer." She caught Lacey's lifted eyebrow. "No, not with my firm."

"How well did you know him?"

"Pretty well." Katya fluttered her hands almost as if she were trying to forget him. "We dated for a while. He was very— pretty. We made a pretty couple. Back then. But it's kind of hard when you always have to wonder which one of you everyone is looking at, you know? And it was all about Maksym, all the time, never about me. He was one of those performers who just suck all the air out of a room. Now he performs in the courtroom. He's good."

"Does he still dance?'

"I think he teaches a few classes at Kinetic sometimes. But he basically quit the theatre after Saige died. Not everyone is meant for a life on the stage." She picked up her latte.

Apparently that statement included at least three performers in *The Masque of the Red Death*: Katya Pritchard, Saige Russell, and Maksym Pushkin.

Katya sighed deeply. She and Lacey checked their watches simultaneously. Katya said she needed to get back to work and stood up. Lacey did too.

I have a psychic to call on.

THIRTEEN

*T*HE LITTLE SHOP OF HORUS, the books and curiosities shop owned by psychic Marie Largesse, would be open for only another hour. Exiting the King Street Metro, Lacey knew she could be at Marie's shop in fifteen minutes.

The tidy store off King Street in Alexandria near the river offered all sorts of books on the psychic world and New Age phenomena, and it always had a pungent aroma of rich herbs, scented candles, and incense. There were aisles of candles and sage for smudging. But no Ouija boards. Marie believed they opened the door to darkness, and she preferred the light.

It was a steamy stroll but Lacey was at Marie's shop before she realized it, and the door tinkled its familiar chime. The place looked deserted, but a musical Southern voice called out from the back room.

"Hello, Lacey. I've got some iced raspberry tea ready, cher."

"You were expecting me?" Lacey said.

"You have to ask?" Marie laughed.

Lacey had debated about even calling on Marie. As a psychic, Marie was usually able only to foretell positive or neutral events. When she caught vibes of death or disaster, fear or foreboding, she tended to faint, and later she seldom remembered anything very useful. Today, however, Marie seemed perfectly upbeat. She bustled into the shop with two tall glasses filled with ice and sweet Southern raspberry tea, and she wore an ethereal white flowing blouse with angel wing sleeves and a long blue denim skirt which flattered her voluptuous figure. Marie would never wear grey or beige or something as mundanely professional as a mere *suit*. Her clients, she said, didn't want to see their psychic looking like an aging Congressional staffer.

"Of course I knew you were on your way. Come in and sit down."

"I didn't call you," Lacey said, teasing her.

"Not on the phone." Marie handed her a glass of tea.

"You caught my vibes?" Lacey wasn't really surprised, but Marie's powers came and went and it was hard to predict whether they might be on or off.

"Big vibes. You wanted to ask me something?"

"It's about a dress, a costume I'm researching."

"Not your own dress?"

"No. A friend's."

"And it's red, isn't it? Red on red on red."

Lacey nodded. "It's at Vic's. At least he took it somewhere for safekeeping."

"Red is a powerful color, strong, sensuous. Too much of it can turn dark and overpowering."

Lacey touched her hand. "I don't want you to faint, Marie."

"No, no, cher. I'm fine. Gregor's sister, you know Olga, she's been helping me with that. Deep breathing. Lots of deep breathing. And centering."

"Why would Marie be fainting, Lacey Smithsonian?" The Russian-accented voice belonged to Olga Kepelova, who entered from the back room.

Olga was the sister of Marie's fiancé, Gregor Kepelov. She was a perennial houseguest of the happy couple and one of Marie's biggest fans. Olga had a shadowy background in the Russian intelligence services, and Lacey sometimes wondered if she had worked on psychic experiments with them. After emigrating to the U.S. she was now working as some kind of weapons expert, consulting with American law enforcement agencies.

There was a severe but wild-eyed quality about Olga. Her brown hair was cut in a razor-edged pageboy. Her brown eyes stared hard and seldom blinked. Lacey thought she vaguely resembled the Russian émigré writer Ayn Rand. She was too slender and wore pants and matching shirts in brown, black, or gray. Today, Olga was a monochromatic picture in brown, from her severe brown haircut to her booted feet.

Lacey briefly imagined her as Ayn Rand working for the United Parcel Service, but Olga wouldn't appreciate that whimsy. The woman rarely displayed even a shred of lightheartedness.

"I know she's a tad frightening," Marie whispered. "But Olga has a good heart. Under the hard angles. And Gregor's here, too," she said without looking.

Olga's brother, Gregor Kepelov, appeared behind her, a former Russian spy whose American dream it was to own a ranch in Texas and could usually be found, like today, wearing blue jeans, a cowboy shirt, and cowboy boots. He had blue eyes and close-cropped hair and sharp features that always seemed a quarter-turn off to Lacey. Marie lit up at the sight of him. She always saw something no one else could.

"Hello, Kepelov," Lacey said.

"Lacey Smithsonian. Marie said you would come by. And here you are. Let me see the ring." He grabbed her left hand and studied her engagement ring.

"You've been talking to Nigel?"

"Of course. Jewels excite him. Ah! Is beautiful antique setting. Good-sized diamond. Very nice. A family heirloom?"

"The stone was in Vic's family."

"Family. Always a good sign," Olga said. "Stability."

Marie crowded in for a look. "I wondered when you were going to tell everyone, cher."

"Some things I like to keep private," Lacey said, pulling her hand back.

Kepelov laughed. "Trust me, with friends like your Stella and Nigel Griffin and my Marie, who knows all, privacy is a fantasy."

"I didn't want to press you for details," Marie said, taking Lacey's hand gently. "It was obvious from the start. The first time I met Victor Donovan I knew you would wind up together."

Lacey grinned. "The first time you met Vic, you fainted."

"Well, yes. At the warehouse, but not when I saw you two together. My, that is a lovely ring, it has such good energy! The setting and the diamond. Both have been much loved."

Marie invited Lacey to take a seat in the cozy blue- and gold-starred psychic reading corner. After Gregor locked the front door of the shop and turned the OPEN sign to CLOSED, he and Olga squeezed in as well. There was barely room for the four of them.

Was this a Russian thing, Lacey wondered, *from growing up in a once-Communist country where everything was constrained, intimate, crowded? Marie will never be lonely with these two around.* Lacey took a deep breath and searched for the right words.

"I didn't want to bother you, Marie. I'm not really sure why I came."

"You came because you had to, sugar," Marie said.

"You have some mystery, Lacey Smithsonian?" Gregor said. "Something of grave interest?"

"No diamonds this time, Kepelov."

"You are among friends," Olga assured her.

"True." *Sort of.* Lacey was slowly warming to Gregor Kepelov, but his sister was another story. She imagined Olga hitting her over the head with a copy of *Atlas Shrugged.*

Lacey described the events of the weekend, the theatre garage sale, the tug of war over the red dress, LaToya's victory, and the break-in. She gave them the big-print version, not the fine details. She held back the bizarre costume parade the burglar had staged with LaToya's wardrobe.

Let's see if Marie picks up on that.

"That red dress is very valuable to someone," Marie said. "As valuable as a memory. Tell me more about the dress."

"It was a theatrical costume," Lacey said. "Made for a production of *The Masque of the Red Death.*"

"Ah, Edgar Allan Poe. Famous American depressive." Gregor nodded. "Continue, please."

"It was a Kinetic Theatre production, more than a decade ago," Lacey said.

"Kinetic? What is this Kinetic?" Gregor asked.

"Kinetic is a theatre company in the District, run by performers from the former Soviet Union. Mostly Russians, I think."

"They are Russians?" Olga and Gregor shared a look. Gregor clearly felt affronted not to know every single Russian in the D.C. area. "How do I not know of this group of Russians?"

"I don't know. Maybe they're not KGB spies."

"You are so funny, Lacey Smithsonian," Gregor said. "Tell me what you know about this theatre."

"They've been around for a dozen years or more, and they have a playhouse on Sixteenth Street near the Circle. It's a small theatre, but they've won some big awards," Lacey said. "Like the Helen Hayes."

"But not a big theatre, like Kennedy Center or Arena Stage?"

"No, much smaller, even smaller than, say, Source or Woolly Mammoth or Studio. Apparently they have this unique style combining acting and dance, a very muscular type of movement, and they tell stories through choreography, dance, music, and a minimum of dialogue. I haven't seen their shows, but I've read about them."

"Ah, dancers! Russians are the best dancers in the world," Gregor said.

"They learn to dance in Russia," Olga added.

"I'm trying to run down a story about this costume and whether there is a connection to LaToya Crawford's break-in. It seems far-fetched."

"You specialize in the far-fetched, sugar," Marie said. "And so do I. The only thing I feel sure about is that theatre woman, the one who fought with your friend LaToya, is not going to get back to you."

"Figures," Lacey said. "You'd be surprised how many people never call me back."

"You are a reporter," Olga said. "The enemy."

"I'm not the enemy, I just ask questions. And I write about fashion, not the theatre or backstage intrigue. It hardly puts me in the enemy camp." Lacey put the iced tea glass to her warm forehead. "Maybe she's just embarrassed about how she behaved, making a scene and all."

Marie frowned. "Tell me more about the dress. I see it as a deep red, many shades of red, dark, layered, long, flowing—"

"And very beautiful. It was worn by the character of Death in the play. And the young actress who wore it, Saige Russell, died right after the last show."

"Oh, cher, I was afraid of that."

"Supposedly she was *not* wearing the dress at the time. As far as I know."

"Did you touch this dress?"

"I had to. LaToya practically threw it at me. The story spooked her."

"Take my hand and visualize it," Marie said. "Send me a picture."

"I'll try."

Lacey closed her eyes. She could see the layers of fabric, the tulle, the taffeta, the silk and satin. The blood-red splash of lace at the throat. She could see the substance of it and almost feel its weight, feel the way it would swing and sweep as you wore it, as you turned and stalked and spun across the stage—

Marie's eyes rolled back and her head started to wobble. Gregor grabbed her before she hit the table and held her up. She shook her head, conscious but woozy.

"Oh my God. Marie, I'm so sorry," Lacey said.

"You have done it again, Smithsonian." Gregor smiled grimly. "Someone is dead."

"Yes, of course, I told you, the actress is dead! The one who wore the dress. A dozen years ago."

"What did you see?" Olga demanded of Marie.

"A face." The psychic blinked. "It was just a face. Changing. Dissolving. Changing. Dissolving again. Over and over. Made me dizzy." She rubbed her eyes.

"How many faces, Marie?" Gregor asked. "Five faces? Twenty faces? A thousand? Or all the same face?"

"I don't know. I wasn't counting."

This vision sounded very theatrical to Lacey. What did changing and dissolving faces have to do with the red dress? She didn't have a chance to ask. Marie suddenly slumped in Gregor's arms and fell fast asleep on his shoulder.

"We don't know what this means," Olga said. "Yet. But it means something. It is a good start, yes, Smithsonian?"

"More like a finish." Lacey rose to her feet. "I have to go. Please take care of Marie."

"Of course," Olga said.

"We will take good care of her," Gregor said, nodding goodbye.

The faces. Was it possible that Marie saw all the actresses who had worn the dress since the demise of Saige Russell? She was glad she hadn't mentioned LaToya's break-in and the oddly life-like presentation of her empty clothes. *But why hadn't Marie seen that? Why the faces?*

Lacey exited, stage left, so to speak. It didn't occur to her until later that Marie hadn't given her the usual weather report. No doubt that meant no change, she decided, and the Washington summer would be blisteringly hot for the foreseeable future.

Maybe forever.

Lacey walked home from King Street alone. The sun dipped below the west wing of her apartment building, taking with it the scorching heat of the day. At home she changed into a casual cotton dress, moved to the balcony, and watched the boats on the river as the light faded.

Vic was busy this evening, with a surveillance and a client hand-holding session. He'd left a message on her phone. She wouldn't have a chance that evening to look at the dress, wherever he'd taken it, but he assured her it was safe. As she sat on the balcony she polished her engagement ring and thought about the man she had promised to marry. It still felt unreal. The ring had been on her finger for over a month and she still hadn't told her family. It was complicated. She wanted Vic all to herself.

Mimi, what would you do? Lacey wondered.

Honey, put on your war paint and stick to your guns, she imagined her Aunt Mimi saying. *It's your life!*

The balcony and the river were getting dark. Lacey went inside and put on some big band music. Mimi's trunk was calling her.

Some relax after a stressful day by watching TV or surfing the Web. For Lacey, often it meant diving into her Great-aunt Mimi's trunk of vintage clothing and other wonders. An ancient wooden steamer trunk banded in leather with tarnished brass buckles, it was filled with patterns and fabrics and half-finished clothes from the late 1930s and 1940s, old magazines and letters, clippings, photographs, mementos, memories. It was a trunk full of dreams.

It was Lacey's personal treasure chest, and it always made her feel close to her favorite aunt, dead now for years. Mimi had left her trunk of dreams to Lacey, and it kept their connection alive, as if Mimi spoke to her through what it contained. She wondered what Mimi would think of Vic, of her engagement ring, of their potential wedding plans, of Lacey's life and career in Washington, of everything. Unfortunately, it was a one-way conversation. The trunk was full of wonders, but there had been no guest appearances of Mimi's ghost.

Mimi was the infamous rebel of the Smithsonian family, the one who had felt liberated in the East, the only one who had changed the family name back to the original Smith, of the Cockney Smiths of east London.

Mimi had moved from Denver to D.C. during World War II for all the right reasons: to do her part for her country and the war effort. And to get away from her clingy family. She landed a job with the wartime Office of Price Administration, which oversaw, among other things, price controls, rationing, and investigating black markets. Mimi always wanted to be where the action was, Lacey knew, and not where her family was. Letters took weeks to arrive back then, and long-distance phone calls were costly. Distances were, well, *distant*.

What do you think, Mimi? Yeah, Vic's a doll. Satin or lace? And yes, a veil is a bit jejune. *Oh, maybe dressing my hair with pearls? Yeah, I like that. And the dress? Of course it would have to be vintage, or a vintage pattern. Maybe a pattern out of your trunk...*

Lacey put her family out of her mind and opened the trunk. She spotted a large scrap of re-embroidered lace in a beautiful claret color. It was clipped to a photograph of Mimi in a dress made with that same material, standing next to a handsome young man in a sharp tuxedo with a silly grin on his face. The dress featured a sweetheart neckline with satin piping. On the back, Mimi had written, "Valentine's Formal 1940." Nothing else.

Who's the pretty boy with the grin? A big romance or just a random date?

The picture was black and white, which added to its glamour, but Lacey was seeing it in color. Mimi looked like Rita Hayworth and had a million-dollar smile, her auburn hair was pulled back behind one ear, where she wore a flower that matched the pink sweetheart roses in her corsage. Mimi's date was handsome and wore a sheepishly proud look. It always struck Lacey that although Mimi was very young—in college at the time—she looked impossibly sophisticated in her old photographs, like a movie star caught by a candid camera. Like so many people in old photos from the Forties.

Times were different then. Courtships, and clothes, were formal. *Must have been nice. Not the inequality of the times, the unspoken sexism, but the formality, the stability. The clothes.* And Mimi never had to worry that her mother was reading about her exploits on the internet.

A song called "The Lady in Red" came on the radio. Serendipity. Lacey looked back at the red lace in her hand. The workmanship was beautiful. Something like that today would cost dearly.

What is it about a red dress? Lacey thought.

The color red attracts the male of the species, studies claimed. Red gets the blood flowing, red means passion, fire, life, love, lust. Lacey wished the red dress Mimi made from this lace had survived and ended up in the trunk. Even though it was gone, Mimi must have been sentimental about it: She saved the photo and this one remnant of lovely red lace.

Does every woman have one great red dress in her life? Many did, but Lacey did not. Her thoughts turned darker. For Saige Russell, a red dress presaged her demise and became part of her death story. It hardly mattered that she wasn't wearing the costume when she died. *Or did it?*

Few people know the hour of their death. Did Saige have any inkling she was about to die? Or did she intend to die? Lacey wondered.

Out, out, brief candle.

Lacey Smithsonian's Fashion *Bites*

What Is It About a Red Dress?
(Red Never Makes You Guess)

Every woman deserves a red dress.

A white dress may speak of purity, and a black dress may speak of power, especially in Washington, D.C. But no color announces your *presence* quite like a red dress. Nothing makes a man say, *Well, HELLO,* faster than a fire-engine red dress. Even in D.C., where they might say it in a whisper, or a sidelong glance. A red dress speaks of presence, passion, the very life force, POW! Red is a signal flare shot into the air. Red makes a statement, and it never makes you guess what that statement is.

Here I am, world! Red on arrival! Deal with it.

Yes, even you, you devotees of beige and gray, in your neutral leggings and hoodies. You who fear the bolder hues provided by nature or art, open your eyes to the possibilities of red. Wear it to wake up your boyfriend, husband, partner, *yourself.* Let him or her wonder what you've been up to—or what you're plotting. Planning to paint the town red, beginning with your wardrobe? Let them wonder. Red has the power to unleash the real you, or at least the *you* you might want to be, once in a while.

It's not just for the pale blondes, who think they look good in red. Far too many women say, *Oh I can't wear red!* Really? Even Snow White looked fabulous in red, as do women with darker skin tones. Women of every shade and hue were born to wear some shade of red. Never fear, there is an array of reds, from blue reds to orangey reds, from burgundy to ruby to cabernet to crimson. There is a red that will flatter your particular skin tone.

And redheads too! Don't believe those jealous voices who would steal your crimson glory and convince you to never wear red. Redheads, from those with titian locks to curls of deepest auburn, can and should rock shades of red. Be brave, fire goddess, and shine on. But here are a few cautions.

- **Not every rosy shade is meant** for everyone. Test different reds against your skin. Some will warm your skin tone, and others will chill it.
- **Be discriminating with your reds.** Shades of "red" can be as different as pink and scarlet, cherry and crimson, innocence and experience
- **Be careful when you reveal skin** in a red dress. Red turns up the volume, so a little goes a long way. You don't have to look like a KarTrashian on a spree. A buttoned-up red dress can be just as sexy as a scarlet scrap of nearly nothing. And classier.

It's no surprise that here in the Nation's Capital red is a power color, a particular choice of many strong women. This season, and every season, the red power suit will be on full display. It can be buttoned up, buttoned down, or a little more free and easy.

But you believe you're too shy to wear red? You have my sympathies. So why not try a red shirt or a sweater? Okay, how about a shawl? A scarf? And there's always red lipstick. Every woman should know how powerful red lips can be.

Start small with a splash of scarlet, an accent of crimson, and feel the energy of red. And someday you may just find yourself shopping for that perfect red dress for the perfect occasion.

And you'll be the Lady in Red who lingers in everyone's memory.

FOURTEEN

*E*ARLY TUESDAY MORNING, Tamsin Kerr arrived at *The Eye's* offices with a news tip for Lacey.

The theatre critic's appearance at that hour was unusual, as startling as an apparition. During the day, the newsroom was barely controlled chaos, and Tamsin didn't care for chaos unless it was on stage and neatly choreographed. Because she attended the theatre in the evening, Tamsin generally filed her reviews late at night, and she often filed from home. Occasionally, however, she found it soothing to visit *The Eye* after dark when the newsroom resembled a graveyard.

Before she came into view Tamsin's long, tall shadow preceded her, stretching down the hallway toward the reporters' cubicles. Her shadowed curls stretched into long fingers of amazement, reaching across the walls. As she emerged corporeally, Tamsin's dark curly coiffure, exploding with the humidity, seemed even more fierce than usual. She wasn't about to let an insignificant thing like the weather daunt her. Even in the D.C. heat she wore a perfectly tailored, deep burgundy Armani suit, contrasting dramatically with her pale skin. People stopped dead in their tracks to stare at Tamsin Kerr, proving Lacey's theory about the authority of *red*. Tamsin paid no attention to them and focused on Lacey.

"Smithsonian, there you are! Did you find what you needed? *The Masque* reviews, the tragic death of ingénue Saige Russell, the fabled red dress?"

"I found what I found." Lacey waved at her stack of copied articles about the Kinetic production. "What I don't know is still a mystery. Saige did die on closing night. No one knows how or why. No foul play suspected, so far as I can tell. Nothing indicates she was wearing the red dress at the time, and Yuri Volkov, the director, says that's just a stupid rumor. Still, that dress seems to have an awful aura about it." Lacey flexed her fingers. "And how are you, Tamsin? Lovely to see you too. Have some hot coffee?"

The office A/C kicked on, blasting Lacey's neck with an icy breeze. She shivered in her sleeveless lavender dress and grabbed her cream-colored felt jacket. In the breast pocket was a vintage violet lace hanky, which she had secured with a vintage pin of purple irises. She tugged the jacket on, happy she'd brought it with her. It felt as cozy as a hug.

Tamsin seemed to be immune to mere heat and cold. She commandeered the infamous Death Chair, which always seemed to roll its way back to Lacey's cubicle, and sat. Either she didn't know its reputation or, more likely, she didn't care. She would consider the painted skulls droll. She leaned forward almost touching Lacey's desk, her dark curls hanging down.

"So the rumors weren't entirely wrong. A dramatic curtain scene for an actor, I suppose, though a trifle obvious." She paused for effect. "I don't want to be an alarmist, Smithsonian, but I have some alarming news." She smiled, clearly not at all alarmed.

"About the red dress?"

"You be the judge. You remember that other woman, the one who got into the fight with LaToya over the dress on Saturday?"

"Yes."

Tamsin paused for effect. "She's dead."

"Excuse me?" Lacey shook her head as if she didn't hear. "I don't think so."

"Oh yes. The one who sparred with our dear LaToya and lost. Short, blowsy blonde? Dead. *Mort, muerto, mortuus est.* I have this information on excellent authority."

Lacey sat bolt upright. "The woman from Kinetic? *The Masque of the Red Death* red dress?" A bolt of dread hit her in the pit of her stomach.

"The very one. Amy Keaton, I believe her name is. Was, rather."

"What are you saying?" Lacey sounded stupid, even to herself.

"Didn't I say? I thought I said it quite clearly. Amy Keaton is dead."

"Yes, but why is she dead? And when did it happen, and how, and who told you, how do you know this?"

"Aren't you a good little journalist, all those W questions! Who, what, when, where, why!" Lacey glared. "Really,

Smithsonian, it's very impressive, and just when we hear
journalism is dead."

"Some answers, Tamsin. Please."

"DeeDee Adler. She's always around Kinetic. A stagehand
or something. She witnessed the titanic tug of war last
Saturday. Apparently she worked the event and saw me there.
Called me this morning at the ungodly hour of nine a.m."
Tamsin's expression made it clear that this was unacceptably
early. "She thought I'd want to know. And I suppose I do,
though I don't cover death. Unless it's on stage. Or the head of
a theatre, an artistic director, an acting legend, someone like
that. The requisite retrospective, cultural context, artistic
legacy, et cetera. But I didn't know this Keaton person. A
backstage type. What was she, a stage manager?"

"Who is DeeDee Adler? How does she know Amy Keaton is
dead?"

"Those W questions again." Tamsin wagged her finger. "I
suppose they were friends. Worked together. After all,
DeeDee was the first to know. Adler has been wardrobe
mistress or—oh God, I suppose that term's been changed to
something like wardrobe *master* now or wardrobe *wrangler*
or something—at Kinetic, and she had something to do with
the yard sale. What exactly, I don't know. I saw her there.
And that is all I know."

Lacey was still trying to wrap her head around the news.
"Dead? Tamsin, are you sure? Absolutely sure? She was alive
just the other day."

"That's how it happens, doesn't it? Here today, gone
tomorrow." Marie's words came back to Lacey. *That woman is
not going to return your call.* "DeeDee seemed quite certain,"
Tamsin said.

"I didn't know you saw the fight over the dress."

When Tamsin smiled, as she did now, she looked impish.
"It rather made up for having to go to that sale in the first place
Saturday. These early mornings are going to kill me."

"What did you think? About the tug of war?"

"Very convincing. One thing you have to say about LaToya
Crawford is that she *commits.*"

"Commits? What, murder?"

"No, she commits to the *action.* To the moment, the
emotion. Fully. Without restraint. Very impressive. Maybe it

was something about that dress. Or maybe LaToya. She could be a great performer. You have to *commit*."

It wasn't surprising that Tamsin gave the critic's-eye view of the action. After all, she once wrote up an attack in the newsroom as if it were opening night of a new play. She gave it five stars.

That article raised Mac's ire to a dangerous level, but there was nothing he could do, it was already in print. According to the paper's algorithms, it turned out to be popular with the readership, the most read article that week, beating out a presidential news conference by a mile.

"Okay. Keaton's death. Accident?" Lacey asked, trying to get back on track. "Foul play? How was her health? Is there a police report? A medical examiner's determination of cause and manner of death?'

"Good lord, Smithsonian! I have no idea. Do you suppose it was murder? Never mind, of course you do, murder is your thing." Tamsin leaned back, hands behind her head. "It doesn't matter, vis-à-vis the dress. Its reputation will only grow. An unearthly object of unhealthy curiosity. That is your bailiwick, isn't it, Smithsonian? And dumped right in your lap. Fashion and death and grim tidings. Lucky you."

"Yeah, lucky me. And lucky for the red dress. Assuming it likes publicity, and notoriety, and being associated with death."

"Well, it is the Red Death dress, the so-called Red Dress of Doom. It ought to be used to it by now. A monstrous myth, helped along with theatrical superstition. I'm surprised it isn't the subject of a bad new play already," she mused. "Or worse, an opera: *The Masque of the Red Dress*. What do you think?"

"God forbid. Somehow it's become a talisman of good luck-bad luck. But people must believe in the good luck, or else all those actresses wouldn't want to wear it to the Helen Hayes awards."

"Two deaths now," Tamsin pointed out. "Possibly more. Who knows what the tally really is? What's it been up to all these years?"

"Tamsin, you're suggesting a connection where there may be none. There's a decade between these two deaths. You're being dramatic."

"God, I hope so. Drama is my job. To cover it, of course, not to live it."

"Droll. Very droll."

Tamsin stood up and sniffed the air. "You said something about coffee. Is there any coffee around this hellhole?"

"How strong is your stomach?"

"Strong enough to go to the theatre every night and face the ever-present possibility of dreck or delight."

Lacey grabbed an extra Fashion *BITES* mug for Tamsin and gestured for her to follow her to the newsroom's kitchen. As usual, the coffee was drained to the dregs and on the verge of burning. Lacey made another pot. As they watched the coffee maker expectantly, Lacey wondered how much to tell Tamsin about recent developments.

"Unfortunate on many levels," Tamsin was musing. "Sad that the Keaton woman is dead. Sad for Kinetic. Tomorrow is press night for their new show. Stage managers are utterly indispensable, so someone's got to take over her duties and they may not be completely up to speed. Could be a disaster."

"I hadn't thought of that."

"No doubt there's an assistant and lots of tech people because of the complexity of a Kinetic show, but still. The stage manager makes the trains run on time."

Tamsin's beat seemed very exciting to Lacey, even glamorous, though it was a lot of late-night hours. There were days Lacey grew weary of the fashion slog. There were only so many ways to describe the latest and greatest look that could change one's life or the newest "blue is the new black."

"Does it get old?" she asked. "The plays, I mean?"

"Not really. Of course there are disasters, but on press night or opening night, there is always the possibility something magical will occur. You always hope for the best. Or the worst. And in a small theatre like Kinetic, the energy is completely different than the huge theatres, where they often present big fossilized warhorses of plays, like frozen dioramas. A small theatre with no money and no resources but passion and talent can sometimes build wondrous things out of hope and dreams."

"Illusion. Smoke and mirrors. Making something out of nothing."

"Yes. It's a relief that the little theatres don't have the money to land helicopters on stage just because they *can*. Or spray the audience with a stupid rainstorm. Just make us imagine that rainstorm, we'll feel it."

"What if a play is bad?"

"Better than boring! Passionately bad can be just as interesting as good, if everyone is committed to it. A strong but wrongheaded choice is still a strong choice. And then of course there are—disappointments."

"Have you seen work by Nikolai Sokolov? He designed the infamous *Red Death*."

"Did he? Before my time, but I've seen his work. At Kinetic and elsewhere. He's very good. I've seen him create amazing sets and costumes with practically no money at all."

"And now Amy Keaton will miss all that."

"Yes," Tamsin agreed. "She'll miss all that."

"What's a press night like?"

"Just part of the job. When you're the critic, you get stares from near and far, trying to decode your every little reaction. Does she like it, does she hate it? Is she falling asleep? Is she taking notes or looking at her phone? What did that little smile of hers mean? Exhausting."

"I never thought about it that way." Lacey generally didn't wonder how others reacted to her or her notebook and pen. But then, she was usually in the background, and she believed no one actually read her fashion columns. At least, she wanted to believe that.

"I arrive at the last minute, I stay in my seat through intermission, if there is one, and I always leave as soon as the lights come up. I never want to be interrogated by actors, directors, friends of the actors, the understudy's mother."

"Acting must be a very strange profession."

"Yes. Funny thing about theatre people. Actors. Actresses too. Though the women all want to be called *actors* now. They hang on to the dream of making it. And when they do, the few who do, when the money rolls in, they firmly believe the stuff that made them great were the bleak days, when it was creativity and alchemy that turned nothing into something."

"And people like Amy Keaton?"

"People like Amy Keaton keep the theatre going, but they're never seen and rarely thanked."

"Kinetic is about to open *The Turn of the Screw*." Lacey rinsed out her coffee mug. "I never considered Henry James as an inspiration for music and dance."

"Who would?" Tamsin stared at the coffee pot. "And a strange show to do in the summer. Of course, they're filling the gap between the big theatres' seasons, and that's part of their niche. I merely hope to be writing a rave and not an obituary. I write about the illusion of life and death on stage, not life and death. I'm not that important in the grand scheme of things. Critics are mere cogs in the show biz machine."

"Don't underestimate yourself."

"I don't. However, the critic is the first to go in a recession, and if newspapers survive in the future, who knows whether critics or reviewers will remain as well. I expect to get the ax every week. When *The Eye* cuts back, this theatre reviewer will be among the first to go."

"And the fashion beat too," Lacey said.

"Au contraire, Smithsonian. Not *your* beat, it's *sui generis*, off the beaten path, what with all those fashion crimes. Torture and tulle, murder and mannequins."

"You sound like Wiedemeyer."

"Do I? Why is that coffee so slow?" The pot was only a quarter full.

"Did you know LaToya's apartment was broken into the other night?" Lacey asked. "Sunday night or early Monday morning."

"Burgled? Were they after the dress? Better and better. Not better for LaToya, of course. You understand what I mean. Better story value, more plot twists."

"I do. Nothing was taken, but there was a very strange—"

"Curious, isn't it?" Tamsin interrupted, looking pensive, yet somehow delighted. "A contretemps over a dress, a burglary, and now a death. The dramatic arc is provocative, suggestive yet inconclusive."

"That about sums it up."

Tamsin reached for the coffee pot before it finished and poured herself the first cup. She inhaled the fresh aroma and sipped, closing her eyes. A few drips sizzled on the burner, adding to the kitchenette's distinct aroma.

"You must need that pretty badly," Lacey observed, filling her coffee mug.

"Are you joking? I'm not usually up till the crack of noon. Coffee is my blood, my ink, my drink of choice. I leave my information about Keaton to you. Do with it as you please."

"Thanks for the heads up."

"Any time. After noon. Keep me posted." Tamsin glanced at her watch. "I'm here so early, I might as well go torture my section editor. Cheers." A nod of her head and Tamsin was gone.

Lacey's stomach was still unsettled and it wasn't the coffee. The facts made her head spin. Unless by some chance Amy Keaton had died of natural causes, everything that had happened since the theatre sale on Saturday was connected: the tug of war over the scarlet costume, LaToya's break-in, Keaton's death.

The battle between Amy and LaToya. Was that the thing that led to everything else? Lacey wondered. *Or did something else happen before the sale? How did the dress wind up on the rack if it wasn't supposed to be sold? And by the way, wasn't there an actual mask to go with that dress? Where did the mask go?*

Too many unanswered questions. She peered into her coffee as if she could read the grounds. It wasn't her particular talent.

It occurred to her that the break-in at LaToya's, particularly the way the dresses were staged, was terribly *theatrical.* This burglar was sending a dramatic message. The trouble was that Lacey didn't know what the message was.

Maybe: I'm just messing with your head? Playing dress-up with your things? Taking an inventory? Or, I know where you live, I know how you dress, and I know who you are! Or could it also mean, *I know what you bought on Saturday and I want it BACK!*

Lacey returned to her cubicle where the air was freshly chilled. She kept both hands around her mug for warmth. *Amy Keaton.* While Lacey thought Keaton had looked unhappy and unhealthy, her gut told her that wasn't the cause of death. But first she needed facts, even if facts were slippery. No doubt Damon Newhouse would soon be nipping at her heels with some mad conspiracy theory, and Brooke right beside him, demanding information.

I need facts! Where to start?

Should she call Detective Broadway Lamont and inquire about Keaton's death? And get involved in an endless police interrogation? Call LaToya about Amy Keaton's death? And freak her out completely without knowing what was going on? *Later.* Lacey made her first call to DeeDee Adler. And got nowhere.

"Like I told Tamsin, she's dead. That's all I know," the woman said on the phone, obviously in a hurry to hang up.

"How did you find out?"

"I got a call. It's out there. The drums. The theatre grapevine."

"Do you know what happened?"

"No, she's just dead. But she'd been depressed," Adler volunteered. "Always up or down. She was either hyper or the world was totally noir. Everything was important. Details drove her crazy."

"Suicide?" That hadn't occurred to Lacey. It was a sad and lonely thought.

"I don't really know. Gotta go." Adler hung up. Lacey didn't have a chance to ask Adler about the theatre sale, her part in it, and what she might have known about the red dress.

The Web and social media were another dead end. Amy Keaton had a surprisingly small footprint on the internet, though her name appeared on the odd theatre program. No one was setting up any memorial pages for her yet.

Lacey left a message on the Kinetic Theatre's voice mail for artistic director Yuri Volkov. He would have to know something about her death. She was his stage manager, an essential role, and he'd been annoyed at her the day before. Volkov seemed the type to resent someone's untimely death if it interrupted his show schedule.

Next up: Tony Trujillo. If Keaton's demise was due to a car accident or something criminal, *The Eye*'s police reporter would know something by now. Lacey was about to call Tony's cell when she looked down the hall and saw his cowboy boots strutting her way. Today's boots were black cowhide with proud gold longhorns on the toes, a flashy contrast to his black jeans and black shirt, gussied up with a bolo tie anchored by a large turquoise.

"Hey, Tony." He didn't even glance at her. He strutted with a purpose toward Felicity's cubby of caloric delights.

"Tony!" Lacey waved, but he danced across the aisle to Felicity, who was waving a plate of fresh homemade chocolate-iced moon pies. The aroma almost made Lacey weaken her resolve not to fall prey to Felicity's master plan.

"Moon pies, Tony," Felicity said. "My own recipe."

"You are my angel, Felicidad," Tony said, lifting one moon pie. "If you ever leave Harlan, let me know."

At the mention of Harlan's name, Felicity's lips trembled, but she caught herself and smiled bravely. Harlan was mad about moon pies, yet he was nowhere to be seen. It was troubling. Without saying a word, Felicity was broadcasting her despair in today's outfit, a dreary gray purple sack of a dress. A shabby gray sweater hung on the back of her chair. She might as well have worn a neon sign: *THE WORLD IS CRUSHING MY SPIRIT. HAVE A MOON PIE.*

Poor Felicity. Lacey found herself wishing for another of Felicity's bright dresses and garish sweaters, trimmed in eye-popping felt flowers in colors unknown to nature, created by some mad knitter in the online shopping universe. At least it would signal Felicity's happiness and optimism.

"You'll have to get in line behind Broadway Lamont, Tony," Lacey said.

"Oh, hey Lacey. What's up, Brenda Starr? Black orchids? Mystery man?" Tony grabbed another moon pie for later.

"Too many mystery men to mention."

"Heard you witnessed a smack down with LaToya and some woman at some theatre yard sale. Over a dress." He grinned. His teeth were big and white, his wolf smile.

"What can I say? This fashion beat is a gift that keeps on giving."

"Word has it LaToya's pretty fierce."

"Very fierce. I should take lessons."

"More fierceness is the last thing you need, Lacey. Trust me. So what's up?"

"A woman named Amy Keaton died. Probably accident or natural causes. But as you are the crime newshound--"

"And Lacey Smithsonian wants to rule out foul play. Why do you want to know? I'll bite." He did, into the nearest moon pie. "Who is Amy Keaton?"

"Don't be difficult, Tony."

"Don't be evasive."

"She's just a name for now."

"Call Lamont." He savored another bite. "You know, these are exceptionally light and fluffy. The chocolate is just right."

"So you haven't heard her name? You're the police reporter."

"Glad you acknowledge that point. She died recently?"

"Yesterday maybe, or the day before. I don't have an exact TOD." Amy was missing in action on Monday. Today was Tuesday. Someone probably knew when she died, but Lacey did not.

"Unless she died in a hospital, it's unlikely that a cause of death has been ruled yet."

"But you can find out if it's reached the attention of the boys and girls in blue, or whether it hints at suspicious causes."

"Also true. Is this a hot story?" He narrowed his eyes at her.

"I have no idea." She looked away. She didn't want that chocolate moon pie in his hand taunting her.

"Liar. If it turns out to be a story, you have to share."

"Don't I always?"

"No. You don't." He flashed his smile again.

"You might not even be interested. You, know. Fashion. Girly stuff."

"I love girly stuff. Okay, some girly stuff. And the more you protest, the more interested I get." He munched on a moon pie and winked. "Double byline."

"Maybe." *Later. After I have a few facts.*

"I'll look into it. You owe me."

Lacey cocked one eyebrow at Tony and turned her attention to her desk, the usual piles of papers to sort, and what little she recollected about Amy Keaton.

Could the Red Dress of Death, that lovely crimson costume, possibly be something Keaton personally cared about? *Unlikely,* Lacey decided. It wasn't hers, it wasn't her size, and from Kinetic's point of view it was ancient history. Another point: Amy Keaton looked like any number of women in the District of Columbia who'd given up on their appearance and escaped to the comfort of stretch pants. Katya Pritchard, the once-lithe dancer and Saige Russell's understudy, was another.

When Lacey had seen her, Amy Keaton's frizzy blond curls were pony-tailed in a black scrunchy. With her white lashes and eyebrows, paler than her hair, she looked like a plump rabbit ready to run. Tight black pants, a black T-shirt with the Kinetic Theatre logo, and black canvas sneakers. Where did the long ruby dress fit into that picture?

Maybe Amy was afraid she'd lose her job somehow because of the mix-up. Was Yuri Volkov so unforgiving? He'd bitched to Lacey about everyone around him, but they'd all worked for him for years, and he said he didn't care about the dress. Perhaps it was the last in a series of Keaton mistakes? Some people had a knack for screwing up. Maybe she was always getting blamed for something. Maybe she had no hopes for ever getting another job.

Like Harlan Wiedemeyer.

Harlan wasn't causing catastrophes all around him, Lacey was certain, but he certainly took the fall for them. Lacey turned around, suddenly expecting to see him hanging around. He wasn't there. But Lacey heard a sniffle and a stifled sob from the next cubicle.

Felicity sat in front of her screen, miserable and blocked. The fluffy food copy she could usually toss like a salad wasn't flowing. No "luscious clouds of whipped cream," or "layers of angel food cake lighter than air," or "dark and sinfully delightful and delicious chocolate."

Before Lacey could think of something to say, Mac arrived in his usual sartorial conglomeration, a short sleeve plaid shirt in yellow and lime green over bright purple slacks that belonged on a golf course. His girls must have slept late this summer day and left him to dress himself, but they would have approved of his footwear: He proudly wore the cowboy boots he had picked up in Steamboat Springs, Colorado, where he also bought boots for them. He lifted a moon pie and observed Felicity staring blankly at her computer screen.

"I don't know what's up with you, Pickles, but get it together. We're on deadline here. And you didn't tell me there were moon pies."

Felicity whimpered loudly and hit a key at random. Mac bit into the moon pie, briefly closing his eyes in bliss.

"You're not helping, Mac," Lacey said pointedly. "Can't you see she's got troubles?"

"Who does?" Mac looked at her blankly.

"Men!" Lacey realized she had to find a way to make things right in the office, or she'd never get any work done. On the other hand, if Harlan and Felicity didn't get married, Lacey wouldn't have to wear a hideous bridesmaid's gown. *How does that stack up against an eternity of sighs in the cubicle next door?* She couldn't take it any longer. She stood and grabbed her bag. "I have to get out of here."

"Where are you going?" Mac asked.

"Lunch."

"It's eleven o'clock, Smithsonian."

"I'm hungry, and I have an interview."

"With whom?"

"Two women who wore the dress, if you must know. *The* dress, Mac. The Red Dress of Death, the crimson costume, the fatal frock. The ruby gown of ill renown."

Mac's eyebrows rose in interest. "That crazy LaToya dress?"

"Bingo."

"Okay. Go. Just don't bring any bad fashion voodoo back here. We got enough weird stuff going on." His eyebrows indicated the downhearted Felicity.

"You and Broadway Lamont are hilarious. You know that?"

Lacey left Mac staring at his moon pie and Felicity staring at her blank monitor.

Men.

FIFTEEN

*O*UTSIDE *THE EYE'S* cool lobby, a blast furnace hit her with an oppressive wall of humidity as clingy as a wet sweater. It wasn't pleasant, but it was better than hanging around, playing an extra in the newsroom's third-floor drama.

Lacey bought a bottle of cold water from a street vendor and trudged up Connecticut Avenue to Krispy Kreme Doughnuts in Dupont Circle, where the "Hot Doughnuts Now" sign beckoned. Lacey strode in and was greeted by the March of the Doughnuts, in all their sugar-glazed glory.

As she suspected, Harlan Wiedemeyer was there. He sat hunched in a corner in misery, with his head lolling on his chest, which only made him look shorter and rounder than usual. Predictably, he wore a white shirt and gray slacks, today paired with a bright orange tie. He had a large collection of ties, usually accessorized with crumbs. Except for his ties, his office wardrobe palette was stuck in neutral. He had told Lacey he was content to fade into the background and let Felicity be his "fair bird of paradise."

Harlan didn't notice her. His hand reached into a flat box full of hot glazed doughnuts.

"Drowning your sorrows, Harlan?"

Lacey stood over him. His hand stopped in midair. He glanced up at her.

"Smithsonian! What are you doing here?"

"Following a trail of doughnut crumbs, Hansel. Your Gretel misses you, back at the gingerbread cottage."

I actually think of Felicity as the witch in that story, but whatever works.

"Oh." He automatically brushed off the front of his shirt. "Sorry."

It was well-known that Wiedemeyer had a serious jones for doughnuts. He'd take any kind, but Krispy Kreme was at the top of his doughnut tower. He licked a crumb off his lips.

"You're going to have a serious sugar hangover, Harlan."

"Only if I stop." His eyes glistened. "Lacey, I can't marry her. I can't ruin her life."

"You're ruining it now! She can't concentrate, she can't work. Soon Felicity won't even be able to cook."

"My Dilly Pickles? Not cook?" His doughnut hand wavered. "Baking is her life."

"She's worried."

"At least she's not dead." He bit into another glazed puff of paradise. "I'm a jinx."

"Stop it, Harlan."

Somewhere behind them, a platter of hot doughnuts fell with a tremendous clatter. He tilted his head toward the sound.

"Exhibit A."

"Harlan, she made you moon pies today. With glazed chocolate."

"Moon pies?"

His eyes lit up for a moment, then dimmed into misery. He wiped his eyes with a paper napkin.

"And you're missing them," she said.

That statement got his attention. "No!"

"Trujillo ate the first one. The first three. Or four. And then Mac arrived. You know what that means. Are you telling me you're turning down a lifetime of moon pies, caramel rolls, and cakes? A lifetime of culinary bliss?"

He wavered. "When you put it that way—"

"I am putting it that way." The sweet aroma of *hot doughnuts now* was getting to Lacey. She was hungry. She wavered. He offered his white box full of fresh doughnuts. She took one and contemplated it, not taking a bite. It was still warm. "She's miserable, Harlan, and so are you, and it's making me miserable. Please, go back to the office and talk to her. You guys were made for each other."

Heaven help us.

"I know we were. But I can't."

"Listen to me! You are not a jinx, Harlan Wiedemeyer!"

A man at the counter slipped in the remains of someone's spilled drink and slid across the floor, crashing into a couple just walking through the door. All three hit the ground. Lacey ignored them and snapped her fingers under Wiedemeyer's nose.

"Focus! I need your help, Harlan." She finally bit into the warm doughnut. It was heavenly.

"Help? How can I help you? How can I help anyone?"

"I'm working on a delicate story and I can't concentrate when Felicity is sighing and sobbing over you."

"Poor kid's got the blues. Me too. I could sing her a blues tune. 'Am I Blue'? And Lacey, I am blue. Too blue to croon."

Wiedemeyer had started a retro swing band in college, Harlan and His High-Stepping Hipsters, and they still played parties and events. Harlan sang and played the trombone, which conjured up a rather comical picture for Lacey.

"Croon anything, Harlan. Go to her. Sing to her."

"Wait. What's the story you're working on? You said there's a story."

His death-and-dismemberment beat antennae were up. Lacey hesitated. Harlan Wiedemeyer could be a little too enthusiastic. He was ridiculously fond of stories of the bizarre, the obscure, and the deadly. And this was a story involving a fellow reporter. It would be irresistible to him. But Lacey thought about Felicity, endlessly moping about the newsroom, and Wiedemeyer eating every last Krispy Kreme doughnut on the planet. She took a deep breath.

"Have you heard of Kinetic Theatre?"

"Heard of them?" He perked up. "We played in one of their shows. Harlan and His High-Stepping Hipsters. One of our first paying gigs after college."

"Really?" That was a surprise. "You didn't play for *The Masque of the Red Death*, did you?" Harlan's jinx, or whatever it was, could not possibly be involved in Saige Russell's death, she told herself.

"No, not that show, but it wasn't too long after. Oh, Kinetic was already notorious all right, especially after that actress died. It was all anyone could talk about. Tragic of course. And just downright weird."

"What was your role?"

"We played the music for their modern interpretation of a Shakespeare play reset in the Thirties to swing music. *Much Ado About Nothing*. I thought they should call it *Much Ado About Swinging!* But they didn't go for it. Think of all the great shows you could produce to a swing music soundtrack. Why, the music would practically be a character."

"Like what, for example?"

This is promising, Lacey thought. *Get him excited about something, anything, get him back together with Felicity, and all will be well in the world of* The Eye.

"How about *A Midsummer Night's Swing,* or *All's Well That Swings Well.* And you could do *The Swinging of the Shrew, As You Jive It, The Swinging Wives of Windsor, Romeo Swings Juliet.* And why not *Titus Swingdronicus?*"

"Why not indeed? Tamsin Kerr would love it."

She'd shred it to pieces.

"Aha! This story of yours has something to do with LaToya and the fatal frock from *The Masque of the Red Death.* Doesn't it? Don't hold out on me, Smithsonian. They're a bunch of crazy Russians over there, you know."

"How crazy? And what do you know about the costume she was wearing? The red dress?"

"I mean artistic crazy. Theatre crazy. Crazy Russian crazy. I don't know anything about the— Wait a minute. Hold the presses." He sat up straight and stared at her. It was unnerving. "Is the old EFP twitching, itching, pitching you forward into another dangerous story? It is! I can feel it. Tell me, Smithsonian, my life may be in crisis, but my nose for news is always sniffing. I'm a born newshound, you know I am."

"Hold on, Harlan." She put up her hand to stop him, but he was on a roll.

"And Kinetic, you say? Let me add this up. So LaToya has a slap-down snit over the fatal gown and then she gets burglarized. What aren't you telling me?"

"Are you giving me any time to talk?"

"Ha. Not really. Sorry. Boy, Smithsonian, you get all the best stories."

"Lucky me," she said. "And I didn't think you were paying attention."

"I always pay attention. I was just letting my fear for my future children and grandchildren take over. But enough of that. Tell me more."

"More?" She finished the last bite of the doughnut. A sugar rush hit her brain. *Have I really done it?* Wiedemeyer was coming alive. News! Weird, disturbing news, that was the food that really nourished the chubby little reporter.

That and doughnuts.

"What can I do to help, Smithsonian? Unless you think I'm a Jonah, a jinx, a catastrophe."

Lacey hadn't actually thought about Wiedemeyer helping her. She just wanted to shift his attention from his own misery to Felicity and her moon pies. But what if he could really help? He'd worked on a Kinetic show. He must know people who knew people, and they might know something.

"I don't know how to say this—" she started.

"Just let the EFP do the talking," he urged.

"Don't get too excited. There may be no connection."

"Me, excited?" He was practically panting. "I'm as cool as a cucumber! I'm chill! I'm good! Come on, there's more, I know there's more. What is it?"

"The woman who fought over the dress with LaToya?"

"Yes." He leaned into her.

"She's dead."

"DEAD?!" Harlan shot out of his chair. "How? When? What happened?" His eyes darted around as if he could see clues floating in the air.

"Don't know yet. Trujillo's asking around."

"Holy Moses, Smithsonian. The poor luckless wench. What's her name?"

"Amy Keaton."

"NO!" He threw the empty doughnut box into the air. "Amy Keaton? Not *my* Amy?"

"*Your* Amy? You know her?'

"Do I know her? I had a— Well, *we* had a— Ah, we had a *thing*. Together."

"A thing?"

"Not really a *big* thing. Sort of a thing. A casual thing. Casual but intense. Sort of. We went out a few times. She was nice, really cute too, but well— Not like Felicity Pickles. My little gherkin. It happened long before Felicity and me, and ultimately it wasn't meant to be. But jeez, poor little Amy Keaton. Wow."

"Little?"

"Yeah, she was tiny. I haven't seen her in years— Oh my God, do you think I jinxed her?"

Lacey blinked. "Harlan, don't be ridiculous. There has got to be a statute of limitations on jinxing. Especially if you haven't seen her in years."

"You're right. Still, poor Amy! No, I didn't jinx her, I couldn't have, not after all these years. So you think some sleazy bastard killed her?"

"We don't know what happened yet. I don't have enough information to draw any conclusions."

"That's right. Sure." Wiedemeyer seemed lost in thought. "Too soon."

"And this is between us right now. Just the two of us. Got it?"

"Of course it is. How could you even say such a thing?"

"Listen, I have an interview to get to." She pulled herself out of the chair. "This has to be on the QT, the down low."

"You're interviewing suspects?" His eyes were wide.

"Not suspects. A couple of actresses who have worn the costume that Saige Russell wore."

"Ah yes, the Red Dress of Doom, the fatal frock, the gruesome gown, the murderous moire, the treacherous toile—"

"Stop right there, Harlan. Let me reiterate: This is just between the two of us, right? Not anyone else. Not Mac. Not Tony. And don't edit me, not even in your mind."

It was well known at *The Eye* that Harlan Wiedemeyer meant well, but he had no filters. No discretion. And an over-fondness for adjectives.

"You have my solemn word on it." He made a zipping gesture across his lips. That was exactly what Lacey was afraid of.

The spirit is willing, but the mouth must squeak.

SIXTEEN

I SHOULD HAVE TAKEN a taxi.

By the time Lacey reached Trio's Restaurant, her lavender dress was sticking to her ribs, her face was glowing with perspiration, and her hair was beginning to frizz like it had been electrified. She pinned it up on top of her head to avoid an imaginary lecture from her stylist, Stella, who thank God wasn't there. The jacket she carried over one arm felt like a soggy five-pound sack of wool.

She dashed into the eatery's considerably cooler air and wondered if she'd catch pneumonia from all the temperature changes. Trio's was an unpretentious establishment in D.C., not far from Theatre J on Sixteenth Street and the theatres on Fourteenth Street. It was a hangout for actors, directors, the odd playwright and journalist, and probably many ordinary people, too.

Lacey spotted Susannah Kittredge and Noelle Pepper from their photos on the web. They were already seated at a table. She introduced herself and sat down.

The two actresses were about the same size and shape. Like LaToya, they were tall and trim, which of course would be necessary for any actress who wanted to borrow the infamous ruby-red dress. Today they both wore black sleeveless sheathes. Black summer dresses seemed to be a style note this summer, Lacey decided, as if by wearing black they were defying the heat. Also, black was a perennial staple for an actor—and for any Washingtonian's day job.

Susannah was blond, and even though she was sunburned, she seemed too pale for the rich reds of the *Red Death* costume. The sunburn looked painful. She noticed Lacey's look and explained she'd just been at their group beach house in Delaware. She forgot to wear sunscreen and was paying for it.

"I hope I don't peel." She picked at some loose skin on her arm. Her hair was short and spiky, white at the tips where the sun had bleached it.

"I never go out in the sun at the beach," her companion said. "Too many auditions where they want you dead pale."

Noelle Pepper's hair was black, and her green eyes were large and round, almost doll-like. Her white skin and red lips made her look like a cross between Snow White and a southern belle, and she had a hint of a southern accent. She would have been stunning in the crimson costume, Lacey decided, like Snow White wrapped in the peel of a poison red apple.

A waitress stopped for their lunch orders. Predictably, she was another actress, who squealed hellos and air-kissed both of Lacey's lunch companions. Also predictably, both actresses ordered salads, dressing on the side. After eating a glazed doughnut earlier, Lacey threw caution to the wind and ordered the old-fashioned grilled cheese sandwich. She blamed the carbs she'd already eaten, and the heat. She craved comfort food, and solid information.

"You write for *The Eye Street Observer*?" Susannah asked. "Do you know Tamsin Kerr?"

"Yes, but I don't write for the theatre section. I'm in fashion."

"You're writing a fashion story on the theatre?"

"If it develops. At the moment I'm just seeking information."

"So that's why you want to talk about the dress," Noelle said.

Lacey nodded. "I understand each of you wore the red costume from *The Masque of the Red Death* to the Helen Hayes Awards. Different years, of course." Both heads nodded.

"And you'll really mention us?" Susannah asked.

"Of course." Lacey was amused by their eagerness.

Dark-haired Noelle weighed in. "I wore it last year because I heard it was good luck. And it's pretty spectacular. Heavy too, and it swings and swishes when you walk."

"It's very heavy," Susannah said. "By the end of the evening I was exhausted. But it's really beautiful. It was a trip wearing it."

"So you liked wearing it?" Lacey asked.

"Sure, and I didn't have to pay for it."

"And you, Noelle?"

"Basically, I wore it on a dare," Noelle said. "I wasn't sure I wanted to wear something that had been worn by so many other women. One of the crowd, you know. Then I saw it and I just flipped for it. I didn't even know that Saige Russell died in it. I was totally appalled when I found that out."

"Did you know her?" Saige Russell worked and died a little before these young actresses' time.

"No. But still."

"She didn't actually die in it," Lacey pointed out. "That I know of."

"Right, but she wore it right before— You know. Curtain. End of play," Noelle said. "It's hard to separate the two events. The timing was so close. Too close. By the time I found out, though, I was committed. And I think she would have understood, you know?"

"In a way, wearing her last costume keeps her alive." Susannah was quite the philosopher.

"I guess." Noelle seemed more pragmatic. "Besides, Helen Hayes tickets are so freaking expensive, even the insider tickets for actors in shows. I just felt lucky to get to borrow it. I couldn't afford to buy a formal dress, or even a cocktail dress."

"I can imagine." Lacey was impressed that someone knew the difference between *formal* and *cocktail*. She hadn't been to the Helen Hayes Awards, but she had attended the White House Correspondents' Dinner, which was as formal as you could get in the Washington journalism world. Even so, some reporters always refused to dress up. "In the theatre world, 'formal' has a little more leeway, right? 'Creative black tie,' they call it?"

"Sure, which means sort of anything goes," Susannah said. "Like that costume."

"Once I saw it, I did yearn to wear that long ruby-red dress," Noelle added. "I felt glorious in it. Like Susannah said, it's heavy, it has weight and consequence. And there you are, with all those photographers taking your picture."

"The Helen Hayes is very glamorous," Susannah added. "Like Cinderella's ball."

"Did the costume turn out to be a good-luck thing for you?" Lacey inquired.

"I guess so," Noelle put in. "I didn't win any awards in it, but it was a fabulous night, and no one else has died in it. Or fallen off a platform, or whatever. When all was said and done and the evening was over, I felt like it was a bit of a letdown to take it off."

"Exactly," Susannah agreed. "In a dress like that, you expect wonderful things to happen."

"And they didn't?" Lacey asked.

"It's such an honor just to be *nominated*, you know?" Both actresses laughed. "No luck for me either, but it was a great night. And then Cinderella has to go back to her ashes." Susannah poked at her salad. "The next day you get up and go back to work. Life happens."

"Like everything else," Noelle added.

"Why do you think Kinetic has let people borrow the dress?"

"It keeps the legend alive," Noelle said. "And Kinetic always gets mentioned when someone wears it, so it's good publicity for them too. A little gruesome that it has to be about a dead woman, I guess, but press is press."

"How did it work? Borrowing the dress, I mean."

"Oh, you just go over to Kinetic on Sixteenth and put your name on the list," Susannah said. "Not online, in person. You have to be exactly the right size and height, 'cause they don't let you do any alterations, and you submit your headshot. And then Nicky chooses."

"Nicky?"

"Nikolai Sokolov. The designer. The guy who made it for the *Red Death* show."

"Right, Nicky."

"He decides," Noelle agreed. "But I mostly dealt with someone called DeeDee." DeeDee Adler seemed to be the woman in the know. Lacey made a point to see her in person and not get shrugged off in another phone call. "She takes your headshot, she takes care of physically lending the dress out and collecting it afterwards," Noelle continued. "But Nicky picks who wears it. And if you say a word about the dress to Yuri Volkov, he yells at you and goes storming out."

"I know!" Susannah started giggling. In a broad Russian accent she proclaimed, "Leaf me alone! I haff no time for stupid costumes! I am *beezee* man!"

They all laughed. It was a pretty good impression of the artistic director Lacey had met the day before.

"Did the dress come with a mask?" Lacey asked.

"I never saw a mask," Noelle said. "Besides, even if it did, it's not a masked ball, it's the Helen Hayes. You want your face to be seen there, even though it's turned all big-corporate-money-ish."

"What do you mean?"

"It used to be this fabulous theatre evening, a great party for theatre people. Insiders get cheaper tickets, a little cheaper anyway, and actors who couldn't afford a ticket, they knew they could always crash the after-party. You saw everyone from the other shows in town, people you'd been in shows with, all your friends, Broadway people on tour, directors you've been dying to meet. It really was a celebration for the community, the actors and directors and designers and writers, all the creative people. But now— Everything's so controlled, major security, and it's flooded with business types. All the money people, the sponsors and the Board of Directors types." Noelle mock-shivered at the horror of it. "Boring."

"Yeah, the party has totally changed," Susannah said. "But actually winning a Helen Hayes award? Wow. That would be *something.*"

Time to change the subject, Lacey decided. "Did you know Amy Keaton?" They both looked blank. "The stage manager at Kinetic." Neither one had known her, and they obviously hadn't heard of her death. "Have you been in any Kinetic productions yourselves?"

"I haven't," Susannah said, and Noelle shook her head too. "I've auditioned. They're really all about dance. You have to be incredibly good. And impervious to pain. And then there's Yuri."

"What about Yuri?"

"She just means they're very exacting," Noelle added. "Kinetic is wonderful, their shows are amazing, they do incredible movement, they win Helen Hayes awards. But personally, I hate to cry every damn day in rehearsal, unless the part calls for it. And then I want to save it for the performance."

"Me too," Susannah agreed. "Crying is pretty much a given with Yuri, I hear. He likes to break down your defenses. But personally? Ick."

They all agreed on that point.

No one wants to cry at work.

SEVENTEEN

*B*ACK AT THE NEWSROOM, a much more cheerful Felicity Pickles informed Lacey she was wanted in the conference room down the hall.

"What's up?" Lacey was wary of sudden meetings in the conference room in the middle of the day.

"I don't know. But Harlan came back! And he's just like his old self." Felicity was glowing.

"Really? I wonder what could have happened. And who's in the conference room?"

"Mac."

"Just Mac? What's so important he couldn't tell me in his office?"

Felicity shrugged and waltzed away with an empty platter, as if walking on air. Her moon pies were a big hit, and her Harlan was back.

Lacey felt relieved, but a bit rumpled and crumpled by the weather and *dumpled* by the cheesy carbs she'd consumed. She detoured to the kitchen for a fresh cup of tea. It was always good to have something warm in her hands if the room was cold. The door of the conference room was closed, but the blinds were open and Lacey could see Mac, Trujillo, and Wiedemeyer. All three seemed to be having a fine time, laughing, joking, munching moon pies.

This can't be good. Mac saw her and gestured for her to enter. Lacey opened the door and there was a sudden silence.

"Hello, boys. Get me rewrite," Lacey greeted them. They didn't get the joke. Mac spoke first.

"I hear we've got a situation."

Oh, Wiedemeyer. You little tattletale, what did you tell them? She gave the round little man the Look.

"I had to tell!" he whined. "This is bigger than you and me, Smithsonian. Some crazy bastard killed my Amy."

So much for promising to keep quiet.

"It's murder?" Lacey threw a look at Trujillo. "You found out something?"

"The dead woman you're so interested in? One Amy Keaton?"

"Who do you think we're talking about, Tony?" Lacey regretted the grilled cheese and fries she had at lunch. She blamed them for the queasiness she felt. "The cops think it's murder too? Or just the little squealer here?"

"Unknown. Could be some freak accident in her apartment. That's where she was found. Right now, it's still under investigation and the D.C. police aren't saying much. But you're involved, so—"

Lacey slumped into a chair. It was going to be a long day. Mac was glaring at her.

"Smithsonian. It seems you didn't mention to me that this was yet another fatal and possibly felonious fashion story."

"Apparently that's officially unknown, Mac. How did she die?"

"M.E.'s report isn't in yet, of course," Trujillo said. "Off the record I was told it looks like a broken neck."

"No." She put one hand on the table to keep steady.

"Yes." Trujillo was maddeningly calm.

Mac cleared his throat. "The first woman who wore that red dress, Saige Russell, also died of a broken neck." He tapped the stack of articles Lacey had so thoughtfully copied for him.

"Who'd you talk to?" she asked Tony.

"A source in the department. Not Broadway Lamont. So feel free to pump him for info if you want. Spill, Lacey. What's really up?"

"Yes, Smithsonian," Mac stared at her and his eyebrows looked like fists. "Do tell us what's going on."

"Our own Tamsin Kerr called me with the news. I started calling sources. Some people in the theatre world know she's dead, but not everyone. Nobody seems to know any more than that."

"Poor little Amy," Wiedemeyer put in. "Not many friends, a woman all alone, a sad little spinster—"

"Enough, Wiedemeyer," Mac said. "Write up what you know, and go easy on the adjectives. Fact is, we don't even know if we've got a story yet."

"No story! Of course we have a story," Harlan protested. "At least an obit!"

"We can't draw a line from that silly tussle over the dress to Amy's death," Lacey said. "All we have are a few incidents. No proven connections."

Trujillo sat back. "Lois Lane's got a point, Mac. Besides, LaToya's probably already put herself in Lamont's custody. Or she's about to. So she's probably safe."

"We know she got into a fuss with this woman over the dress," Mac pointed out, "and now the woman is dead. It's always a dress."

"It's not always a dress," Lacey said. "There was a shawl. That one time."

"I heard LaToya was fierce," Wiedemeyer mused. "I knew she had a fight with someone, but I didn't know it was poor little Amy."

"If there is a story, it's probably about Amy Keaton, not LaToya. I don't know where the dress fits in," Lacey said. "And she wasn't poor little Amy that day. She was right up in LaToya's face."

"Is that the EFP talking?" Wiedemeyer asked.

Lacey glared at him. "Shut up, Harlan. LaToya's apartment was broken into. Remember?"

"Maybe LaToya staged it for you?"

"Don't be ridiculous. No woman would go to that much work to fake some screwy message. You weren't there. You didn't see it."

The image of the stuffed clothes in LaToya's apartment surfaced in Lacey's imagination. *All dressed up and nowhere to go.*

"What about LaToya, then?" Tony asked. "How is LaToya involved in this mess?" His voice carried well beyond the closed conference room.

To everyone's surprise, LaToya Crawford opened the door and stomped in on her four-inch heels. She looked as fierce as ever, from her shiny patent-leather black bob to her dangerous stilettos. Her bright purple sheath dress was drawn in at the waist with a narrow pink belt, and a rose-colored scarf was looped around her neck. Her nail polish and lipstick were glossy and violet, like hard candy. It was a look that said, *Here I am! I will stomp you with my high heels. I will gouge out your lungs with my nails. I will tap dance on your heart. Bring it on!*

"What about LaToya?" she repeated, with her fiercest glare. "My ears are burning! And I've got a city council story to file, so talk to me quick, people."

"Better come on in." Mac didn't look happy to see her.

"I'm already in!" LaToya gazed from one face to another. "I've rarely seen a motleyer crew. What the hell is up?"

"We were discussing the Red Dress of Doom that you fought over, and won," Wiedemeyer said. "From poor little Amy Keaton."

"I bought that dress, Wiedemeyer! She tried to take it away from me. I've got a receipt for that dress." The receipt was clearly a point of honor for her. "And for your information, your poor little what's-her-name is a *mean* little thing. Not so little, either."

"LaToya," Lacey said. "Amy Keaton is dead. She died sometime in the last couple of days."

"What?" LaToya shook her head as if she didn't hear it right.

"She's dead," Mac repeated.

"Oh no, she didn't! That beeyatch is not dead! No, she did not, that pale frizzy piece of— Dead? I don't believe it." They were brave words, but LaToya was shaken. She pulled out a chair and sat down. "How did she die?"

"No determination yet," Trujillo said. "There is a slight chance it could be a freak accident."

"Freak accident. Sure. These things happen all the time in this town."

"They do, but when there is an unusual old dress and two of my reporters involved, I have questions," Mac said. "So far, we have interesting incidents, but not a through line. And we won't have it until we know what happened to Amy Keaton and why."

"This is ridiculous! My condo, my sacred home turf, was broken into. My security was breached. That crazy woman was my number one suspect. And you're telling me she's dead?" She put her hands flat on the table. "What's going on, Smithsonian? Is it the damn dress? Are you telling me I'm in some kind of danger?"

"All I have are questions too," Lacey said.

Was LaToya in danger? Only if the dress was hiding a secret. But all clothing hides secrets. *That's what it's for.*

"What are you going to do?" Wiedemeyer asked LaToya.

LaToya rubbed her bare arms. "I can't write one word about this. I've got a conflict of interest. I'm calling Detective Broadway Lamont. I'm pretty sure he's going to want to protect a citizen of the District."

And if Lacey wasn't mistaken, LaToya had a gleam in her eye. *A gleam called Broadway Lamont.* "LaToya, tell me what you think about Amy Keaton."

"Hell if I know." She took a deep breath. "I thought she had something to do with my apartment break-in. Now I don't know."

"When do you want the dress back from me?"

"You out of your mind, Smithsonian? Never! At least not till I'm sure it's free of bad juju. And even then—" She shivered. "I'll let you know."

So I'm stuck with it. For now. Better take a closer look at it. Wherever it is. She needed to call Vic, she remembered. *Is this really a killer dress? Or is someone pulling the threads for reasons that have nothing to do with the dress?*

"Um, Mac—" Lacey began.

"No, Smithsonian, I'm not giving you another beat. After wreaking havoc on fashion, you think I'd unleash you on something else?"

"I didn't do this. I'm not responsible."

"You never are! But you're like a magnet for weird fashion mayhem. I don't know how you do it, but you do. Now go write me a story about the red dress."

She stood up. *I'll never get off this beat. Maybe it's just as well.*

Lacey was developing a unique expertise on *The Eye*'s strange version of a fashion beat. Fashion was a language she spoke fluently. She found fashion fascinating. Although there were times she wondered why she worked so hard. *A little less sweat and no one would know.* All she really needed to do was to turn her copy by deadline; she could churn the same phrases over and over and no one would be the wiser. *Like the sportswriters.*

But she couldn't help herself. Lacey took pride in her beat and the stories it threw in her path. There were always threads that somehow came together. Lacey didn't know what thread connected the red dress and a long-dead actress and the lonely death of Amy Keaton. There must be one, and she was going to find it. It was her curse.

Let's begin with a young actress who danced her way to the top. And then fell.

Saige Russell had just scored the biggest success of her career, and it lifted her up like a pair of wings. And then it let her drop. Why? Saige would never know that young actresses kept her memory alive by wearing that infamous gown, if only within theatre circles, in their attempt to defy death and flirt with fame and fortune. They saw something in Saige's last costume, a totem in red taffeta. Wearing it gave it power, if only the power of superstition. And in the end, the crimson gown seemed to have taken on a life of its own.

"Anything else, Mac?" Lacey asked.

"Stay on this story, Smithsonian. Stay safe," Mac said. "And get out of here, everyone, we're on deadline!"

EIGHTEEN

*M*AC, TONY, WIEDEMEYER, and LaToya! Lacey's potential story was becoming a circus. She wanted out of the lion's den. The article wasn't even written, she already felt exhausted, and yet she had nothing to write. A woman was dead, it was murder or it wasn't, and an old dress was involved, or it wasn't.

She'd already turned in a "Fashion *BITE*" and some news briefs that morning. Therefore she declared herself at liberty to flee the scene of the "Crimes of Fashion." Besides, it was five o'clock. She grabbed her bag and loped out of the newsroom, making a break for freedom.

Vic wasn't expected at Lacey's office on this Tuesday afternoon, but there he was, waiting for her downstairs in the lobby. At the sight of him she felt her lips lift into a smile and her face light up. The weight of that heavy red dress slipped right off her shoulders. She concentrated instead, and gazed with satisfaction, on Vic Donovan. He was looking splendid in khakis, a light blue shirt paired with a dark blue tie, and a Brooks Brothers blue blazer slung over one shoulder. Lacey decided he must have had a business meeting with a client.

Or a photo shoot with Brooks Brothers.

He returned her smile. He reached for her hand and kissed her with conviction, before the moment turned serious.

"I understand the woman who tangled with your LaToya is dead."

"Word travels fast," Lacey said. "And hello to you too, darling."

"Sorry." He drew her into a tight hug and whispered. "Hello, sweetheart. So tell me about this other fine mess we're into."

"We? Vic, how sweet. You used to warn me off things you thought might be dangerous. Now you want to jump right into the swamp with me."

"I have found out, like most reasonable men, that resistance is futile."

"Careful, darling. You're sounding mighty romantic. However, we don't know if this is dangerous. We don't actually know anything, in fact."

As he opened the lobby door for her, he put up his hand and started counting fingers. "Let's see. We've got two women in a tangle over a dress, your basic apartment break-in with your not-so-basic freaky dress display, and one newly dead woman, maybe an accident, maybe not. What do they have in common, class? Oh, wait, I know! One ridiculous red dress. With a killer backstory."

"When you put it that way, it does sound dangerous," Lacey said. "Do you have the killer dress?"

"I do. And I checked out your apartment, just to make sure no one else has."

"You don't trust all those fancy locks and alarms you installed?"

"Trust, but verify. They're doing their job. Your shabby little abode above the river is secure."

They strolled to his Jeep through Farragut Square, where he'd snagged a rare parking space.

"Do you have dinner plans?" she asked.

"I do. I have a date. With a lady. Could I interest you in being the lady?"

"You certainly could. And I have an idea about afterwards."

"Afterwards? What could top a date with my lady?"

Nineteen

A *DATE WITH A RED DRESS.*
As promised, the red dress was in a secure location under lock and key. That location was currently at the Donovans' private security firm in Arlington, Virginia. Vic's offices occupied an entire upper floor of a steel-and-glass building in the Rosslyn neighborhood, across the river from the District. He and Lacey signed in with the security guard (one of Vic's employees) and rode the elevator up. It was quiet and most of the building occupants had emptied out. Cleaning crews were on the premises, but Vic mentioned that they were never allowed on his floor, for security reasons. The Donovans had their own personally vetted crew.

Although it was just another anonymous modern building, the large windows boasted fabulous views. From the darkened conference room Lacey could see the Washington Monument across the Potomac to the east, and to the north the spires of Georgetown University and the glittering lights of traffic crossing the Key Bridge.

She paused to enjoy the sight. Vic flicked on the lights and she turned to see him crossing the room to a set of doors.

"Don't tell me. It's in the closet?" she asked.

"In the closet. But not just any closet."

Vic keyed in a combination, pressed a few fingerprints to a sensor, and the closet doors swung open and the lights inside switched on. The "closet" revealed itself as a giant steel walk-in weapon safe, specially constructed behind, and camouflaged by, a pair of regular closet doors. It doubled as a heavily armed safe room, complete with its own HVAC, cots, lockers, a kitchenette, and secure communications to the outside world. There was even a tiny bathroom with a toilet and shower. Though it had never been used as a safe room, Vic said, the structure made an impressive statement to prospective clients. The Donovans had sold more than one replica of their safe room.

Vic beckoned Lacey inside. There hung the flashy crimson costume, surrounded by weapons, handguns, rifles, ammunition, and emergency equipment of all kinds. Lacey started to laugh.

"Well, the dress certainly looks safe, hanging there with its own armed guard."

"Best I could do on short notice."

"Have I ever told you I love you?"

"Recently? Let me think."

She grabbed hold of him and kissed him. "I love you, Vic Donovan."

"You want to get frisky in front of *that* thing? I hear it has a mind of its own."

"See, you are a smarty pants. And I don't believe it's actually sentient."

Vic gathered the crimson gown in one arm and hung it in the doorway so she could see it lit from both sides. It was the first time she had gotten a really good look at Death's Red Dress.

The dress was just material and thread, a lot of it, and a lot of care had gone into it. And yet there was something more to it. The long skirt flowed in layers upon layers of half a dozen fabrics, tulle and taffeta and silk, satin and lace and velvet, all of them in slightly different tones and textures of red, ruby, claret, crimson and more, giving it depth and mystery. Lacey realized there must have been a dozen or more layers.

But what does it tell me? What made it so amazing in the Kinetic show?

"Vic, darling, you wouldn't happen to have something like a black light on hand?"

"Part of the arsenal. And you need that, why?"

"Theatrical smoke and mirrors, maybe. I see some kind of residue or something on this dress that's not very clear in regular room light."

"As long as it's not a bloodstain. I don't do bloodstains on dates. Generally." Vic returned bearing a forensic flashlight with a black light bulb. He handed it her. The flashlight was heavy and cool to the touch.

She grinned with delight. "You have the greatest toys."

"I aim to please. And they're tools, not toys. Okay, they're toys too. What are we looking for, if it isn't blood?"

"Maybe nothing."

"Right. Or maybe something?"

"I hope so. I just don't know what it might be."

Vic turned off the lights and she turned on the flashlight, revealing the hidden effect the costume designer had devised.

"Skulls," Vic said.

"Skulls on skulls on skulls. Small skulls intertwined to make larger skulls." She stepped closer. "Look at that."

"Black light skulls." Vic breathed out heavily. "Theatre people are creepy. I was prepared for bloodstains. Blood is routine. This is just weird."

"Remember, it's only a costume. They must have had turned on black lights on stage to make these pop at the right moment."

Lacey was glad she hadn't set her heart on owning this garment. Would LaToya still want to wear it, if she could see it now? Lacey stepped back and gazed at it. The costume was even more dramatic from farther away. Up close, she could see the brush strokes of whatever it was that created the illusion of skulls. Some kind of black light paint, she supposed. For the audience, the effect must have been magical and shocking.

Behind her, she heard Vic taking photographs, with an ultraviolet flash on one of his big Nikon DSLRs. When he was finished, he switched the overhead lights back on. Lacey moved the dress to the conference table, laying it flat.

"Looks pretty harmless now, Vic."

"Of course it is. It's just a dress, right, not a secret weapon?"

"As far as I know. Of course it was designed by a Russian."

"Uh huh. Like Kepelov?"

"I hope not."

"Yeah. Me too. I mean, he seems to be a good guy, but— Are we finished with this thing?"

"Not quite." She fluttered her hands over it, delicately touching it here and there, noting the different finishes and feels of the various luxurious fabrics. The dress was expertly made, but it was beginning to show some wear from so many borrowers. On the inside, the hem appeared to have been resewn in several places. Small tight knots were visible from the repairs.

She leaned in and examined it carefully. The hem was weighted to keep it from flying up when the wearer whirled and spun. Seamstresses sometimes employed old-fashioned lead curtain weights to make a garment hang just right, or such things as coins and metal buttons. Coco Chanel famously sewed gold chains into her jacket hems so they would hang perfectly. Lacey was curious about what this costumer had used.

"Vic, do have a small pair of scissors handy?"

He raised a dark eyebrow at her. "You plan to cut the dress open? That doesn't sound like you."

"I just want to open a few little stitches and take a peek inside the hem."

"Why?"

"Curiosity."

"Killed the cat. Would a pocket knife do?"

She smiled. "You want to do it yourself, don't you?"

"I want to feel useful, and in the field of Swiss Army knives, I am an expert. First, however, let's take a few more photos. You want the hem, right?"

"And these little knots, if we can get them. There are weights of some kind sewn in the hem. You want to do it? Your cameras are better than mine."

"Here, you know what you're looking for." Vic's office was fully stocked with every kind of camera used in surveillance. He handed her the Nikon DSLR he'd been using and she focused on the hem, the knots and the different threads and styles of stitches. When she was done photographing it, Vic pulled out his Swiss Army knife and flipped open the scissors. Lacey showed him which threads to snip. She'd worry about resewing the thing later. *And what to tell LaToya.*

"Very nice. Now do this one."

"I do tailoring and alterations too, you know."

Lacey reached inside the folded material of the hem and pulled a weight out of the little pocket Vic had snipped open. It was round like a coin, but not a coin she recognized. It wasn't a button or a washer or a lead curtain weight. It looked like some kind of gold and silver medal.

"Who is this guy? Is this Lenin's profile?" She held it up to the light.

"Lenin? You're kidding." Vic moved closer. "Let me see. Yup. Looks like Lenin. With a red star. And look, a hammer and sickle."

To make sure, they googled Vladimir Lenin on the conference room laptop. It was him: Vladimir Ilyich Ulyanov, known as Lenin. This appeared to be one of the innumerable medals handed out, apparently like popcorn, as service medals to Soviet civilians and military personnel in the old USSR.

"Pretty odd thing to hide away in a dress," she said.

"Well, darling, that's why they pay you the big bucks."

"As if." She scowled. She set the Lenin medal down next to the pocket from which it came and shot more photos. She felt the rest of the hem. There was more than one medal, but she left the rest of them in place for the moment.

"What do you think?" Vic asked. "EFP-wise?"

"Your guess is as good as mine." Lacey shook her head. "The dress was made by a Russian designer, at a theatre run by Russian émigrés, so that fits. But if someone was proud of these Lenin medals, or even considered them a curiosity, wouldn't they be on display or something? Or did they have so many of them laying around they could just use them as weights?"

"You remember what Churchill said about Russia?" Vic asked her. "He called Russia a riddle wrapped in a mystery inside an enigma."

"Inside a red dress," she added.

Until this moment, Lacey hadn't realized how tired she was. She slumped into a chair and propped her head on her hands.

"What's our next move, Lace? Besides my place."

"And besides falling asleep? I need to find out more about this dress. And these medals. Soviet medals, right? Who do we know who might know something about these?"

"Oh no." Vic groaned. His eyes were deep green in this light. His dark eyebrows knit together. "Kepelov? You want to talk to Kepelov? Voluntarily?"

"We may have a Russian doll of a mystery here," Lacey said.

Gregor Kepelov once told Lacey a mystery was like a set of *matryoshkas*, Russian nesting dolls. Each doll opened to reveal another doll inside, and another and another, each doll becoming smaller and smaller. The key to a mystery, he said, was like the smallest doll, perhaps the size of an acorn, usually something unexpected and overlooked.

Kepelov had once been in the Russian intelligence services. Now he worked as a freelancer within the D. C. security world, sometimes crossing paths with Vic—and with Lacey. They had worked together, once or twice. Kepelov was always on the hunt for artifacts he could sell to wealthy collectors in Russia. On anything involving his former country's artifacts, he was an expert. But there was also a danger the ex-spy might be tempted to interfere.

"Gregor can be exhausting, sweetheart. And it's getting late."

"I know. But Kepelov is the only Russian I know. Except for Yuri Volkov at Kinetic, and I don't think he likes me. And then there is Kepelov's sister, Olga. I suspect she's got more spook history than we know. But—"

"Tonight?"

"It would get it out of the way." Lacey paused. "Gregor may not want to come here anyway. After last time."

The last time Gregor Kepelov had visited Vic's offices he'd been shot. The ex-spy was wearing a bulletproof vest, fortunately, but it was a terrifying assassination attempt.

"That would be a shame. How about tomorrow?"

"Better tonight, Vic. He'd be hurt if we didn't ask him." Lacey was half kidding. Their eyes met.

"Me too. Do you want to call him, or shall I?"

They flipped the Lenin medal. Vic called heads and Lacey lost. As she picked up her phone, it lit up: It was Gregor Kepelov, calling her.

"This is weird, Kepelov," Lacey said in greeting. *It's him,* she mouthed at Vic. Vic's eyes went wide. "I was just about to phone you."

"Lacey Smithsonian. It is late, but Marie told me to call you," Kepelov said quietly. "Now you tell me why."

"She didn't fill you in?" Lacey asked.

"She says she does not know. Only that you have some important question."

"Um, yes. I do. Would you mind coming to Vic's office? I know it's late. If you'd rather not, I understand. Because of last time."

"What are you saying? Last time was nothing. Bullets bounce off Gregor Kepelov."

"I'm sure Marie doesn't feel that way."

He grunted. "What is this problem?"

"It's a kind of a *matryoshka*."

The unexpected sound of Kepelov's laughter surprised her.

"Ah. A mystery. And you need Gregor Kepelov's help. I will come." Lacey heard animated chatter in the background. Kepelov came back on the line. "I will bring Marie. And Olga. She insists. It will be a party. Do you have vodka? Vodka is necessary. For luck. Not to worry, I will bring. See you soon." He clicked off.

Lacey looked at Vic. In her worst Russian accent she intoned, "Night is young! Commander Kepelov says must have vodka! Not to worry, he will bring!"

Vic shook his head, laughing. He locked the safe room and shut the outer closet doors, leaving the scarlet suspect lying on the table. Lacey replaced the Lenin medal in its original pocket in the gown's hem. The red dress looked as innocent as the day she had first seen it, which, she reflected, was *not very*.

And as far as I'm concerned, Lacey thought, *Vladimir Lenin has no business hiding in any woman's skirts.*

TWENTY

*V*IC AND LACEY GREETED the trio in the lobby and got them signed in with the security guard. The humid night air that swept in with them reminded Lacey it was still steamy outside. She longed for a rainstorm to blow some of the heat away.

"Ah, cher, cooler weather soon," Marie said in the elevator. "Tropical storm headed up from the Gulf. Gonna be rain. It'll clear the air."

"Raining Katzenjammers?" Lacey asked.

"And cats and dogs too."

Inside Vic's office door Gregor Kepelov presented Vic with a paper bag containing a large bottle of clear liquid. The label was in Russian.

"Vodka," Kepelov announced unnecessarily. "For luck. You have glasses?"

"Make yourselves at home," Vic said. "Glasses coming up."

Marie and Gregor settled on the brown leather sofa in the suite's lobby, while Olga took the matching chair. She flipped through a *P.I. Magazine*. Marie closed her eyes and Kepelov waited with a sleepy smile for the vodka to arrive. Lacey decided she needed to help Vic, not make small talk. Vic was in the office suite's kitchenette, rounding up glasses, sodas, and juice.

"Vic honey, why are there so many cocktail glasses in your cabinets?"

"We're Boy Scouts around here. Always prepared." He hugged her for a quick kiss, then he stacked glasses on a tray and filled an ice bucket. "Tell me again why Olga is here," he whispered softly.

"I assume Olga assumes she's welcome wherever Gregor and Marie are welcome. Part of the family. You know."

"She is welcome. A little spooky, though."

"Don't I know it? But Olga has her moments."

There was another side of Olga, a sentimental side. She had once gifted Lacey with a small rosewood box. The delicately decorated container was oval and lacquered in black with brilliantly colored figures and flowers, inlaid with mother of pearl and delicate gold leaf. It was Olga's token of gratitude after Lacey uncovered the identity of a woman who had tried to kill her brother Gregor.

Because it was old and beautiful, and Russian, of course the empty box contained a legend. According to Olga, it held the scent of roses—but only if the woman who opened it knew her true love. Those who were not in love would detect no aroma at all.

For Lacey, the pretty box held a powerful scent of roses. Obviously just the rosewood, she thought, but on the other hand, she was definitely in love with Vic, so who knew? She tried to keep in mind that tender side of Olga Kepelova, rather than her uncanny resemblance to Ayn Rand.

Vic grabbed the tray of glasses and the ice bucket. Lacey carried the sodas and Kepelov's big bottle of vodka.

Olga stood as they entered. "*Spaseeba.* You have a new mystery, yes?" She inquired with her unnerving stare. She looked very old-fashioned tonight, rather like a vintage Soviet factory worker in a socialist-realism poster.

"First things first, Olga." Gregor poured out healthy shots of vodka. He handed one to Vic, one to Lacey, then to the others. "*Za vstrechu!* To being with friends."

Lacey sipped her vodka delicately and soon exchanged it for a glass of soda water, but she and Marie were the only ones holding back. After another toast in Russian, she produced her copies of the old articles from *The Eye.*

"Gregor, these stories discuss the Kinetic Theatre production of *The Masque of the Red Death.* Twelve years ago. I'd like you to look over them, if you don't mind."

"That's why we are here, no?" Gregor said.

"Well, yes, actually. And the vodka, of course."

Olga, Marie, and Gregor studied them intently, as if there would be a test. The last article drew a gasp from Olga and Marie: Saige Russell's death after the last performance of *The Masque.*

"The woman died." Olga gazed at Lacey expectantly.

"Yes. And I want to show you the red dress she was wearing that night." Another gasp from Marie.

"We are honored," Gregor said.

"And I have a question for you. About the dress. It may be nothing, perhaps just a curiosity." Lacey paused for breath. "There is an—*anomaly* in the dress. I think it's something of Russian origin. Probably Soviet-era."

"You make me curious, Smithsonian," Gregor said with a smile. "I see the vodka has not gone to waste."

"We will be the judges of Russian anomalies," Olga said. "If we can answer your questions, it is our pleasure to be of assistance."

"They're dying to know, Lacey," Marie laughed. "Please end the agony, cher!"

Vic whisked the tray with the vodka into the conference room, and everyone followed. The dress lay in the center of the large table, as if it knew it was the star attraction. Gregor refilled their glasses with vodka, and Marie's with juice.

"Don't worry, Lacey, cher, I am driving tonight," Marie said.

As long as there's no fainting, Lacey thought. Gregor inspected the dress closely.

"This is the dress, yes? From the Russian theatre you told us about? And it has secrets?"

"It has secrets. If I tell them all at once, Gregor, it won't be any fun," Lacey replied.

"Very well." He smiled that off-kilter smile. "Let the fun begin."

Showtime. They all stared at the dress. Vic held it up and flicked on the overhead lights in the conference room, so the red gown was flooded with light. They watched intently, as if it might come to life and sing and dance.

"It's more than just a dress, cher, isn't it?" Marie reached out for the material and caressed it.

"Yes. It's the Red Death costume, made to be worn on the stage, under stage lights, designed for and worn by the actress Saige Russell, who played the character of the Red Death."

"It's a memorial, to— To—" The psychic backed away and took a seat. Everyone turned to her. "Don't worry, I'm not going to faint. I just need to sit."

"A memorial, Marie? A memorial to Saige Russell?"

Marie waved her hands. "Not clear. Faces again. I see so many faces. I'm okay."

"I want to show you something. One of its secrets."

Lacey nodded to Vic. He handed her the forensic flashlight and switched off the room lights. In the sudden gloom Lacey flicked on the black light. Skulls on skulls on skulls appeared, covering the dress from neckline to hem, dancing with the dress as it moved. She heard a sharp intake of breath, and then unexpectedly, applause, first from Olga, then Gregor.

"This is a little taste of what the audience saw during the show," Lacey said. "Imagine it on the young actress it was made for, as she spun and whirled across the stage."

"Very beautiful," Olga said. "Very Russian."

"And there's more," Lacey said.

"This dress was sold?" Gregor moved closer. His teeth glowed almost lavender in the black light. "But why? You say it was a mistake?"

"Apparently." Lacey turned off the flashlight, and Vic flipped the room lights back on. He carefully placed the dress back on the table.

"Did I mention that my coworker LaToya Crawford's apartment was broken into?" Lacey said.

"Burglary?" Kepelov asked.

"Breaking and entering, nothing taken, but the perp left a message."

"What kind of message?" Olga asked.

"LaToya's clothes. Whoever did it spread her clothes around her apartment in dead silence," Lacey said. "Complete with accessories, and the clothes were stuffed to— "

"—To look like invisible bodies, sitting in her chairs." Marie shook her head. "Very strange. More than a violation of her privacy. You saw them, didn't you, Lacey?"

"Yes, it was a little unsettling." The Kepelovs said nothing, but they nodded in unison. "What? Do you have an idea?"

"The connection is obvious," Gregor said. "The dress, the break-in, and you. Once again, Lacey Smithsonian is in the middle."

"That must be terribly annoying for LaToya," Marie said. "But this event will draw that big man to her. There is a big guy in her life, isn't there?"

"But he's a little reluctant, Marie," Lacey said. "Let's see how it unfolds."

"There is another secret, Smithsonian?" Kepelov rubbed his hands in expectation.

Lacey lifted the skirt of the red dress and turned up the hem. She showed them where she had opened a small seam, and then she carefully extracted the medal she'd found earlier and tucked back in place. It was about the size of a silver dollar. She placed it on the table.

"These were sewn into the dress to weight the hem down, so the skirt will hang and flow properly. An old costume designer's trick. You put a little extra weight right at the hem to make it swing. And there are others, with room for many more."

Marie leaned forward. "Why, that looks just like— Gregor, darling, isn't that—" The Kepelov siblings exchanged another look.

"Vladimir Lenin," Gregor said. "The past follows us, like an orphan looking for a home."

"What can you tell me about this thing, Gregor?" Lacey handed him the medal. "Vic, can you snip out the rest of them for us?"

Vic went to work carefully with his Swiss Army knife scissors, and soon six more medals lay on the table in a row. They were all slightly different in size and style and the design on the back, but each of the seven bore the same distinctive profile of Vladimir Lenin.

Lacey handed a second medal to Olga, who examined hers with great care. She turned it over and over. The siblings shared a look amid a torrent of Russian words. Gregor switched back to English.

"KGB medals. You were right to call us. These are ordinary KGB Lenin medals, and yet they are not ordinary. These have a very special purpose."

"Not just to weight the hem of a red gown, I'm guessing," Vic said.

"Look." Olga held hers up like a teacher showing it to the class. "A very particular kind of Lenin medal. You see?" She deftly popped it open with a fingernail, revealing a tiny secret compartment. Olga displayed it to them all with a grim little smile, and it was Lacey's turn to gasp. "Fortunately this one is empty. Or perhaps not so fortunately, for someone."

"Like those hollow spy coins that open up," Vic said. "You can buy them in the gift shop at the Spy Museum, in the District."

"Yes, but not like these," Gregor said. "These are the genuine artifact out of the Soviet past. And who knows, the FSB may hand them out even today."

"So something could be hidden inside the medal?" Lacey asked.

"Secrets," Gregor said. "Usually microfilm. But these particular medals?"

"Poison needle," Olga said, very matter-of-factly.

TWENTY-ONE

"*P*OISON NEEDLE? WHERE?" Lacey peered into the medal Olga was holding up to the light.

Brooke cannot hear a word about any of this, or DeadFed and Damon Newhouse will be stalking us all.

"Where? Good question." Olga pointed out the tiny slot in which it would have nestled, against a tiny spring. "Needle is now presumably in deceased target."

"Deceased target?" Lacey's head was spinning.

Olga opened the rest of the medals, very carefully. "No needles. All gone."

"Are you sure?" Lacey asked.

Olga leveled a look that brooked no argument.

"My sister is sure," Gregor said. "You see, these were not sold in spy souvenir shops. They contained poison needles, at one time."

Seven poison needles? If the Kepelov siblings were to be believed, and Lacey had no reason not to believe them, these medals represented seven deaths. Or if as Marie said, the dress was a memorial, perhaps they represented seven tombstones. *A killer's trophies?*

"What kind of poison?" Lacey asked. "Cyanide?"

"Better than cyanide," Gregor said, picking up another medal. "A secret Soviet poison. There is a Russian name for it. Stops the heart, disappears quickly, cannot be traced, and if other plausible evidence of cause of death is present..." He shrugged.

"Are you talking about a super-secret Soviet knockout juice?"

"No. Super-secret Soviet knockout juice merely renders you pleasantly unconscious, it does not kill." He smiled at her and they shared a memory. For Lacey, not a pleasant one. "And we do not call it that."

The first time Lacey encountered Kepelov, he'd approached her from behind, covered her face with a monogrammed handkerchief, and rendered her unconscious with that secret Soviet juice. *But not so "pleasantly."*

As if answering her unspoken comment, Gregor said, "That was before we were such good friends, Lacey Smithsonian."

Yes, good friends indeed. "Wait a minute. LaToya told me something odd. During that break-in, she never woke up. She claims she's a light sleeper and she's up at the slightest sound, but she never heard a thing."

"Ah. The burglar made her sleep more soundly," Olga said. "This is a very polite burglar."

"How is that polite?"

"If she had awakened, the thief would have had to deal with her. Perhaps even kill her. Obviously this was not the plan."

"Exactly right," Gregor said. "Well executed. Saves on excess corpses and questions."

"Okay. First, I don't like where this is going. And second, I am not going to tell LaToya this," Lacey said.

"Good," Olga said. "No unnecessary explanation."

"Please hand me one of the medals, Gregor, honey," Marie asked.

He put one in the palm of her hand. She breathed deeply and nodded her head in a brief prayer. He handed her all the rest. She cupped the seven medals in her hands, blinked, and started to sway. She managed to whisper, "Murders. Memorials. Faces. Why are there so many faces?"

Marie's eyes rolled back and she crumpled into a faint. Kepelov caught her gently before she fell out of her chair and held her tight against his shoulder.

"My darling, rest now. Gregor is here."

"I was really hoping that wouldn't happen," Lacey said, catching her breath.

"Delayed reaction," Olga noted. "Still, she is getting much better."

"How is this better?"

"See how softly she fainted? No shock, no terror. And she was able to tell us there was a murder *before* she went under. She has given us so much more information than she could have before. Marie is very gentle person. It is a mercy she doesn't remember everything. She leaves it to us to find out more. Or in this instance, to *you.*"

"But why so many faces?" Lacey said. "Who are they? Victims? Or killers?" Olga said nothing.

"Are you sure there were poison needles?" Vic asked. "Not microfilm, microdots, whatever?"

"Needles," Olga stated. "I know this concealment method. Watch me." She held up one medal. "Hold like this. Press like so. There is a tiny spring. Concealed needle pops out. Can be delivered by stealth or in formal ceremony. Can even be done while pinning medal on target. Mission accomplished. These needles have served their purpose. Found their targets."

"And who were those targets?" Lacey asked, knowing that was a question that couldn't be answered. Not yet.

"Not the aging family pet," Gregor said. "Human targets. The only target where you must conceal the weapon. But the killer?" He lifted his glass of vodka and realized it was empty. "Who can say?"

"How old are these things?" Vic asked. "Cold war stuff? Or current issue?"

"Good question, Victor," Gregor said. "Not necessarily old. Possibly they have been made to look old."

The Kepelovs launched into another debate in Russian. Figuring that her fingerprints were already all over the medals, Lacey picked them up and felt the weight of them in her hand.

"But you've seen these Lenin medals before?" she asked Gregor. "This exact kind of medal?"

Gregor nodded. "Never before hidden in a dress."

"A costume, Gregor," Olga corrected. "In the theatre, everything is illusion."

Lacey turned the medals over, face down. They were scratched on the back. She lined them up in a row. All had distinct marks.

"What are you thinking, Lacey?" Vic rubbed his face. He was clearly ready to go home.

"I'm not sure. Look at these markings."

"Could be a code," Gregor said.

"A code?"

"Fascinating," Olga said. "But useless without the key."

"Can you figure it out?" Lacey asked Gregor.

"Lacey Smithsonian, I am flattered that you think I have such powers."

"And to answer your next question," Olga added, "premature to call in expert Russian cryptographer. These are troubled times. So many deaths. "

"So these marks are Russian?" Vic opened another soda. Gregor poured more vodka.

"Possible. Some are Cyrillic letters. Badly done. Other scratches are not. Perhaps unique to the one who marked them."

"We all want to know what it means," Olga said. "But it is wise never to seek out expert opinion until you know whose side the expert is on."

"A code. This makes my night." Vic leaned back in a chair and propped his cowboy boots on the conference table. "Thoughts, anyone?"

"Someone hid these medals in this scarlet costume," Gregor said. "Why? A dressmaker's reason, of course, to make it hang just so. But there is another reason. Is it meaningful or trivial? For example: Medals found forgotten in a closet at this Russian theatre, used innocently without knowing their original purpose? Trivial. But if meaningful, the concealer is possibly also a killer. A killer is unlikely to want such things lost to some unknown buyer. If selling it to LaToya Crawford was a mistake, this killer will be most unhappy."

"Uh oh." Lacey said and everyone turned toward her.

"Are you all right, Lacey?" Vic sat up and reached for her.

"Amy Keaton, the woman from the theatre, the one who fought to keep the dress, was panicked when I ran into her on Sunday. Maybe she knew the dress's secrets and knew there would be hell to pay if it were lost. She begged me to get LaToya to give it back. And if it wasn't a freak accident, she paid a price for that sale."

"Explain, please," Olga said. "Freak accidents are Russian government specialty."

"Amy Keaton is dead."

"Aha! At last the heart of the mystery! Someone had to be dead, or we would not be here." Gregor poured more vodka for Olga. "Another woman connected to the dress is dead? That makes two?"

"That we know of," Lacey said. *This part isn't nearly as much fun. Maybe I should give that vodka a try.* Vic stood behind her and rubbed her shoulders. "The medical examiner hasn't released a cause of death. Off the record, a police source told Trujillo at *The Eye* that it looked like a freak accident. Or maybe murder."

Olga nodded with satisfaction.

"And of what did Ms. Keaton die?" Gregor persisted.

"Looks like a broken neck. Again, no determination yet."

"Is that not the way the actress died? Broken neck, falling off the set?"

"Yes, and I know what you're thinking," Lacey said.

"Then we are all thinking the same thing. We are ninety-nine percent sure this was no freak accident." Olga seemed very cheerful. She was about to continue, but just then Marie emerged from her faint. The psychic blinked and wiped her eyes.

"It happened again, didn't it?"

Olga clucked like a mother hen and poured Marie a glass of water. "Not to worry, dear. You had good information for us. You are feeling all right?"

"Yes, Olga honey, I'm fine, but I went out like a light. It must have been bad."

"Yes, my darling, but you were magnificent," Kepelov cooed into her ear. "And I caught you. I will never let you fall."

"Lacey, the woman you wanted to speak with," Marie said. "The one I said wouldn't return your call?"

"She's dead," Lacey said.

"Yes. I saw that. There is no light there, where she used to be."

"We will let Lacey find out what happened," Olga said. "She is good at finding secrets. How did you put it? Secrets behind the seams."

"Answers will come, Lacey, but keep your wits about you." Marie reached out for Lacey's hands. "And your mask. Don't forget your mask."

"What do you mean—my mask?"

"I haven't the slightest idea, cher." She giggled unexpectedly. "Sometimes words just slide out. It must mean something."

"But why would anyone keep this thing in a costume shop," Lacey asked, "with all these ominous things sewn into it? Why lend it out to actresses every year?"

"I don't know, sugar. But we need to be getting home, and I have to drive."

She wobbled as she rose from the chair with Gregor steadying her. Olga patted Marie's purse and deftly produced her car keys. *A pickpocket in a previous life? Or just more KGB training?*

"Not to worry, Marie. I will drive, very carefully. I have not drunk as much vodka as Gregor."

Vic put his arm around Lacey's shoulder. "It strikes me that by dangling that dress in front of the world, and letting all those women parade around in it unknowingly, this nut job is laughing at everyone. Thinks he's smarter than everyone else. Any other symbolism is probably personal."

"Excellent point, Victor." Olga took Lacey's arm. "Take warning, Lacey. You are very smart journalist, but you must tell no one what we have discovered here tonight. Is not safe at present time. Every day another death: Russian agents, ex-agents, persons of interest, spies, witnesses, family members, they die every day. Someone is erasing footprints."

Gregor nodded. "Olga is right. Could be agent of foreign government. And we all know exactly which government. Very dangerous."

Oh please. "But is it any more dangerous than usual? There are thousands of spies in D.C.," Lacey said. Brooke had repeated that often enough. For Brooke, spy conspiracies were as fun as aliens and Bigfoot and killer rats in Congress.

"True, but only one such as this. This spy is an assassin."

"Do you know someone like this?" Vic asked Gregor.

"Premature to say. I know many assassins, but none who sews red dresses." Gregor reached for the gown. "Let me take this costume and keep it safe for you, Lacey Smithsonian."

Vic stepped between the spy and the red dress lying on the table. "It's safe, Kepelov. Trust me." If it wasn't well protected in Donovan's walk-in safe room, Lacey thought, it wasn't safe anywhere. Vic put his hand out. "And Gregor, the medals? Please."

Kepelov hesitated. "They have more information. On the other side."

"Chain of custody. Come back and visit them. You're always welcome here. But it's late."

"Perhaps a good idea." Olga put her hand on Gregor's arm. "Victor understands security too."

"Please, sugar," Marie said. "I'm dead on my feet."

It was clear that Gregor Kepelov didn't want to part with the seven little Lenins, but he smiled his crooked smile and dropped them into Vic's hand.

"You know something, Gregor," Lacey said. "Something more. Tell me, who put the medals in the hem of the dress?"

He shrugged. "I do not know. Only a suspicion. A tiny little suspicion. I can say nothing more. Not yet. Keep close watch on this building. I will be in touch." *Just like Kepelov to go all inscrutable after being so chatty.* But Lacey was too tired to try and worm more out of him. Vic wanted to go home, and Marie was practically in slumberland, so she let it lie. "Please. Do nothing for now," the Russian ordered her. "Tell no one. Write nothing."

Lacey and Gregor locked eyes. Normally, Lacey would bristle at his authoritarian tone, but she wasn't in any hurry to break this story.

"Okay. For now."

What could I write, anyway? She had too many questions, not enough answers.

"Call me. We will get together for big evening on the town." With that, Gregor ushered Marie and Olga down the hall to the elevator.

"What was that about?" Vic asked after he shut the door. "Get together? On the town?"

"You got me. Maybe it's some kind of secret spy code. Like saying 'let's do lunch.' Only with plenty of vodka."

؃

The red dress was back under armed guard. Lacey was nestled in Vic's arms in his townhouse in McLean. She'd had only a sip of Kepelov's vodka, for solidarity, but now she consented to a sherry. Vic was opening a Dos Equis. And Lacey was very relieved she didn't have to go home tonight.

"It could all be nonsense, you know," Vic was saying. "Hollow medals, poison needles, spy versus spy. Seems more like an elaborate inside joke. Or an accident. That whole theatre is full of Russians, right? So one of them inherits a shoebox full of Lenin medals, thinks they're just corny old Soviet junk, uses them for hem weights in a stage costume. That's as good as any other explanation."

She snuggled a bit closer, trying not to yawn. "Do you think Kepelov was telling the truth? At least some of the truth?"

"From his reaction, I'd say yes. I was watching him, and his eyes popped open when Olga opened up that first medal."

"She opened up a can of worms too." Lacey sipped her sherry.

"Another can of worms. The real question is, Why does Lacey Smithsonian keep finding all the weird fashion stories?"

It was her turn for a raised eyebrow. She sat up and grabbed his lapels.

"No, Victor Donovan. That is *not* the question. The question is: Why do crazy Russians hide weird things in their clothes?!"

He laughed and pulled her into a hug. "Oh, *that's* the weird thing. Thanks for enlightening me. Now, what is Lacey Smithsonian hiding in *her* clothes?"

When they came up for air, Lacey said, "I just wish the obvious solution didn't add up to spies."

"Like you said, D.C. is full of spies. But what I want to know is, in all this crazy mess, how did you end up with someone else's dress?"

"It's a gift." Lacey groaned and pulled away to rub the headache beginning to flutter above her forehead. *First vodka and now sherry. What was I thinking?* "This is nuts, Vic. LaToya wants to me make sure it's 'psychically cleansed.' Or something like that."

"Yup, clean into another mystery." Vic yawned and stretched. "Much as I want you to get rid of that thing, I can't see you giving it back to LaToya. Not yet. Not until we find her a psychic dry cleaner. And will she even want it back?"

"Oh, Vic, you don't know LaToya! It's a matter of honor for her. She won't give it back to the theatre. I'm just afraid she won't take it off my hands either. I mean, how can you tell when something is really 'psychically cleansed' or not?"

"A dilemma. What to do?"

"Hush." She put her finger on his lips. Lacey was tired of talking. She started kissing him and unbuttoning his shirt. "Let's do this."

"Now you're talking," Vic managed to say, before forgetting all about red dresses and Lenin medals and sweeping Lacey off to bed.

Things were looking up.

TWENTY-TWO

*O*N WEDNESDAY MORNING, Lacey was still practicing her excuses for coming up empty on the Red Dress of Death story.

Perhaps that was why it was her turn to wear red today. It was a sleeveless red-and-white vertical striped dress. The white collar fluttered around her neck and the red cotton bolero jacket warded off the indoor chill at the newsroom. She wrapped a long red scarf around her neck for extra warmth. She hoped she looked crisp and cool and not like a peppermint stick, although at least that had a breezy and fresh connotation.

It was barely half past her first cup of coffee. Too early to fully engage the brain. She was distracted by Harlan Wiedemeyer's story on Amy Keaton in the morning edition of *The Eye*. It ran in the editorial section for some reason. *Obviously too many adjectives*, she thought.

TRAGIC MISHAP OR SOMETHING MORE SINISTER?
DEATH OF A SAD STAGE MANAGER
By Harlan Wiedemeyer

When you hear of a friend's death, even one you haven't seen in years, it hits you in the gut. It takes your breath away. It fells you like a runaway truck. And so it was when I heard that Amy Keaton, stage manager at Kinetic Theatre in the District, had died in an incident the police are calling a "freak accident." Amy was a friend. No. She was more than a friend. Keaton was a beacon of hope in the theatre world...

Lacey had been unaware of Keaton's beacon-like attributes. Although the writing was florid and full to the brim with tortured phrasing, Lacey was pretty sure Mac had done his best to edit the piece before relegating it to an op-ed slot. To her amazement, Harlan didn't mention the fight over the dress between Amy and LaToya. *Or did Mac cut that part?*

The deceased paragon celebrated in the article bore no resemblance to the woman who confronted Lacey in Baltimore, and Lacey had no idea what Felicity thought of Harlan's former relationship, now enshrined in deep violet prose. Perhaps she wasn't entirely displeased that Amy-the-paragon was now even more definitely history. And Felicity must not have felt too threatened: The aroma of baked goods permeated the newsroom air. She had cooked up a storm of fruit tarts, possibly in a flurry of love-induced hormones.

Felicity appeared right behind that aroma in a clash of crayon colors. Her sack-like dress was bright orange, and the fruit-themed sweater was glow-in-the-dark yellow with cutouts of bright red cherries and apples and royal purple berries. Felicity's style brought to mind a kindergarten teacher on the first day of school. *A seasonal calendar of delights. Isn't love grand?* Lacey thought, while applauding the eye-popping outfit in front of her.

I wouldn't be caught dead in that, but it's fun to look at.

It seemed the balance had been restored to Felicity and Harlan's relationship. At last, the newsroom could look forward to more recipes with summer's ripened fruits, for Felicity announced she had picked her own cherries and blueberries for today's repast. In fact, she had some kind of membership at an orchard or a farm. There would be semi-healthy, although drenched in sugar, baked goods for the rest of the season and into the fall, until the apples turned crimson.

Lacey was still pondering the meaning of those home-baked goods, and reading Harlan Wiedemeyer's opinion piece, when the shadow of her editor loomed. She peered at him over the newspaper.

"Pretty exuberant piece of prose," she said. "Harlan's little op-ed."

Mac's bushy eyebrows knit together like two caterpillars mating. "It was so awful there was nothing to do except shovel it over to editorial."

"Good call. It will keep Harlan happy."

"Smithsonian. Listen. You find out anything more about that creepy crimson costume?"

She put her fingertips together, as if in contemplation. "I need to talk to the costume designer. I haven't heard back from him yet."

"You need any help?" His lips formed a sadistic smile. "Wiedemeyer would love to sink his teeth into it. He volunteered."

"For the love of heaven, Mac." She waved Harlan's purple prose in front of him. "You'd do that to me?"

"Something's got to give, and soon. This story's got my newsroom in an uproar. Wiedemeyer's turned the hysterics on high. Crawford's jumpy, and when she gets nervous, she gets mean."

"LaToya is fierce," Lacey said.

"One way of putting it. It's because of that dress. It's haunted or something screwy, isn't it?"

"I'm trying to find a connection. Some threads to follow. A red thread."

Felicity moved out of earshot, heading to the kitchenette with a bag of her special personal coffee. Mac sniffed the air, his gaze following her.

"And Pickles— I hope she's back to normal."

"I don't know, Mac. Anything could happen. The Harlan-and-Felicity nuptials aren't until next month. Long time around the newsroom."

"Yeah. And the hottest damn month of the year." He picked up a cherry tart, looked at it, and picked up a blueberry tart as well. "A July wedding in Washington. Everybody sweating in the church like pigs. What do you have for me today? Crime of Fashion-wise?"

Grasping at straws, Lacey grabbed her notebook. "Street fashion! Popular looks this summer on the streets of the District." Of course most of the same looks were popular last summer and the summer before, so it wouldn't be difficult. "Gotta go outside. Commune with the street."

"You aren't fooling me. You just do that when you're out of ideas."

"And yet it always works, Mac." She smiled and tossed the notebook and pen in her tote bag and stood up. She figured she could scan some denizens of the city in their summer togs, ask a few questions about their outfits, and voilà, instant column. To save the day, and her beat. And while she was out, she would stop by Kinetic Theatre and try to finagle some more tidbits on the fatal frock.

But how? Did anyone there even know that those Russian medals were used in the hem? Had they replaced earlier weights? Had the dress been designed with weights in mind? The resewn threads indicated the weights were added at different times over the years. Why? To add even more weight? Or had others fallen out and been lost? Once, those weights were deadly spy weapons. Heeding Kepelov's advice, Lacey decided it was wiser to refrain from mentioning the face of Vladimir Lenin, or even the hem of the gown. At the moment, her head felt as hollow as those seven Lenin medals.

"If you have time, figure out what's going on with that red rag LaToya bought, so my newsroom can go back to normal. Or whatever passes for normal around here." Mac took a bite of the blueberry tart. "Let me know if there's something I can do to push this along."

How the world had changed. Even Mac wanted to jump on her story.

"I'll see what I can do."

"You think it was more than an accident? This Keaton woman? Is this one of those feelings of yours?"

"I prefer to call it intuition, but honestly I don't know what it is. Yet."

"Okay. Get out of here. Work on the dress story. I know you will anyway."

"It's touching, your faith in my work ethic."

"Will we have anything on fashion from you today?"

"Yes, on a Fashion Bite. No, on the crimson costume."

He harrumphed loudly. "Throw something together by deadline. What did you say, street fashion?"

"I did."

"So hit the street, Smithsonian."

Felicity returned with a fresh platter of tarts. Lacey briefly wondered if the paper actually paid for all those fattening dishes she made.

Of course they do! With their waistlines, she realized, *if not with their wallets.*

Lacey hugged her notebook to her waistline and fled the premises.

TWENTY-THREE

*I*T WAS ANOTHER steamy June day in the Nation's Capital. The District's inhabitants appeared to be moving more slowly than their normal brisk trot. The sun's blazing rays and the soaring humidity made the air as thick as syrup. Lacey settled into the tempo and headed up Seventeenth Street, taking her own sweet time to scout potential candidates for her fashion column.

She spotted a couple of men strolling down the street in seersucker suits, one blue and one gray, bright white shirts, and crisp bow ties. And to complete their summer attire, one wore on his feet light blue bucks and the other light tan. Lawyers, she decided, possibly lobbyists. They carried on as if the heat were no big deal, but at a leisurely pace. *Definitely from the South, and a much deeper South than Northern Virginia,* she decided. Together they seemed the epitome of preppy self-assurance and retro cool. Or were they heading for a magazine photoshoot somewhere? Maybe for *Southern Living*?

She observed other men in one of the District's summer uniforms: khaki pants, loafers or boat shoes, pastel shirts with short sleeves or long sleeves rolled up, and no ties. All covered with a thin layer of sweat. Apparently from cooler climates, they found the heat and humidity oppressive. Women in the muggy D.C. summer fought a never-ending war against frizzy hair, exploding in the humidity. They wore it up and off the neck, clipped back in oversized barrettes, or controlled by the ubiquitous ponytail.

Not everyone seemed exhausted by the heat. Delivery workers in blue and brown looked well put together in their summer uniforms, happily in shorts. For young women who worked in offices, the sleeveless dress was a perpetual winner, in seersuckers, striped or flowered prints, or basic black. It was simply too hot to wear long pants, but she spotted a number of capris and sleeveless tops, as an alternative to the sundress. All had that dashing-to-lunch look. No doubt there were sweaters and jackets waiting for them in their frigidly air-conditioned offices.

Armed with an iced chai to keep her cool, Lacey was still relatively crisp by the time she reached Kinetic. She wanted to touch base with Yuri Volkov and if possible meet the elusive costumer, Nikolai Sokolov. But first she ran into a woman who hadn't been helpful the day before.

It never failed to impress Lacey that talking with someone in person was so much more valuable than doing it over the phone, or worse, via email or text. *The Eye's* shyer reporters, the ones who preferred to stay in the office and cover their beats via C-Span and the Web, didn't know what they were missing.

Lacey was a throwback to an earlier style of reporting, and she preferred to believe her journalistic brain was better off for her anachronistic skills. Most of the time, she inked her rough notes with fountain pen on paper, saving the computer keyboard for the mad dash to deadline. But she knew working journalists who had lost the ability to write by hand. It was rather like strutting in high heels, she thought. Women who stopped wearing them found their ability and desire had vanished, and they would be stuck with flats forever.

Aha, another Fashion BITE!

Lacey opened the theatre door and stepped into the lobby. A woman edged around cartons of wine stacked in front of the bar for tonight's show to greet her, and Lacey inquired after Volkov and Sokolov.

"Yuri stepped out for a minute, and I have no idea where Nicky is. I'm DeeDee. Can I take a message?"

"I'm Lacey Smithsonian. From *The Eye.*"

"Oh hi. We talked yesterday. About Amy."

"You're DeeDee Adler?" *The woman who couldn't wait to get off the phone.* "I didn't know you worked here."

DeeDee was small and muscular, with a gymnast's physique. Short dark hair and dark upturned eyes made her look a bit like an elf, an elf wearing cutoff blue jeans, a long-sleeved blue T-shirt, and running shoes. She appeared to be in her early thirties.

"I'm the assistant stage manager, and I help out in the costume shop and whatever else needs doing. Looks like I'll be picking up some more hours now."

"Because of Amy Keaton's death?"

"Sadly so. It's a big job. Well, a lot of responsibilities." DeeDee waved at the bar stacked with stacked cases of wine. A Trader Joe's grocery sack sat on the counter, filled to the top. "I just bagged up all the personal items Amy left here at the theatre."

"Is that it?"

"Yeah. One bag. There's not that much, mostly stuff from her desk drawers. Her tea collection. She must have had every brand of tea. It's just that Yuri wants everything of hers gone ASAP. It's because of the show. Press night jitters. Superstition. You know."

"That's pretty cold."

"You have to understand, Yuri's a genius. He's the motor behind everything here. Offstage, he just can't deal with personal stuff. To him, people are too messy when they're not on stage. Too much information, or something."

"I'll make a note of it. Do you mind if I ask you some questions?"

"I guess not." She scratched her head.

"Was Amy your friend?"

"Yeah, sort of. Not like best friends. We hung out sometimes." DeeDee paused to stuff some of the overflow back in the Trader Joe's sack. "This is such a drag. It's not a cool thing to have to clean up after someone who died suddenly. I'm supposed to give all this stuff to her brother."

"Her brother?"

"Yeah. Don't know why he called me. Maybe Amy had an address book at her place? Maybe I was the first name, you know. Adler. Always up front in the A's. And I had to tell Yuri about Amy dying too. That was a treat."

"Messy? Like people?"

"You got it."

"You suggested suicide, on the phone."

"I have no idea why I said that. She wasn't a happy person. But turns out it was some freaky accident. That's what her brother said."

"So I heard. When was the last time you saw Amy?"

"Saturday. Working the sale."

"Did you see the fight? Over the red dress?"

"Yeah! What a scene! That lacked dignity." DeeDee laughed at the memory. "I don't think Amy even saw the *Red Death* costume on our rack until that woman bought it. Then she went ballistic. Like a crazy person. Insisted it wasn't supposed to be in the sale. It wasn't on the sale inventory."

"She blamed an intern," Lacey said.

"Did she? That's weird. We don't have any interns right now. They're a mixed blessing anyhow. All I know is the costume was on the rack and one of our volunteers rang it up. This pretty black woman handed over the cash. I can see why, she'll look great in it. I told Amy to chill. Wrong thing to say! Boom! I just thought it was her anal side, you know. Us stage managers, born control freaks. But she was all flipped out, like she thought she'd lose her job or something."

She lost a lot more than that.

Lacey didn't know what to make of DeeDee's story. Nobody saw the costume on the rack until it was sold? Did someone deliberately hang the dress on the rack, hoping to rid the theatre of it? Was lending it to all those actresses becoming a burden? Did they know how the dominoes would fall? And where did the hollow Lenin medals fit into the whole thing?

"How did you find out she died?"

"The police called her brother and he called me. Some kind of accident. In her apartment. The landlord found her. He had complaints about loud music and said she wouldn't open the door."

"Did she listen to loud music?" Amy didn't seem the type.

"Maybe after a hard day with Yuri." DeeDee paused and checked her sack again. "Amy meant well, but she could be frantic about details. She got very stressed."

"Why do you work here?"

"Me? Theatre major in school. Always loved theatre. Working here? You gotta let things roll off your back. Lots of people are intimidated by Yuri. Mostly, I find him funny. He barks at everyone, but he treats people okay. That's why I've been here so long. You have to understand that right now, before a new show, he has to maintain focus. Things like death? Losing his stage manager right before press night? That's a big deal. Kinda freaks him out."

Things like death. "What else freaks Yuri out?"

"Oh, man. Missed cues. Misplaced props. Actors. Anything out of place. Basically anything." DeeDee lifted a small plastic superhero figure out of the Amy Keaton bag. "Wonder Woman. Kind of sad, don't you think?"

"Very sad." The contents of a life reduced to a shopping bag struck Lacey as beyond melancholy, right into tragedy. But surely there was more to Amy Keaton than this sack of office detritus? "This was just her job, right? What was the rest of her life like?"

"This job was pretty much her life. She lived in a tiny studio apartment up in Mount Pleasant. She loved the theatre. I'm not sure it loved her back. Oh damn, I forgot her mug, the one she used for tea. I bet it's still on stage." DeeDee turned and marched out of the lobby, down one of the side aisles toward the stage. Lacey followed and watched while the other woman picked up a big black coffee mug. It didn't look valuable.

"Sentimental value?"

"No, I just don't want someone to walk away with it, or use it. This may sound superstitious, but I don't want bad luck hanging around just before opening. Nobody does."

DeeDee boosted herself up on the lip of the stage to sit. Lacey leaned.

"Doesn't sound any stranger than anything else I've heard lately. What can you tell me about Amy as a person?"

DeeDee sighed. As if she couldn't stay still for very long, she jumped to her feet and adjusted some furniture on the stage, matching it with squares of glow-in-the-dark tape that marked the stage. The set was swathed in drapes of blue velvet and white sheers. She sat down again on the lip of the stage.

"She was a good stage manager. Stage managers aren't really like anyone else in the theatre," DeeDee said. "Actors care about their art. Their lines, their marks, their cues, their applause, nothing else. Techies care about physical stuff, like lights and sound and costumes and props and furniture placement and the set not falling down. Nothing else. Directors care about everyone following orders. Nothing else. But the stage manager worries about *everything*. Everything! About getting everyone and everything on stage, on time, in place, in the right order, and then off again. It's like running an entire railroad. All night, every night."

"Big job," Lacey said. "Will you be the head stage manager from now on?"

"Just temporarily, as far as I know. Believe me, it's intense working directly under all these mad Russians. But *dramatic*." She grinned, indicating that was a little joke. "Never boring. I like it when this place is empty, though. It's amazing that we can create a show out of almost nothing. An empty space, a few pieces of painted wood, some scraps of material and glitter, and a bunch of actors. It's a kind of alchemy."

"What do you do, when you don't work here?"

"I'm working on my master's in theatre right now, so I can teach and stop living in poverty." She grinned. "With a little help from the long-suffering parents who are desperate to see me become a valuable and viable member of society. I also part-time at Starbuck's. And when I can get another paying gig, I help out with lighting, set building, costumes. Whatever."

"Have you always worked here, at Kinetic?"

"Off and on for years. Since college. A liberal arts degree with a theatre major gives you only so many options. I didn't want to be somebody's administrative assistant, so I started working in the shop here."

"Are you familiar with their production of *The Masque of the Red Death*?"

DeeDee stared at Lacey for a moment before answering. "Yeah. *The Red Death*. I worked on it. That was a trip. Kinetic blazed its path to fame and fortune with that show. My first big production out of undergrad. Definitely a trial by fire."

"You knew Saige Russell?"

She rolled her eyes. "Ah, Parsnips! That's what we called her, backstage." DeeDee giggled wickedly. "Her real name was Patience. Didn't fit her at all. I guess she thought 'Saige' was a more interesting stage name, earthier or something. But *nothing* could make Parsnips more interesting."

"Parsnips?"

"You know. Like that old song?"

"The song?"

"You know, 'Parsnips, Sage, Rosemary and—'"

"You mean 'Scarborough Fair'? I thought that was parsley, not parsnips."

DeeDee laughed again, an unexpectedly musical laugh. "Right, sure, but in my theatre crowd in college we used to sing it as 'parsnips, sage,' and Saige was like a vegetable you don't want on your plate, so she'll always be Parsnips to me."

"You didn't like her, I take it."

"I didn't." DeeDee leaned back on her arms and studied the catwalk and lighting grids. "Parsnips was temperamental and bitchy, and not very good. If she were bitchy and brilliant, well, all right then, but bitchy and bad is a terrible combo. Every time there was a problem, every time she blew a line, Parsnips yapped about how she was a *professional*. She was the *lead*. She shouldn't have to help move props or take care of her costume or clean up after herself. Or God forbid, learn her lines. And she barely had any lines."

"A professional?"

"When people have to tell you what a professional they are, they aren't. She wasn't even Equity. Real pros don't bitch about the little things." Lacey had to agree. There were "professionals" she'd had to deal with who were anything but. "I don't know why Yuri didn't kill her. Or can her ass. And he was a total madman after Parsnips died."

"Why? Was he in love with her?"

"Oh, the farthest thing from it. He was just greatly offended that she died in his theatre. Like how *dare* she."

"And the night she died, where were you?"

"Oh, I was at the cast party. Didn't hear about Parsnips till the next day."

"You were there all evening, then?"

"The whole crew and I. We got to the party really early, 'cause we didn't have to strike the set. The children's theatre show was going to use it. If we'd had to strike, we'd have been working till dawn, instead of partying."

"How was Parsnips in the role?"

"Barely adequate. And that was because everyone was covering her ass. She could dance, but she had no chemistry with Maksym. And that's weird, because he was such a babe."

Maksym Pushkin? Lacey recalled the name from the clippings.

"The actor who played Prospero?"

"Good memory, Smithsonian. Prospero tries to keep Death out of his castle, but when she appears anyway, he falls in love with her, et cetera. But Maksym couldn't stand to be in the same room with Parsnips." DeeDee shook her head and sat up, hugging her knees. "She hated him too. I don't know what her problem was with him, except he didn't think she was the stars and the moon. Major offense with her. She was a total narcissist. Like some politicians I could name."

"She had a wonderful dress," Lacey said.

"Agreed. And she wore the hell out of it. She looked amazing in it. That costume Nicky made was really something. You could have put a robot in that outfit and it would get raves. And when the spotlights dimmed and the black light hit it, you could hear the whole audience gasp. Every night."

Even Gregor and Olga were impressed. "So if clothes make the man, costumes make the actors?"

"Sometimes. When Nicky designs them, they do." DeeDee was loyal. "It made Parsnips seem a lot more fabulous than she was."

"That's Nikolai Sokolov? Is he around?"

"He's been in and out today, but you should probably catch him later. Tensions are running high."

"Because of Amy Keaton's death?"

"No. Press night. Well, Amy too. But I'm here, I'll get it done."

So press night outranks death. "Can you tell him I dropped by and I'd like to talk to him?" Lacey handed DeeDee her card.

"Sure. You know, if you want to get another insider's view of Parsnips, I mean *Saige*, you should talk to Gareth. Maksym wasn't crazy about her, but Gareth—"

"And Gareth would be?"

"Gareth Cameron. I think it's a pen name. He's the playwright who adapted *The Masque* for the stage. If you want to find someone with another opinion about Parsnips, try him."

"Playwright? That's right, the Poe story was only a few pages," Lacey said.

"Right, it had to be fleshed out. And Kineticized. Honestly, a lot of the visual design was inspired by that cheesy old Vincent Price movie version, did you ever see that? This was sort of an ironic homage, Kinetic style. But Gareth wrote all new dialogue for it in iambic pentameter, in blank verse. Not that anyone noticed. Anyway, Gareth is dreary and miserable enough to adapt Poe."

"He's a tortured artist?"

"He's the tortured playwright's poster boy. He can write, though. He also adapted our new show, *The Turn of the Screw*."

"He sounds perfect for that. Where do I find him?"

DeeDee pulled out her phone and gave Lacey the number.

"That's his work, I don't have his home. It's some kind of trade association. Gareth is some kind of assistant to someone who lobbies Congress about—something. Not sure what. He hates it."

Lacey smiled at DeeDee. "I'd be disappointed if he didn't."

Pounding started backstage. It sounded like jackhammers. A few sweaty and sleepy-looking people started trickling into the theatre, armed with large cups of coffee.

"Rehearsal. Caution, Men Acting!" DeeDee grinned. Lacey picked up her tote bag just as Yuri Volkov stormed up the aisle to the stage.

"I was just leaving," she told him. He pointedly ignored her and jumped up on the stage.

"DeeDee, I have changes, many changes! We must go over these. Now." He dismissed Lacey with a wave of his hand. "Next time you come to my theatre, Smithsonian, buy a ticket."

Maybe I should. I'd like to see Kinetic in action. She wondered if there were any cheap tickets available.

I'll see if Tamsin can get me a comp.

TWENTY-FOUR

EEDEE ADLER PROMISED Gareth Cameron was a downer. Even in D.C., sometimes promises come true.

The playwright agreed to meet her in the lobby of the K Street building where his plastics association was located. She assumed he didn't want to be seen in his office in some lowly day job, but he left her cooling her heels for nearly half an hour. Portentous things must be popping in plastics, she decided.

It gave her time to write most of today's Fashion *BITE* in her notebook. She tried out a couple of headlines: *D.C. STREET STYLE IN THE SIZZLING SUMMERTIME.* Or maybe, *KEEP COOL! SEERSUCKERS RULE!*

In between sentences, Lacey admired the building's décor. The lobby was grand in an old-school kind of way, with leather couches and coffee tables settled around an abstract rug. WPA art decorated the walls, brawny working men and women with sinuous arms and chiseled jaws, all with a look of noble purpose in their visage.

Lacey shivered. She'd strolled from the steamy sunshine into subzero air conditioning, but even with the shivers the chilly air felt good. *Until that shiver turns into a dreaded summer cold.*

When Cameron finally appeared, his misery was palpable. Lacey found him instantly comical in his gloom, as if he carried his own private raincloud around with him, shedding thunder and lightning as he went. Every furrowed line in his forehead reflected an artist's anguish: a badge of honor, like his pilled brown sweater vest on this miserably hot day. The vest was paired with a tan shirt and khaki slacks, and his shaggy hair, which he kept sweeping off his forehead with one hand, was as brown as his eyes.

After the preliminaries, wherein his hopes were dashed— she was not writing a piece on *him*—Cameron asked, "Let me get this straight. You're not a theatre reporter?"

Gareth Cameron was attractive in a shaggy, poetic, even-featured way, and in his mid-thirties. He spoke with a slight New England accent with a twinge of preppy. In his hand was a bottle of kombucha. It looked revolting. He didn't offer Lacey any of it. *Just as well.*

"No, but as I mentioned on the phone, I'm researching the Kinetic production of *The Masque of the Red Death*," Lacey said. "I understand you wrote the script."

"The adaptation, yes."

"There were some very impressive reviews." *A little butter can't hurt.*

"Thank you. First time out of the gate." He smiled ever so slightly. "It was so long ago. Before I got my master's in playwriting. Yale School of Drama." This was clearly meant to impress. Lacey knew Yale Drama was a major force in the theatre world, but she wasn't about to let it show. "After Yale I worked in New York theatre for a while, then back to D.C. Frankly, I don't know why I came back here. But of course there's Kinetic." Cameron settled his lanky frame into the faux-modern sofa angled next to Lacey's.

"That must have been a great opportunity. Yale, I mean." Yale, Harvard, Princeton, Dartmouth, William and Mary, those had all been unattainable dreams for her.

"It was. I was lucky enough not to need financial aid," he said.

Lacey admired Cameron's ability to casually drop such credentials into the conversation. He might have said, *I'm rich enough to pay for Yale and you are not,* but this was so much classier.

Lacey's journalism degree was from a giant public university that later abolished its Journalism School and replaced it with a "School of Communications," whatever that meant, which was reported to have become a safe haven for football-team mouth breathers. Lacey suspected her J School degree was now invalid. She was glad she already had a reporting job and didn't have to produce her worthless diploma.

"My degree impresses no one," she said.

"There's no place like Yale," Cameron said, successfully achieving the dramatic rule of three repetitions of his theme, the importance of Yale and an Ivy League education. He smiled, a slightly superior-yet-sorrowful smile. "Though I expected more from Yale, to be frank. And these days, theatres prefer younger playwrights. I'm thirty-five. I might have missed my window of opportunity."

"Surely not," she said, thinking that anyone thirty-six or older would find this ridiculous. *Flatter, remember to flatter!* "And you look so young."

"You're too kind. You're a writer too, of a sort," he acknowledged grudgingly. "Are you working on a book, or anything important?"

"Depends what you call important."

Unless you count investigating seven possible deaths related to poison needles hidden inside KGB medals.

"I thought every D.C. reporter was working on a book."

"Maybe someday." *If I live that long.* "Let's talk about you, Gareth. You're a produced playwright. You wrote the script for Kinetic's *Masque*, and now you've done their new *Turn of the Screw*. That's quite an accomplishment."

He dismissed the compliment with a shrug. "Adaptations. I'm currently working on a new play, a new original work."

"Can you tell me about it?"

"It won't be produced here in D.C. I'm talking to a major New York theatre. But I really can't talk about it yet."

But he can talk about Yale Drama.

"I appreciate your seeing me. I'm writing about the costumes from *The Masque of the Red Death,* one costume in particular. Could you tell me what it was like to work with Saige Russell?"

Gareth Cameron wrinkled his nose and mouth into a sneer. "Not to speak ill of the dead, but—" He let a dramatic pause hang in the air.

"But?"

"It was so long ago." *And every moment enshrined in memory*, Lacey was willing to bet. "It's hard to remember. It was a challenging production. We got through it." He ran his hands through his hair.

"I'm guessing there's more."

"To be perfectly honest, Ms. Smithsonian—"

"Call me Lacey."

"To be honest, Lacey, Saige was a dreadful, dreadful actress. DeeDee Adler and the rest of the crew started calling her 'Parsnips' and it stuck. It suited her. Parsnips. Pretentious little bitch."

"Dare I ask for an example?"

He swigged some kombucha. "Saige couldn't learn lines. Pretty basic requirement for an actor, wouldn't you think?"

"The most basic," Lacey agreed.

"Every time Parsnips went up on a line, she'd blame me, or the script. It was never her fault. I wrote it all wrong, or the line doesn't make sense, or nobody talks that way, or whatever. And I had to explain very carefully that even a slow child could learn these lines. They were easy, it was rhythmic, it was blank verse. The cadence was essential. She couldn't do that. She'd simply stand there looking blanker than the verse."

"Sounds like you should have replaced her."

"I would have, but I wasn't the director. Yuri Volkov said no. And Katya would have been great. Katya Pritchard. Understudy. She had the lines down cold. She was a better dancer. Unfortunately, Yuri said we were too far into rehearsals for that. Frankly, I don't know what Parsnips had on him." Lacey was about to ask a follow-up, but Cameron was just getting started. "Maybe she was sleeping with him too, as well as Nikolai. I don't know. For God's sake, she only had a handful of lines! I mean, *really*. She must have had a learning disability or something. And temperamental too." Cameron's kombucha must be kicking in. "There was this one time, she refused to go on because she didn't have the *right* false eyelashes. False effing eyelashes! They had to hold curtain while someone ran to the drugstore to buy her more eyelashes, in five different sizes. For the love of God, she was wearing a mask! Nobody could even *see* her eyelashes! She simply shouldn't have been an actor. I don't know what she thought she was doing, but it wasn't acting."

"I heard she was a dancer."

"Mediocre at best. She was a better dancer than an actor."

"She wasn't either one for very long," Lacey pointed out.

"No. That's true. The theatre world dodged that bullet."

That's cold. But Saige was beginning to sound like a nightmare you wouldn't want to wake up to. "Here's another question, Gareth. Do you think Saige's death was an accident?"

He studied his kombucha. "I don't know. I don't actually care. You shouldn't play the diva when you haven't got the chops. You're suggesting something else? Murder?" He looked interested in the dramatic potential of murder.

"Just a question," Lacey said. "She doesn't seem to have had a lot of fans."

"I've never really thought about it." *That sounds like a lie,* she thought. "If someone pushed her, at least whoever it was waited until the run of the show was over."

"What happened after the last performance? What do you remember after she was found on the stage floor?"

"I didn't find out until the next day. Of course the press went crazy. FINAL CURTAIN FOR ACTRESS WHO PLAYED DEATH, stuff like that. Her death took away any attention my play would have had. To be honest, it felt very unfair."

Life is so unfair to us wealthy graduates of Yale Drama: I went to Yale but I'm not on Broadway! I'm so old at thirty-five! A woman's death inconvenienced me! Lacey wondered if she could hold back the tears: *Yup, I can.*

"What about Amy Keaton's death?"

"Amy. The stage manager. Yes, that was terrible news." He looked slightly distressed. "I heard it was an accident."

"Did you know her well?"

"Not really. She was very efficient and kept things moving, and that is something I appreciate. I mostly stayed out of her way so she could get her work done."

"Was she ever temperamental?"

"More bristly, like a brush. She could rub people the wrong way.'"

"Worse than anyone else?"

"This is the theatre we're talking about, Lacey. Everyone can be—prickly. Amy Keaton would have to take her place in line."

"What's the cast of this show like?"

"Mostly young. Well, you'd have to be, the show is so physical. They're eager, and good-looking, and they're willing to learn their lines *as written.* Not as *forgotten.* Not as *improvised,* not ad-libbed. Not rewritten on the fly. I told Yuri that was my bottom line. Now, Anastasia is wonderful in the part, for example."

"And who is Anastasia?"

"Our leading lady. A wonderful dancer. She had the script down cold the first week of rehearsal. Off-book, just like that."

"I can see how that would be attractive. How's it going?"

He preened, finally a dark cloud of gloom no more. "Not to be immodest, but it's brilliant. Henry James, now *that's* material you can sink your teeth into. And Yuri's choreography is impeccable as usual."

"And the actors?"

"They know their lines."

At least there's no cause to murder anyone this time around, Lacey decided. Not yet, anyway. *Could Gareth Cameron be a little too self-involved to be a murderer? Or is "too self-involved" the definition of a murderer?*

I really need to see this show, she thought. *It might even be good.* Lacey wondered if Tamsin Kerr might actually have an extra ticket to Kinetic's press night preview this evening. *Maybe I can slip quietly in at the back of the house with her.*

And the costumes for The Turn of the Screw *might be to die for.*

TWENTY-FIVE

ITH MINUTES TO spare before deadline, Lacey's "Fashion *BITE*" was finished and sent to Mac's editing queue. Seersucker was the thing. *So sayeth Smithsonian.* She'd merged her two draft headlines into one: D.C. SUMMER STREET STYLE SIZZLES IN SEERSUCKER!

Mac will just change it anyway.

She waited for Mac to edit and approve the piece so she could leave for the day. In the meantime, Lacey's head was spinning with style notes and theatrical gossip. Her perception of Saige Russell was evolving, like Saige's multilayered crimson costume that morphed with each change of light, revealing the skull beneath the skin. It only served to complicate rather than clarify matters. Her cell phone rang. She hoped it was Tamsin Kerr returning her call about a free ticket or two, but she didn't recognize the number.

"Hello, Lacey Smithsonian," the Russian-accented voice said. It was Kepelov, using an unfamiliar phone number. Lacey's voice dropped and she looked around for eavesdroppers.

"Have you found out anything about the medals?"

"All in good time."

"Okay. Take your time and hurry, as they say." She leaned back in her chair. "What's up?"

"We are going to hang out tonight." His words weren't making a lot of sense to her. "You and Donovan, and us."

"Hang out?"

"I have tickets for the Kinetic Theatre show tonight. A preview, but still a chance for all of us to see the foxes in their den."

"Tonight?" She wouldn't have to badger Tamsin for a ticket after all.

"Da. I am assured it will be a packed house. You and Donovan will meet us, Marie and me, at the theatre. Doors open at seven thirty."

Lacey was taken aback. She wanted to see the show, but Kepelov's invitation was practically a command performance. What if she'd had plans for the evening?

"I don't know if Vic is free tonight," she said carefully.

"Ha. For you he will make himself free." One of Kepelov's charms was his invincible confidence. "Will be fun. Olga is coming too." He clicked off without a goodbye.

Olga Kepelova at the theatre? Well, even Ayn Rand wrote plays.

Lacey's computer beeped. Mac approved her article and she was free to flee. She called Vic and relayed Kepelov's command to meet at the theatre at seven-thirty. He greeted the invitation with laughter.

"Could be interesting," he said. "I'm in."

"Really, you want to come?"

"Wouldn't miss it. With the Kepelov siblings and our favorite psychic, the company is bound to be entertaining, no matter what the show is like. Bring smelling salts for Marie."

"You haven't asked what the show is."

"Doesn't matter, I'll be with you." His deep voice, with its slight Southern tinge, sent a wave of relaxation down her spine. She could hear him tapping on his laptop, consulting the Web for details. "Here it is: *The Turn of the Screw.*"

"Appropriately enough," Lacey said. "Ghost story, two naughty children, a half-mad nanny, and the truth is elusive. What could be better?"

Change the characters to interfering coworkers and a half-mad reporter and you could be talking about ME, she thought. *I'm being driven mad by the ghost of a story!*

"I promise you a drink afterward," Vic said.

"Deal. But no vodka. Bonus: Several people who worked on the production of *The Masque* will almost certainly be in attendance tonight. Director, costume designer, playwright, and a stage hand, now stage manager."

"Even better. Why do you suppose Gregor wants to go?" Vic asked. "Other than the pleasure of our company and sniffing after the Soviet medals?"

"Isn't it obvious? He's taking an inventory of all the Russians in town. He's just peeved that I know a few he doesn't."

They arranged to meet at Lacey's place and said their goodbyes. Lacey's desk phone lit up with another call, and this time she recognized the number.

"Hello, Brooke."

"How could you not tell me that Amy Keaton is dead?" she accused. "Murdered in her own apartment?"

"What? It doesn't exactly say she was murdered." Lacey glanced at Wiedemeyer's article, still on her desk: TRAGIC MISHAP OR SOMETHING MORE SINISTER?

"Not in so many words. I can read between the lines. What's up, Lacey?"

"The article says it was probably an accident. And you know Wiedemeyer. He gets all excited. Um, sort of like you."

"Murder is implied. And that crazy blond woman who was fighting with LaToya is dead. And one more thing, why is he writing this story and not you?"

"As you can see, Brooke, Harlan knew Keaton. They had a relationship once. He's overwrought. That is why this is a personal piece and running on the op-ed page, not in the news section. Also because Mac thought it was too purple."

"Well, it is purple. But what about you? Are you ignoring this story?"

"Are you my guest editor today, Brooke?"

"I should be." Brooke sniffed in disdain.

"I'm looking into it. You know I don't want to put out a half-baked story. Especially one that could so easily be misconstrued by Conspiracy Clearinghouse and Damon's DeadFed gang. This story is still baking."

Holding her phone with one hand, Lacey gathered her things together with the other and gauged how long it would take her to get home and change clothes.

"That implies there is a lot more to this story."

"There is a *little* more. I've been interviewing people who knew her."

"And the dress? What's the through line?"

"There is no proof of a connection yet."

"Yet! I knew it," Brooke snapped.

"I'm not saying there is anything to it or not. Fact is, I don't know."

Lacey wondered if she should cross her fingers behind her back. Brooke was her friend, but Damon Newhouse complicated everything. Brooke was often torn between her loyalties to Lacey and to her all-things-conspiracy boyfriend.

"But why didn't you tell me? I'm hurt."

Brooke wasn't hurt, Lacey knew. It was a courtroom ploy to get Lacey to spill her guts.

"Listen, Brooke, I'm sorry. I have to leave now. Vic and I are going to the theatre."

"On a school night?"

The District of Columbia: not a late-night town. Many denizens of the District preferred to be safely tucked in by TV news time, for very Washingtonian reasons. They were due at seven a.m. the next morning in a staff meeting on the Hill, or in court, or at the office, or with their legal team. Or they were up working till all hours on documents, briefs, press releases, congressional testimony, or plausible denials. Or they were hoping to catch a glimpse of themselves on the ten p.m. news.

Or they're hoping not to.

"I know, but Kepelov got us tickets. And listen, I have to run, I need to change before Vic picks me up."

"Where is the show?"

"Kinetic."

"Aha! I knew something was up. This Keaton woman worked in that nest of ex-pat Russians, didn't she? I'll see if I can still get tickets for Damon and me. Bet I can. See you there." Brooke hung up.

This story was turning into a farce, but not the kind Gareth Cameron would write in blank verse. Then again, he didn't seem like the type to write comedy. Lacey grabbed her purse and ran for the door.

TWENTY-SIX

*H*AD LACEY KNOWN A trip to the theatre was in the offing, she'd have worn something different to the office. Something that would go from day to night, so she wouldn't have to rush. It wasn't going to be easy to race back to Old Town Alexandria, hop in the shower to wash off the heat and humidity, and race back to D.C. with Vic. She hailed a cab from the Metro station instead of walking home.

Vic was already in her apartment, looking dashing and semi-dressed up, in khakis and an emerald green polo shirt that highlighted his eyes and weakened her knees. His navy blazer was at the ready. His hair was combed back and she had the urge to loosen the one adorable dark curl that tended to droop over his forehead. He was calmly perusing *The Washington Post* and sipping iced tea.

Vic and her blue velvet sofa, and his grin when he saw her, looked very inviting.

But it was nearly show time. She kissed him and hurried through a quick shower, changing into a basic little black dress that had enough stretch to be comfortable and enough fit to show off her shape. She stepped into black patent leather high-heeled sandals. The black-on-black effect seemed a bit severe, so she added a sparkly crystal necklace and a matching bracelet.

In case the theatre was cold, she grabbed a vintage black cashmere bolero jacket, a sassy wrap from the early 1950s. It was lined in white crepe and trimmed in braiding and white-and-black felt leaves.

She quickly touched up her makeup, adding bright red lipstick. She brushed out her hair and took one last look in the mirror before sprinting into the living room. Vic whistled in appreciation. She laughed and did a spin for him.

Sometimes the effort is worth it.

☙

On the way to the theatre, the wind started to blow. The sky grew dark with charcoal storm clouds, and the temperature dropped ten degrees by the time Vic parked the Jeep, not far from the theatre. The wind rearranged Lacey's tresses, but she felt better than she had all day. The relief from the heat was welcome but short-lived: The curtain would be rising soon.

Marie and the Kepelov siblings were waiting outside the front doors of the theatre. Marie hugged them both, Gregor and Olga did not, and Gregor gave his name at the ticket counter. The lobby was decorated with red-and-orange flower arrangements that brightened the blank walls, and of course actors' headshots were prominently placed on easels. The bar was open for business in one corner.

There was an air of promise to the show, like every show before the critics get their hands on it. Lacey realized she was looking forward to the play almost as much as figuring out what the Lenin medals meant. The thought of sitting quietly in a theatre for a couple of hours while others entertained her was, in itself, delicious. She hoped she wouldn't fall asleep.

Around their little group, the lobby began to fill up. Some theatregoers were well dressed, well groomed, even creative. Others had arrived from mowing the lawn or cleaning the garage, Lacey thought, or perhaps they were tourists. Or perhaps they had no idea that dressing for an event was about an exchange of mutual respect.

For heaven's sakes, actors dress for their parts, why can't the rest of us?

Lacey ruminated gloomily on the fall of Western Civilization. But as she could do little to avert that fall, she took mental notes for a possible "Fashion *BITE*." Her own theatre party was a mixed message: Vic looked perfect, Gregor had come as himself, Olga was another story entirely, and Marie was dazzling, as sparkling as the sequins that decorated her multicolored shawl, beneath which she wore a long dress in a swirl of greens and blues. Her dark curls flowed down her back and her red lips matched her red nails. She was a beautiful and zaftig picture of happiness.

"Did you suggest this outing to Gregor?" Lacey asked Marie.

"Oh no, this was all his idea, cher. I'm just excited to be out on a date with my man."

"Don't you two go out much?"

"Not often. Gregor doesn't like to be in crowds much these days. Since the shooting. With so many Russians around D.C. and so many recent troubles, so many of his countrymen recently dead, he doesn't know who's a friend or a foe. You remember he switched his loyalties to our side long ago."

"Do you think he's a target?"

"Anyone who gets in the crosshairs of Russian interests could be a target."

"Can you help him out? Any feelings, speaking psychic-wise?"

Just don't faint, Marie. Please.

"Not tonight. When I'm with Gregor, I feel so safe it sort of keeps the vibrations at bay. Though I suspect Olga would like it better if I manned the psychic hotline twenty-four-seven." She chuckled. "Gregor wants me to enjoy tonight. I took a tiny bit of Valium, which also blocks any nasty impressions I might have. I don't do it often, only when that other world threatens to become too intense. And with all these Russians around and that red dress all tied together somehow, a Valium was the way to go."

"I had no idea," Lacey said. "And you do deserve a break."

"We all agreed, Marie needs rest," Olga said, popping in between them. "Tonight, Gregor and I keep watch."

Olga made no apologies for eavesdropping, and her outfit was very un-Olga, or so Lacey thought. She wore a brilliant blue silk swing jacket decorated with gold embroidered birds over her simple black slacks and shell blouse. The peacock color did wonders for her sallow complexion. Olga's dark hair was still severe but shiny and clean, and someone, presumably Marie, had persuaded her to add a hint of makeup and a dash of color on her lips. Her eyebrows were still an untouched forest, but the Venus de Milo wasn't sculpted in a day.

"Olga, you look wonderful," Lacey said.

"Is good, no? I am not a crime of fashion?"

"Not at all." *Not tonight.*

"Is not too much—the makeup?"

"It's perfect."

"Good. I tell Marie I don't want to look like a painted *matryoshka* doll." They laughed together. Olga looked as pleased as Lacey had ever seen her. She rubbed her hands along the silk. "A long time since I have been to the theatre. In Moscow I used to go often."

Lacey tried to imagine that. But after all, Olga's lookalike, Ayn Rand, attended the theatre, and even wrote plays.

"I didn't know you liked the theatre."

"Da. I love the dance and the plays, though I have not seen much of it for years. Perhaps I will start again. After all, we are here, in a Russian theatre."

"Not everyone here is Russian."

"No. But majority. And in America, majority rules."

"Perhaps Olga will buy our tickets next time," Gregor said to his sister with a smile. He was wearing black jeans, cowboy boots, and a pink-and-orange Hawaiian shirt under his rather tight blue sports coat. He topped this sartorial splendor with a cowboy hat. *Home-on-the-range-meets-Moscow-on-the-Potomac,* Lacey thought with a smile. Gregor put his arm around Marie. "Here we are, Lacey and Victor, hanging out together. As I promised. And Victor—"

Conversation swirled around her, but Lacey found it difficult to relax and "hang out" while those hollow Lenin medals were still in the hem of the red dress. And hanging over her head. Tension was coiling inside her like a snake waiting to strike. Whoever hid them, and stitched them out of sight, had a connection with this theatre. Was there another medal involved in Amy Keaton's death? Another trophy for the dress's hem? Or a memorial, as Marie had said? And did someone feel thwarted because he or she could no longer stitch that memorial into the red dress?

"Don't worry, I will give you *my* review of this show over vodka later," Gregor was saying, shaking her out of her reverie. The others were laughing. The lobby crowd was in a state of high anticipation, and Lacey picked up a phrase here and there.

"It's supposed to be amazing—"

"Well, I've read *about* it, but I've never actually read any Henry James—"

"I read it in school. Can't wait to see what Yuri's done with it—"

"I've seen every single Kinetic production since they did the *Red Death* in that little dump of a theatre—"

Please! No More Red Death *tonight!* Lacey's stomach growled. She eyed the snack counter and excused herself, with Vic following her.

"Don't look now," he whispered. "But isn't that one of your loony coworkers?"

"That could describe any number of my coworkers."

"Do the initials H.W. mean anything to you?"

"No! Not Wiedemeyer." She tried to be subtle as she spun around in the direction of Vic's gaze. "And Felicity. What are they doing here?" *Honoring Amy Keaton, of course,* she thought. And Wiedemeyer and his swing band had played in a Kinetic show or two.

Harlan had dressed up for the theatre in his white dinner jacket and brown trousers, a brown-and-white striped shirt, and a brown bowtie. His brown-and-white saddle shoes looked spiffy, and well-polished. The old-fashioned outfit oddly suited his short, chubby frame. It was easy to imagine him crooning a Forties love song to his lady love.

And his lady love, Felicity, was something out of a Day-Glo dream, beaming in a shocking pink dress topped by a sweater in neon shades of yellow, green and orange. The pattern looked like radioactive gumdrops. No doubt, Lacey speculated, from the pantry at Felicity's gingerbread house in the forest where she fattened up bad little boys and girls. Felicity and Harlan made quite a colorful pair, and heads turned their way. Lacey and Vic slipped away to the snack counter.

Vic bought a package of nuts to share and a couple of lemonades, and they moved to a tall round table as Harlan and Felicity disappeared from view. She opened the nuts just as someone appeared at her elbow and made her spill her cashews.

"What's our strategy, Smithsonian?" Wiedemeyer stage-whispered.

Vic exchanged a look with Lacey. He was grinning behind Wiedemeyer's back. She glared at the chubby intruder.

"My strategy is to enjoy the show! And to forget you said that."

And maybe eat something before I die of starvation.

"Sure, don't tell me. The great Smithsonian can investigate anything she wants, but she doesn't share." Lacey gave him the Look. "Okay, I get it. Too many people listening."

"Sure I'll share, Wiedemeyer. Have some cashews. And where's Felicity?"

"Getting us some wine."

Felicity arrived with two plastic glasses of overpriced red wine from a box. Her pink plastic purse dangled on one arm.

"Hi, Lacey, isn't this fun?" She craned her neck to take in the crowded lobby. A new voice chimed in and Lacey didn't have to answer.

"Harlan Wiedemeyer, is that really you? Wow, where are your High-Stepping Hipsters? Are you playing tonight?"

Harlan spun around to bask in the attention of a music fan. He took one of the wine glasses and pulled Felicity along with him. DeeDee Adler pushed past them, steaming through the lobby from one side to the other. Armed with her digital tablet and headset, she seemed to be enjoying herself, turning to a friend here and there with a smile and a wave. Yuri Volkov was hot on her heels, muttering something about "picking up the light cues." The new stage manager took it in stride.

"Relax, Yuri, I got this," DeeDee responded coolly, slipping through the theatre doors. The woman was in her element. DeeDee seemed very capable, and Lacey remembered how efficient she had been about disposing of the dead woman's belongings. *Had erasing Amy's presence really been Yuri's idea, or her own?*

Lacey briefly wondered how much of what DeeDee had told her was true. Maybe she'd secretly coveted Keaton's job and wouldn't stop at pushing someone out of the way. Or off a scaffold high above a stage right after the last show—

Stop it! I'm imagining murderers everywhere! Just because DeeDee likes her job, that doesn't mean she had anything to do with anybody's death—

"Having fun yet, sweetheart?" Vic asked.

"You have no idea," Lacey said. "As soon we're in our seats and the lights go down."

"I promise you a steak after this is over."

The double doors to the theatre opened. Gregor Kepelov, who'd been surveying the crowd, gathered them together. Marie was floating on a Valium cloud and Olga seemed happy to be there. The five of them flowed with the rest of the audience through the entry into the theatre. The preshow music was playing, something that sounded vaguely Russian.

An usher handed out programs and escorted them down the aisle to their seats, close to the stage in the center section. *How did Kepelov get such great seats at the last minute? Maybe he does have connections.* Vic went in first, then Lacey, followed by Olga and Marie, with Gregor on the aisle. Lacey settled into her cushioned seat, and her first deep breath turned into a yawn. She covered her mouth with her program, trying not to be too obvious.

"Smithsonian!"

Wiedemeyer's voice somewhere off to her left jarred her. He was waving at her, Felicity too. People were staring. *So much for slipping in unobserved.* She peered around the theatre, hoping for no more surprises.

Uh oh. Brooke had come up with tickets too, and she and Damon were just being seated, a few rows back on Lacey's right. Brooke, fresh from the courtroom in a gray sleeveless dress, carried her briefcase in one hand and a white jacket in the other. She'd unbraided her hair, which cascaded in waves around her shoulders, a stark contrast to her standard lawyerly apparel, and her makeup was Full Evening for this outing to the theatre. She spied Lacey and smiled brightly, lifting her briefcase in salute.

Damon waved at Lacey with his phone and grinned. Summer or winter, Damon Newhouse never varied his nouveau beatnik-hipster attire, basic black with the occasional shot of gray. Tonight that shot was a little gray hipster fedora trimmed with a black ribbon, which he took off when he sat down. He had delicate features that were almost pretty, but he tried to hide them with a goatee.

The lights were dimming when Tamsin Kerr was ushered to her seat in the back just before the show started. Her stealthy last-minute arrival was deliberate, Lacey knew, to cut down on theatre insiders staring and pointing, warning their friends that the grand dame from *The Eye Street Observer* was in the house.

But this was press night, and the critic watch would be in effect for all the reviewers, not just Tamsin. Lacey knew theatre critics for *The Washington Post,* the *City Paper*, the *Blade*, the smaller papers, and all the suburban dailies and weeklies were probably somewhere in the house, or would be slipping in just as the lights went down. Tamsin seemed to be alone, but then Lacey caught a glimpse of Tony Trujillo, who apparently caught Tamsin's extra ticket tonight.

I'm surrounded.

At least she didn't see Broadway Lamont or LaToya Crawford, a small relief. But Brooke and Damon, Felicity and Harlan, and Trujillo and Tamsin all knew there were two deaths connected to this theatre and the red dress. Lacey consoled herself that they were all ignorant of the Russian medals sewn into the hem. But *someone* knew about them, besides Lacey's little theatre party. *Is that someone also here tonight?*

A voice came over the music, asking for all electronic devices to be silenced, first in English and then in what Lacey assumed was Russian. She opened her program. One loose slip of paper fell out, black with white type.

THIS PRODUCTION IS DEDICATED TO THE MEMORY
OF KINETIC THEATRE'S LATE STAGE MANAGER
AMY KEATON.

The date of her death followed, and then apparently the same message in Russian. Nothing else.

The house lights faded to black. The music grew louder and the stage lights came up for Act One.

TWENTY-SEVEN

ILING OUT OF THE theatre at intermission as the applause died away, Lacey overheard a few snippets of other theatregoers' conversations.

"Weirdest show I've ever seen! Sexy as hell though. How did they do that thing with the—"

"That was amazing! Do they still sell soundtrack CDs?"

"Is this thing running through Halloween?"

Lacey thought Kinetic's interpretation of *The Turn of the Screw* was thrilling and strange. Heavy on dance and music, and light on Henry James's words, it was a moody and enigmatic exploration of a moody psychological ghost story. The dancers' own bodies became walls and tables, candles and apparitions that sailed through the air. Lithe bodies writhed in tangled bedsheets, danced with pure light on staircases, and crept like shadows. Stagecraft that seemed more like stage magic made actors suddenly appear and vanish, and then reappear in two places at once. A dizzying collage of shifting lighting effects through windows and mirrors illuminated corners of the set, and the story, that were dark and foreboding. The ceaseless music veered wildly, from horror movies and Russian folk into mournful blues and jazz, and something the program notes described as "gypsy cabaret noir." The script by Gareth Cameron was sparse and poetic, and the spare dialogue effective.

Played by the amazing Anastasia "who learned all her lines," the nameless governess seemed lonely and timid, trapped by her surroundings, and bewildered by the children she was supposed to care for, pretty Miles and Flora. She felt the walls press in on her, the children taunted her, and the phantoms of the doomed lovers who appeared on the periphery of her vision tormented her. She became convinced the children were likewise haunted, by the evil ghosts of Miss Jessel and Peter Quint. But soon the timid governess and wicked Miss Jessel seemed to have traded places. Both women were vying with fierce little Flora to seduce the elusive Quint, and who was making violent love with whom in the tower room? Do ghosts really have sex?

And that was only Act One. Whatever Kinetic was doing, Lacey thought, they were doing it well. She wondered if *The Masque of the Red Death* had been a similar extravaganza. With Yuri Volkov at the helm and most of the same Kinetic creative team, it probably had the same kind of theatrical signatures, she decided. She sat back and let the story take over, and there was no more yawning.

Blinking in the lights of the lobby, Marie and Olga headed for the ladies' room and Gregor and Vic headed for the bar. Lacey was happy to linger by one of the tall tables, waiting for Vic. Someone opened the front doors for fresh air and a few people gravitated outside, some for a smoke break. *Theatre people still smoke,* she noted with dismay. The breeze felt lovely.

Yuri Volkov approached Lacey with something like a smile on his face. He was either much more relaxed now that the show had opened, or he'd been indulging at the wine bar. Or maybe this was his "press night" face. He was followed by another man.

"Ms. Smithsonian. Don't say I never did anything for you," Volkov said.

"Okay, I won't," Lacey said.

"This is Maksym Pushkin. He used to be a fabulous dancer for us until he abandoned the theatre for the law."

"Yuri is too kind. I was just okay as a dancer. And the law pays better," Pushkin said. "So pleased to meet you, Ms. Smithsonian."

She shook his offered hand, and the name clicked into place. He was tall for a male dancer, as Katya Pritchard had told her, and still very fit. He smiled, revealing large immaculate white teeth. His eyes were brown and his dark hair was beautifully styled. Height was always an advantage in the courtroom, according to Brooke, and he was very handsome. Lacey detected no trace of a Russian accent.

"You played Prince Prospero in *The Masque of the Red Death*," Lacey said, trying to picture the photos from the old news stories.

He seemed surprised she'd heard of him.

"That was a long time ago."

"This one is a nosy reporter," Volkov said, referring to Lacey. "Not even a theatre critic, who could do us some good." Volkov met Lacey's eyes and winked. "I had to let her in though, someone bought her a ticket. So what do you think of my show, Ms. Smithsonian?"

"It's wonderful. But then I'm not a theatre critic."

He laughed. "Then you can stay. I leave you now." Yuri backed away and was swallowed up by a throng of well-wishers.

"You're a reporter?" Pushkin asked. "Your name is familiar."

"Fashion reporter," she explained. "With *The Eye Street*—"

He snapped his fingers. "That's it. You're the one who found the Romanov diamonds." His smile grew even wider.

"You read about that?" She wasn't exactly surprised, but the whole adventure seemed very long ago to her.

"Everybody read about that. A coup for your newspaper, as well as for you. Not to mention, exciting reading for any Russian. Sad and bizarre. Where are the diamonds now?"

"Still tied up between the State Department and the Russian government, as far as I know."

"They'll be tied up for some time, then. However, I predict they will eventually come to some agreement. A timetable for the U.S. to turn them over."

"To somebody," Lacey agreed. "But to whom? The Romanov heirs want them back."

"Yes. But the Russian government might get there first. They have a history."

"It's a blood-soaked history," she said. She refrained from making a further crack about Russia and its history, and its current activities. Annexing Crimea, for example. What would stop Russia from annexing the diamonds if they saw their chance? "And those diamonds are a blood-soaked treasure."

Bloodstains marked the small corset in which a Romanov princess died. Bullets and bayonets had torn the delicate fabric, revealing the diamonds in their hiding place. There were rubies too, but most people remembered only the diamonds.

"It will be years," Pushkin said. "I predict many lawsuits and finally a grand exhibit. Somewhere."

"In Washington, at the Smithsonian, I hope."

"And a venue very appropriately named, for their discoverer," he laughed. "I'll be the first in line. And what are you working on now?"

"Not diamonds. I'm interested in the costume worn by Saige Russell when she played the character of Death. Opposite you. The dress was sold at the big theatre garage sale last weekend."

"Yuri really sold it?" He reacted with the slightest lift of his brows. "Well. Don't expect to find a Romanov treasure in that dress."

"Do you remember anything about the red dress?"

"Not much. Except it was very dramatic. Very red. Parsnips loved it. She gloried in it."

"You called her Parsnips too?"

"Not to her face. It was the crew's name for her, but it suited Saige. Poor Saige. Anyway, she didn't really have to dance, not like the rest of us. So athletically, I mean. So her costume was much more elaborate than the rest. It was big and it was every color of red. Now, if you ask me about *my* costume, it was velvet, in seven different colors, for the seven rooms in the castle. That's all I remember. No, I remember it was hot. Even hotter under the stage lights. And like Prospero, I was ready to die by the final scene. Covered in sweat every night."

"Do you still dance?"

"Only the tango." She realized he was probably flirting with her now. *So unusual in D.C.! Or maybe it's me, maybe I just don't recognize flirting anymore. Except from Vic.* "We came from Russia when I was a child," he continued. "I wanted to play football like an American boy. My mother insisted that I dance. She had big plans for me. Ballet. Now I play touch football with my friends on the weekends."

"How old were you when you came to America?"

"A toddler. My family emigrated when I was three. I don't remember much about Russia."

"Is your family related to the famous *Boris Godunov* Pushkin?"

"I wish we were. My mother tells everyone we are."

"And you don't dance. Except the tango. Do you still act?"

Brooke and Damon made their way through the crowd to Lacey's side.

"No, my theatre is the courtroom," he said, eyeing Brooke. "Hey, Brooke."

"And he's not bad," Brooke said. "Hello, Maksym."

"You know each other?" Lacey asked.

"Of course," Brooke said. "We've occasionally crossed paths. Even swords."

"She accuses me of working for the Evil Empire."

"Only because it's true," Brooke said.

"She would," Lacey said. She wondered which conspiracy theory in Brooke's file drawer had Maksym Pushkin's name on it.

"How are you, Counselor?" Pushkin turned on his bright white smile again. He took Brooke's hand and held it for a moment, until Brooke extracted it. Maksym Pushkin looked huge next to the smaller Damon Newhouse, who popped up between them.

"I'm well, Maksym," Brooke said. "I didn't know you were a theatre lover."

"I have unsuspected depths."

"Oh, I suspect everyone."

Damon stuck out his hand. "I'm Damon Newhouse. Conspiracy Clearinghouse. DeadFed dot com."

A pause. There was an undercurrent to the conversation between Maksym and Brooke. Was there an attraction there? Was there more? Brooke had some explaining to do. Lunch would be in order.

"Ah, of course. DeadFed." Pushkin shook the smaller man's hand. "A very popular site. How's the wine here, by the way?" Without waiting for a review, he turned back to Brooke. "We will have to talk soon. Ms. Smithsonian, so nice to meet you." He smiled at Brooke and backed away through the crowd before turning around.

Brooke looked mildly annoyed. *At whom, Lacey wondered. Damon or Maksym? And was Pushkin a DeadFed fan?* She hoped he hadn't read Damon's crackpot "Romanov Revengers" articles. Half of them featured Lacey and the Romanov diamonds.

"Who wants some wine?" Damon asked.

"Vic's getting me some coffee. I think." Vic was still at the bar with Gregor. Brooke said she'd love some wine. After Damon left the table, she whispered to Lacey.

"Tomorrow. Lunch. You and me. Debriefing."

"I agree," Lacey said. "Where?"

"Spy Museum. For inspiration. This little theatre is one gigantic hotbed of intrigue. Can't you feel it?"

Nothing lit Brooke up like a conspiracy and she was glowing like a nuclear reactor. And even better than mere conspiracies: *spies!* Lacey assumed Russian spies would be on the lunch menu.

"Not everyone is a spy, Brooke." Lacey tried to keep her face straight. "Only one in six Washingtonians, according to you."

"Probably five out of six here tonight. Listen."

Russian words were flying all around them, quickly, excitedly. Neither Lacey nor Brooke had any idea what was being said.

"Okay, there are a lot of Russians here. Russian theatre, you know. They might be discussing the show," Lacey said.

"You just *want* everyone to be a spy."

"Not true. Did you hear that another healthy young reporter from Moscow who criticized government policies was found dead in a hotel room?"

"Here or in Moscow?"

"London this time. And did I mention the Russian who was thrown off a roof on election day, in Manhattan?"

"I have to admit that's disturbing. How did the reporter die?"

"Right now, it's all very hush-hush, and obviously, 'natural causes' are being blamed. But he is another in a long line of dead journalists," Brooke said. "Journalists working on stories involving Russia."

Thanks a lot, Brooke. A tiny finger of fear danced down Lacey's spine. In other countries, journalists risked their lives to report the news. American reporters believed they were protected in their craft by the Constitution, and because they dealt with the truth. But the truth was also subject to interpretation, and there were unpredictable loons out there. Now, unfortunately, the loons were in control, and truth was under attack on a daily basis. Even Lacey's fashion beat had received death threats.

"Don't spook me," Lacey said.

"Exactly. Spooks. Spy Museum, tomorrow at noon."

She couldn't help smiling as she watched Brooke glide off to join her boyfriend and fellow conspiracist. She spied Trujillo across the lobby, chatting up a blonde. There were always blondes for Tony. He seemed more interested in the woman than in joining the rest of Lacey's inquisitors, for which she was grateful. She knew Tamsin was most likely still in her seat, as she didn't care to mingle with the intermission crowds.

"Ms. Lacey Smithsonian? I heard you have been looking for me," a man's barely Russian-accented voice said, and Lacey turned around. The speaker was about six feet tall with a tight, slender frame, wearing black slacks and a black shirt. *Another theatre type.* He was pleasant-looking with close-cropped light brown hair and even, unexceptional features. But he had bright blue eyes, a blazing shade of blue.

Lacey realized he must be the costume designer for this show, as well as for the decade-old production of *The Masque*. The man who made the red dress.

"I'm Lacey. Are you Nikolai Sokolov?"

"Call me Nicky. All my friends do." He smiled as if delighted to meet her.

"Yuri must have pointed me out to you?"

"And DeeDee as well. Forgive me for not getting back to you earlier. So much to do before press night. I was still adjusting costumes this afternoon." He bowed slightly and took her hand in his. "It's a pleasure to meet you."

"Then you probably haven't read my fashion columns," she said with a smile.

"But I have. Very insightful, as well as humorous."

"You're flattering me."

"Why lie when the truth is flattering?"

"Why indeed." She smiled back. *So many lies, so little time.*

Vic arrived with a beer in hand and a decaf for Lacey. He eyed the new arrival. Gregor Kepelov was close on Vic's heels and Marie and Olga arrived from the ladies' room. Lacey introduced Nikolai "Nicky" Sokolov to the others. He and Kepelov evaluated each other, exchanged a few words in Russian, and finally shook hands carefully, the handshake accompanied by wolfish smiles. *What's all that about,* Lacey was wondering, when someone bumped her elbow and almost spilled her coffee.

"Hey, watch it, buddy," Vic said to the elbow-bumper.

"I'll kill her if she misses another cue," the bumper said matter-of-factly to Vic. There was venom in his tone. Lacey recognized Gareth Cameron, the miserable-yet-superior playwright, in a froth over some actress—could it be Anastasia?—who had flubbed a cue. Wearing the same clothes he'd worn the other day, Cameron looked as if he hadn't slept since then.

Probably subsisting on kombucha. And hurt feelings.

"Playwrights." Sokolov chuckled. "Everyone knows it's the director's job to kill the actors! Playwrights must stand in line." The group laughed.

"Do you think he's drunk already?" Lacey asked.

"No, no, just press night." Sokolov turned his head slightly, watching the playwright careen across the lobby. "Probably going to the men's room to be sick. Our Gareth has a tender stomach."

Lacey thought he looked more like a man heading off to confront hungry lions in the Colosseum, and fight back.

"Press night nerves?"

"Exactly," Sokolov said. "After all, if the show is a flop, everyone will blame the playwright. If it is a great success, everyone will applaud the director. And all is right in the kingdom."

"That's cynical."

"That's the theatre."

The lobby lights flashed three times to signal the second act would soon begin. "Nicky, I—"

"You wanted to ask me about Death's ruby-red costume, from *The Masque of the Red Death*."

"You anticipate me," Lacey said.

"Saves time. And Yuri told me. What can I tell you? In three minutes?"

The others in the group stood by, and Lacey felt the tension increase at the mention of the dress. Vic put his hand on her shoulder.

"I was at the sale when the dress was sold,." Lacey began. "Amy Keaton tried to keep it. But now—"

"I know. Tragic news. I wondered where she was on Monday. Not like her to miss work. I read about her unfortunate accident in the paper." He dropped his voice. "Amy would have been right here tonight. She was very efficient. We will miss her."

"Very sad news," Lacey agreed. "Amy told me it was a mistake that the costume was at the sale."

"These things happen." He gestured as if swatting a fly away. "You met her there?"

"Sort of."

"It was nice of you to remember her. Not many people connect the name with the woman. Poor Amy. She was very exacting. Made her a great stage manager. But she was seldom recognized for her work. As for the costume, I don't know whether Death's red dress was supposed to be in the sale or not. That show was so long ago."

"You aren't concerned about it being sold, then?"

"Why?" He lifted his shoulders and let them fall. "A rag from so many years ago."

"Kinetic let many actresses wear the dress, for example to the Helen Hayes awards. But I heard you always had to approve them personally."

"You have been busy, Ms. Smithsonian." He laughed with appreciation. He seemed very different from Yuri Volkov and Maksym Pushkin. *But why would I think all Russians were alike?* "Yes, I always approved the actresses who wore the costume. Kinetic, that is, *Yuri*, always wanted the red gown to be presented at its best. For both the actress and the theatre. We have exacting standards. Also, it had to be a perfect fit for the wearer. We didn't want to have to tailor it every time, or let someone else butcher it."

"But now you have no costume."

"No costume?" Sokolov found that amusing. "Kinetic Theatre has many wonderful costumes. Hundreds, even thousands. Perhaps we will start a new tradition with another outfit." He gestured at the dozens of posters lining the lobby walls. "Perhaps we could loan out the Lady Macbeth? Such a dress! Gold and black damask, very impressive. Have you seen it?"

"I'd love to see it."

"I will be happy to show you."

"That would be lovely. I have so many questions."

Sokolov glanced at Vic and then back to Lacey. "I must go now. I would be delighted to offer you a tour of my costume shop. To show you how I put together the concept for a show's wardrobe. But maybe you're not so very interested in theatrical costumes?"

Not interested? The offer was pure sucker bait for Lacey, and he knew it.

"Of course I'm interested. When?'

"May I call you tomorrow?"

"So soon. You love your work."

"I have a talent. Or so it seems." He picked up her hand again for the briefest moment, leaving a card in her palm before he disappeared into the crowd streaming into the theatre. The lights flashed again and this time a set of melodic chimes sounded.

I didn't have a chance to ask him about Saige Russell. Parsnips. She glanced at Nicky Sokolov's business card in her hand. *Next time.*

Vic took her other hand. "Come with me. Act Two."

TWENTY-EIGHT

"*A* MUSCULAR SHOW" was Gregor Kepelov's considered opinion after it was all over. "Very powerful. Obviously the second act was a metaphor for mind control."

Lacey didn't think that was the subject of the play. However, she granted that Kepelov's interpretation had merit. According to Gregor, the ghosts on stage represented deception, illusion, and confusion, what he said was called in Russian *maskirovka*, a deliberate masquerade of misinformation, so that in the end, the governess didn't know if she was crazy or being haunted, under attack from within or without. And neither did the audience. It was up to each of us, he said, to discover the truth.

As they walked, Gregor was practically shouting over the storm, which had finally broken and was pouring down sheets of rain. The heat and humidity tangled head-to-head and scattered thunder and lightning across the city. The wind blew umbrellas inside out and skirts upside down. Lacey didn't mind, the wind was soothing in its fury. It felt good after the heat.

Gregor had insisted they needed to share their reactions after the show, and Vic was up for it. They agreed on the bar at the Tabard Inn, not far from the theatre. It was only four or five blocks away, and as usual in D.C., once the cars were safely parked, everyone agreed it was foolish to move them. And also as usual in D.C., everyone had an umbrella. Or a cowboy hat. What was one little rainstorm?

The five dropped their umbrellas inside the door and tucked into a snug corner at the Tabard, decorated with dark wood and sofas. The Tabard was a classic D.C. establishment, comprised of three old townhouses, creating a warren of interesting spaces. *If only I can keep my eyes open.*

"It's lovely, no?" Olga said without irony. She wiped raindrops off her face with a napkin. "A brisk walk in the rain after a hot day. Reminds me of Moscow. And no one followed us. I was on guard."

Vic and Gregor ordered the meat-and-cheese board for them to share. Marie gathered her soaked curls and wrung them out over her shoulder. Lacey twisted her rain-frizzed hair into a knot and pinned it out of her face. She leaned her damp head on Vic's shoulder. *What a day.*

"What I like most about the play are the ghosts," Olga was saying as they settled in. "Like life. Life is full of ghosts."

Marie sat close to Gregor and hugged his arm. She looked sleepy too. "I loved the ghosts too! So exciting and strange, yet so familiar. But there was that one ghost in a red shroud, remember her? Toward the end? I'm not sure what she was doing there. Has anyone read the story? Who was she? She seemed so sad and lost."

There was a pregnant silence. They all looked at Marie. Lacey caught the eyes of everyone around the table before she broke the silence.

"Marie, we didn't see anyone in red," Lacey said quietly.

"Perhaps you saw something else," Olga suggested. "There were so many shadows, all those effects with light and—"

"No, I saw her. Why, she was just as plain as day. Oh dear. I didn't realize she was a ghost. I don't generally see them, you know."

"She was wearing red?" Gregor asked.

"Yes. But it's not what you're thinking, sugar, she wasn't wearing that red gown, the costume with the medals, and she didn't wear a mask. Just red cloth, like a shroud. What did you say her name was, cher? The dead actress?"

"Saige Russell," Lacey said. "Her real name was Patience Russell. Although they called her Parsnips behind her back."

"If there was a ghost," Vic said, always the sceptic, "and I am not saying there was, we don't know it was Saige Russell. Aren't theatres always supposed to be haunted? I mean, look at Ford's, with the ghost of Abraham Lincoln." His lifted eyebrow told Lacey he thought this apparition was the ghost of Marie's Valium.

"Or else Saige is a ghost who loves red." Lacey liked that image. "If that was Saige, I guess a woman's favorite color survives the grave."

"I really thought she was part of the show," Marie said sadly. "Perhaps she was merely smoke, an afterimage, the last wisps of a lost soul. She seemed to be looking for someone, but it wasn't me. She had nothing to tell me. Sorry." Marie looked even more exhausted now.

"Ha. What do ghosts know anyway?" Olga asked briskly. "They are dead. And not reliable."

"But beautiful," Lacey put in. "At least on stage."

"I thought the on-stage ghosts were exceptional," Vic agreed.

"Dancing ghosts," Lacey said. "Ghosts having sex on the staircase."

"Spies and mind control," Gregor asserted. "Though I wish I could have seen your ghost in red, Marie." There was another pause.

"Have you found out anything about the Lenins?" Lacey asked Kepelov, speaking very softly. Their corner was secluded, but in Washington, even walls had ears.

"In a word, no," Gregor said. "You think I go around asking obvious questions? No. I carefully assess situation. Tonight was advance reconnaissance."

"And what did it tell you?"

"Not as much as my gut. Gut says caution. There are secrets in that theatre that are not in the plays, not on the stage."

Olga dismissed him with a wave. "Gregor. You are merely being Russian, and it is Russian theatre. Of course there are secrets."

"What are you saying, Olga? Putin is growling like bear. Agents are everywhere. Spies and ex-spies are dropping like flies."

"You're sure Kinetic is a hot bed of spies?" Vic asked.

"Yes," Gregor said. The waiter arrived with their appetizers, and they fell silent until they were alone again. "Audience too. Many Russians."

"So you overheard something in Russian?" Vic pressed.

"I overheard many things. All very innocent," Gregor said. "This is how I know things are not so innocent."

"I hate it when Brooke is right," Lacey said.

Olga seemed unimpressed by her brother's gloomy assessment of Kinetic. She lifted a glass of vodka to Lacey in salute.

"You were big success tonight, Smithsonian. Everyone is fascinated by Lacey Smithsonian. To you!"

"Me? No way. I'm more adrift on this story than ever."

Lacey was not the type to think that people whispering— especially in a foreign language—were discussing her. It startled her when people quoted her column. She picked up a cracker and some cheese and popped it in her mouth.

"You missed all the looks in your direction, all the talk?" Olga asked her.

"To be fair, Olga," Gregor pointed out, "the talk was in Russian."

"Apologies." Olga didn't look apologetic. "I am spontaneous translator in five languages. I forget not everyone is."

"The diamonds, Smithsonian. The Romanov gems in the corset. Your discovery of the gems was in the air tonight. You have an ability, the EFP," Gregor said. "You beat even Gregor Kepelov to that treasure. I salute you, like Olga. And now with the Lenin medals, you have done it again." He lifted his glass to her.

"But what exactly have I found? And what does it mean?"

Another pause. *I'm always stopping conversations tonight.*

"Marie, I just want to know, do you sense any danger for Lacey?" Vic finally asked. Lacey was surprised. Vic the Skeptic had come a long way in his opinion of their friend Marie. He might not completely believe in Marie's powers, she knew, but he didn't quite disbelieve either.

"No, cher. I am quite blank right now." Marie closed her eyes. "I don't even know why the crimson ghost was part of the show."

"Don't worry, Victor. She is Lacey Smithsonian," Gregor said. "Danger walks by her side wherever she goes. And yet leaves her untouched."

"That's not exactly comforting," Lacey said. She took a sip from her cranberry and seltzer.

"It's not exactly news either," Vic said.

"Not every Russian émigré is dangerous, however." Gregor paused. "I, for example, am paragon of American democratic values. Olga as well. However, there is cause for concern. You know of the Russian billionaire who was beaten to death in a Washington hotel?"

"Yes." Brooke had already filled Lacey in on that story, and DeadFed was running wild with it.

"And the reporter in London? And the Russian who died on election day? And many more who handled a certain damaging dossier on a certain moron of a politician. They are dead, but the Kremlin is alive and well, here and in Moscow."

"We like to think the problems of the past do not follow us. But is not true," Olga said. "Old Soviet Union may be dead, but still haunts us. Like the red ghost."

"What does all that have to do with the red dress, and LaToya's break-in, and Amy Keaton's death?" Lacey asked, exasperated.

"I hate coincidences," Vic said. "Coincidence is usually an illusion."

"Victor is right," Gregor said. "There is a connection."

Marie snuggled against Gregor's shoulder. Lacey had never seen her look so peaceful, and she was glad that her favorite psychic had taken the night off. And a Valium. Or there would be fainting now for sure.

"Okay. By now, everyone in Washington knows I've been asking about the red dress," Lacey pointed out. "At least everyone connected with Kinetic."

Marie opened her eyes. and addressed Lacey. "It was your destiny, cher. And this is as well. Remember you have friends who will do whatever they can to protect you."

She closed her eyes and promptly fell sound asleep. *I hope that doesn't count as fainting.* Gregor adjusted her head gently on his shoulder.

"Fear not, Lacey Smithsonian, we will discover who it is, who opened the Lenin medals, who delivered the poison needles," Kepelov promised. "The Delivery Man."

"Or woman," Lacey said.

He nodded. "Or woman."

"What about the red dress?" Lacey asked. "What happens if the Delivery Man finds out where it is?"

All eyes, except the sleeping Marie's, were on Vic. He smiled. "On the theory that he or she, or they, were watching you during the show, sweetheart, I had the dress moved to a secondary location during *The Screw.*"

"Turtledove?" She knew he was reliable. He'd had a hand in moving Aunt Mimi's trunk out of her apartment when Lacey feared its contents were at risk. She trusted both men with her life.

"Not mentioning any names. But it's handled. I got a text at intermission."

"Smart move, Victor," Gregor said. Olga nodded.

"It's as secure as it was in our offices. Possibly more. And if anyone does breach our security, they'll get a surprise."

"What, you moved it to Fort Knox?" Gregor asked.

"Almost. Company secret."

"Did Turtledove think it was silly to move it?" Lacey asked him.

"No more than usual, sweetheart."

"Not to worry, Smithsonian," Gregor assured her. "We have a plan."

Uh oh. "What kind of plan?"

"To keep you safe. To be ready when the Delivery Man arrives, which he will, sooner or later."

Brooke would love all this spy stuff. Too bad I can't tell her anything. And damn, Kepelov thinks I'm a target!

"She has the ExtraFashionary Perception," Gregor continued. "Whoever put the medals in the hem of that dress is no doubt aware of her interest in the dress, and her abilities."

"There is no way to be sure of that, Gregor. Some of those medals could have been in there for years," Vic pointed out. "Our so-called Delivery Man might be long gone."

"Despite that, it is true," Olga said. "Lacey Smithsonian will be a target."

"You're exaggerating my super-powers," Lacey said tiredly. "All of you."

"You have a gift, Smithsonian."

"Or a curse."

"And me." Vic lifted one beautiful dark eyebrow at her. He stood and reached out his hand for her, and she took it. It was time to go. He put money down to pay for their share of the bill.

"Like Boy Scout, Smithsonian," Gregor cautioned her at the door, "you must be prepared. You are the flame that draws the moth."

Normally statements of that kind would keep Lacey up all night. But she was too weary and this all felt too fantastic.

"Don't worry, Gregor. I have my own personal Boy Scout."

TWENTY-NINE

"*Y*OU'RE A LITTLE LATE, Smithsonian."
Mac greeted her on Thursday morning by pointedly looking at his watch. He was just lifting the last whatever-it-was from a platter on the food editor's desk.

Tell me something I don't know. Lacey had overslept, but to her relief she'd had no nightmares.

"Sorry. I was up late. And the Metro was dead on the tracks for a half hour. Blue Line."

The Blue Line train in front of hers was declared Out Of Service for unknown reasons and unloaded at Pentagon City. That trainload of passengers raced back to Lacey's train, holding it up and packing it like proverbial sardines. Lacey was lucky to have snagged a seat before the crush, which spiked the ambient stress levels in the train car. She was trying to write a column, in between dodging elbows and knees and the occasional swinging backpack.

She didn't mind Mac's sarcasm. *Go ahead, fire me. Good luck getting someone else to work this beat.* She took a second look at Felicity's morning treat: some kind of frosted chocolate and vanilla marble cake. Tempting, but not enough to be worth the calories.

Judging by today's swirly delicacy, Felicity must have enjoyed the show a great deal the night before. She had already produced something fattening for the troops. Quite a feat for being out late on a school night, Lacey mused. *Maybe she doesn't need sleep, baking all night in that gingerbread house in the woods.*

"Excuses, excuses. What do you have for me today?"

"Fashion Bite: DRESSING UP OR DRESSING DOWN—A MATTER OF RESPECT. Or something like that. You'll have it later this morning."

She had penned the first draft by hand in her notebook while the train was stalled, inspired by the attire of the theatre crowd the night before.

"Sounds okay." He scanned the half-empty newsroom. Many staff members were missing, and Lacey knew they weren't occupied in government hearings. "Looks like half the office was on your train. Blue Line?"

"Blue Line."

"It's the worst."

"This week." Lacey was just happy not to be a rumpled mess after escaping the packed train, and she was impressed with the material in her "new" vintage dress. Wrinkles just fell right out: the magic of vintage. Today's outfit was a sleeveless pink "wiggle dress" dating from the 1950s, with a kick pleat, suitable for a garden party, as if anyone gave such an event these days.

It's a shame there's never a garden party around. I'm ready!

Lacey was breaking one of her own rules about pink with this dress. Pink sent a message, especially in Washington, and could be construed as weak or "girly." She usually avoided pink at work, and she didn't know why today felt different. Maybe it was a reaction to the red dress, or all that Theatre Standard Black last night. This pink confection was a soft polished cotton with dots woven into the fabric, and a wide shawl-collared sweetheart neckline that dipped into a V in the front. Lacey wore it with a matching black bolero jacket with three-quarter length sleeves, her summer go-to jacket. Her hair was pulled back in a French twist, which went with the dress's vibe, and her white wedge sandals were comfortable enough to see her through the workday and a quick trip through a museum.

Her editor didn't seem to notice the outfit. Mac rarely did, and he was also blind to his own fashion crimes. Lacey averted her eyes.

"And Mac, I'd like to take this afternoon off."

"Does this have anything to do with LaToya's crazy red dress and the story I don't have?"

"Possibly. And possibly related to me getting some sleep."

"What aren't you telling me?" He took another bite of the marble cake.

"Mac, I can't tell you what I don't know."

"Nightlife getting to you?"

"Research. I was at Kinetic Theatre last night for *The Turn of the Screw.*"

"Aha. The scene of the crime, theatre-wise?"

"No, the show was great."

"Tamsin gave it a thumbs-up too."

Lacey hadn't seen the review yet. She reached for *The Eye*'s morning edition, already on her desk. There it was, in the Entertainment section: KINETIC DAZZLES IN NEW TAKE ON CLASSIC GHOST STORY.

"Is that the same theatre where the actress died?"

"Same group, but not the same building. Kinetic was in a different space back then, off Fourteenth Street."

Mac's fork dangled above his plate. "Police say Keaton's death was an accident. What do you think?"

"Nothing tangible yet, Mac." Lacey's gut—and a handful of hollow Lenin medals—said murder. But there was no evidence. She tossed the paper on her desk and grabbed an empty coffee mug.

"But you're not buying it," Mac grumbled. "I suppose you won't be happy until you have some maniac coming at you with a pair of scissors."

"Oh ye of little faith. Why does everybody assume that? It might not be scissors. It's not always scissors. There could be a peaceful resolution."

"We can always hope. Yet if history is any indication—"

"You make it sound like I plan these things."

Mac's eyebrows narrowed in a way she wasn't particularly fond of. They were their own editorial statement of gloom.

"Hear me on this, Lacey. I know you're going to pursue this. If you get that Spidey sense going on, you better have backup. I mean it, Smithsonian. No dress is worth dying over."

"Agreed." She headed toward the newsroom's kitchen.

"Is there some more wacky backstory to that thing that you haven't told me about?"

"Undoubtedly. Exactly what, I'm not sure yet. Costumes tell stories, just like everyday clothes. Costumes are designed to tell stories. But so far it's simply a dress that's been worn by a lot of actresses, on stage and off. All but one still alive." She raised one eyebrow. "Why don't you ask Wiedemeyer what he thinks? He's the death-and-dismemberment guy."

Mac gave her the eye, under a cloud of black eyebrows. "I'm not interested in science fiction. Besides, he's got a personal ax to grind. He knew Amy Keaton."

"He wants part of this story, doesn't he? It's my story, Mac."

"He had his shot. That sob story I shoveled over to the op-ed section."

"He wants to horn in on my story."

Lacey didn't want Harlan dogging her steps or meddling in her process. She also didn't want him to get hurt. Wiedemeyer, for all his glee in the death-and-dismemberment beat, struck her as hopelessly naïve. She couldn't trust the chubby little rascal not to throw himself headlong into danger. And losing Harlan, even temporarily, would affect Felicity's baking. It might even shut down the cake-and-cookie train. *Worse than shutting down the Metro.*

"I ordered him to back off. Whatever good that will do."

Mac finished his marble cake with a satisfied sigh.

"About this afternoon," she reminded him. "My time off?"

"Fine. After I edit your piece. Get some rest." He headed for his office. Over his shoulder he added, "And stay out of trouble!"

Lacey retrieved Nikolai Sokolov's business card. She didn't want him to forget about his offer: a tour of the Kinetic costume shop. Still, she was surprised when he answered the phone, instead of letting it go to voice mail.

"Lacey Smithsonian, I've been expecting your call."

She checked her watch. "Isn't this early for theatre people?"

"I don't sleep as much as other people. And I like the quiet of the theatre this time of day. I finish more work when I'm alone." They set a time for her to visit Kinetic on Friday, tomorrow.

Lacey hung up as several of her coworkers finally arrived, complaining about the Metro breakdown of the day. Tony ambled her way, another late arriving victim of the subway. He usually drove his car, Mustang Sally, but she was in the shop for an oil change and minor maintenance.

"What's up, Brenda Starr? Looking very French today."

"Really? I'm not sure they wear much pink. And what's up is I'm writing a Fashion Bite. Fashion never sleeps."

"I need a bite of food, not fashion."

Trujillo was a fashion plate in his own way, and his clothes always had a personal stamp. He was looking fine today in a navy western shirt with the sleeves rolled up over his tanned arms, crisp dark jeans and the inevitable boots. Trujillo would never be one of those guys who wore Hawaiian shirts in the summer, like so many men in D.C. who declared the entire summer luau season, especially Casual Fridays. Spotting the marble cake, he lifted a big slice, took a bite, and closed his eyes.

"Yum."

"Hey, I saw you at the show last night."

"Yeah. Saw you and Vic, too. I figured it was worth a look, and Tamsin had an extra ticket. That's the theatre that's been in the news, right?"

"News? You're talking about Wiedemeyer's piece?"

"That sob story. That and your forthcoming piece about Amy Keaton's death. You've got LaToya all in a twist, a dead actress from long ago, and a brand-new corpse. Well done."

"You've been busy too. Reading the archives?"

"Listen, Lois Lane, if there's a hot story here with bizarre encounters and your signature loony sources, I want in."

"You think there's more to it?" She was enjoying toying with him, and she still hadn't had her coffee.

"There's always more to it with you, Lois."

"Why not team up with Harlan? He wants in on this story too. And let me caution you, it isn't necessarily a story yet. Not everything I write is a big crime drama, you know. Usually it's just clothes."

"You find enough drama. Here's the deal. I help. Double byline."

"If you really want to be part of this story, Tony, shake down the M.E. for a cause and manner of death for Amy Keaton. And if we go in together, we go alphabetical. Smithsonian before Trujillo." She picked up her empty mug again.

"Damned alphabet." Trujillo groaned. "But I'll take it. I'll see what I can do." He finished the cake and tossed his crumpled napkin into her wastebasket. She headed in the direction of the coffee. He followed her.

"What did you think of the show last night?" she asked him.

"It was, um, different. I was more interested in everyone else who was there. Let's see: You and Donovan, the lovely

Brooke and her boy toy, that screwball Russian spy of yours, and your Marie, our favorite psychic. I didn't recognize the other woman, but she looks like some dead writer, I can't remember the name."

"Kepelov's sister, Olga Kepelova. I think she looks like Ayn Rand."

"Ayn Rand! That's the one. Intense. Crazy eyes." In the kitchenette Lacey checked the coffee pot. It was half full and didn't quite qualify as a toxic spill yet. "There are really two Kepelovs? Brother and sister? The mind reels." Tony took the pot and poured coffee into their mugs. Evaluating the thickness of the brew, Tony added a healthy heap of sugar and non-dairy creamer to his and stirred.

"Anything else?" she asked. "About the show."

"Saw Wiedemeyer in his glad rags, with Felicity of course. What a couple. It was old home week. Tamsin. Me. I didn't see Mac or Claudia or the sportswriters there, but either we have an unsuspected hotbed of theatre lovers at *The Eye Street Observer* or something is afoot."

"Something is always afoot, Tony." Lacey sipped the coffee: *Could be worse.* "I'm sure you have a medical examiner to shake down."

"I'm sure I do. Double byline." Winking, he spun on his heel and strutted back to the newsroom ahead of her.

Lacey avoided the last crumbs of the marble cake and finished keying in her hand-written notes from this morning's commute for her "Fashion *BITES*" column, bumpily penned on the Metro. Her head was down as she reread her article.

"Smithsonian. What's the scoop on my red dress?"

The clicking of LaToya's shiny black patent heels could be heard several desks away. Lacey glanced up from her screen. LaToya looked crisp and professional in a black and white sheath dress, dangling a black linen jacket in one hand. It must be new. After all, LaToya had a good excuse to buy new clothes that hadn't been handled by an unknown burglar.

"Not yet," she said carefully. *I can't talk about the Lenin medals.* "Any news about your break-in?"

"Not yet." LaToya looked disgusted. "I mean, what's taking everybody so long?"

"Don't know. Amazingly enough, this story isn't just jumping into my lap. However, it is giving me a headache."

"It's been that kind of week. I sympathize."

There was a moment of silence between them. Finally Lacey spoke.

"I do believe your scarlet costume has a distinctly tangled history."

"I knew it. It's too damn beautiful." LaToya leaned against Lacey's desk. "To tell the truth, I'm not sure I should have bought it. But that red demon called out to me like some unearthly thing and grabbed ahold of me. Some damn costume voodoo. I got caught up in it. And that particular shade of red looks fabulous on my skin. However, between you and me, I'm not sure I'd ever wear it."

"There's always the odd formal event," Lacey suggested. *As long as she doesn't know about the skulls that glow in the dark, and the strange secret sewn into the hem.* "You know, LaToya, you really could just give it back. Or I bet they'd buy it back from you. I could handle it for you. How much did you pay for it, anyway?"

"It's not the money. It's mine. I won't give it up without a fight. I already fought for it once." LaToya's face was grim with determination.

"Give it up? You don't even have it."

LaToya suddenly laughed out loud and fluttered her fingers at Smithsonian. "That's right. You have custody till it's clear of evil spirits. Evil spirits and the weird women who covet it. You are the committee to free my dress from doom and disaster. Let me know."

I tried. "You bet."

"Any ETA on arrival?"

"Nope, but it can't be too soon for me. Aside from my troubles, LaToya, how are things with Detective Broadway Lamont?"

"He can run, but he cannot hide."

"How long are you going to chase him?" Lacey leaned back in her chair and stretched.

"As long as it takes. I got it bad for that handsome hunk of man." *Broadway is doomed.* "By the way, exactly *where* is my dress, Smithsonian?"

"A secure undisclosed location. Under lock and key."

"Sounds like CIA stuff."

"Safer. The best part is, even I don't know where it is."

Lacey always appreciated Vic, but even more so when he pulled off a surprise like this one. "Vic hid it away."

"Just as well. I can't stop thinking about my apartment, some stranger breaking in and touching my things. And I didn't even wake up! Gives me the creeps. And doing what he did, leaving my clothes dancing like phantoms around my rooms."

A perceptible shudder passed through her. Lacey could almost feel it herself. She had never seen anything quite like the scene at LaToya's.

"Are you staying there?"

"I'm staying with my folks. Until the new locks and security system are in."

"I thought your building looked pretty safe."

"Me too. Till this thing. One more reason to get Broadway to comfort me in my time of distress."

It's just a matter of time before the big man caves. Boom.

LaToya winked. She gathered her things and clicked away on fearsome patent leather heels.

Lacey sent her "Fashion *BITE*" to Mac's reading cue. She tapped her fingers on her desk and sipped her bad coffee, waiting. Waiting and thinking. Thinking about Russian theatres. Russian red dresses. Russian medals.

Russians. Aside from LaToya, and the creepy burglar and Keaton's possible killer—perhaps the same person—who did she know who might have some conceivable interest in Death's Red Dress, a dress from a Russian theatre? A dress full of secret KGB medals that once held secret Russian murder weapons? Could that person possibly be Gregor Kepelov? Gregor had wanted to hide the dress himself and hang onto the medals. He yielded gracefully when Vic put his foot down, but was he secretly dreaming of, say, brokering its sale to some Russian collector? Or even to the Spy Museum, for example? The very place where Lacey was due to meet Brooke in less than an hour.

Mac poked his head out of his office and gave Lacey the good-to-go sign. She ditched the last of her coffee and made her escape, making sure no one saw her slip out.

Nothing but freedom awaited her for the rest of the day.

LACEY SMITHSONIAN'S FASHION *BITES*

DRESSING DOWN MEETS DRESSING UP
OR, COME AS YOU ARE!

One of the most misunderstood invitations is the fashion conundrum known as *Come As You Are*. Your sister's wedding? Grandma's funeral? The company's Big Formal Event? Just *come as you are*, dude! Oh, you're practically naked, because you were washing the dog? Well, whatever. *Just be you!*

Sadly, hordes of Americans have taken the freedom to "come as you are" to heart. Come-As-You-Are-Ism can be an invitation to sartorial anarchy, on the assumption that it's somehow liberating to be dressed inappropriately. Well, it's not liberating if they won't let you in, or they throw you out, or look at you "funny" all evening. I'd call that limiting, not liberating. James Bond wears that great tux because it *liberates* him to go anywhere he wants to in Monte Carlo, not because it *limits* him.

But determined Come-As-You-Are-Ists have laid waste to perfectly reasonable dress codes and even the most rudimentary of formal events, in the belief that whatever they throw on to wash the dog ought to be acceptable attire *anywhere*. Let me say it here and now. Please, do NOT "come as you are"! You can wash the dog later.

Today, men and women *come as they are* to the office, the garage sale, the wedding, the funeral, the picnic, the business dinner, and the awards ceremony, perhaps not understanding these are different things with differing social rules and functions. Different events require different wardrobes. Most people understand what to wear while riding a bicycle or working out at the gym, but many people haven't the faintest idea what to wear to the theatre or a holiday dinner.

My advice: When you are invited to an event that does not involve lifting weights or going on a fifty-mile bike ride, absolutely do not Go As You Are. This is a fashion trap if ever there was one. And people are waiting to see you fall into it.

In your home, you can wear whatever you want. You can paint yourself blue and wear feathers, become the work of art you knew you were always meant to be, and no one else has to see it. On second thought, invite us all over, that would be something to see. However, the world is different outside your front door. When you leave your kingdom, as great or small as it may be, you have an opportunity to present yourself at your best, and an obligation to respect the rest of us. Life is a social contract even when the invite says "casual."

Your clothes express more than your taste and personality, your social status and annual income. They reveal your attitude, your courtesy or lack thereof, your respect for yourself and others. The simple rule of what to wear is this: If you are going somewhere special or you want to impress people with what a cool, civilized human being you are, make an effort to learn the social rules for the occasion, which includes your clothes. You don't want your clothes to say you don't care.

When your hosts issue an invitation for a "casual" event, they don't want to create a burden, they don't want you to stress about your outfit. They do, however, expect you to be clean and presentable, and with your tresses combed or under control, even if they are dyed blue or green.

Casual in the steamy Washington, D.C., summer might mean slacks or a skirt, a madras plaid shirt, and boat shoes sans socks, a la the ultimate preppy. It never means filthy jeans and a grass-stained hoodie, or paint–spattered overalls. (Unless Senator Tom Sawyer has invited you over to help paint that fence. Then it's your very best paint–spattered overalls.) You don't want to look as if you just mowed the lawn, washed the dog, didn't shower, didn't change, and don't care. That's the ultimate insult to your host. And the rest of us.

When you're next at a formal or formal-ish event, look around. Note the wide variety of garments people are wearing. You'll see some underdressed Come-As-You-Are-Ists. You might consider some overdressed. Inside the Beltway, for example, many Southern women believe it is always better to be slightly overdressed than underdressed. If you have questions, check with a friend to get her take on the event and what she's wearing. You'll be on the same page, but not in the same outfit.

If a cocktail party takes place at the end of a business day, most partygoers will arrive in what they wore to work. Washington lawyers who are *coming as they are* may have spent their day pleading a case before the Supreme Court, in dark suits and sober accessories. Others may be dressed down, in pressed slacks and pearls. And some attendees coming from work may change accessories and shoes to transform an outfit to fit the event. It's a matter of perspective.

So why do some people always look appropriate to the moment? What's their secret? They listen to the unspoken social rules and regulations. They don't attend a cocktail party in shorts. They don't wear a formal to a pool party, or a bikini to a formal dinner. They find it liberating to find a way to fit in while still standing out, rather than "sticking out like a sore thumb." They might even read this column for a clue, so here it is:

Rules usually make dressing easier, not harder.

Some places and events have very strict rules. They make it easy: They'll simply ask you to leave if you are not garbed appropriately. There are restaurants that require men to wear jackets and people to refrain from shorts and tank top. Tennis "whites" are required at many tennis clubs. Natty attire is expected on the golf course or in the clubhouse, or at least "natty" by golf standards. For tennis and golf, you can even buy the correct and coordinated outfits in sports shops, everything from shirts to slacks to shoes. And even woebegone media types are "requested" to dress appropriately when covering Congress (or you might be asked to leave the Press Galleries).

And yes, there are places and events that don't spell out their requirements, but they still exist, as unwritten rules. These are more difficult to master. Pay attention to unspoken dress codes, those are the strictest of all. Consider the theatre or the opera or a symphony concert. These are events where the performers are dressing their part, often extravagantly. This shows respect for the part, the play, and for you, the audience. Take your cue from the actors. Theatre is a performance, not a punishment. No need to don prison togs or complain about dressing up. I would point out that of course you're not five, but five-year-olds love to dress up, and will willingly suit up as Spiderman or Wonder Woman if the mood strikes. A five-year-old knows that you simply can't be Superman without the cape. Now *there's* a strict dress code!

How do you know when you're clad appropriately? Here are some thoughts:

- **If you're uncomfortable** around other better-dressed people at the literary soiree or play reading, you need to up your game.
- **If someone dresses up for you,** return the compliment. Dress up for them. Dress for the play. Dress the part.
- **What's your imaginary style?** The fantasy of clothing is a great place to start. When you see a frothy little frock, do you immediately picture yourself wearing it for cocktails on the beach? So maybe you can't go to the beach this year, but you can indulge in the great little dress and find an occasion to suit. You don't have to pass it by, it won't kill you. Don't let opportunity slip by in the twinkle of the tulle.

And when someone says the weekend get-together is casual so just *come as you are,* you'll be able to *come as you wish you were.*

THIRTY

*T*HE STORMS THE NIGHT before blew away the cloud of heat and stale humidity that had hung over the town for a week, leaving in its wake a lovely breeze. It was a wakeup call. Thrilled to be done with her column and out of the office, Lacey felt wide awake and free.

She purchased an iced coffee that was finally drinkable and hailed a taxi to the museum-rich Gallery Place neighborhood near Chinatown. The International Spy Museum complex was located just south of the Smithsonian American Art Museum and the National Portrait Gallery, and among its other neighbors were Ford's Theatre, Madame Tussauds, the Shakespeare Theatre Company, and the FBI. Lacey wove her way down the F Street sidewalk through groups of happy tourists in their newly purchased museum T-shirts, baggy plaid shorts, and dazzling athletic shoes. She ducked out of the throng into the Spy Museum shop to meet Brooke.

And there she was, breezy and professional in a sleeveless blue-and-white seersucker dress, Brooke's own spin on that traditional Southern summer fabric. She wore flats and carried a matching jacket and a light blue tote for her courtroom high heels.

Dressed in pastels in pink and blue, the two friends looked like a throwback to more elegant days, as if they had walked out of a vintage movie—if Rita Hayworth and Grace Kelly had ever made a movie together. Lacey noticed tourists staring at them. While she despaired of Washington's stodgy style, she was always surprised when out-of-towners seemed impressed with the city's prevailing business attire. To be fair, there were people who dressed well in Washington, D.C. Most of them were people who had the money to spend on personal shoppers, expensive clothes, and fine tailoring. A few, like Lacey, were able to find rare vintage pieces of great quality for less money. And then there were those like Claudia Darnell, Lacey's publisher, who could do both.

Lacey caught up with Brooke checking out the spy toys. "What's up, Mata Hari?"

Brooke grinned. "Mata Hari was a fool. We'll discuss her later." Brooke produced museum tickets for both of them.

"I'm starving, Brooke. Can't we have lunch first? Maybe the District ChopHouse?"

One of Lacey's favorites, the steakhouse and brewpub was a mere block and a half away, a bank in a previous life. It had lots of retro charm, comfortable booths, and a beef-heavy menu.

"How about Asian?" Brooke always countered with Asian. "We're right by Chinatown."

"I need comfort food. Protein, not rice."

"ChopHouse it is, but the tickets are timed entry. We'll have to eat afterwards. How much time do you have?"

"Before I collapse from hunger? Well, I am taking the afternoon off."

"Wonderful!" It had been a while since they'd spent much time together.

"What about you? You must be busy."

"I have a few hours. I shoveled some briefs off on Ben." Brooke's younger brother Benjamin, who also worked at the family firm, apparently owed her again, for something. He was eternally in his big sister's debt. "Okay, first spies, then lunch."

The Spy Museum was one of Brooke's favorite places, and Lacey was sure she knew the place as well as the staff. She pulled Lacey through the store and the museum entry and into the elevator, where screens lit up with an introduction to the lore of spies.

"I love this place. Let's just walk and talk. I'll show you my favorite stuff."

"From the Land of Paranoia?"

"It's not paranoia when it's true. And it's fun, right?"

"It is," Lacey agreed. "I feel like I'm playing hooky."

"Me too! We'll play hooky like champs."

They stopped to watch a film of a woman being disguised, step by step, as a young man, emerging in a turban and a thin beard. It was an amazing transformation, but one that an actor or a spy might do routinely. For the actor, just another performance. For the spy, perhaps life or death. Lacey thought again that spycraft and stagecraft had so much in common.

Each dealt with illusion and fantasy. Each told a story that their audience found believable (if they were good, and lucky). Although on the stage, no one died at the end of the play (despite the body count in *Hamlet*). Not permanently. Not usually. Saige Russell was an exception.

Was the person who hid the Lenins in the red dress a theatrical spy? Or an espionage-obsessed actor?

"Hey, I've seen that actress," Lacey said to Brooke. "The one in the disguise video. She's a Washington actress, I've seen her on stage somewhere. I don't know her name, though."

"Neither do I," Brooke said, "and speaking of Washington actors, I don't trust Maksym Pushkin and neither should you."

"The dancer-slash-lawyer at Kinetic last night? He seemed nice."

"Obviously he *seemed* nice." Brooke frowned. "He seems nice in court too, but he's a total shark. He's a smooth attorney with a very smooth courtroom demeanor, but he's a liar."

"He likes *you*," Lacey said.

"Oh, please." Disgust registered on Brooke's face.

"Really, he's very attracted to you."

"Well, of course, that's an entirely different thing," Brooke replied. "I know he oozes charm and empathy, and he's very handsome, but—"

"But what?"

"He's a sneaky bastard. *Charming* is just a performance for him. Agents in place are programmed from an early age, and Maksym Pushkin is exactly the type who would make a very good agent-in-place for Mother Russia."

"A spy? You really think he's a spy?" Lacey treated Brooke to an obvious eye roll. "Pushkin is an American. Or so he told me."

"Born in Moscow. He's a naturalized US citizen."

"He told me he was brought here when he was just a kid." Brooke shook her head. "Okay. I see you've done your homework."

"A smart attorney always does her homework. And when any Russian national comes into my professional view, and keeps coming into view, my antennae go up."

"The Russian thing again."

"The Russian thing is a threat to our democracy. They hacked into our elections and colluded with American traitors,

traitors who are now in the highest levels of our government. And they are everywhere, Lacey. Russian plants in the White House, Congress, the FBI. And Putin! Don't get me started on Putin."

"I'll try not to. However, not every last Russian in this country can be a spy."

"Maybe not, but nearly every Russian in this country could be a target for Russian *kompromat* and could be tempted or corrupted into collaboration. Money, power, sex, glory, whatever it takes."

Lacey looked at Brooke. Most of Brooke's conspiracy theories struck Lacey as tongue in cheek, as much comedy as conspiracy, but her passion about this felt very different.

"Maksym Pushkin's won against you in court, hasn't he?"

"Just once. And he had to cheat to do it." Brooke narrowed her eyes. Lacey had seen that look before. It was a look to be feared. "You don't understand, Lacey. I don't lose. I *don't.*"

Brooke collected herself while they lingered at an exhibit about female spies, Mata Hari, Belle Starr, and the female heroines who spied for George Washington's famous espionage ring and helped turn the tide in the American Revolution.

"Okay, Brooke," Lacey said. "Let's say Maksym Pushkin is a smart, handsome, charming, unscrupulous man. Oh, and tall too," she added. "He plays dirty and he won one he should have lost. That doesn't make him a Russian spy."

"No, it doesn't. But I don't trust Pushkin. Everything about him is too good to be true, and you know what that usually means. There are home-grown operatives here and foreign agents working to undermine America. Pushkin is Russian by birth. He has family in Russia. He travels to Russia all the time. He defends Russian oligarchs in court. He was at Kinetic last night, a hot bed of Russians. And he's danced with them."

"But has he kissed them too?" Brooke mock-glared at her. "I'm kidding. You have no proof, do you?"

"I don't. But Damon is working on it."

Oh, great. I can hardly wait for that story. It's bound to be insane.

"We were all at the show, Brooke. Doesn't mean we're all double agents. And by the way, what did you think of the show?"

Brooke pursed her lips and pondered before answering. "Technically perfect. Visually brilliant. Relentlessly musical. But somehow heartless."

"The source material is pretty grim."

"The problem is the heart is missing, lost in all that athletic proficiency and dazzling stagecraft."

"Mathematically precise," Lacey agreed. While she thought the show was beautiful, there was something very analytical about it. She was almost sorry now that she hadn't seen the apparition Marie had. "You're right, the heart was missing."

"The telltale heart, so to speak."

Marie's ghost in red: Was that the missing heart of Kinetic?

"Brooke, did you see a ghost on stage last night?"

"Of course, the stage was full of ghosts! I lost count."

If I don't tell Brooke, she'll never forgive me. And Marie didn't say not to.

"Listen," Lacey said quietly. "Marie saw a ghost on stage in a red shroud, a ghost who seemed lost, not part of the action. Did you or Damon see anything like that?"

"No!" Brooke shivered and rubbed her arms. "Did you?"

"None of us did. Just Marie."

"Good God, Lacey. I have no idea what that could mean. But it doesn't sound like a *good* omen."

"Well, maybe it just means Marie sees things the rest of us don't. It may not mean anything. But Brooke, we can't paint every Russian with the same brush. It's wrong. Aside from the spies—and we don't know who they are—most of these people are here because they had to flee Russia. They cherish freedom. Like the Kepelovs."

"Some of them, yes. You're forgetting the opportunists and the agents in place and the Russian Mafia. They all cling to each other."

"If I were in living in a foreign country, I'd seek out other Americans sometimes too," Lacey argued. "I might miss speaking English once in a while."

"But we can't be too careful. Putin is beating his chest, playing chess with our dim-bulb diplomats, and corrupting Americans from the swamp to the White House."

"Don't forget, he does it all shirtless too! On horseback. And he's very white. Not terribly appetizing." *Fashion clue, or ego clue?*

"I know! Putin, beating his pasty-white shirtless chest! Brrr! Russian agents are flooding this town like never before. They want nothing less than the complete destabilization of our government. And the road there is littered with Russian bodies. Russians who opposed Putin, Russians who got too close to Putin, Russians who know too much for Putin's comfort."

"Brooke, this is different from your usual conspiracy theories."

"This is different from anything we've ever faced. As real as all those dead bodies," Brooke said. "And one of the creepiest things is that the Russia-backed alt-right crazies have taken over most of the big conspiracy websites. But not DeadFed and Conspiracy Clearinghouse. Damon and I are a voice crying in the wilderness."

They fell silent, still standing before the exhibit on George Washington's spy ring. Around them swirled a mob of laughing children, playing Spy vs. Spy. They were giggling and whispering, running through the child-sized tunnels, squealing at the exhibits and their parents.

A city of spies, Lacey thought. That's what these kids would remember most from their trip to the Nation's Capital.

ψ

"So tell me," Brooke asked. "What was Kepelov doing there? *Really* doing there?"

They paused by the Bond Villains exhibit to admire those super-villains who had tried to destroy the world—and who could only be stopped by one man: Bond, James Bond.

"He wanted to see the play because it was performed by a Russian émigré theatre troupe he'd never heard of. I think he was annoyed that I knew more about them than he did. Gregor is not really a theatre person, my guess."

"He was speaking Russian with a number of people. I saw him. Not that I understood a word of it."

"Gee, Brooke, did they sound like *spies?*" Lacey arched her eyebrows.

"Hmph. What did Marie have to say? Did she faint?"

"No, she took a Valium. Dulls the psychic vibrations, she says, and Gregor wanted her to enjoy herself last night. A rare night out for them."

"And why is that?" Lacey wondered what she could say. "Lacey?"

She fixed Brooke with a look. "This must never appear on DeadFed. Don't even tell Damon. I mean it." She waited for Brooke to nod. "They don't hang out with the D.C. Russian crowd because Marie is afraid. That someone might try to kill him. Polonium or ricin, or something equally unattractive."

Brooke nodded again. "Well, she might be right. He's ex-Russian intelligence, so he's potentially a target. If he's really as pro-American as he says, that makes him a different kind of target. Tell him not to stand in front of windows. Or fall off any balconies. That's popular this year."

"All natural causes, too, I understand."

"You know I've never trusted Kepelov, Lacey, not completely. We met him under, let's say, unusual circumstances. Sure, he's been your friend and ally, but he's a treasure hunter at heart, always after *something*, like phantom Fabergé eggs."

Lacey couldn't argue with any of that. "You know what they say: Keep your friends close, and your enemies closer? Either way, I should keep Gregor Kepelov close."

"I agree. And Lacey, I respect the fact that you're holding something else back. Don't bother denying it. You're on to something on the Amy Keaton death and you're not telling me." Brooke's shoulders slumped a bit. "And I'm really sad that if it weren't for Damon you would tell me."

There was nothing Lacey could say. There were rules, even among friends. Feeding Brooke any information about the hollow Lenin medals in the dress was out of the question. It might put Brooke in danger. Lacey had promised Kepelov, and Vic, and Marie. Damon would print some garbled version of it and that might ruin any chance to get at the truth.

And I still have no idea if there is any connection to Keaton's death.

"Damon respects you," Brooke insisted. "Really."

Like a puppy dog who wants a biscuit. Brooke dug into her bag and produced the program from *The Turn of the Screw*. The page with the dedication to Amy Keaton was circled in red. Taped to it was the news brief Trujillo had written for the police column, and last, but not least, the overwrought editorial that Wiedemeyer produced.

"What do you know about Amy Keaton's death?" she demanded. "I promise it won't go any farther."

"Honestly, Brooke, I don't know anything except that she's dead. There's not even a cause of death determination yet. I have Trujillo trying to get something from the M.E. Cops say it's an accident."

"She had a knock-down drag-out fight with LaToya over a dress. Don't forget I saw that too. Forty-eight hours later, Keaton is dead. And that's an accident?"

"I don't know! LaToya had nothing to do with that. That so-called fight was just a warm-up for LaToya and you know it. I don't have any inside dope on Keaton's death. Besides, reporters are interested in reporting the news, not making it."

"So you've talked to Broadway Lamont?"

"I have. I'm sure Damon has too."

"And Damon says there was something weird about LaToya's break-in, but Lamont wouldn't talk about it." Brooke waved her small collection of papers. "You know there's more to this story."

"Isn't there always? I've talked to a lot of people, but I don't know anything else about Keaton's death. I promise. I don't know if there is a connection to the dress."

"So far."

The famous Aston-Martin DB5 from the Bond film *Goldfinger* was just ahead of them, surrounded by a knot of tourists. The *Goldfinger* theme music played as the Aston flashed its lights, twirled its license plate, and raised the bulletproof shield protecting the rear window. Simulated machinegun fire thundered and whirling blades ejected from the wheels to slash pursuers' tires.

Hollywood magic, Lacey reflected. *Theatre and espionage once again converge.*

Lost in their own thoughts, Lacey and Brooke wandered through more exhibits, past the Third Reich's Enigma machine, past mockups of famous dead drops and other classics of espionage tradecraft. They sat through the videos on rogue Americans who betrayed their country to the Soviets. And for what? Nothing but a few dollars and endless shame.

Welcome to the Spy Museum, Lacey thought. *If you weren't paranoid going in, you will be coming out.*

Brooke's phone rang inside her tote bag, and she looked at the number.

"Benjamin," she said to Lacey, annoyed. She answered the call. "What now, little brother?" She listened. "Yes, you are interrupting us." Dramatic sigh, and then a laugh. "Don't panic, I'll be there. Keep your shorts on."

"Let me guess," Lacey said. "Something legal came up."

"Sorry. Have to go."

"Off to save democracy, no doubt?"

"We live to serve. I'm so sorry, Lacey. I'll make it up to you."

"It's okay, Brooke. We'll do lunch next time. I would never stand in the way of you preserving Truth, Justice, and the American way."

Brooke hugged her and slipped on her baby blue sunglasses. She saluted Lacey and headed briskly toward the EXIT sign.

On her way out, Lacey decided she deserved a souvenir. There was one big red coffee mug in the Spy Museum gift shop that she liked. It was emblazoned with the image of a slinky female spy in a trench coat and the warning, BEWARE OF FEMALE SPIES! And knowing Brooke would have argued her into lunch in Chinatown at a Chinese restaurant (which would have given Lacey a headache), she headed directly for the ChopHouse.

C&#x8;

Seated in one of the cozy upholstered booths all alone, Lacey felt positively decadent. Housed in an old bank building, the District ChopHouse's stately décor was dark and soothing, and American comfort food called to her, in the form of savory steak tips and good bread and butter. She would order a cappuccino later to top it off.

Eating alone gave her time to decompress and to people-watch. Judging by their clothes, most of her fellow diners seemed to be enjoying a break from work, or else conducting business over lunch. Suits and tailored dresses were the order of the day. The occasional tourists, complete with fanny packs, loud T-shirts, and giant sunglasses propped on their heads, looked out of place, but they didn't seem to care.

Tourists in D.C., Lacey had observed, usually looked either happy or miserable. There was no in-between setting. This bunch looked pretty happy.

Lacey was slathering butter on a piece of bread when her phone rang. It was Vic. For a brief moment, she hoped he was there in the restaurant. She raised her head and looked for him.

"Where are you?"

"My office. Finalizing a contract for a new client."

"Contracts and clients. Sounds boring." She settled back in the booth. His voice sounded wonderful.

"Not when I start sending them bills. That part is fun. Where are you?"

"Lunch at the ChopHouse. By myself."

"Thought you were lunching with the conspiracy queen."

"She got a call. The law never sleeps."

"How about you? Are you available tonight?"

She smiled into the phone, thoughts of a romantic evening with Vic dancing in her head. "What do you have in mind?"

"Kepelov wants us to have a meeting. To come up with a plan."

"No!" Her spirits sank. "A night at the theatre is one thing, but every night this week has been a Kepelov night."

"Under the circumstances, darling, I'm inclined to believe a plan is in order. And maybe Gregor's got some old KGB tricks up his sleeve."

"I am not going anywhere tonight, Vic. I am going home and I am not moving a muscle."

"Okay then. We'll meet at your apartment. Say seven?"

"My place? I am not providing snacks and drinks, Vic Donovan! I mean it. I am going to lie on the sofa and eat grapes. Which you will peel for me. For getting me into this thing."

Vic found her way too funny. His laugh was deep and soothing, and vaguely mocking. "Grapes it is. I'll take care of everything. You won't have to move a muscle. Gotta go. Love you, Lacey."

"Love you too. But I'd rather love you alone tonight."

"Me too. But this will be our last night with the spy who came in from the cold." He signed off. She stared at the phone after he hung up,

Against her better judgment, she used her phone to check Conspiracy Clearinghouse, to see what Damon Newhouse had written, if anything. Turns out he had been inspired by the previous night's play.

RUSSIAN THEATRE'S *TURN OF THE SCREW*: GHOST STORY?
OR THEATRICAL ANALOGY FOR DESTABILIZING
U.S. GOVERNMENT?

It was the usual journalistic goulash that Damon had perfected. Spies were everywhere, even in the theatre, even in the afterlife. Even in Henry James.

Lacey ordered that cappuccino she'd promised herself and pulled her brand-new Spy Museum mug out of its bag. She contemplated its message: BEWARE OF FEMALE SPIES!

But was it necessarily *female spies* that she should be worried about?

THIRTY-ONE

*R*ESISTING THE URGE to run home and make sure everything was freshly vacuumed and the pillows fluffed for the soon-to-be-descending troupe of Russians, Lacey decided instead it was the perfect day to pamper herself—and pick up some gossip.

"Well, well, well! Look who the cat dragged in."

Stella was at the counter of Stylettos with a freshly coiffed patron, who had apparently wanted aggressive highlights. Her hair resembled a black-and-white zebra, but the woman left looking happy. Lacey gave her friend a look.

"What? It's what she asked for. Mine is not to question why. Mine is but to do and *dye*."

"Cute, Stella."

Stella was still channeling the Fifties and Sixties today, from her thick cat-eye makeup to her outfit beneath the salon smock. She wore her hair up, in a moderate beehive wound around with a ribbon headband. All the backcombing required for a beehive was bad for the hair, she often told Lacey. ("Totally wrecks the strands. Fractured split ends, who needs that?") But it added a few inches to her petite height. Her legs were encased in tight red capris. Under her smock was a tight leopard-patterned bustier. No one else in D.C. seemed to dress like Stella. At least not during the day.

Together, she and Lacey looked like two ends of those decades' spectrum. Lacey, in pink with her French twist, was prim and proper. Stella, pushing the envelope, and her Girls, in her corset top, was always the wild child.

"Look at you, Lace," she said. "Pink wiggle dress! Very sexy, Pollyanna."

"Hi to you too, Stella. Do you have time for a tiny trim?"

"So that's why you've got the up do going on. Hiding those ends."

"And?"

"Depends. As long as you spill everything you know about that Amy Keaton. You know, the dead woman who rumbled with LaToya last weekend?" As if Stella had to distinguish between all the dead women they might have in mind.

"Not you too." *Rumbled?* Was Stella watching 1950s motorcycle movies?

"What do you mean *me too*? I should be first in line with the info. Me first. Stella Lake Griffin. Now, what happened?"

"The short version is I don't know."

"Okay, now the long version of *why* you don't know and *what* you don't know." Stella examined Lacey's hair critically, pulling the hair pins from the French twist and combing through the locks with her fingers. "You are overdue for a trim, girl. You see these ends? These ends are ragged and dry."

"Half an inch." Lacey measured with her fingers.

"Ha."

"I mean it, Stella."

"An inch, or no deal. You got an inch of damage. I will not be held responsible for these ends. Look at it my way. You're advertising my work."

"And that zebra-striped job I just saw?"

"A different audience."

Drama, it's always drama. Lacey pulled her hair back. All she wanted was to close her eyes and have her hair washed, trimmed, and blown dry into something sleek, so that every strand fell into place. Something to take her worries away. Perhaps a manicure too.

"May I put on the smock before I get the obligatory lecture?"

"Make it snappy. And we're doing a deep conditioner too."

Lacey donned the black Stylettos smock and Stella personally guided her to the shampoo bowl.

"I don't have much to report," Lacey said.

"You'll talk, and you may remember more details, if you get a nice long head massage shampoo. I'll do it myself."

"You're on."

Stella didn't disappoint. The massage was great, and with her head back in the shampoo bowl under the warm suds, Lacey almost forgot everything, including where she was. She started to doze.

"Hey. I'm talking to you, Lacey. Wake up." Stella smacked her arm with a comb. "You need some vitamins or something?"

"I need more sleep." *And fewer distractions in my life.*

"This should wake you up." Stella rinsed her hair with cold water.

Lacey's eyes popped open. "Hey! That's freezing!" She covered her face with her hands.

"Cold water's bracing and it closes the cuticle." She sprayed the last of the suds away. "You're finished, and you've had your little nap. Time to talk."

Stella marched Lacey back to her station and brought out the sharp scissors.

"Half an inch," Lacey pleaded.

"You're not talking to Sweeney Todd, you know." The stylist paused. "On the other hand, we wouldn't want to experience an unfortunate slip of the shears, would we? So start talking. That woman we saw: Amy Keaton." She parted Lacey's hair into sections and clipped them up. "She pops up like a bad penny on Sunday in Baltimore? And now she's dead."

"Have you been talking to Brooke?"

"Brooke keeps in touch. We're like *this.*" *Snip.*

Lacey didn't want Stella seeing Russian spies in every shampoo bowl. Or jump to conclusions about what might be going on. *I don't KNOW what's going on.* Or worse, announce everything she thought she knew on the Stella Broadcasting Network.

"Take it easy, Stella." Lacey glanced down to see how much hair was floating to the floor. *Snip.*

"What does LaToya think?" Stella asked.

"She thinks I'm going to make sure the costume she bought doesn't retain any bad vibes. Any bad fashion juju. And the last time I looked at my job description, that wasn't in it."

"But who else could do it, Lace? No one. You're everyone's go-to fashion guru. You got that EFP thing going on. Still, why blame the dress when it's some *person* who put the bad vibes in it in the first place?"

"Right." Lacey yawned.

"You still got custody of that burgundy bitch of a dress?"

"Sort of. It's in a safe location. Vic knows."

Stella tapped a fingernail on Lacey's nose. "No sleeping. You know what I think? It's all tied up with that theatre."

"You think?"

"I'm sorry we couldn't make it last night. To the theatre. Me and Nigel." Stella never struck Lacey as a playgoer. Rock concerts, yes. The theatre, no. "Brooke told me about it and it sounded cool. Well, interesting anyway. Unfortunately, I had to close up late. And to tell you the truth, I'm not so big on plays and that kind of thing. Especially when I got Nigel waiting for me at home. And we're still in that newlywed phase. 'Course he knows all that Shakespeare stuff, 'cause he's English and it's like a law or something over there."

"Right. English law. Don't worry, you didn't miss that much." *Except Marie's Red Ghost.*

"We were busy last night, anyway. You know how I may have mentioned my clock is ticking?"

"I remember. You really want a baby?"

"I want a baby, Lacey!" Stella gazed in the mirror above Lacey's head for a moment, perhaps envisioning the perfect baby. Or the perfect baby bump. "So maybe I'll go to the theatre when I'm old."

"And when you need a break from the kids."

"That's right." With the conversation turning to babies who would have "Nigel's awesome hazel eyes," Lacey hoped she was off the hook for the moment about Amy Keaton and the red dress. Stella concentrated on cutting the back of Lacey's hair straight.

"You know, you could try something new, Lacey. Like layers."

"No layers. I see women with layers and it looks like some feral animal chewed off the ends."

"That's not what I'd do to you. It would be cute."

"No layers. No short hair. I mean it."

"Spoilsport."

Lacey gazed into the mirror to monitor the snipping and caught a glimpse of Lady Gwendolyn with her bottom deep in a massaging chair, her toes in hot soapy water. Her eyes were closed and she looked transported. For someone who previously had no sense of style, since meeting Stella Lady G had become a fashion fiend. She'd tossed many of her tweeds in favor of chic linen suits. But it was summer. Winter would tell if the makeover had really taken hold. She looked very different, stylish. Lady G's English overbite, however, was still English.

"How's it working out with your mother-in-law? She's here a lot."

"She's a doll. Strangest thing, Lacey, it's like having a real mom. Yeah, I know I got a mother and we haven't even fought since the wedding. Course we haven't talked either—knock on wood. But Lady G and me? Who'd of ever thought we'd get along so great? It's like a miracle."

"And how's Nigel?"

"He's a doll too. Who'd of thought a year ago, I'd be here today and happy?"

"Who indeed." Lacey thought of the past year. Stella's marriage. Lacey's engagement. "How's your leg coming along?"

"Better. Course I can't wear high heels all the time anymore. And that grieves me, Lacey. It really does."

She glanced down at Stella's feet, laced up in a pair of black leather boots with a small heel and a lot of ankle support. Stella had broken her leg in a frightening confrontation last winter with a woman who was obsessed with Nigel. On that cold and snowy day at Great Falls, Brooke had brought a gun, but in the end she couldn't use it. With Stella's life at stake, Lacey had used the gun. The memory still gave them both nightmares, and it left Stella with physical scars. It could have been worse.

"But I could have died. Lots of us could have." Stella said what they were both thinking. "Instead, I got the man of my dreams and a perfect mother-in-law. That other bitch, she's getting prison."

Stella picked up a piece of Lacey's hair and watched it fall. "Everything Nigel and I have been through has just brought us closer together."

"I can tell. I'm really happy for you, Stel."

"Hey! New subject! Notice something new?"

Lacey gazed around the salon. Three elaborate period wigs that Stella had scored at the theatre sale were perched on wig stands in the front window: Cleopatra, Marie Antoinette, and Queen Elizabeth I. The faces were painted with exaggerated makeup to approximate the period of the wig. At least a theatrical version of the period. Stella's handiwork, no doubt.

"Wow. I like what you've done with them. Have you tried them all on?"

"Totally!" Stella's grin exposed her inner imp. "They're getting lots of action after hours, and Nigel loves them too. He gets to be with a new woman every night. Well, a new woman from the neck up, you know."

"Do I really want to know all this?"

Stella laughed. "The Cleopatra's my fave so far. She was a complete temptress. Without the asp, if you know what I mean. What a weird way to die. Snakebite? And speaking of dying, what do you think happened to Amy Keaton? I haven't forgotten about her."

I was afraid she hadn't. "Police say it was an accident."

"Ha. That's what the paper said." Stella snipped one more piece of hair. "I want the story behind the story."

"That's all I have."

"It's weird, Lace. It doesn't make any sense."

"What do you mean?"

"That Keaton woman looked like the last person on earth to go crazy over a dress. I'm not being mean when I say she was dumpy. Clothes, hair, grooming, attitude, what a mess. On the other manicured hand, LaToya is always styling. What a contrast in types. I wish I'd taken a picture."

Pictures! How could I forget? Lacey gave herself a mental head slap. Todd Hansen was there on assignment last weekend, taking pictures of the theatre yard sale. Tamsin had used some with her piece in *The Eye*. Had he caught LaToya and Keaton fighting over the dress? If so, why hadn't he told anyone? Time to find out.

"You're working on it, right?" Stella prompted. "You're not giving up?"

"No, but I'm a little stalled. I'm trying to find out more about the dress and the first actress who wore it. I'd like to find out why it wound up on the sales rack. If that leads to Amy Keaton, then it does."

Stella grabbed her hair dryer. "Now you're talking." She hit the switch and the dryer whined. It was too loud to talk anymore. And when Lacey's hair was finished, Nigel arrived to escort his ladies away. Lacey was off the hook and looking fabulous.

Too bad it's not Friday already.

ᙘ

Freshly coiffed and window shopping in Dupont Circle on her way to the Metro, Lacey was interrupted by a phone call from a number she didn't recognize.

"Ms. Smithsonian? Lacey? It's Maksym, Maksym Pushkin. We met last night at Kinetic."

After discussing him with Brooke, this was unexpected and a little spooky. *Were his ears burning? Is there a hidden microphone somewhere?*

"I remember you, Maksym. What's up?"

"You're still interested in *The Masque of the Red Death?*"

"Always."

"I don't think I gave you a satisfactory answer."

"Well—" Not satisfying the press was a time-honored tradition in D.C., and anywhere politicians and lawyers dwelled.

"Perhaps we could discuss it further."

"Why not?" Lacey always wanted to know the whole story. Maksym Pushkin might have an interesting take on Kinetic, and according Brooke, he was a possible spy. Lacey was willing to bet he was interested in her attorney friend. If she was right, perhaps he wanted to ask Lacey about Brooke, and Lacey might have some conversational leverage. In fact, she realized, she must have. *Or else Pushkin wouldn't be calling me.*

"The phone is so impersonal," Pushkin said." Could we meet in person?"

"Is tomorrow soon enough?"

"Tomorrow is fine for me."

"Tomorrow afternoon? I have an interview in the morning." *With Nicky Sokolov.*

"Would the Portrait Gallery be convenient?" he asked.

"That's an interesting choice," she said. It was a public place, which was good. So far, Lacey believed Pushkin was probably harmless, but she wasn't about to meet him in a secluded environment.

"My offices are just a block away from there, and the Gallery is more interesting than a coffee shop," he explained. She agreed. They set a time to meet and signed off.

The Portrait Gallery was across the street from the Spy Museum. Lacey suddenly wondered if Pushkin had caught sight of her there with Brooke earlier that day. Outside the building, perhaps?

It didn't really matter. Lacey far preferred face-to-face meetings and interviews to phone or email. Body language, facial expressions, and gestures were always telling. Besides, leaving the office was a perk of her beat. External inspiration was better than waiting for ideas to hit her over the head while staring at her computer screen.

Her phone beeped again. She had a text from DeeDee Adler: Amy Keaton had been cremated. Her brother was taking her home in a box and if there was a funeral service, it would be family-only. DeeDee didn't know yet whether a memorial service would be held later at the theatre. She said she would text again if they got around to planning something.

Lacey doubted it. *Amy Keaton is gone, and Kinetic is moving on.*

THIRTY-TWO

*V*INTAGE CLOTHES command attention and carry their own kind of magic. However, after wearing a wiggle dress all day and standing at attention to show off the pink dress to perfection for Stella, Lacey was happy to change into a comfortable pair of white capris and a patterned top. Alas, she had no time to chill out before company was due.

She hoped her favorite man would arrive ahead of "the Troika," as she was beginning to think of Gregor, Marie, and Olga. *Two Russians tonight and two more tomorrow. All of a sudden it's raining Russians.*

There was a knock at her door, and a voice. "Sweetheart, open the door. Please? My hands are full."

She found Vic bearing a gigantic aluminum platter and miscellaneous sacks and bags. He rushed through her living room and set it all down on her dining room table. He kissed her, smelling of barbecue.

"Provisions, as promised, ma'am. Wings. And things."

"Wings?" She peeled back the foil on top of the big platter and peeked inside. "Just wings?"

"Not just any wings. All kinds of wings. Crispy wings. Grilled wings. Right wings, left wings. Red, white, and blue wings." They were piled high. Vic sounded proud of himself.

"Chicken wings." She contemplated them doubtfully.

"Sauces too. Blue cheese, red chili, ginger Thai, ranch. It's not like you wanted a salad, did you?" He picked one up and bit into it. "Yum."

"Not salad." She shook her head. "But a hostess could get a reputation for this kind of thing."

"The hostess with the mostest."

"Yeah, the mostest chicken wings. What happened to those grapes you were going to peel for me?"

"In the bag." Sure enough, one of the bags was full of plump purple and green grapes. He grinned at her and threw some of the bags in the refrigerator. Lacey's larder, as usual, was rather bare. Eggs, yogurt, and a variety of cheeses were on hand, but little else, except Dos Equis for Vic and a couple of bottles of champagne. She kept champagne on hand in case moments of celebration surprised her.

"Why wings?" They smelled delicious.

"We serve them at staff meetings. They're very popular."

"Do only men attend these meetings?"

"Women too. Hey, if anyone wants to provide something different—" He picked up another wing and dunked it into the blue sauce. There seemed to be plenty.

"He who provides the food, chooses the food?"

"Exactly. Them's the rules."

Vic cleaned his hands with a wet wipe from a pile that came with the wings. He took something out of his pocket. It was the size of a small cell phone and had an antenna. Lacey had seen one before: a bug detector. He switched it on and methodically moved around the apartment, sweeping every room for hidden surveillance equipment.

"This is new," Lacey commented.

"You mean the *wings*, right?" Vic gave her a wink.

"The wings? Oh, the wings! Right. I usually leave the *wings* up to Brooke."

"My wings are better." He continued the sweep. It only took a minute before he said, "Clear."

"Phew, I was holding my breath," she said. "No spies have been in Smithsonian's lair. Until this very moment."

"You're a smartass. But such a cute ass."

"You say the sweetest things, Wingman."

Another knock at the door announced Gregor Kepelov, with Marie and Olga. As Marie was hugging Lacey, Gregor put his finger to his lips and did a bug sweep of his own, with his own detector, which he pulled out of an old leather briefcase. The gizmo looked a little different from Vic's but seemed to work the same way. *Probably Russian-made,* Lacey decided. Vic watched, amused.

"All good," Gregor said as he finished. "Can't be too careful."

"Or theatrical," Lacey remarked.

"Ah, a little joke." He smiled but did not laugh.

"So you begin all your meetings this way?"

"Many of them."

Lacey didn't even find this odd. Maybe it was the peculiar day, the Spy Museum with Brooke, or the odd call from Maksym Pushkin. The thought of LaToya's break-in still gave her the creeps. She was doubly relieved to have a second opinion that no one had breached the sanctity of her shabby apartment. Lacey certainly didn't want to be paranoid all by herself. It was better to have paranoid company.

And plenty of chicken wings on hand to feed them.

This was the first time that Gregor and his sister had ever visited Lacey's apartment, but they felt free to tour her rooms and opine on the décor. They liked everything she'd inherited from her aunt. And why not? Mimi had great taste.

The Troika were most impressed with her balcony and the river view of the Potomac and Maryland across the river. Lacey's building was old, a little scruffy, and the elevators were iffy at best. But the seventh-floor balcony with its French doors and incredible view made up for the rest of the place. It felt like an eye in the sky. It was still light outside, but the sun was dipping behind the west wing of the building. Ships with white sails dotted the water and the shadows grew long. The evening was perfect. *Almost.*

"Smithsonian, why do you not invite us here before?" Gregor asked.

It was a question she couldn't answer. Not politely. "I never had a Red Dress of Death before."

"You have million-dollar view," Olga said.

"Not counting inflation, Olga," Gregor declared. "Perhaps two million in today's market."

"Dollars or euros?" Vic asked, and everyone laughed.

Marie leaned against the brick wall. She seemed sleepy and content, ready to stay right where she was on the balcony. "I can see why you love it here, Lacey. It's very peaceful. And I love your hair. I bet you saw Stella today?"

"Yes, she worked her magic."

"Yes, everything is wonderful. But enough talk," Gregor decided. "We have much to discuss."

He ushered everyone back into the living room, closing the French doors and pulling the blinds over both doors and windows.

At least I don't have to coat the room in tinfoil. I'm fresh out of Reynolds Wrap.

"Is that necessary?" Lacey switched on some lights.

"Perhaps not. But there are telephoto lenses and lip readers and that building across the way. Why take chances?"

"Gregor is right," Vic said.

"Let's get to work."

"Nyet, Gregor," Olga said. "Refreshments first. We are company."

"Oh, we have refreshments too," Lacey said. "Vic brought wings." Vic pointed at the big platter, still covered with foil.

"Excellent! We love American wings. But first we have something for you." Olga Kepelova offered a bag to Lacey. "You have a plate? For the caviar?"

"Caviar?" Lacey peeked into the sack. *Caviar and chicken wings! All my favorites!*

"And a small silver spoon. Da?"

"Yes, I have a plate and spoon."

"Must be silver."

Gregor's sister always carried an air of unimpeachable authority, even in someone else's home. She marched into Lacey's small galley kitchen, fingers trailing the counters, touching the cabinets. Perhaps she was doing a sweep of her own.

Lacey produced a delicate silver platter with a fluted rim that had belonged to Aunt Mimi, and one of Mimi's best silver spoons. Olga deemed these acceptable. She placed the caviar in the middle and surrounded it with crackers.

"It will do." Olga dipped the spoon into the black goo and spread it on a cracker. She tasted it, and closed her eyes in bliss. "Try it. Is good." Olga gazed at her intently, insistently.

One cracker's worth is polite enough, Lacey decided. She took a bite. It was incredibly salty and made her mouth pucker—not in a good way. Her palate was more prosaically American than one accustomed to exotic fish eggs.

"That's really something," she said. Olga smiled, satisfied. *Whew.*

Marie scooped a dollop of the dark delicacy on a cracker and popped it into her mouth.

"I didn't know you liked caviar, Marie," Lacey said.

"Cher, down in Nawlins we eat alligator and frog's legs and suck the brains out of crawfish. This is delicious." She picked up a plate, filling one side with crackers and caviar and the other with chicken wings and sauces. The others followed suit. Except for Lacey. She dug into the grapes.

"With caviar we must have vodka," Gregor announced. "Olga?"

"Of course, brother. You must pour the vodka," Olga said.

Gregor looked at her. "I thought you brought the vodka!"

"I thought you had it!" Olga looked wildly at Lacey. "Smithsonian! You must have vodka!" Before Lacey could answer, Olga flung open the refrigerator door. There was a long silence.

Oh my God, Lacey thought. *No one brought the vodka. We're doomed. Doomed!*

"Ah! Champagne!" Olga emerged triumphantly with one of Lacey's bottles of champagne. The best one. "Excellent! Even better! You have champagne glasses?"

No, I drink it straight from the bottle. And I may start.

"In the cupboard over the sink, Olga. Make yourself at home."

"So nice of you. A very good champagne. Perfect with caviar."

Marie sent Lacey a smile and a little shrug. Her look said clearly, *There's nothing to be done about Olga, just chill.* Lacey smiled back.

Wings, caviar, beer, and champagne were flowing freely when another knock sounded on her front door.

"I'll get it." Vic strolled to the door and peered through the peephole. He opened it, and a large yet graceful man stepped into the entryway.

"Turtledove," Lacey said.

"Lacey." He lifted his head and sniffed the air. "I smell wings." His teeth were large and white and looked fearsome when he grinned.

"Lots of wings," Vic said. "Help yourself, Forrest."

"Vic invited me," he said to Lacey. "Hope you don't mind."

"You know you're always welcome." She ushered him into the living room. "And thank you for moving the crimson costume."

"My pleasure. Course I'm a little curious to find out why it merits the James Bond treatment."

"And you will. But first, have some chicken. Beer. Caviar. Champagne."

Kepelov soon called the meeting to order. Lacey curled up on the sofa next to Vic. The others pulled up chairs in a circle.

"As you know, we are here because our friend Lacey Smithsonian has once again pulled on a red thread and tickled a terrible tiger," Gregor said, mixing metaphors.

"I wouldn't put it quite that way," Lacey said. "And we don't know about the tiger yet."

"I think we do," Vic said.

"You have a gift," Olga said. "A dangerous gift."

"I'd be willing to bet on it," Turtledove added. "I just gave the five-star protection service to a dress. The story has got to be the best part."

"This is the truth, Lacey Smithsonian, no use arguing," Gregor said. "This EFP is more than just paying close attention to clothes, noticing things others do not see."

"I got that." Lacey leaned her head back against the sofa. "I don't have anything solid yet."

"You have more than you know," Gregor said. "And more than I know."

Lacey wondered if Marie had taken another Valium. She seemed to be on a very even keel. *Maybe it's the caviar and champagne.*

"That is why we must proceed with the utmost caution," Gregor added.

Turtledove paused over a wing. "Caution. How so?" Everyone looked at Lacey.

"There is something very unusual about that dress, Turtledove." Lacey sat up straighter. "Every garment has a hem at the bottom. It seems insignificant, but it protects the fabric's raw edges and helps give the skirt its shape. Sometimes the hem is weighted down to enhance the movement of the dress, especially in a long formal gown, like the red dress. The weights can be nearly anything small and heavy. Coins, buttons, metal washers. Coco Chanel weighted her jacket hems with gold chains. With this particular costume, someone weighted the hem with commemorative medals of Lenin."

"Lenin? As in Vladimir Lenin?" Turtledove asked. "Russian revolutionary, famous communist? Corpse kept on display?"

"That is the Lenin," Gregor said.

"These particular medals were hollow. Apparently used by spies," Lacey said.

"Not 'apparently.' They were used by a spy. One spy. And better to say agent."

"The ones in the hem were empty," Lacey continued.

"Empty? What were they for originally?" Turtledove asked.

"Microfilm?"

"To explain," Olga began. "These medals were KGB, or perhaps FSB or GRU. They once contained poison needles."

"An assassin," Turtledove said. As a friend of Damon's and a loyal reader of DeadFed dot com, he was well versed in spies and conspiracy theory. "A dress is a pretty weird place to put something like that."

"Exactly," Vic said. "So it fell to Lacey to discover them."

"How?"

"I peeked. I felt the weights and I was curious. I asked Vic to snip open the hem, and there they were." Lacey wondered why others didn't see what she saw.

"You're onto an assassin, presumably poisoning people?" Turtledove devoured another wing.

"Let me summarize," Gregor said. "We have a red dress, or crimson costume, if you prefer, which comes from Kinetic Theatre, a theatre run by Russian émigrés."

"They are quite good," Olga interrupted. "It is a mix of music and dance and beautiful bodies. We saw a show last night."

Gregor cleared his throat. "As I was saying, we have two dead women, both connected with the theatre. An actress and the stage manager."

"Twelve years apart," Lacey said. "Could be a coincidence. Both were described by the police as accidents. But both had broken necks."

Gregor put up a hand for attention. "What do they have in common? Kinetic Theatre and the blood-red costume. One wore it in a production. The other tried to prevent it from being sold. More curious, it was sold to Lacey's colleague LaToya Crawford. The stage manager fought with LaToya over it. It was witnessed by many. Including Lacey Smithsonian."

"It was more of a schoolyard tussle than a fight," Lacey interjected. "LaToya bought it at that the multi-theatre yard sale thing. Last Saturday."

"But then at the last minute," Gregor went on, "Miss LaToya, very intelligently, decided Smithsonian should make sure for her that it was free of clothing voodoo."

"Who told you that?" Lacey asked him.

"Sorry, darling," Vic said. "It must have slipped out."

"That part makes sense, Lacey," Turtledove said. "You have the touch, you know you do."

"You've been discussing this behind my back. The three of you."

"Private investigator here. Occupational hazard," Vic said, sheepishly.

Turtledove reached for a napkin and another wing. "No worries, Lacey, I'm sworn to secrecy."

"You thought it was funny."

"No, ma'am." He tried to keep from laughing.

"Not so funny for LaToya when her apartment was broken into," Gregor said. "And something was strange about that as well, is that not so, Smithsonian? Tell our friend."

"Her clothes were taken out of her closet and set up around the room. Stuffed with paper to look like they were almost human. Like the Invisible Woman's costume parade. They were deliberately arranged around the room in outfits, the way she might wear them, with matching shoes and bags and scarves. Creepiest thing I ever saw. The next day, I found out Amy Keaton was dead."

Turtledove took it all in with a nod of the head. "Do you know why they're dead? Were they targets of an enemy operative? Do you have a person of interest?" He finished his plate.

"When the killer is in disguise, in deep cover, it's difficult," Gregor said. "No way to know yet, but we will try to bring the threads together."

"In disguise?" Lacey wondered if she had missed something.

"He is not revealed to you yet," Marie said. "But you have met him. He is close."

"So it is a man?"

"I'm eighty percent certain, cher."

Gregor took Marie's hand and gazed into her eyes. "Of course, my wonderful one, you are right. Lacey has met our person of interest."

"It would be easier with a name," Lacey said. "And if he was at the theatre— There were hundreds of people there last night."

"But you only met ten or twenty," Olga said.

Marie closed her eyes and tried to cover a yawn. "I'm trying, y'all, but information comes when it comes."

That's convenient, Lacey thought. "I have two meetings tomorrow. One with the costume designer Nikolai Sokolov, and one with Maksym Pushkin."

"Both Russians, but who is this Pushkin?" Gregor asked. "Related to the famous Alexander Pushkin?"

"He says not. He played Prince Prospero in that production of *The Masque of the Red Death.* He was the male lead, opposite the actress who died. She played Death."

"He's a dancer?" Olga looked at Lacey intently.

"In the past. Now he's an attorney. Brooke's run up against him in court."

"And what does Brooke think of this guy?" Vic asked.

"That he's a tool of the Evil Empire, and possibly a Russian agent."

"Many of us are *from* the Evil Empire," Gregor said with a grin. "We are not all evil. Counselor Brooke makes me laugh. Tell me more about this Maksym Pushkin."

"He supposedly came to this country when he was a kid. I think he might be sweet on Brooke. She says he's a smooth liar who cheats in court."

"Poor guy. Doesn't stand a chance with her," Vic commented. "But why do *you* need to talk to him?"

"He might remember something from the original show, or something about Saige Russell, the actress who died," she said for Turtledove's sake. "He might know who hated her enough to send her flying off a set. Or he may know something that seemed insignificant then, but that might be interesting now. And he called her Parsnips, her pet name from people who didn't like her."

"And this has something to do with the medals?" Turtledove asked.

"I don't know, but Saige was the first woman to wear the dress. It was made for her. I don't know if the medals were there from the beginning, or they were added later. Or one by one, over time."

"We believe there are other deaths we have not discovered yet," Olga said. "One death for every empty Lenin medal."

"If Amy Keaton was murdered, there is no Lenin for her, because LaToya Crawford bought the dress before Keaton died," Lacey pointed out.

"So we presume the killer wants the dress back to put another medal in it?" Turtledove asked.

"If it's a memorial to the people he killed, then yes," Marie said. "Memorial, or trophy."

Turtledove took a small notebook from his pocket. "I have to jot some things down to keep this straight."

"Right now, we don't know the exact reason for the medals, except they appear to be a tally of seven poison needles that had to have ended up somewhere," Vic said.

"Exactly right," Gregor added. "More important, we are dealing with a monster."

"This is always my favorite part, sweetheart," Vic whispered in her ear. "You and the monster."

She poked him in the ribs. "Really, it's not *my* favorite part."

"This is important," Gregor said, commanding their attention. "We are talking about certain people in Russian intelligence services. They are not like me. KGB is gone, but many intelligence agencies live on. Bigger, harder, smarter, even more dangerous. They recruit, when they can, a certain very special type of person."

"Not like you?" Lacey said.

Gregor smiled. "I am happy-go-lucky fellow, Smithsonian. I have done dark things when my profession demanded, but I have a light soul. Full of love. Honor. Humor. Hope." Marie was smiling at him and she hugged his arm.

"They have no sense of humor, then?"

"Worse than that. They have no souls."

Where did that come from? Lacey looked to Marie for a clue, but Marie was concentrating on Gregor.

"What do you mean?"

"There is no light in their eyes, Smithsonian. No humanity in their hearts. You stare into their eyes and nothing looks back."

"I'm not feeling very secure here, Gregor."

"Another psychopath? Not like the last one, I hope." Turtledove leaned forward tautly, at full attention. His muscles rippled beneath his polo shirt.

"You make it sound like this is a habit," Lacey said. "It's not."

"No, Lacey. It's your mission," Marie said. "Life chooses you because of your talents."

"That is one word for them," Gregor said. "Of course not every psychopath is a stone cold killer. Many are smiling politicians."

"We've all met a few." Turtledove turned to Lacey and winked. "Some of us have stabbed a few."

"Tell them, Gregor, "Marie said.

"Very well. Olga and Marie and I believe we know who this person is."

THIRTY-THREE

"WHO IS IT?! AND WHY? And how do you know this?" Lacey was suddenly standing up and shouting.

"*Who* is complicated. And *why* is question of the ages," Gregor Kepelov replied calmly. "I only have an old codename for this person. I believe we are dealing with a legendary operative. Legendary in a very quiet way."

"Wait a minute, Kepelov," Vic said. "A spy? Or not a spy?" He stood up too, to stand by Lacey. But Lacey couldn't stand still. She was pacing the room.

"Are you telling me," she asked Gregor, "that this *someone* is not only connected to Kinetic somehow, but he or she might also be a Russian agent?"

"Everything points to this. And I fear this person has our Lacey Smithsonian in his sights. This of course is no surprise. But this is an amazing opportunity. You have drawn him out."

"And how do you know this?"

"The existence of this person is spoken of in select circles. You have heard of the Russian businessman beaten to death in his Washington hotel room?"

"Brooke mentioned it. And a few others. First reported as a heart attack."

"Brought on by a severe beating and head trauma. Seems to be going around." Gregor inclined his head. "Your charming attorney friend is crazy, but often right."

"Brooke sees connections we don't see," Marie said. "Not with the psychic eye, but with her mind, and her sense of right and wrong."

"She does that, all right," Lacey agreed. "Does this monster have a name?"

"Many names. Many faces," Olga said.

"He is a man of a thousand faces, cher," Marie added.

The psychic had described faces changing continually, morphing into another and another and another. "He's what you saw? A master of disguise?"

"That's what I saw, cher," Marie said. "He is connected to the dress, and to Gregor, because he is a former spy, and now to you, because— Well. More champagne, anyone?"

It was definitely time for more champagne, even though this was hardly a celebration.

"Sure." Lacey lifted the bottle.

"Yes, please, more champagne, Lacey." Olga put out her glass.

"How do you know this man, Gregor?" Lacey asked.

"I know *of* him. Brilliant Russian operative, almost mythical. Some people think he was made up, just a story, or a composite of many agents. He was suspected in many deaths. Disappeared long ago. Or perhaps in very deep cover."

"But it's a man?" Lacey said. *Volkov? Sokolov? Pushkin? Cameron?*

"So far as we know. Remember the different faces. Male, female."

DeeDee Adler? Katya Pritchard?

"Most were men, some were women," Marie said. "Whether they were him or her in disguise, or victims, I don't know. They sped by so quickly."

"Until he is caught and his true face is revealed," Gregor said, "he is a man of a thousand faces. In Moscow a name I heard him called most often was 'the Centipede.' Killer, spy, assassin, cold-blooded son of a bitch. But very successful."

"The Centipede?" Lacey pondered that image.

"One drawback to our theory, Smithsonian," he continued, "is that the Centipede is dead."

There was a silence. Lacey stopped pacing. "Dead? That is a drawback," she said.

"Perhaps not to the Centipede. Everyone Olga and I know who knows of the name 'the Centipede,' they say to us in the next breath, 'But the Centipede is dead!' But who is to say? He disappeared long ago, became apparently inactive, perhaps in very deep cover, perhaps awaiting activation, perhaps imprisoned, perhaps dead. Everyone who knows of him says he is dead. But to become 'dead' might have been a clever career move for the Centipede."

"A centipede is swift, poisonous, and carnivorous," Turtledove said. "Sounds like an interesting character."

"If this character is alive and caught, he'd just be deported," Vic said. "Or traded."

"Unclear," Gregor said. "Depends on many things. If he even wants to survive. He may not want to return to Mother Russia and Papa Putin."

"If he wants to survive?" Lacey said. "After being already dead?"

"He may not want to live in captivity. He must have more needles, at least one he keeps for himself," Olga said. "If cornered."

"He'd kill himself?"

"A matter of policy, if not honor," Gregor said.

"If it keeps him away from Lacey, I'm all for it." Vic pulled Lacey into his arms.

Gregor demonstrated with a chicken wing. "Understand what the Centipede is like. He is a man who snaps a neck as easily as a chicken bone." *Snap.* "The KGB sought him and others like him as children. Other Russian agencies do the same now as well. The chosen children have no fear and no conscience, so they are easily trained to kill. Smithsonian, because you are tenderhearted, you must not fall for his tricks. He is a thing without a soul, not a man. No soul. No guilt. He was selected for this life as a child because he had no light inside of him."

"No light," Marie repeated.

"If he has no feelings," Lacey said, "what does he want?"

"We believe he has no attachment to *humans*," Gregor replied. "But to things, objects, places, habits, who knows? This costume means something to him. And of course he has feelings. Not for others. For himself, for his power, for his accomplishments."

"Proud of his work?" Vic said.

"Yes. The Centipede is very professional. A true psychopath. And enjoys demonstrating his power, his mastery."

"Why am I not feeling reassured?" Lacey asked.

Olga lifted her glass and contemplated it. "These men can be very charming. They do anything to reach their objective. I may have dated some of them."

Lacey stared at Olga in her monochromatic gray slacks and blouse, her severe straight haircut. Her crazy, penetrating eyes. Olga had hidden depths. Lacey didn't know what was more alarming: The thought of all the psychos out there. Or Olga Kepelova dating them. *Or Olga dating anyone.*

"Smithsonian, this is not just any spy," Gregor cut in. He said it as if Lacey had been dealing with a lot of run-of-the-mill spies. "Operatives, they are mostly ordinary people. They have goals, objectives, follow orders. The Centipede's goal is a mystery."

"I know how much you care about your work, darling. But would you consider dropping this story?" Vic reached for her hand. "I don't ask this lightly."

"I'm not sure I can, Vic." Lacey had been thinking that very thing. "Not as long as the dress is out there. If this person broke into LaToya's looking for the costume, and took the time to send a creepy message, he or she is pretty dedicated to the hunt. I could put it on the front page of *The Eye*. 'Call it off, I'm not looking for anyone anymore!' And it probably wouldn't matter."

"Maybe LaToya could give the dress back," Marie suggested. "If she knew how dangerous it might be."

"I tried pushing her to do that. No good. I could push harder, but she'd just dig in her heels. And I don't want to tell her anything that could put her in danger." Another thought occurred to her. "If the Centipede was in LaToya's condo looking for the dress, he didn't find it—and yet he didn't harm her. It all happened while she was right there, asleep. So maybe she's safe from him now? Because he knows for sure she doesn't have it? I don't want to upset the balance."

"Interesting." Olga freshened Marie's glass of champagne, and her own. "This is one good thing. We know he doesn't kill *everybody* in his path. She did not get in his way. There was no need. Shows he is a practical killer."

"But *we* have the dress, Lacey," Turtledove pointed out. "What if you gave it back yourself, medals and all? Sew 'em back in. Tell LaToya the truth, that you just couldn't make it safe from the bad juju it's got. So it had to go back."

Gregor shook his head vigorously. "For Smithsonian to hand the dress back herself would be to tip her hand. With her reputation, the Centipede, wherever he is, would know she has found its secrets. He would assume a trap. Our Smithsonian would never be safe again."

"If this monster has no feelings, at least not for other people, why does he want the dress back?" Lacey asked.

"Perhaps a loose end," Gregor offered. "Tying up loose threads. So to speak."

Lacey whispered to Vic, "You are staying with me tonight, right?"

He wrapped his arms around her. "With a shapeshifting boogeyman out there? Yeah, I'm staying."

"That's a relief. But listen, if metamorphosis is his genius— a thousand faces and all that—how will we know who it is?"

"Excellent question," Gregor said. "For that, I think you must rely on your special talents."

I'm screwed.

"Okay. Let's say these disguises and the theatre are tied together. However, the people I've met at Kinetic all have jobs, busy jobs." Lacey couldn't imagine how they'd have time for the skullduggery Kepelov suggested.

"Oh, please," Olga said with a wave of her hand. "All operatives have convincing covers and careers. The theatre is perfect cover."

How Brooke would have loved this party, caviar and all. "He's been hiding here in D.C. in plain sight all these years?"

"Why not?" Gregor answered. "The theatre is a safe haven for all his tricks of disguise. Perhaps it has given him a home, an identity."

Kepelov had a point. Whoever had sewn the medals in the hem of the dress had been free to come and go at Kinetic.

"That could be a lot of people," Lacey pointed out. "Over the past twelve years that might be hundreds! Actors, dancers, designers, directors, tech people, stage managers, wardrobe assistants, friends and family, even interns."

"Who knows? Or someone less obvious."

"Even a playwright?" she asked. Everyone laughed.

"You met a few of the regulars, Gregor," Vic said. "And you were eavesdropping on all those Russian conversations, right? Any suspects?"

Olga laughed suddenly. "Gregor suspects everyone. That's why he is counting on you to draw the Centipede out of the mud."

"So you didn't overhear anything that would give us a lead?"

Gregor looked glum. "Nothing. They spoke about the theatre, Russian dancers, Kinetic. Where they would go to drink later."

"They knew you were Russian?"

"I look Russian. To the trained eye. And like all Russians, they were suspicious."

Vic rubbed his face. "You said we've got a plan."

"Go ahead, Gregor," Lacey said. "Against my better judgment, I want to hear the plan."

"Gregor sugar, everyone is tired." Marie countered with a yawn.

"And we are running out of champagne." Olga emptied the last of the bottle into her glass.

"Fine, fine. We have a plan. Here is what we do," Gregor said. "Anytime Smithsonian is with anyone from Kinetic—"

"And we mean *anyone*," Olga said. "At any time."

"Thank you, Olga. As I was saying, Smithsonian, when you are with anyone from Kinetic Theatre, even the janitor, you contact us. We listen in, and we arrive as back up."

"Just like the cavalry in a Western?"

Gregor looked pleased. He loved Westerns. "Yes, like that."

"You want me to wear a wire?"

"Nobody actually wears a 'wire' anymore. Not with digital technology," Olga said. "Wireless remote microphone. Everything is wireless."

"Sorry, sweetheart. That's only on TV," Vic said.

"Disappointing." It was funny how deflated that made her feel. "How are we going to do it then?"

"A phone. We can turn it on remotely," Vic said. "Anytime, anyplace." He handed her a new phone.

"Okay. D.C. has one-party consent, so it's legal to record a conversation in the District if I'm a party to the conversation," Lacey said.

"This is not necessarily for recording, it's just for listening," Vic said. "And when it comes to saving your life, sweetheart, I don't give a rat's ass about legality. Besides, we'll have your permission."

"You are dealing with a Russian mole. Assassin," Kepelov said. "If necessary we would dispose of him. It would never get to court."

"I feel so much better now. Sarcasm." She turned to Vic. "You said you could turn this phone on remotely. Any time? Any place? At will? I'm not really comfortable with that."

"Darling, no one is spying on you."

"Except perhaps the Centipede," Olga chimed in.

"Here's the deal, Lacey. You let me know when you're heading into the lion's den and I turn it on. It's for your safety."

"Good. Everything is settled," Gregor said. "Everyone is happy now."

"I wouldn't put it that way," Lacey said. "How is this a plan?"

"She wants a *real* weapon. I applaud you, Smithsonian!" Olga was sounding a little tipsy. "There are probably real weapons at hand in a Russian theatre. Perhaps a sword. You would like that better?"

"No swords! Let me get this straight. The first plan is to throw me into the lion's den, while you listen to the lion growl at me, wherein the lion—"

"The Centipede," Gregor corrected.

"The Centipede admits he killed Amy Keaton, or sewed hollow Lenin medals into the hem of the ruby red dress. Or both. Then all of you will arrive like Theodore Roosevelt with the cavalry."

"Not all of us. Victor Donovan, Forrest Thunderbird, or myself."

"One of us, or all of us," Vic said. "I'll be right there behind you."

"Not me, cher. Sorry. I'm no good at this stuff." Marie wasn't made for physical altercations. There was always the chance she might faint.

"Wait. Wait a minute. You are not including me?" Olga complained to Gregor. "I am a better marksman that you, baby brother."

"Debatable point. However, we do not need a sniper, Olga," he said. She started to protest.

"Sniper?! Quiet. Please." Lacey stood up and held up her hands for silence.

Gregor spoke more softly. "Lacey. A contingency plan is also necessary if Smithsonian, in typical Smithsonian style, finds herself in trouble before cowboys and cavalry can arrive." He looked around for his battered leather briefcase. Marie handed it to him.

"And what is the contingency plan?" Lacey hoped it would be good.

Gregor pulled out a small spray bottle, of clear plastic, about three inches tall. It looked like a travel-size bottle of hairspray. He held it high for dramatic effect.

"This is our contingency plan. Let me caution you, is very volatile."

"That's it? Your contingency plan is that tiny bottle? What's in it?"

"Oh, I don't think you want to know, Lacey," Marie said.

"I think I do. Gregor?"

"The formula is proprietary," he said. "A very powerful self-defense weapon. Will drop a charging bull elephant in his tracks. But the effect does not last long. When used like this, perhaps only a few minutes."

"He wouldn't tell me either," Vic said. "Be careful with that stuff."

"Don't be curious like the cat with no lives left. Don't even think of smelling this," Gregor cautioned, still holding the spray bottle. "One sniff and you wind up on the floor."

"On the floor?" Lacey narrowed her eyes, remembering the first time she encountered Kepelov. She didn't actually remember much of it. "Like before? In France? Is this the same stuff you used on me?" Gregor opened his mouth to speak, but she cut him off. "You know what I'm talking about. You called it your Super-Secret Soviet Knockout Solution. The secret stuff you dosed me with. The farmhouse in France. Remember how we met?"

"You make everything so dramatic, Smithsonian," Gregor grumbled. "That time when we first met in France was not so dramatic. I don't know why you go on about that. It was a little moment in time. We were competitors, rivals. We had not yet been introduced. I did not know you. I could have harmed you, but I did not."

"So it was okay to just render me unconscious with your secret knockout juice? Leave me face down in the cobwebs in a filthy basement?"

When Lacey came to, there was a drunken cancan line high-kicking behind her eyes and around her temples and performing somersaults on the top of her head. The terrible taste the stuff left in her mouth lingered for a day.

LaToya complained of a terrible headache the morning after her break-in. Same stuff?

Lacey realized she was still angry. She'd never quite forgiven Gregor Kepelov, though they'd become friends.

"Cher. I believe Gregor is trying to apologize," Marie said. "In his own way."

"You're right, Marie." Lacey realized her glass was empty. Olga grabbed the second bottle of champagne from the fridge and filled their glasses. Lacey fought the urge to douse Kepelov with champagne. And she realized she was breaking her Do-Not-Open-Except-in-Case-of-Celebration champagne rule.

But this doesn't feel like a celebration, so that's okay.

"Is that how you met? On that treasure hunt? I didn't know the details," Olga said. "I am very glad there were no ill aftereffects. You never know."

I'm feeling an aftereffect right now.

Gregor Kepelov sighed. "As I have explained many times before, I did not kill you, Lacey Smithsonian. I never would have done so. You came away with no scars and now we are good friends. And I have deep affection for you and respect for your talents. Your EFP." He handed her the spray bottle.

"Can everyone please stop calling it that?" she complained.

"Okay, gang," Vic said. "Let's not fight. Ancient history. Moving on."

Lacey looked at the little bottle. "What, no gun? You made me take your gun that one time, remember?"

"We talked about that, but—"

Olga jumped in. "Normally a good idea, but not when dealing with trained assassin. Too easy to lose control of your weapon. Even this little bottle carries a risk."

Lacey held the clear liquid up to the light. "So now Doctor Kepelov's Secret Sauce is my best friend. How do I use it?"

"Carefully. First," Vic said, "be very sure he's the right guy. The Centipede."

"I don't plan on dropping everyone in my path. Like a charging bull elephant." *But some days it might be just the thing.*

"You don't have to wait till he starts swinging, or throwing something, or gets too close, you know."

"In other words, get him to admit he's the killer and blam?" She sipped some champagne. It was very bubbly.

"You are not taking this seriously, Lacey Smithsonian." Olga helped herself to another glass of champagne.

"She does take it seriously, Olga," Marie said. "This is how she handles it."

"Very well," Olga said. "Make jokes. Just do the job. Bring down the Centipede."

"You must be cautious." Gregor frowned. "If the Centipede gets close, shut your mouth, hold your nose, and spray directly into his face. Make it a direct hit. Run like hell. Oh yes, don't breathe."

"That's the contingency plan?! Hold my nose and run like hell? Are you insane?"

"Insanity has been alleged from time to time. Now, it is better to take him alive, but—"

No doubt there was a reward, she thought. "When you used this stuff on me, it was on a cloth."

"I planned a surprise, I was prepared. And I am bigger than you, more body mass. Also that was older version, is much stronger now. You do not want to get that close to him. This is only a precaution, Smithsonian. If all goes according to plan, you will have no need to use it."

She grabbed a plastic zip bag from the kitchen to store it in. Lacey looked at Vic and held his glance.

"Do you think this is a good plan?"

"I don't plan to let you get that close to this guy. But I don't want to take any chances." He handed her a small package in clear plastic.

"Paper respirators? Whoa, I'm feeling better already." She pulled one out. "Very chic. I'll wear this at our next masked ball."

"If the worst happens, darling, and you have to use that stuff, and I hope you don't, one of these should buy you some time to get away. This is a basic N95 respirator, painters and furniture refinishers use them. It filters out liquid and airborne particles. You press the metal part around the nose and snug the bottom around your cute little chin. There's an elastic strap. I chose these because a big respirator would be hard to conceal. I bought extras, so you can practice putting them on. Sweetheart, don't let him get close."

"Ah. Personal protective equipment. Good idea," Gregor said. "Smithsonian, hold your breath until it is safely on your face. *After* you drop him. The Centipede we have heard of is a slippery creature. Keep the bottle concealed. Be sure nothing else you carry with you can be used against you."

"Lacey, we have your back." Turtledove leaned in close. Sitting down, he was practically as tall as she was. "One of us— or all of us—will be right outside the door. Wherever you are."

"What if he doesn't make a move or reveal himself," Lacey asked. "What if he isn't someone I've already met, and what if he isn't there?"

What if we've made him up?

"Then back to drawing board," Gregor said with a smile.

Lacey collapsed on the sofa and pulled Vic down with her. "So after I drop this Centipede like a bull elephant, then we call the police?"

"No police," Gregor said.

"If this is really the Centipede, we'll be contacting other authorities," Vic said. "Federal. Then international. Kepelov has contacts."

"Just how sure are you that this guy is the so-called Centipede? Who's supposedly dead?" Lacey's voice was ice.

"Seven Lenins worth," Gregor said. "Seven empty Lenins. Two women are dead. A Russian businessman is dead. Many other Russian agents, diplomats, operatives. Someone put those medals in that dress."

Olga sat down next to Lacey and refilled her glass. "It will turn out all right. You will see. Do not worry. You are the only one who can unmask the Centipede. Have some more champagne."

THIRTY-FOUR

*O*N FRIDAY MORNING Detective Broadway Lamont scanned the newsroom like a hunted man, which of course he was. Hunted by LaToya Crawford. He looked both ways and glanced over his shoulder before charging down the aisle toward Lacey's cubicle. It wasn't often the big detective looked less than totally in charge, and Lacey was enjoying it.

"LaToya isn't here, Broadway."

"I'm not looking for LaToya. I'm looking for you." He couldn't help looking over his shoulder again, though.

"You found me." Lacey glanced at Felicity's desk. The food editor wasn't there, but she'd left *blinis*, thin Russian pancakes, for the day's treat. Apparently, *The Turn of the Screw* had inspired her to try something Russian. The blinis were accompanied by bowls of sour cream and various jams with silver spoons. Felicity had also thoughtfully left plates and forks, to reel in more innocent victims. Broadway followed Lacey's gaze.

"Don't mind if I do."

He stepped across the aisle, picked up a plate and made a selection. His attitude generally improved after intake of Felicity's sweet treats. She didn't know what was up, but she wanted Broadway happily fed before he unloaded it on her.

"Coffee?" she asked. "I'm getting myself some."

"That swill you serve here? Fine." He nodded while he bit into the blinis. "Not bad. Ms. Felicity can surely cook. What are these things, Smithsonian?"

"Blinis. They're Russian. She's engaged, you know."

"Shame. She generally stays out of trouble too, unlike the rest of you."

"Generally. But there was that one time when you thought she nailed our copyeditor in the head with a giant candy cane."

Lamont waved a blini in one big hand, as if that could happen to anybody.

Lacey slipped down the hall to the staff kitchen with a couple of her specially ordered Fashion *BITES* mugs. The coffee smelled bitter. Perhaps *The Eye* was buying cheaper beans, or maybe it was just scorched. Whatever the reason, this brew was bound to be bracing.

She filled two mugs and ventured a sip from one, wrinkling her nose. She managed to return to her desk without spilling any or fainting from the aroma. The big detective was sitting in the Death Chair with his pancake snack. She handed him the pink mug. He frowned at the color but he took it.

Swill in a pink mug is still swill.

"What you got on that red dress?" he asked.

"Not much. What do you have on the break-in?"

"Not much. It's unique. No one else is going round emptying closets and playing with the clothes."

"Sending a message to LaToya alone?"

"I wouldn't say that just yet. However, this thing's got fashion weirdness all over it. And you and LaToya are smack dab in the middle of it." He waved his fork with a piece of the pancake. "Man, I wish she hadn't bought that dress."

That makes two of us. "LaToya is getting to you, isn't she?"

Broadway fixed her with an evil eye. "That woman. She— I— I mean, I can't say I don't think she's one— But—" The intimidating detective was at a loss for words.

"She likes you, Broadway."

"Hell, I like her. But she's always all up in my grill. And she's a reporter. Kind of a conflict. I'm a cop. In the District. Homicide, major crimes, bad hours. And people hate cops. That's no life for— Well, it takes a toll on loved ones, let us say."

"Loved ones?" Lacey tried hard not to look too interested. She failed.

"Don't jump to conclusions, Smithsonian. I ain't here to talk about me and LaToya Crawford. We got to close this thing down."

"Which thing?"

"This dress thing. So we can put LaToya's mind at rest and get back to normal. That woman is relentless. She's got to leave me alone. But she won't, because she says she doesn't feel safe. Hell, nobody feels safe."

"And you?"

"I wish I was safe from insane fashion crimes. Before I met you—" He graced her with an especially fierce glare. "Oh, never mind. So, what do you got, Smithsonian?" The big detective sat up in the Death Chair and brought his fists down on her desk.

"Honestly, Lamont, I've got nothing right now. Nothing solid." *Like hell I don't. I have seven Lenin medals. And a codename for a dead spy.*

"Nothing solid, you say, so you got *something.* Maybe you can't put your finger on it. And the vibes. The fashion voodoo you do. What do they tell you?"

She had to give him credit. He actually believed she had a special kind of insight into clothes. In spite of his rough, gruff, blow-your-house-down style of interrogation, he was a good cop. He deserved an answer.

"If I said there might be international ramifications, and I am not saying there are, what then?"

"International ramifications? What the hell? What country are we talking here?"

She busied herself with straightening her desk. "I don't know. Wild guess, let's say, oh, maybe Russia."

"Oh man. Russia. The same scummy Russkies who screwed up the elections?"

"There's Russians and then there's Russians. I don't know if they're the same ones. I have no proof."

"Just to be clear. Russians are the ones who wear the funny fur hats?"

"Lots of fur and snow, caviar and vodka."

"Well, all right!" Broadway brightened visibly. "Russians would be way the hell out of my purview. Jurisdiction in D.C. is a multilayered blessing, as you know. Sounds like this damn red dress mess might just belong to some other agency. FBI, CIA, ICE, Homeland Security, whoever." He took another bite of Felicity's pancakes, licking his lips. "It don't solve the LaToya situation for me though." His frown was back. "She wants the perp locked up so she can go spit at him. Locked up by *me.*"

Circling back to LaToya again. He IS attracted to her. Typical man. Typical D.C. Hand him a potential for real intimacy with a woman and he panics like a little boy. Lacey wondered how long it would take for LaToya to reel him in. She hoped it was soon. The tension was getting to her too.

"Why don't you check out the new show at Kinetic Theatre?" she suggested.

"Oh yeah? Why?"

"Practically everyone here has seen it. Except LaToya. Lots of Russian dancers, very physical version of *The Turn of the Screw*."

"Damn. *Turn of the Screw*? I had to read that thing in school. About killed me." He grimaced. "And more Russkies? You gotta be kidding me."

"LaToya would love it. You could take her. I'm sure she'd clear her schedule for you."

The grimace turned into a scowl. "You ain't funny, Smithsonian. And I ain't getting involved with any Russians and tempting fate. Not if it's not my case."

"You know Gregor Kepelov."

"Yeah, well, I'm not going to watch him or anyone else jump around on stage. My name might be Broadway, but I don't sing and I don't dance. I don't do theatre."

"I've heard that one before. Come on, Broadway. Give LaToya a chance. Take a chance on romance. You might enjoy it."

"That's what I'm afraid of, and I ain't afraid of anything." He finished the last of his blinis, tossed the plate and fork in a trash can, and hefted himself out of the chair. He pointed a finger at her before leaving. "Keep me apprised of the situation, Smithsonian. Call me."

Lacey watched the big detective as he strode urgently down the hall, looking around like a man fleeing a tiger.

As for her story, Broadway and everyone else could read about it when it hit the front page, or the LifeStyle section, depending on how the story played out. As Lamont disappeared from sight, she called Todd Hansen and asked if he still had any photos from last Saturday's theatre sale.

Hansen arrived shortly with a memory card. He'd taken hundreds of frames, he said, and this was easier than trying to decide which ones she might be interested in. He folded his tall frame into the same Mariah Death Chair just warmed by Detective Lamont, leaned his head on the wooden back, and closed his eyes. Lacey popped the card into her computer.

"What are you looking for?" he asked, his eyes still closed.

"I don't know."

He opened his eyes and squinted at her. "That's always helpful."

"If I was looking for something specific, I might not see the other thing."

"The other thing?"

"The surprise," Lacey said. "The unexpected. Could be something in the background or the foreground. Something that I'm not expecting."

"Oh, right. The clue." He smirked.

"Yeah, wise guy, the clue. Or not."

Scrolling through the photos, she was dismayed at the multitude of them. Hansen was thorough. He'd made the rounds of the entire event and shot almost all of it. Lacey clicked rapidly through frame after frame: stacks of props, mounds of stage furniture, makeshift counters with costumes, wigs, makeup, hats, and more. She slowed down when the clothing racks appeared. There were perhaps fifteen or twenty photos with various people rummaging through the costumes hanging there. She didn't see the dress.

"That's funny. Maybe someone was looking at it, trying it on. Or was this after LaToya bought the dress?"

"No. This is before you were there. I came back again later," Hansen said. "When I saw you and Tamsin. Have lens, will travel. What are you working on, Lacey? I thought you already wrote the story with the Mad Hatter photos."

"I did. This is the yard sale that keeps on giving. I want to see the costume that LaToya bought. The red dress." She turned back to the screen and scrolled through more photos. Everything seemed to go by in a blur.

"I heard she had a fight with someone over it. Hey." He pointed. The red dress suddenly came into focus. "That's the one you're talking about? I am so sorry I missed the drama. Can't be everywhere at the same time."

She kept her eye on the screen and, sure enough, Hansen doubled back to the racks of clothes, as he said. Lacey was surprised to see not just the dress, but herself in several of the shots.

She cocked her head at Hansen. "You just can't help yourself, can you?"

"You're always looking good. And you never can tell when Smithsonian will bring down some nefarious fashion criminal. Good times." He gave her two thumbs up.

"I'm appalled."

"You wouldn't want me to miss those special moments, would you? Moments that wind up on the front page? Now that's teamwork."

He was enjoying himself. Hansen's eagle eye wouldn't have been so bad, she thought, if he hadn't caught Smithsonian so often in embarrassing circumstances, usually on the floor in an undignified position. True, she had taken down a killer or two, and he had it caught on film. Still, it was embarrassing. And her mother always saw those photos.

"Hope you're not disappointed that I didn't do anything embarrassing," she said.

"Never disappointed." He reached for his coffee. Something caught his eye and he pointed to Lacey's screen. "Look, there's LaToya eyeing that dress."

Lacey compared it to the first photos Hansen had taken of the costume racks. "And this is before we came on the scene. Nothing."

Even more interesting to Lacey was that Amy Keaton was on the edge of the frame in the first photos, the ones not graced with Death's Red Dress, apparently greeting people, showing them costumes.

"They're time-stamped," Hansen said. "Check it out. Ten minutes apart."

Ten minutes between the first photos of that rack and the later ones. Ten minutes during which Hanson strolled around the grounds of the sale. Ten minutes until he circled back to confer with Tamsin and take more photos. Ten minutes in which someone added the ruby red frock to the rack. Lacey held her breath.

She blinked. In the later photos, the dress in all its blood-red glory was hanging there and Lacey and LaToya were staring at it. Another photo featured LaToya lifting the dress for a better look.

It was clear: Someone deliberately added the scarlet frock to the rack *after* the compulsively meticulous Amy Keaton had stopped monitoring the dress sale, presumably to go handle something else. Why? To get rid of it on purpose? Without Amy stopping the sale? To send Amy into a tizzy?

Lacey zoomed in on the photo to see whether she could identify the people in the background. Hansen lifted himself out of the chair and peered over her shoulder.

"You know, photography is not like in the movies. Blowing up the photograph doesn't make things clearer," he said. "Much to my chagrin."

"Not like the movies. Isn't that always the way?" Enlarged, the figures became grainy and blurry. Lacey downloaded the series of photos from the rack, as well as all the ones with the red dress and herself and LaToya. She gave Hansen his memory card back. "Thanks, Hansen."

"What now?"

"Gotta go. I have an interview."

Lacey stood and straightened her clothes. She had worn a fitted black-knit top with short sleeves and a full cotton skirt, red roses on a black background. It had deep pockets, one where she concealed Vic's burner phone. The other contained Kepelov's knockout juice. Her red wedges were comfortable enough to run in, if necessary, and a sleek red shoulder bag held her notebook, wallet, regular cell phone, and essential makeup. If she needed a pair of scissors to stab someone in self-defense, she would simply have to improvise.

03

Walking up Sixteenth Street to the theatre, Lacey used her regular phone to call Vic. She could have taken a cab, but she needed the exercise to calm her nerves. She felt ridiculous playing Spy vs. Spy. Besides, it was much too hot for trench coats.

"You're on your way now?" he asked.

"Yes, your phone's in my pocket. Do you know how hard it is to find something to wear with pockets deep enough so it's not noticeable?"

"Those are the breaks, sweetheart. With your endless wardrobe, I'm sure you're up to the task."

"It's not endless."

"Ha. You have Gregor's secret sauce?"

"In my other pocket."

"Good. Don't worry, Turtledove will be nearby."

"I hope he'll be bored. Not too bored."

"I don't care whether he's bored, as long as you are safe."

"Love you too."

They signed off. The heat was rising.

THIRTY-FIVE

"*T*EN O'CLOCK, YOU are prompt. How refreshing," Nicky Sokolov said with a smile, as he unlocked the theatre's front door for Lacey.

"Deadlines," she replied. "I like being punctual." Cool theatre air hit her warm skin. She shivered.

"Are you cold?"

"Not really. It feels good to be out of the sun. I'll acclimate."

Nicky Sokolov looked trim and dramatic in black jeans and a tailored black shirt. For many people in the theatre, black was a uniform, a blank canvas to build a performance upon. His sleeves were folded up, and his forearms were surprisingly muscular and defined. "Coffee?"

"I'd love some. What would D.C. do without coffee?"

"I shudder to think."

Lacey watched him pour two cups from the same pot. He handed her a black mug with the Kinetic logo in white.

"Here you go. Tell me if you need anything in it."

"Black is fine." She took a sip and closed her eyes to enjoy it and inhale the aroma. It was surprisingly good, strong but not bitter. "It's delicious."

"From my private stock of beans. So glad you approve."

"*The Eye Street Observer* must supply bitter beans as a punishment."

He smiled in response. "Maybe to strengthen its reporters."

Sounds like a Russian interpretation. "Then we should be the strongest reporters in Washington."

Sokolov nodded in agreement and tilted his head toward the stairs. He led the way through the first floor lobby to the side stairway to the second floor.

They arrived in the upstairs lobby, a pleasant central area between the double doors to the half balcony overlooking the stage and the light booth on one side. Opposite the theatre balcony, sliding glass doors led to the offices and the costume shop, which overlooked the street. A compact bar was set up on the side wall next to the tiny restrooms. The taupe-and-white color scheme provided a quiet backdrop for theatre crowds and the occasional art installation.

Lacey was greeted by costumed mannequins set all around the lobby space, outfitted in selections from some of Kinetic's notable shows. The mannequins came in a variety of colors, white, pink, blue, and black, and in different dimensions to fit the costumes. They were costumed, bewigged and accessorized, but the faces were blank, to show the costumes to their best advantage. The viewer's imagination filled in the details. It was even more theatrical than the creepy little wardrobe tableau at LaToya's place.

"Are these set up all the time?"

"No. Several times a year Kinetic sponsors an exclusive opening night cocktail reception to give our angels, our donors, an inside look, behind the scenes. They pay for much of it, and we like to show it off for them. The costumes, being the most visual items, are the most popular thing to display." Sokolov had a very slight Russian accent, but it was there when he relaxed.

"It's a great idea."

"And for the official premiere of *The Turn of the Screw* tomorrow night, my costume shop will be open too."

The press night production that Lacey had attended was a preview, or a soft opening. Perhaps everyone would be calmer for the official opening, after the glowing reviews came out, she thought. Sokolov seemed less tightly wound than he had been the other night. Perhaps even Gareth Cameron would calm down and stop threatening to kill the leading lady.

"We set up buffet tables in here, we have caterers. The cast serves champagne in costume—carefully, I hope—and they have a meet-and-greet after the show. Let me tell you, it is a lot of work, but these evenings are very popular. And when our generous friends open their pocketbooks, Yuri is most happy."

"And you?"

"I am happy when they don't break anything. They always break something. Or spill champagne on a costume."

"This must be your Lady Macbeth." He nodded. Lacey focused on an elaborate ball gown, an explosion of black taffeta and gold lace. "Gorgeous. Will it replace the red dress from *The*

Masque, for some lucky actress to wear to the Helen Hayes awards?"

"I have been thinking about that."

"It's your decision then?"

"Ultimately, yes. No one else here really cares, you know." *Except Amy Keaton*, Lacey thought. He guided her to the center of the lobby. "We have the costume dress from *The Snow Queen* to offer too. Here she is—the Empress of Winter. Would this do?"

The empress costume Nicky pointed to was the focal point of the collection, set on a pedestal in the center of the workroom. The gown's long, sleek silhouette featured dramatic bell sleeves that dipped low and a flaring pointed collar as wide as the shoulders. Its inspiration seemed a mix of medieval, Renaissance, and pure fantasy. The costume shimmered in white and ice blue, in organdy and tulle, glittering with faux crystals. A tall ice-blue-and-white headdress ended in dangling elongated "ice" crystals that would make the actress appear tall and regal. And frightening.

Kinetic Theatre did not specialize in the warm and cuddly. All their shows seemed to have an overtone of gloom, even the fairy tales. And Hans Christian Andersen wasn't exactly a barrel of laughs, Lacey thought.

"This is dazzling. I imagine any woman would love to wear it."

"And some of the men." He grinned. "So you approve?" It was her turn to no. "That is the answer I wanted to hear."

He turned and threw open the glass doors to the costume shop. The hard-wood floors inside were polished and the windows, which looked out over the street, sparkled. The space felt light and airy.

"Welcome to my little kingdom, Lacey Smithsonian."

Sokolov seemed to like using her whole name, the way Gregor and Olga sometimes did. *Must be a Russian thing.*

Lacey turned around and around, taking stock of the workroom. Bolt after bolt of fabric covered one wall, arranged on multiple shelves by colors, from light to dark in every shade. The materials ranged from bleached muslin, used to make the mockups before the actual costumes, to silks and satins and velvets that invited her to touch. Lacey resisted the impulse. Everything was neat and clean, perhaps obsessively so. She stopped to admire the array of fabrics. She could feel Sokolov staring at her.

"Sorry. Fabric has the power to put me in a trance."

"I can see that. Don't worry. It's charming, really."

"Do you mind if I take some photos?" She had her digital camera in her purse. "I could always send our staff photographer over later, if you prefer."

"Not at all. Be my guest."

She snapped a few shots of the displays and the mannequins. "This place is very organized. You are a perfectionist, I take it?"

"I must confess to a tiny compulsion in that direction. I simply like things organized. Really, it's so much easier and faster. I don't waste time hunting for things, nor do my tailors."

"You produce beautiful costumes."

"Yes," he acknowledged. "Most of the work is made here on site."

His large well-used drafting table was perched near the corner next to the front windows. With his chair against the wall, Sokolov had a view of the entire shop, as well as the streetscape with its old-fashioned apartment buildings and pretty brownstones in a variety of colors and styles.

"It's a lovely kingdom, Nicky. I adore the view."

"As do I."

For the next evening's event, easels were set up with large poster boards where fabric samples were attached to sketches of costumes, colored in pencil. These also represented ensembles from some of Kinetic's popular shows and concepts for future shows. The blond wood sewing tables were pushed against the walls, their sewing machines tucked away under covers. Lacey didn't spot any scissors or any other obvious weapons.

So much for there always being scissors.

"This is a wonderful space," she said.

"Thank you. When we moved to this location, I had to redesign everything."

"You did? How was it different?"

"They wanted to shove me in the back in an airless room and put the costumes up here in the light where they would fade. Can you imagine?"

"They don't understand fabric," Lacey said. "It's lucky you do."

"I think so too." He laughed. "The closets are in the back, where the clothing is better preserved."

"Where? I didn't see closets."

"We own the building next door too. It connects through a doorway. That space serves as the closets and the scene shop. It's very handy. I'll show you later."

They settled in near the windows. Sokolov sat at his drafting table and Lacey sat in a chair near him. She didn't mind that her seat was lower than his. If he was comfortable, he'd be a better interview.

"You wanted to ask me questions?" He sipped from his mug.

"It's what I do." She pulled out her notebook and pen. "Let's talk about the process of costuming. How do you begin preparing for a new show?"

"With the script of course, once the play is selected. I sit in on the first cast read-throughs. I look for nuances and listen to the actors deliver their lines, study their interpretation, and ponder how to express all of that in my costumes."

"Who selects the plays?"

"The artistic director picks the plays. Yuri. Mostly. At least he thinks he does. It's important for him to think so."

"And the costumes?"

"I design the costumes, the overall look of the wardrobe and the production. Occasionally I am busy with another project and they job in someone else, but as the resident designer, I do most of the shows. Once I sewed much of it too, but these days I'm less hands-on with the day-to-day sewing. Before I begin to sketch, there are endless discussions about the setting and time period, the look and feel." He paused for some coffee. "With Shakespeare for example, directors always play with the time period, like a signature. Victorian, the Twenties, the Third Reich, the Old West. Or give me a break: the future. Always a big concept."

"You don't like that?"

"Sometimes, but it is a fight, the setting. Every single time we decide on a Shakespeare play."

"Have an example?"

"Elizabethan settings for Elizabethan plays are so passé, Yuri says. Me, I like it, because it is rarely done. Of course

Kinetic is known for our daring Shakespeare productions. Yuri must have it different. Provocative. Far-fetched. Crazy. It must have a point that hits you over the head with a bat. Tell me, why must Richard the Third always be portrayed as a Nazi or a Fascist? Everyone in black and gray. So boring. *The Tempest* must be set on Mars like *Forbidden Planet*, or in New Orleans during Hurricane Katrina. Yes, Yuri wants to set it in the French Quarter next spring. Prospero will be a Doctor John-type voodoo wizard, Caliban his Creole slave. Ariel is a psychic. Miranda is a showgirl."

Sokolov shook his head as Lacey smiled, taking notes.

"And with *Romeo and Juliet*, why does it always have to be set in the Fifties with motorcycle gangs?" he went on. "A mixed-race couple. A same-sex couple. I have no objection, but it is quite the fashion, so it is overdone. Fine, I say to Yuri, why only black and white people? Be brave. Paint the Capulets green and the Montagues purple! That would at least be colorful." He sighed and reached again for his coffee.

"That too would be a statement." Lacey had to stifle a giggle. "Interesting, though. Does Yuri interfere with your work?"

"Of course he does. It's his job. The artistic director is the prince of our little island, the boss. He has a PhD, he has done everything, he can do everything I do, costumes, makeup, music, choreography, set design, more. But I am better at *some* of those things. That is all I am saying, though perhaps you shouldn't put that in your article."

"Perhaps not."

He again sipped his coffee, then waved his cup. "It's all been done. Really, all these concepts make me tired. Trust me. Kinetic Theatre produces classic stories with original music and dance. We don't need another concept. I am always telling Yuri, we don't need this concept, that concept. This is one concept too many. Sometimes two, sometimes three too many. Then it's just concept, concept, concept. You lose the play."

"Are they always so dark? The plays?" she asked. "I mean, your examples all seem to be dark."

"We have presented comedies and they are very popular, but few and far between. Like Chekhov, Bulgakov, Gogol. Perhaps it is our Russian character, you know what I'm saying?"

"A professor once told me the reason Russian novels are so long is because the Russian winters are endless and gray and cold."

He clapped his hands. "Excellent analogy. Perhaps that is what makes us so somber. Winter always comes again. You have studied Russian history?"

"Only a little, in high school. Napoleon said he wasn't defeated by Russia, but by General Winter. I was defeated by Russian history."

"There is a lot of it. Like winter. And winter in Russia is something I don't long to experience again, but perhaps it is in my bones."

"When did you come to America, Nicky?"

He paused. "About fifteen years ago. I was lucky that Yuri had a job waiting for me."

"You're an actor as well. And a dancer?"

He put both hands up. "Only occasionally. A small role with a few lines is my preference. A little cameo turn. Make a plot point, get a laugh, get a tear, get off the stage. Like the Apothecary in *Romeo and Juliet*, my kind of part. But it's instructive to put yourself in the actor's shoes now and again."

"You don't feel the need to take a leading role?"

Now he laughed. "An actor's life is not for me. I am content on the edge of the stage. I am not perhaps as serious as Yuri. Yuri is all theatre, all the time."

"And Yuri decides the parameters of a production, including the setting?"

Sokolov picked an imaginary piece of lint off his sleeve and flicked it into the air. "We have many discussions. I plant my seeds. Often he sees it my way."

"When you design the costumes, time and place are important, as well as the script. What else do you consider?"

"The colors. The texture. The characters. The time of year, summer, winter, fall, or spring. Sometimes a play has more than one season."

"And the fabrics, how do you choose them?"

"So many variables. How will they evoke the characters, whether he or she is rich or poor, rough or smooth, someone from the nobility or the working class. A doctor dresses differently from a lawyer or a teacher. I look for the essence of each character. Because our shows involve dance, I have to think how the materials will move, if they will stretch, how they look under the lights. I have to know how well they hold up and still look good when the curtain falls. And even if a character has no money, I never do the costume cheaply, and that is always an argument with Yuri."

"Your costumes are gorgeous. But aren't they a little heavy to dance in?"

"Here's a secret. Usually, the principals act more than they dance. But yes, I always take the weight of a fabric into consideration."

What about adding weight to a dress to make it hang correctly? For example, sewing Lenin medals in the hem? Or would that tip my hand? Lacey felt the tiny bulge of the spray bottle in her pocket. *Let's hold off on that question.*

"In fact," Sokolov went on, "whether the fabric will clean well is the biggest challenge. The cleaning bills here, they are monstrous. Yuri always complains." He gazed out the window. "Yuri is my cousin, did you know that?"

Lacey tried to keep the surprise out of her expression. The men were of a similar build, but they didn't look alike. "No, he didn't mention it. Then again, I don't know him very well."

"He wouldn't mention it. Families. You understand?" Sokolov seemed amused, as if Yuri Volkov would be annoyed.

Ah yes, families. Lacey thought of her mother and glanced at her beautiful diamond ring. She would have to tell Rose Smithsonian about her engagement soon. The sooner the better. "Yes, I understand about families."

"Beautiful ring you have." He noticed her glance.

"Thank you." Every time she admired the way the diamond was tucked into the gold filigree of the antique setting, it warmed her heart. "It's rather new to me."

"It looks like an heirloom. You are engaged?"

"Yes." She touched it with her finger.

"An engagement ring. It's true." He seemed rueful. "The good ones are always taken."

"That's not true. I'm not available anymore, but I have very beautiful and accomplished friends who have nothing but trouble with men. And it was no picnic for me."

"Perhaps you are right, yet I suspect there is only one Lacey Smithsonian," Sokolov said. "I sense a fascinating story there. The way you consider that ring."

Lacey gave the ring a little polish. "I'm just very different from my family. I haven't told them about the engagement yet. Now you tell me, why wouldn't Yuri mention your family connection?"

"It's Yuri's way, and we are not very alike either. And maybe he doesn't want people to think I get special treatment as family."

"Do you get special treatment?" she inquired.

"Obviously. Because I am excellent at my job and because I demand it. Not because I am related to Yuri. Or maybe just a little."

Sokolov was certainly confident of his place in the Kinetic universe. There was no lack of ego there either, Lacey noted silently. However, humble people rarely made news. *Wait, I'm forgetting Mother Teresa and the Pope.*

"You were telling me about your process," she said. "Do you create the lights and set too?"

"Not the set, not anymore. I used to do the light plot myself. With the costumes I have a lot to do. Now I just oversee lighting and sets with the other designers. And the music and sound design, the choreography, that is another universe entirely."

"You work freelance jobs too?"

"Maybe once a year or so. It creates new challenges to work with other companies. I usually find chaos and then they give me a free hand."

"You've won Helen Hayes awards," she said.

"You do your homework, so you know enough about me. I have a question. Is it true what they say about *you*?" He put his hand on her arm and stared intently. "You have something different, some special sense about clothes."

"It's not anything supernatural, if that's what you mean. Anyone could see what I see if they only looked. Clothes have their own language." Lacey gently took her arm back. "I'm merely amazed that people don't realize what they say with their attire, or they think they say nothing. But every outfit tells a story. And too many people don't want you to see who they are, but their clothes give them away. If only you bother to read them."

He nodded. "I knew this about you. But I have heard people say you have something called EFP. What is that?"

"It's a joke, really."

Sokolov lifted an eyebrow imperiously. "I don't believe that."

Lacey played with her pen. "I have friends who say I have what they call ExtraFashionary Perception. As if it were a psychic thing. It's not. It's a joke."

"Amusing to them, perhaps. But not a joke. You do have a sixth sense. You are a style psychic."

She shook her head. "Not me. I'm not psychic." Marie was psychic, and it seemed Russians loved psychics. Most of the time, Lacey was glad she didn't have those abilities.

"Maybe just a little bit," he said.

"I try to pay attention, that's all." She wanted to get the interview back on track, and off *her.* "Nicky, could you tell me about the production of *The Masque of the Red Death.* I know it was a long time ago."

"Yes, long ago and not so long ago." He jumped off his tall drafting chair. "Tell you what. Do you want to see the closets?"

"Of course." She drained her coffee and stood up. "I'd love to."

"Why are you so interested in the scarlet costume and that production?"

"Because they have a mythology. And because the production has a strange reputation. You can partly take credit."

"You are talking about the actresses, yes?" He gestured for her to go ahead of him through the costume shop back into the upper lobby. He shut the glass doors behind them.

"Yes, how did that start? Your tradition of loaning out the dress?"

"With an actress who had small parts here. Not a great talent, but she was lovely to look at. She used to help out in the costume shop. She told me she had no money, nothing to wear to the awards. Wasn't there one dress in the shop that she could borrow?"

"You took pity on her."

"You could say that. I was tired of hearing her whine. I knew she would show off the dress well and that it would add to its notoriety. You could also say she slept with me. She did, but that had nothing to do with me lending her the dress." He paused and reflected. "She was the only one where that happened. You have my word. Actresses. It is not practical to sleep with such flighty women."

This just took a turn. "Did it bother her that Saige Russell had worn it?"

"At first. But she, and I have forgotten her name—" Lacey was sure this was a lie. "She was the one who decided she could turn her luck around by wearing it. And in a small way, it kept Saige alive for me." He breathed softly, almost sighing.

"The dress took on a life of its own?"

"Perhaps. It became a sort of a tradition for someone to be allowed to wear the Kinetic Theatre's red dress. There are always more than enough actresses who need a spectacular dress to wear."

Lacey remembered what the two actresses who had worn the dress had told her. "Do they have to compete to wear it?"

"No, no. I just choose the woman who I think will wear it the best. The one who would show off the dress to its best advantage. Now, this way."

Sokolov opened another door for her at the far end of the lobby past the balcony doors. They entered a long narrow hallway, at the end of which a tall stained-glass window let in colored sunlight. There were doors lining either side.

"Yet, you don't mind that the red gown was sold?" she asked.

"I wasn't going to wear it," he said with a smile.

"Was this costume different because of Saige Russell?"

Sokolov stopped and leaned against the wall at the end of the hallway.

"Saige is gone now and the dress is gone as well. And I have no more tears to weep. The other actresses transformed her dress. They improved its history." *That's one interpretation.* He straightened up and indicated the door to the right of the stained-glass window. "This is the wardrobe closet. At least the beginning of it."

THIRTY-SIX

"*I*T'S ENORMOUS!" LACEY couldn't see the end of it. Behind that door was a maze of storerooms, closets, cabinets, more doors, mannequins, piles of clothes, fabric, and sketches.

"As I said, we own the townhouse next to the playhouse. The upstairs have been combined. It makes quite a lovely labyrinth."

"You don't rent the space, then?"

"Renting is the kiss of death for a theatre. You have to own your building to survive. Once a neighborhood has a theatre, the playhouse improves everything around it. New shops come in, new restaurants, new people. It becomes more desirable. That's when the developers swoop in, like the vultures they are. They can't wait to throw you out, tear down the theatre, the thing that brought in all the people."

"That's terrible."

"The joy of the theatre. But Kinetic is smarter. We bought the buildings."

"We're in the townhouse now?" Lacey turned around and around, looking at the labyrinth of rooms and doors.

"Yes. There is also a connecting door downstairs, and a few others. Some of the offices are on the first floor, so we can pop in and out. We can thank our donors for helping us buy the two buildings, back when the neighborhood was much cheaper."

Lacey wondered about those donors. Would those be foreign governments, or simply wealthy patrons of the arts?

The "closet" seemed to go on forever, with room after room full of nooks and built-ins that sheltered wardrobe items such as hats and bags. Yet even with all the space, and the hanging rods for dresses and coats and suits and jackets, and shelves for shoes and gloves and other accessories, it was still packed to the walls with clothes.

"You can see why we need to occasionally downsize our collections," Sokolov said.

"It must be hard to keep track of everything."

"It is not easy."

A rainbow of *something* overhead caught Lacey's eye, and she looked up and gasped. At least a hundred silk kimonos were hanging above their heads, exploding in a sumptuous show of shimmering colors.

Sokolov glanced up. "Yes, the kimonos. One of our patrons recently decided this theatre was in desperate need of her collection of silk kimonos. Yuri took them in. You don't say no to big donors. You say thank-you and write them a receipt for their taxes. However, it is not likely that Kinetic will be mounting a production of *The Mikado* anytime soon."

"And you couldn't get rid of them in the sale?"

"If only. What if our very wealthy donor had spotted them there?"

"They are beautiful."

"Perhaps I should consider them an art installation." He smiled at the notion. Or possibly at her. Walking further into the room, Lacey realized this first space was set up in aisles. Sokolov pointed out the contents of each aisle as they passed through them.

"Outerwear. Period underwear. Leotards in bins by sizes, though most of our dancers prefer to wear their own. Sometimes we have to order something special for someone."

"The things you donated to the sale were just a drop in the bucket."

"As you can see."

"*The Masque of the Red Death* was one of your first shows, wasn't it?"

"Yes. Kinetic had done several full seasons before that. But it was *The Masque* where everything finally clicked, if you know what I mean."

"It put Kinetic on the map."

"Exactly," Sokolov said. He turned to face her. "I will make you a deal, Lacey Smithsonian. I will tell you what you want to know and you will tell me how you found the Romanov diamonds. You want to know about *The Masque*? I want to know about the lost corset of the Romanovs."

He sounds like Kepelov. Why does this always have to involve some mind game?

"Okay, it's a deal. A question for a question?"

He winked at her. "Works for me."

"You've already read about the diamonds. There were rubies too."

"Lacey Smithsonian, everybody in Washington has read about you and the diamonds and the rubies. In your reports, however, you did not mention the instinct that brought you, step by step, from America to France, to New Orleans, Louisiana. Your EFP."

"As I say, my alleged powers are way overrated. The truth is I had a friend who was convinced the corset really existed, because of information she'd inherited from her family. Very incomplete information, as it turned out, but it was a start. We were planning a trip to France together. She would hunt for the corset, I would write the story. When she died, I decided to follow her dream, at least for a while. Besides, I'd made her a promise."

"It is good to have such friends. I hope we can be friends."

She smiled at him. Didn't he know reporters were never friends with their sources?

"It was over a year ago when I met Magda Rousseau, a corsetiere here in the District. Through a friend. She told me that theatre costumers have a superstition, that if a costumer pricked a finger and spilled a drop of blood on a costume, it meant she was putting her heart into her work, so her blood would bring good luck for the show. 'Bloody thread, knock 'em dead.' That was one version of it."

"Fascinating. I have never heard of that superstition. But I like it. I was familiar with Magda's work," Sokolov said. "She was very good, very precise, very imaginative. An untimely end, as I recall?"

"She was murdered. Magda was descended from one of the Latvian guards who attended the execution of Czar Nicholas and his family. The Latvians refused to shoot the children, so instead they were ordered to strip the bodies."

He tented his fingers and brought them to his lips. "And like many soldiers, one of them grabbed a bloodstained souvenir. But unlike the other drunken Bolsheviks, they managed to hide their booty."

"Yes. Well, one of them did, with the help of his friend."

Nicky Sokolov picked up a stack of gray and black fedoras and started rearranging them by size.

"And that began the strange odyssey of the diamond-filled corset."

"My turn. Other people have told me you and Saige Russell were in love during the production of *The Masque*."

"That is true." He dusted off a hat and took a moment before answering. "I made her the most elaborate costume I had ever made up to that time."

"Yet the character of Death is not the largest role in the play."

"No, yet perhaps the most important role. A pivotal role." Sokolov leaned against a wall and folded his arms. "I wanted everyone to be impressed by her. To see what I saw."

"There was some jealousy and bad feelings about Saige, I heard."

"You must have talked with Katya." He grimaced at some memory. "The understudy. She thought she should have the role."

"She mentioned that."

"Katya was the better dancer. The part didn't call for the best dancer. Only the most magnetic presence. That was Saige. Ultimately, it was Yuri's decision."

"Influenced by you?"

He inclined his head in acknowledgment. "Perhaps. Tell me, why did you go to France to search for the corset, the diamonds?"

"Magda was convinced they were there. She had part of an old family diary. I didn't want her dream to die with her. I was curious." Lacey gazed at him. "I'd never been to Paris and the tickets were bought. I did think it was probably all a pipe dream. There was no reason to think the corset still existed after all these years. The Russian Revolution was a century ago. But if I went on the hunt with Magda, or with her memory, I'd always have Paris."

"Yes, it was the only thing to do." He seemed impressed, or perhaps merely amused.

"My turn again. So Katya was jealous of Saige. But others had issues with her as well?"

"Ah, now you must be talking about Gareth Cameron? I'm afraid it's true. She could not learn his lines. To be fair, the script was bad. Cameron was very young. She blew most of her lines, most of the time. She couldn't remember her blocking.

She insisted her instincts were better than the director's. She drove Yuri out of his mind. Cameron seemed positively homicidal. You would have thought he was an actor."

"And yet you loved her."

"Love is blind. And foolish."

"Saige died sometime after the last show. Are you sure it was an accident?"

"I was wondering when you'd get to that. It's a reporter's question," Sokolov said. "Saige died that night. It was tragic. A tragic and stupid incident." He closed his eyes briefly. *To shut out the thought? Or to relive it?* "What else could it be but an accident? She was alone in the theatre. Put your mind at rest, Lacey. The mystery is why she returned to the stage after the last show. I will never know that."

Maybe to savor her moment of triumph all by herself?

"One more question, please."

"You are wearing me out," he said, but he didn't seem annoyed.

"Nicky, did you go to the cast party for *The Masque*?"

"Of course. It would have been rude not to go. As it turned out, I was late, because of Saige. She was supposed to meet me right after the show and we would go together. She was changing, and I was making sure all the costumes were accounted for, including the Death costume, so they could be cleaned and stored. We agreed to meet in the lobby. She didn't show up."

"Did you look for her?"

"Of course I did." He closed his eyes and pinched the bridge of his nose. "She wasn't in her dressing room. I checked the balcony. I went into the theatre. The ghost light was on, but no one was there. At least, I didn't see anyone. I called her name. She might have been already dead, lying on the floor beneath the scaffolding, the platforms. It's haunted me all these years."

"What then?"

He took a deep breath. "I thought she had left without me. I went first to her apartment, it was nearby. I thought maybe she wanted a different outfit for the party. She was always changing outfits. I didn't know what to think. No one there. I kept calling her phone. She didn't answer."

"So you went to the party?"

"I thought she might have gone ahead, because I had taken so long."

"She didn't answer her phone?"

"If she was already at the party, I thought it would have been noisy, maybe she didn't hear it. Then I thought she must be mad at me, for some obscure reason, or because we missed connections after the show. She could be temperamental that way."

"And Saige never showed up?" Lacey had wondered whether Saige had never left Kinetic, or if she went to the party and then returned to the theatre.

"To be honest, by the time I got to the party and she wasn't there either, I was a little irritated with her. I had a drink, and then another. Everyone was getting drunk, dancing, celebrating. I figured I would eventually get a sob story from her later, some elaborate excuse. But we found out the next day she was dead." There was pain in his face. "Why do you make me remember all this?"

"I'm sorry." Her instinct was to reach out and comfort him, but she couldn't. Sometimes she had to fight to retain her objectivity. *Reporters don't hug sources,* she reminded herself. *And it could have happened that way.* Sokolov's story sounded logical, internally consistent, even a little polished. *He's had twelve years to polish it.* Lacey would have to find out what the others recollected about that night, if anything. "I didn't mean to upset you."

"You haven't." He stared into her eyes and took her hand. "Really."

She took back her hand. What should she make of Nicky Sokolov? Although Saige was disliked by several others in *The Masque* cast, she sparked something in him. And in the director. It was a romantic gesture to fashion a fabulous costume so she would seem to be a better actress than she was. Wasn't it? A funny thing about death: It could bestow sainthood on the unlikeliest people.

"Saige was very lovely. Not a great actress, but she had a great presence on stage." His thoughts seemed far away. He brought his attention back to Lacey. "It was all so long ago. There are days I have trouble recalling her face. Now tell me, why did you go to New Orleans after Paris?"

"It was one last crazy chance. I found an address written on a slip of paper in France, in the place where Magda thought we'd find the corset. The corset wasn't there, but this one little clue was." *The slip of paper that Kepelov never discovered.* "I thought the address was in Paris, but that number didn't exist. But the French Quarter in New Orleans has some of the same Parisian street names, even the same street intersections. That was where the address was. I'm sure I wrote about all of that in my articles."

"I'll have to read them again."

"Whatever happened to the mask that went with the dress?" she asked. "I've seen pictures of it. It was gorgeous."

"I couldn't say. Despite all my careful planning, many little things went missing when we moved to this location from the old playhouse. It's probably hanging over someone's dressing table somewhere."

"The mask was lost?" She felt deflated without knowing why.

"I told Yuri it was a mistake to rely on volunteers."

"Volunteers moved the whole theatre?"

"Not everything. Not the office furniture and files, but they moved a lot of things, costumes, props, tools. They were so happy to help. But it was chaos."

"You don't like chaos, Nicky, do you?"

"That would be correct. My flaw. My turn. How did you finally figure out where in New Orleans the diamonds were hidden?"

Magda had left a hidden note for Lacey, which told her cryptically to look *between the stitches.* That small fact was not mentioned in her articles in *The Eye,* and she wasn't about to mention it to Sokolov. After all, she'd found the Lenin medals hidden between a different set of stitches.

"Dumb luck," she said.

"I doubt that very much, Lacey Smithsonian. However, if I ever find the missing mask, through dumb luck, you will be the first to know."

"What about Amy Keaton, did you get along with her?"

"Interesting question. I got along with Amy very well. She was efficient, well organized. We weren't buddies. I am not a buddy kind of person."

I can see that. "A friend?"

"Not really. She was a coworker. I didn't know anything about her life."

Lacey wondered if he had any friends, but she didn't ask Sokolov that question. It would have radically changed the tone of the interview. "What did you think when you heard she died?"

"Are you really writing about Amy Keaton? She was not really a fashion subject, was she? Forgive me, but she was more like one of your Crime of Fashion victims."

"I was just curious. She didn't leave much of a footprint."

"It is sad, but the majority of people, my friend Lacey Smithsonian, leave no footprint at all."

THIRTY-SEVEN

"*F*IND OUT ANYTHING?" Mac asked over the phone.

"Nothing that merits breaking out the Maalox," Lacey told him.

"Good to know. Don't get in any trouble."

"Nice talking to you too."

After winding down her interview with Nicky Sokolov and leaving the theatre, Lacey called Mac to advise him she was going in search of lunch before her second interview of the day, the one with Maksym Pushkin. She clicked off and dodged traffic, crossing the busy streets near Dupont Circle, a green oasis inside the double roundabout of careening vehicles.

Lacey spied a free spot on a shady bench by the central fountain, dedicated to Admiral Dupont, and claimed it. It was tempting to stay there and pretend she had all the time in the world. Unfortunately, she had another call to make. Her perch under a towering tree with a view of the lovely beaux arts fountain was as good as anyplace.

"Katya Pritchard," the woman answered. Lacey apologized for disturbing her. "No problem. I'm up to my eyeballs in this boring brief. What's up?"

When Lacey explained she was interested in precisely who had attended the cast party for *The Masque*, Katya just said, "Wow. Really?"

"You don't remember?"

"I think I do, but it was so long ago. The night when someone you know dies, you tend to remember everything you did. And I do, at least until the vodka really started flowing. The party was at this little club, more of a dive, close to the old theatre. Still there. I think it was painted purple back then."

"Did Saige ever show up? I don't know exactly what time the accident happened."

"Does anyone? But no, she never arrived. We all thought Parsnips was just playing diva again, or waiting to make a grand entrance, or maybe having her own private party with Nicky."

It was odd that after all these years, there still seemed to be a wistfulness in her voice when Katya mentioned him. But if Nikolai Sokolov wasn't interested in her then, why would he be now, twelve years on?

"Did Nicky go to the party?" It was always essential to confirm what others told her.

"He did. He was pretty late."

That tallied with what he'd told Lacey. "Who else came late?"

"Well, I was. I took my time getting ready. You know, shower and fresh makeup, fresh outfit. Most of the cast and crew were already there. I think only Maksym and Gareth showed up after I did. Oh and Yuri too."

"Why were they late?"

"Not sure. I think they were filming like a two-minute spot with one of the TV stations in front of the theatre. Local arts beat stuff."

"But Yuri was at the party?"

"He was there, in his glory. It was his night as much as anyone's."

"Was he as intense as ever?"

Katya laughed merrily. "So you've met him! Not as much as usual. The show was a big success. They had a little break before rehearsals for the next show. The pressure was off, for a minute or two."

"What about DeeDee Adler?"

"Who? Oh, was she a techie? I have no idea whether she was there or not."

"Did you have a good time, without Saige?"

"I won't lie, I was glad she wasn't there. We drank and we danced. I even had one dance with Nicky. He seemed a little distracted, with Saige missing in action. They were a couple, you know. Overall, it was really fun, but I paid for it the next day. Since then, I have parted ways with vodka shooters. Take my advice, stay away from them."

"I thought you were Russian."

"Only half. Half of me loves vodka, the other half is puking her guts out at the very thought of it."

Lacey thanked Katya for her time and wrapped up the call. Lacey's stomach growled and she reluctantly gave up her pleasant seat by the fountain. She strolled toward Connecticut Avenue, past street vendors, looking for lunch.

She planned to take a quiet break and let her interview with Sokolov sink in so that she could write her lede. *Well begun is half done!* An old proverb, but useful. Returning to the office would just be a distraction. Mac would want a recap, and Wiedemeyer and Trujillo would try to jump aboard the Good-Ship-Lacey's Big Story.

Whatever that is. This ship may be sinking fast.

The restaurant she stepped into was cool and dark and felt secluded. It was new, with a fresh coat of paint and white tablecloths for the professional lunch crowd. The host picked up a menu and guided Lacey to a table where she had a view of the street.

"Want to share a table?" She lifted her head from the menu to see Turtledove.

"How did you know where I was? Oh, right. The phone." She reached into her skirt pocket and turned it off.

"Just making sure you're safe." He grinned and took the seat opposite her.

"Much appreciated."

In contrast to the sleek, compact Nikolai Sokolov, Turtledove was robust and muscled and had an engaging smile. His pale yellow short-sleeve polo shirt strained over biceps the color of caramel.

"What do you think of that Nicky Sokolov guy?" he asked.

"Not sure yet. An interview is like a dance, or a performance. Everyone wants to give the reporter their side of the story, all glossy and friendly. It takes a while to digest it. Like the theatre."

"You got some good information there, though. About the connected townhouse. But I don't know, Lacey, there was an awful lot of clothes talk." He faux-yawned.

"I warned you."

"A whole *lot* of clothes."

"Costumes. So I can relax now?"

"Maybe. Why do you think he wanted to know about the Romanov diamonds? Does he think you've got a lead on something else, some other jewels?"

"Maybe he thinks I'm a diamond dowser." She wiggled her fingers, showing off her engagement ring. "You know I've got the only diamond I want." Turtledove grinned at her. "My take on Sokolov is that he wanted to establish some rules of the game. Information for information, whether he needed it or not."

"And you established your willingness to talk."

"I wanted information, he apparently wanted to talk. I can't imagine he really cares about the Romanov diamonds. Plus, I didn't tell him any secrets."

"Yeah, but my guess is, Sokolov wants to know how you think."

Lacey shook her head. "That way madness lies. I don't even know how I think."

"He's suspicious about the EFP thing. That could spook someone who tucked hollow medals away in a skirt, thinking no one would ever suspect they were there. He wants to find out if you've found them. Or are capable of finding them."

"No way. How could he even know I have the dress? And hey, I *don't* have the dress, you do!"

Another voice broke in. "Pardon me, ma'am, mind if I take this seat?"

"Vic!" She hadn't expected to see him there. "Aren't I Ms. Popularity?"

He sat down beside her and hugged her. She kissed him passionately, even though public displays of affection were not common in the District of Columbia.

"I'm so glad you're here."

"Where else would I be?" he asked.

A server took their orders. Turtledove chose a healthy salad with grilled salmon. Lacey didn't care for salmon. Despite its healthy reputation, it still tasted like fish to her. She asked for a burger with a side salad, no bun and no fries. Vic ordered a burger with everything and a big old mound of fries. The server winked at Turtledove before slipping away with her order pad.

"So what's your take on this Russian?" Vic asked when she was gone. "Master spy, or just anal retentive theatre genius?"

"You were listening in too?" Lacey asked Vic.

"With your sweet butt at stake, what do you think?"

"I'm not sure it was at stake. Nicky Sokolov? I find it odd that he's so creative and yet so controlling at the same time."

"Forrest, your take?" Vic asked.

"A lot of talk about clothes. The fabric, the feel, the fit, how it wears, what it looks like under the lights."

"I got that too," Vic said. "Fascinating, wasn't it? Forrest, you and I should go fabric shopping together *more often.*" The guys exchanged a look and cracked up. Lacey merely raised her eyebrows.

"Guys, you know this stuff is my job, right? Clothes. Fashion. Crimes of Fashion. Remember?"

"It's the crimes part I'm interested in," Vic said. "I leave the fashion up to you."

"Bottom line, he was flirting with you," Turtledove said.

Lacey snorted. "Blather."

The costume designer might have been flirting, for all she knew, she realized, but since she'd become engaged to Vic, she tended not to notice other men as possibilities. Their orders arrived. Lacey assumed the service was exceptionally efficient because there were two attractive men at the table.

"You came out in one piece and I didn't hear any threats, but I don't like him a lot either." Vic bit into his giant burger.

"One interview down. One to go."

"I take it Pretty Boy Pushkin is still up for this afternoon?"

Lacey snickered. "You're cute when you're jealous, Vic."

"Not jealous," Vic said. "Just paying attention."

"Yes, I'll be seeing Maksym Pushkin. He played Prince Prospero, who was taken down by the Red Death."

"Ironic if, in real life, it was the other way around, with Prospero taking down Death," Turtledove said. "Or at least the lady who played Death."

"It would be. I don't really expect a confession, though. At the moment, I'd just like some basic, truthful information. Brooke thinks Pushkin could be a deep cover Russian operative, trained from childhood to be an agent in place. Normally, I'd let that pass as her usual craziness. Yet, in the current political climate, with serious Russian interference in our government—"

"I agree," Vic said. "This time, Brooke could be on to something. Pushkin works for a Russian law firm, worked at a Russian theatre, he's fluent in English and Russian, and Ukrainian too. He is connected. Deeply connected."

"Ukrainian too? Darling, you've been busy," Lacey said. "I just want to find out who put the medals in the dress and whether they truly represent murders. Pushkin doesn't seem to have much connection to the theatre anymore, not with direct access to the costume shop. Although I've heard he teaches dance there sometimes."

"He could have friends with access," Vic pointed out. "Maybe he's buddies with Sokolov. He could be lying about not being connected. Brooke says he's a liar. Liars lie, always."

"Maybe. I hope he remembers something without knowing it's important."

"That's my favorite fact-finder," Vic said. "Anyway, he was born in Russia. He may not be a spy, but simply surrounded by them."

"I think he's interested in Brooke. Attracted to her. A big old crush."

"Talk about irony," Turtledove said. "He doesn't stand a chance."

"You do have the bottle Kepelov gave you?" Vic asked.

"You mean—" Lacey dropped her voice. "Doctor Kepelov's Super-Secret Soviet Knockout Juice? Yes, my skirt has deep pockets."

"And the masks?"

"Check. And my spy phone. Relax, Vic. I'm meeting Pushkin at the Portrait Gallery. It couldn't be more public."

She couldn't say exactly why she needed the security of a public place with Maksym Pushkin, when at the same time she was happy to crawl around the deep closets of Kinetic Theatre with Nicky Sokolov, without anyone else on the premises.

"I'll be nearby," Turtledove said.

"And listening to my every word." She would have to try to keep the snark to a minimum. Unfortunately, it was way too easy to forget they were listening. "Then I'll go back to the office and you will turn *off* the remote mike, right?"

"Word of honor," he promised. "Just one thing. Is this going to be all about clothes again?"

"I hope so, Turtledove. In my book, clothes chat is preferable to murder and running for my life."

ଓଷ

She stopped after lunch at St. Matthew's Cathedral on Rhode Island Avenue. The day was getting hotter and the cool interior of the church was a relief. She often sought the quietude this cathedral provided, a short walk, but a world away, from the news business. The majestic mosaics decorating the walls were soothing, and the jewel colors in the murals and the pillars burst forth from every corner. She smelled candles and the lingering scent of incense. It was after midday Mass, but several people stayed to pray, or just sat in silence. Tourists gazed silently at the Byzantine murals.

Lacey lit a candle and prayed she would be able to discern the truth in this confusing story. The church was a sanctuary where she didn't expect to see people she knew, but she was amused to see a couple of *Eye Street* reporters sitting in the pews, their eyes closed. Meditation was free to all. *Must be a stressful day.*

Yeah, mine too.

THIRTY-EIGHT

*P*USHKIN WAS RIGHT. The National Portrait Gallery definitely beat a typical coffee shop for their meeting.

Even better, it was public and the summer visitors and school classes were out in force. Lacey was grateful for every pair of loud madras shorts paired with a Day-Glo T-shirt and oversized running shoes.

Despite the throngs of tourists, Maksym Pushkin was easy to spot, tall and attractive in a bespoke suit, looking like a menswear ad. He was standing just inside the museum shop, leafing through a large art book. He looked up and smiled as she entered.

"I hope you don't mind this place," he said. "It's handy for me."

"No, I like it. And I like getting out."

She had no idea what Pushkin would have to say. But the feel of the live phone in her pocket, with Vic and the gang listening in, reassured her. As did the bottle of Kepelov's knockout spray in her other pocket.

Pushkin put the art book down. "Shall we stroll? Or do you want something to drink? Coffee? We could take it out to the courtyard."

"Strolling first. Then something cold. I'm coffee'd out." They passed a wall of Mathew Brady's daguerreotypes. "I would have called you if you hadn't called me first. Why did you want to see me?"

"You have a history of getting into trouble," he said.

He sounds like Vic. "I also have a history of getting *out* of trouble."

"After you invite it in."

Pushkin smiled, but he seemed very serious for a friendly afternoon chat.

"And your point?"

"I'm not saying bad things might happen, but why kick around the dusty ancient history of Kinetic Theatre?"

"You're concerned about a twelve-year-old show?"

"Listen to me, Lacey." He stopped and faced her. "It was a bad-luck production. You can't get more bad luck than the leading lady dying on closing night."

"Unless it was opening night," she countered. "Certainly it couldn't be bad luck now, all these years later. Are you superstitious?"

"Me? A rational attorney?" He examined his manicured nails. "Perhaps. Perhaps superstition is part of being Russian. I'm curious, what do you expect to find in that dress? More diamonds?"

"I'm pretty sure those diamonds were a one-time thing. I didn't get to keep them, you know."

"What then explains your fascination with the Death costume and poor old Parsnips?"

"I'm a reporter. It's a story. A sad one, I admit. That crimson costume has become known as a good-luck, bad-luck talisman. There's a story there."

"Are you planning to draw a connection to Amy Keaton?"

She felt the thrill of anticipation of possibly learning something new. No one else had brought up the unfortunate stage manager unprompted.

"What do you know about Amy, Maksym? Is there a connection to Parsnips?"

"I know nothing about her. I know how you write."

Has he been studying my work? Reading about more than diamonds? And why?

"You find the strangest stories to explore," he continued. "Dangerous stories. And I know that ridiculous website follows you faithfully."

"Did you see something on DeadFed? Something new today?"

"No. Nothing today." Pushkin continued strolling down the hall at her side. "But there's something crazy on it every day. My firm tracks social media for some of our clients, and Conspiracy Clearinghouse is always pushing the most insane nonsense. That conspiracy maniac your friend Brooke is with, Newhouse? Sooner or later he'll tie Amy's death to something other than the accident it was."

"How do you know it was an accident?"

He looked away. "The police say it was."

Pushkin was taking a lot on faith, she thought. Or he found it convenient to say he did, especially if he was a Russian agent who might have knowledge about Amy's death.

"So about Brooke. Is she a maniac too?"

He softened at the name. "Not Brooke. She is very sweet, very fine. Sometimes tough as nails and sometimes a little gullible."

"Sometimes conspiracies are real."

He laughed. "Every once in a while," he admitted, pausing to admire a Mathew Brady portrait on the wall.

"Did you know Amy?"

"No. She started there after I went to law school. I only saw her bustling around, shouting orders, when I went to shows. But even Yuri said she was a good stage manager. He's hard to impress."

"You still go to the theatre, but you gave up dancing?"

"I loved it, but it didn't pay. Except in aches and pains. I always go to their shows, I'm a donor, and I help out from time to time, teaching dance. Those who can't do, teach, remember? And sometimes in the shop."

"Sokolov's costume shop?"

"Sometimes. Moving things around. Sometimes I even help paint the sets. I've always loved the theatre. But as I may have said, life interferes."

Lacey mulled this new information. Maksym had worked in the costume shop. He had access to the dress. He hated Saige. He mentioned Amy without Lacey asking.

"*The Masque*. Tell me about Saige Russell. I heard she wasn't popular."

"No. Not at all. First, she wasn't Russian. Not everyone in the production was, but she didn't work as hard as the rest of us. The Russians worked their asses off. And Gareth too. So neurotic. He was the one who started calling her Parsnips, or maybe it was the techies. But we all did, behind her back. Somehow it made her easier to deal with. I have no idea what Nicky saw in her."

"Gareth said she couldn't learn lines."

"Yeah, she had some kind of dyslexia when it came to memorizing. That is not an asset in the theatre. She could dance competently, but not superbly. Not lighter than air, like Katya."

The Katya Pritchard Lacey had spoken with didn't match that description. It was hard to imagine her as a dancer at all.

"Katya was lighter than air?"

"Believe me, she was lovely." He smiled at the memory.

"You dated?"

"For a while. People said we looked good together. I thought so too."

"She told me she was attracted to Nikolai too, but Saige got there first."

"Isn't that always the case? Perhaps she was lucky she didn't get the part. Look at what happened to Parsnips."

"That's what Katya said." She wondered what he would think if he could see Katya now. "Did you keep in touch with her?"

"No. I've heard she's changed a bit."

A bit? Much more than a bit. Perhaps Saige's death killed a lot of Katya's dreams. Of a life in the theatre. Of Nicky Sokolov. They were silent for a moment.

"Hey, I'm thirsty, Lacey, how about you?"

"Sure."

They picked up cold sodas in the café and entered the majestic Kogod Courtyard at the center of the Portrait Gallery's massive stone building. The space was always a welcome surprise, a retreat, a calm place to sit with a cup of coffee, ice cream, or even lunch. The wavy glass ceiling high above allowed the sun to shine through and kept the rain and snow out.

Lacey sat on the wide edge of a cement planter and Pushkin joined her.

"I don't mean to drag up painful memories," Lacey said when they were settled. "I'm simply trying to write a story about a dress."

"Just the dress? That production is a decade old. Old history, old news."

"Are you warning me away?"

"Is that even possible?" He lifted his soda and drank deeply.

"No. I'm afraid that would only make me more interested." She sipped on her cold root beer.

"Just like your friend Brooke, I guess."

"We're not quite the same."

"I'm going to tell you something, Lacey, and then I will deny I ever said it. This is off the record. This is not for your story. This is for your safety. Your safety. Do you understand?"

She felt her eyes go wide and she took another gulp of root beer. "I do. Off the record." *But I hope Vic and Turtledove are getting all this.* "Go ahead."

"I saw something that night. After the show. Something that has always made me wonder."

"The night Saige died?"

Pushkin nodded. He put his face in his hands. Lacey didn't know if it was an act, but she was listening. That was her fatal flaw, she knew. She always stayed for the last act. She had to know the ending.

Hopefully without becoming part of it.

"What did you see?"

He lifted his eyes and stared at the glass ceiling high above. "After the last performance, I just wanted a moment on stage alone. Don't ask me why. I guess to breathe in the theatre, one more time. I loved it, you see."

"A moment alone?" *The big Washington attorney who had once been a dancer.*

"Without all the others. Without that stupid annoying Parsnips. I stood there in the dark, and I heard something. People talking softly, behind part of the set, the castle. They didn't realize the lights were creating silhouettes. Or they thought they were alone."

"Were they taking that last quiet moment, like you?"

"That's what I thought, at first. It was funny. All the actors taking their last center-stage moment, each thinking they're alone? The ghost light was on behind them. I saw their shadows on the walls. I was waiting for them to leave, so I could have *my* moment. So I retreated into the darkness, where I was sure I couldn't be seen. Then the shadows climbed the stairs to the top of the tallest platform. It was supposed to represent the tower of the castle."

"Saige? Who was with her?"

"I couldn't tell. I didn't know who they were. I was an accidental voyeur."

"What did you see?" Lacey felt a terrible anxiety rise in her chest. She reached into her pocket and touched the spray bottle. "There were definitely two people?"

"Yes, and I heard, um, intimate sounds. Laughter. They were making love, up on the platform. I looked away. I knew even then that it isn't wise to know everything in this town. That what you know can hurt you. I was embarrassed too, and I couldn't leave without making a noise, the stage there was creaky, so I just stood there, listening. It was excruciating. I waited in the dark, waited for them to finish, stop and go away. Then I heard something fall. Something heavy. So loud it made me jump. So loud I knew it wasn't good. After that, there was no noise, no screams. I peeked out. The shadows were gone."

"Saige?" Lacey held her breath.

"I waited a long time before I left my hiding place. At least it seemed like a long time. Maybe only a minute. Until I heard the theatre doors open and close. Until I was sure everyone was gone. Then I crept out of the dark. Saige was lying there on the stage. She was broken, dead."

"An accident?"

"It could have been an accident."

"Do you think she was with Sokolov when she fell?"

"Maybe it was Nicky. And maybe not. I couldn't tell, and Saige was always playing around. There were lots of guys around Saige. Never me, in case you were wondering. I don't know who it was, and I don't really want to know."

"If it was an accident, why didn't the person she was with tell the police?'

"A million reasons. It would cause problems."

"If Saige fell, why didn't she scream?" That bothered Lacey. "Not even a gasp?"

"I don't remember hearing anything but the sound of— Of the impact."

"Why didn't you go to the police?"

"I've wondered that myself. I think I was embarrassed. Confused. Shocked. It was late. I was expected at the cast party."

Yeah, wouldn't want to miss a great party because of a nasty little death.

"That's awful." Lacey must have looked shocked.

"I know. But I thought someone else would report the accident. The person who was there. Whoever it was."

"Unless it was murder." *And maybe she didn't scream because she was already dead when she fell?*

Lacey stood up. Maxim grabbed her arm and held her.

"I don't know! I will deny everything I have just told you. You have no proof of what I've said."

Except for a couple of guys listening in. Lacey said nothing. He let her arm go. There would be a bruise.

"As I said, I don't know exactly what happened. All I know is that Saige Russell wasn't alone when she died. And if it wasn't an accident? People can die from knowing too much in this town."

He let the thought hang in the air.

"Are there Russian agents involved with Kinetic Theatre?" she asked.

He looked startled. "What? Is that what Brooke says?"

"I'm asking you."

"It would be ridiculous to answer that. If you so much as suggest that in print, I will deny every word. That I ever even talked to you. Do you hear me, Lacey?"

So much for deep background.

"I do." She gazed at Maksym Pushkin. There wasn't a hair out of place. He looked perfect. He used his calculatingly handsome smile on her.

"Please don't pursue this story. For your own good."

He grasped both of her hands in his. They shared a long silence. Lacey's thoughts were spinning too fast to grab hold of them.

She noticed a bustle of activity in the far end of the courtyard. Among the tourists, catering staff were hauling in bars, glassware, and flowers.

"I didn't know the courtyard here could be rented," she said.

"Yes. It's very convenient."

"Have you been to parties here?"

"Quite a few. The one they're getting ready for tonight is for my firm and our clients. I have to go back to the office, but I'll be back here this evening."

"What exactly does your law firm do?"

"We have a lot of international clients. Mostly private sector, from Ukraine and Russia and other Eastern European countries. We help them through the legal and financial hurdles in establishing successful business relationships in the US. It's mostly pretty boring."

Boring? The lion's den of Russian oligarchs? "It must be helpful to be fluent in those languages."

"Yes, it is. Essential, actually." Pushkin had warned her off, but to what gain? He'd only made her more determined to come out of this with the right answer. And he must have known that's what he was doing. Why?

She spotted Will Zephron, the actor who bought the tuxedo at the theatre sale. Still working in catering, he passed Lacey with a wink, carrying an enormous glass vase with dozens of long-stemmed red roses. She smiled at him and he paused to give her a quick hug, and to eye her companion, before hurrying on, balancing his burden. More of these extravagant flower arrangements followed him. Tall tables were wrapped in burgundy cloth and tied with silver ribbons. Someone was spending a lot of money on this affair.

"You probably have some very nice appetizers," she said to Pushkin.

"Especially if you like caviar."

"Not particularly."

"I must return to my office for a meeting, but I'll be back for the reception. You're very welcome to attend, if you like. As my guest. We can talk more. I don't remember anything we said here this afternoon." He smiled again.

"You must be a great lawyer, Maksym. But I don't speak those languages. And I have places to go, people to harass."

"Undoubtedly." He reached out and took her arm gently. He rubbed the spot that was beginning to bruise. "I'm sorry. Be careful, Lacey. I don't want to see you hurt."

He released her and turned and walked away. She sat back down, feeling shaky. She finished her root beer and watched the party preparations, mentally adding up the costs of the décor and caterers. She came up with the grand sum of *Yowza!* Those Russians were rich, very rich. By her accounting, Maksym Pushkin must be rich too. He was certainly telling the truth about one thing: This paid better than being a dancer.

He had warned her away from the red dress story. Warned off a *reporter*. Never a smart thing to do. A good lawyer should know better than to even try that. So had he made up the story to see how she would react? Or was it true? Pushkin said he was at the theatre the night Saige died. If he was there when her body fell, was it because he was involved as more than a bystander? Perhaps he was the one up on the platform with Saige?

Something moving at a rapid pace caught her eye. *Gareth Cameron?* The Kinetic Theatre crowd was feeling like a very small private club. Their sad-sack playwright cruised past, wearing the same outfit she'd seen him in last, with the addition of a preppy blazer. *Shabby, but raffish.*

"Gareth, what are you doing here?"

"Smithsonian?" He stopped suddenly and considered her. "I could ask you the same thing. You seem to be everywhere I turn. I'm here to seek inspiration and edify my soul with art. And food."

"You're here for this Russian shindig?"

"I'm early. I heard there was free food. And until my fortunes reverse, I rely on the kindness of strangers. And their free party snacks."

"But you have a new hit show. *The Turn of the Screw.* Right?"

"Yes, but you know what they say about the theatre. 'You can make a killing, but not a living'? So I try to take advantage of these little grants in aid to the arts. Maksym told me there would be plenty of appetizers."

"I'm sure they can afford it."

"Absolutely. And some of the lawyers at my trade association will be here. They'll think I'm working overtime. Win-win."

She couldn't blame him. She enjoyed seeing people with too much money spend it on lavish parties for party crashers. Too bad she wasn't dressed for a party. And she had work to do.

"Gareth, I wanted to ask you something. Did you go to the cast party for *The Masque?*"

"The cast party? I made an appearance, after we did some quick TV thing, Maksym and Yuri and I, but it was a blur for me. You have to understand, the entire experience was an overload of emotions. It was, after all, my first play."

"I heard Saige never made it that night."

"Are you still on about her? I mean, why? She's not worth it. But to answer your question, no, she didn't show up. I was relieved there'd be no diva moments from her that night. We hated each other by that time. I think everybody hated her."

"Enough to throw her off a platform?"

"What are you talking about? Come on, these are *actors*. They don't actually *do* anything." He shook his head as if to clear it of the thought. "It was a shock to find out the next day that she'd died in that bizarre accident. I've often wondered if it really was an accident."

"What do you mean?"

"Suicide, of course. Perhaps she finally realized what a bad actress she was and decided to go out at the height of her career. It wasn't going to get any better than it was that night. She'd never get a decent role again." He plucked a leaf from the nearest plant. "I would have made sure of that. She'd practically ruined my play. It was a hit in spite of her. The problem as I see it? Taking a swan dive off that stage set would hardly be a reliable way to kill yourself. Typical Saige, doing it *wrong*. I guess it worked though, and it did have a nice dramatic touch. One of her few really dramatic moments, I have to give her that. If it was suicide."

"You never wondered if someone engineered her accident?"

He frowned and crushed the leaf between his long fingers. "Funny, I didn't. I suppose I never thought she was important enough for someone to murder, dramatically speaking."

"You hated her."

"*Obviously*, but it wasn't exactly a grand passion. I had better things to do."

"Like putting the moves on Katya?"

"Katya? Please! I was interested in Yuri! I thought you knew."

"Really? Did you get anywhere with him?"

"Sadly, no. Yuri is in love with Yuri. And the theatre. Although he had a minor thing for Katya. And at one time I thought he had a thing for Saige, because why else would he have cast her as the Red Death, I mean, really, anybody could see she was hopeless, although she looked great in that red dress, and another thing about—"

Gareth Cameron was still rattling on, waiting for the "free" appetizers to arrive, when Lacey gathered her things and hopped down off her perch on the planter.

The theatre, Lacey thought. *Just one big happy family.*

THIRTY-NINE

*G*REGOR KEPELOV WAS waiting for Lacey as she exited the G Street doors of the Portrait Gallery.

It was impossible to miss that car: Marie's ancient purple Gremlin, which unbelievably was still on the road. His cowboy hat and Hawaiian shirt were equally outrageous. He grinned his lopsided grin, but he didn't speak until she was in the car with the door shut. He took off before she had a chance to put her seat belt on.

"I could have taken the Metro, you know."

"Not while Gregor Kepelov is on the job. Actors can be pushed off platforms! Reporters can be pushed in front of subway cars!"

She had ridden with Gregor before. It was a frightening excursion. Who knew an old purple Gremlin could go so fast? Securing the shoulder harness and locking the side door, Lacey also made sure the phone in her pocket was turned off. At a red light, a man on the street stopped and slid his sunglasses to the top of his head to peer at the Gremlin.

"Gregor. Isn't this car a little too *noticeable*?"

"But of course it is. No one would suspect a man of Kepelov's capabilities would drive a purple Gremlin." He pulled into traffic between two taxis. "I drive in plain sight."

"You were listening in this afternoon," she said.

"Every word. It was my turn. Victor's too."

"What did you think?"

"A man who tries to warn you off does not know Lacey Smithsonian."

"Do you think he had anything to do with the actress's death?"

"Possibly."

"Do you think he's a spy?"

"This one? Could be. Very slick. Like they say, spy from Central Casting. But if he wanted to hurt you, he would already do it."

"Gregor, Marie said you could be a target."

"Occupational hazard when one defects to the West as I did. That was many years ago."

"There are a lot of dead Russians lately."

"What? Are you keeping count?" He hit the accelerator on a yellow light, barely missing an oncoming city bus.

"No, but Brooke is."

"All of natural causes, I am sure. After all, poisons are natural. And heart attack when pushed out of window, also very natural. Hitting the sidewalk at a hundred kilometers per hour would give anyone a heart attack."

It was a grim joke. Lacey held on tight to the passenger grab handle as he took a corner at a ridiculous speed.

"Please be careful. These are dangerous times. Like these streets."

He glanced over at her and grinned again. "See what good friends we are becoming? You care about the safety of Gregor Kepelov?"

"Yes! You're driving! So please get us both to *The Eye* in one piece," she said.

First, however, she insisted Kepelov stop at a CVS, where she purchased the largest bottle of Maalox she could find. A gift for her editor. She also bought two chocolate bars, one for herself and one for her driver.

"Good stuff, Godiva," he said.

Kepelov tucked the chocolate away, stepped on the gas and sped her to *The Eye Street Observer*, narrowly missing a D.C. police car.

 og

It was quiet in the newsroom. About half of the reporters had managed to slip away early. Even on a Friday afternoon in the summer, escaping before deadline these days was an impressive feat. Obviously, certain deals had been cut among Lacey's coworkers to cover each other's beats.

Young denizens of the District lived for the weekend. After work on summer Fridays, they raced to their group beach houses in Rehoboth, Delaware, or Ocean City, Maryland. Their favorite beach bars with their umbrella cocktails were at least three hours away in weekend beach traffic, dodging road construction and Delaware state troopers. Beachgoers watched the clock, counted the minutes, and worked themselves into an exhausted lather.

Lacey was not one of those frazzled beach people. *Relaxing can be so stressful.*

But news was a tossed salad on Friday. Government agencies often waited until after the big media's deadlines to dump unfavorable news, such as the economy tanking, healthcare legislation collapsing, or investigations into Russian espionage, hoping it would be forgotten or buried in the Saturday papers. Which, they hoped, no one would read. Because they were at the beach. Therefore, smart news teams were now on the Friday late-breaking-news watch. Generally, the fashion beat was not part of that news watch.

Today was different.

Lacey ran into Mac, looking for crumbs from Felicity's baking. Alas, the cupboard was bare. Felicity had left for the day. Her editor wearily acknowledged Lacey's presence with a question.

"What have you got, Smithsonian?"

"A headache."

"Take an aspirin. Don't call me in the morning."

"How do you feel about a picture story on the theatre costumer's craft?"

"If you can fill a big hole in Sunday's edition for me, I'm thrilled."

"Those words make my heart sing. I took some pictures with my trusty digital."

"Good. Deadline's at five. Any developments on the red dress?" She handed him the fresh bottle of Maalox. He looked at it and made a sour face. "Oh. My favorite. This doesn't bode well, does it?"

"For a five o'clock deadline, I can work on one story or the other. Not both. And I don't have anything solid on the red dress story. Not yet. The theatre costumer thing is a little more solid."

Mac's eyebrows undulated quizzically. He gave the bottle of Maalox a shake. "I need the costume thing today. And make it solid."

He threw one last look at Felicity's empty desk before walking away. He lifted the plastic bottle of antacid in the air like a trophy.

THE MASQUE OF THE RED DRESS

Breathing Drama into Fabric:
The Art of Theatrical Costume
By Lacey Smithsonian

There's an old theatre saying, "You don't want the audience to go home singing the costumes." Yet the costumer's craft is essential to every show. The costumes express the characters' essences and help give them life. Costume design lets the director's and playwright's ideas and themes speak through the fabric, cut, and color of the clothes, enhancing but not overshadowing the action of the play.

The Kinetic Theatre's resident costume designer, Nikolai Sokolov, is a Helen Hayes Award-winning master of his craft...

Counting photographs, her article would be plenty for the hole in the Sunday LifeStyle section. She pulled some file photos and looked at the frames she took during her interview with Nikolai Sokolov. Perhaps the Lady Macbeth gown and the fantastic Snow Queen? Her story was the lovechild of deadline and necessity. She sent the file to Mac.

Lacey rubbed her neck and stretched. She'd been wrestling with a question all day: Should she let Mac in on the full scope of the potential red dress story, what she had of it, and pass part of her headache on to him? Or wait for further developments?

The lights were still on in Mac's office. He was working and the antacid bottle was on his desk, sitting on a pile of newspapers. She stuck her head through the door.

"Hey, Lacey. Your story's fine. The pictures are okay too. I'm using three. You can go. Have a good weekend."

"I'd love to. Unfortunately, I need to tell you about the other story I'm working on. We can call it the 'The Red Dress Rabbit Hole.' Or maybe, 'Over the Rainbow in My Red Dress.' Or—"

Mac's eyebrows huddled together in that frown she knew so well. "This is about LaToya's crimson monster?"

"And a bit more. Is Claudia still here?"

The eyebrows went sky-high. Claudia Darnell was the owner and publisher of *The Eye Street Observer*, and she only needed to be consulted in the event of traumatic news, or whenever Lacey Smithsonian was potentially going to cause big trouble.

"Oh hell, it's that kind of story?" Mac reached for the Maalox bottle.

"Afraid so."

Mac stared around his office. It was in its normal state of chaos, piles of newspapers covering his desk, more papers stacked in neat piles on the floor and the second chair, papers everywhere.

"We better use the conference room."

"Good idea. I'll close the blinds."

Mac groaned. Not just a closed-door meeting, but a *closed-blind* meeting as well? Reporters loved to peek into the conference room windows, trying to figure out what was going on inside. Closing the blinds was a precaution, but also a calculated risk. Reporters were always nosy, but they tended to be nosier on Monday mornings; less so on Friday afternoons, when they had beach plans for the weekend. But if Claudia was spotted going into a *closed-blind meeting*, the rumor mill would start churning.

Mac and Lacey didn't have much to say during the wait. Presently, Claudia Darnell arrived and made her entrance. She looked glorious, as usual. Today her hair was down, brushing her shoulders, she wore a violet sheath dress and silver sandals, and her legs were bare. A beautiful woman of fifty-something, her money only enhanced her natural assets, her sparkling white-blond hair, her turquoise eyes, and her buttery tanned skin, fresh from her summer home on Nantucket.

"Lacey, so nice to see you." Claudia smiled brightly, and she didn't seem to be in a rush to be somewhere else. "I take it a big fat mess is about to hit the fan?"

"Potentially," Lacey said. "Depends on how you feel about theatre, death, and Russian spies."

"I feel intrigued."

"Oh, boy," Mac said. "Here we go."

"And this is all way beyond top secret, by the way."

Claudia nodded. Lacey launched into a summary of what she had learned so far and what she had yet to find out. She began with a thumbnail history of the red dress and what she found inside it, the seven hollow Lenin medals and the missing poison needles, and the Kepelovs' suspicions about "the Centipede." She ended with her interviews with Volkov, Sokolov, and Pushkin, including Maksym Pushkin's confession of *almost* witnessing Saige Russell's suspicious death.

"Wait, what I don't get," Mac interrupted, "is why you felt like tearing up the hem?"

"I didn't tear it up. I opened it up. Carefully."

"And what made you do that?" Claudia was also curious.

Good question. Why did *I have to do that?*

"The dress has a lurid reputation, starting with the actress who wore it as Death and died in that fall on closing night. It's good luck, it's bad luck, it's cursed, it's haunted, it had this brush with death, it's become a theatre legend, and so on. Then Amy Keaton died, also supposedly in a fall. I know the police say they were both accidents. Even Pushkin seems to think Saige Russell's death might be an accident, though he seems haunted by it. Unless that's an act. But I saw Amy Keaton a day or so before she died. She was distraught, wildly upset about losing the dress when LaToya bought it. And after LaToya's apartment break-in, where it seems increasingly obvious that someone was after the red dress, I wanted to take a closer look at it and see what the dress could tell me."

"Why can't you write like other reporters?" Mac complained. "They do an interview, take a picture, write a story, done! Your beat is just fashion. Not how to have fun with killer spies."

"Clothes have a language, Mac," she said, trying not to stare at his Tower of Babel of an outfit, the lime green pants, the purple and orange shirt. Could he be color blind? "And this dress has a tale to tell, even if I don't know the whole story yet."

"Stop interrupting her, Mac. You found the medals in the hem," Claudia said. "Then what?"

"When I saw Lenin on the medals, I called the only Russians I knew who might understand what they meant."

"Seven medals," Mac said.

"Seven medals, but no poison needles."

Claudia laced her fingers together. "And the Kepelovs think the hollow medals signify seven deaths?"

"It's a theory. And if what Gregor and Olga say about the medals is true, yes," Lacey said. "And we really have to protect these sources. The two of them and my friend Marie."

"That goes without saying," Claudia said.

"So far, everyone is safe," Mac said. "Even you, Smithsonian."

"Do they think the costume is some kind of gruesome trophy case?" Claudia said. "A repository of a killer's memorabilia?"

"Possibly. Some kind of memorial. There could be other explanations, but I don't know what they might be."

"And what about this Centipede character?" Mac shook his head and scowled. "Sounds like a spy thriller."

"I don't know. Possibly part truth, part myth. Presumably somehow connected to Kinetic. Whoever sewed the KGB medals in the hem certainly could have been a Russian agent, either active or in the past. Perhaps even the legendary Centipede. Who is supposedly dead. Did I mention that? Volkov, Sokolov, and Pushkin are all viable suspects, but there might be any number of Russians who've had access to the dress over the years."

"Run through those three again for me, Lacey, if you would," Claudia asked. "All those Russian names run together."

"Yuri Volkov is the artistic director of Kinetic. The boss. He directed *The Masque*. He's always at the theatre, he's always had access to the dress, but he says he couldn't care less about the stupid dress. Can't stand to hear about it. Also doesn't want to talk to me. Intense, driven, not a charmer. Nikolai Sokolov is their costume designer. He made the dress for *The Masque*. He had a passionate affair with Saige Russell, the actress who died. He runs the costume shop like his little kingdom, so he's had the most access to the dress, but he also said good riddance to the dress. Also intense, but more charming. Maksym Pushkin played opposite Saige in *The Masque*. Couldn't stand her. Very charming, matinee-idol handsome, now a smooth big-money lawyer for Russian interests. Says he was an *ear*-witness to Saige's death, says she wasn't alone, but doesn't know who was with her, doesn't know if it was an accident or murder or what. Tried to warn me off the story."

Lacey took a breath and then rushed on.

"Oh, and the moody playwright says Saige was a justifiable suicide, the wistful understudy dated Pushkin but seems to still have a thing for Sokolov, and the sharp new stage manager hated Saige too, thinks they're all nuts, but seems awfully comfortable taking over for Keaton."

"And if LaToya's break-in is any indication, whoever sewed the medals in the dress is probably the one who wants it back. Sokolov," Claudia said, jumping to the most likely conclusion. "This Sokolov made the dress for Saige Russell, because he loved her. But if he also sewed the medals into it, he doesn't seem to want it back. So that argues against Sokolov. Where is the gown now, by the way?"

"In a secure, undisclosed location."

Claudia smiled in appreciation. "Of course. I assume your handsome Vic Donovan is taking care of it."

Mac was not amused. "And you've got some maniac after you again?"

"There's no indication of that, Mac," Lacey said. "No one seems to be on my trail or lurking in my closet, playing with my clothes. I've been chatting with suspicious Russians all week long, and no one has come after me yet."

"Yet. Stupid fashion beat. Should be as safe as obituaries. No one ever comes after the obit writer. And this time, what do we have? SPIES AND THE RED SILK ROAD!"

"Not a bad headline," Lacey said.

"Calm down, Mac," Claudia told him. "Lacey, you know we don't expect our reporters to be targets of violence. Or bait for killers."

"Smithsonian's got a special talent for it." Mac lifted his blue bottle and took another slug.

Claudia ticked points off on her fingers. "This all started a dozen years ago with a red dress and a dead actress. A little Russian theatre in D.C. A rogue spy-slash-assassin keeping trophies there. And then nothing happens for twelve years? Until the dress is sold? Why the gap? And what bothers me too is the current alliance of high officials in our government with Russia." She massaged her temples. "Are all these things connected somehow?"

"Maybe there's no gap at all. If the dress is a trophy case of his kills, he's been executing targets all along, without anyone connecting it to him," Lacey said. "And if he killed Amy Keaton just because she let the dress escape—"

"He'll stop at nothing."

"Yet one puzzling thing is that LaToya wasn't harmed, although she was certainly freaked out."

"What does she know about this?" Mac asked.

"About what I've found out since the break-in? Nothing."

"Small blessing, but I'll take it," he said.

"Please keep it that way until we break the story," Claudia added.

"We *are* going to break the story, right?" Lacey took another deep breath. "I'm afraid the U.S. government, Homeland Security, FBI, or some obscure agency will get involved. They might try to cover it up."

"You mean they'll lie," Mac said.

"Of course they will," Claudia replied. "And then they'll deny lying."

"This Russia-loving administration might try to kill this story, Claudia," Lacey said. "So I'm making a record of everything I know, or think I know. If I get thrown in jail, you'll get everything. Send me a care package. And protect my sources."

"I will, Lacey. And you think I wouldn't run this story?"

"Well, there might be a lot of pressure on you—"

"Bullies can't intimidate me. They can cry fake news till the cows come home." Claudia's blue eyes took on a hard-edged glint. "Everyone is safer, the public is safer, if we break this story in *The Eye*. The public has a right to know about Russian agents in our midst, a right to know about the Centipede, dead or alive, about how two women died in this town. Whatever the truth is. If we act first, bring the story public, the bastards can't do anything. Knowledge is power and if I can't use that power in a good cause, then I don't deserve to own this newspaper."

There was a wonderful spine-stiffening effect in being the odd woman out, Lacey decided, and never being invited into the good old boys' inner circles. The beautiful and impressive Claudia Darnell was steel-belted, and she believed Lacey's story had the power to rock D.C.

Maybe. And it still wouldn't win us a Pulitzer Prize. We're immune.

"Send everything to Mac first and copy me," Claudia directed. "Nothing goes live until we're absolutely sure of what is going on. I might feel out a few sources myself. Just general information. Nothing specifically about the Centipede. The ambient temperature, vis-à-vis our current relationship with the Kremlin. I know a few people I can ask, without revealing anything." Claudia had friends in high places. "And this story will run," she assured Mac and Lacey. "We can't be silenced."

"What if we don't unmask the assassin?" Lacey asked. "What if it all falls apart?"

"We still have a hell of a story," Claudia said with a smile. "Two women dead, a local theatre legend, and seven fake Lenin medals baked in a pie. Now, Lacey, do you have a personal protection plan in place?"

Someone knocked at the door. Lacey opened it just enough so they could see who it was.

"Hope I'm not interrupting," Vic said. "Evening, everyone. Mac, Claudia."

"So this is your protection plan?" Claudia remarked with a smile. "Good timing, Mr. Donovan." Vic lifted one eyebrow at Lacey.

"We've been discussing the red dress," Lacey told him. "I had to tell them."

"In for a penny, in for a pound," Vic said. "Old family saying. Are we all on the same page?"

"Front page," Mac said. "Barring disaster."

Claudia stood up. "No one tells us what to write or what not to write. Nobody intimidates me or *The Eye Street Observer*. And now if you'll excuse me, I think there's a margarita waiting with my name on it. Have a lovely weekend, everyone, and stay safe."

Claudia knew how to make an exit, as well as an entrance.

"I gotta go too," Mac said. "Kim is holding supper for me and I promised Jasmine and Lily Rose we'd go find some fireflies. They love fireflies."

Back at her desk, Lacey printed the theatre yard sale photos she copied earlier from Hansen. Vic settled into the skull-painted Death Chair.

"I guess your summit conference went well. So can I take you to dinner?" he asked.

"No surprises from our friends, the Troika?"

"As far as I know, the Kepelovs and Marie are busy tonight. No one has raised a warning flag."

Lacey leaned over to Vic and kissed him. "That is music to my ears."

"I was happy Gregor drove you back to the office and kept you safe."

"Safe? You wouldn't say that if you ever rode with him." Lacey stuffed the photos into an envelope and slipped them into her tote. She grabbed Vic by the arm and pulled him out of the Death Chair. "We have a date, darling. And tonight I'll be your firefly."

FORTY

"$\mathscr{I}$ HAD TO TELL THEM, Vic."

Lacey lifted her margarita and eyed the tortilla chip basket. They stood at the bar waiting for a table at Cactus Cantina, a Mexican restaurant in northwest D.C., near the National Cathedral. Inside, the air was cool and scented with chili spices. Children were enjoying watching the hot tortilla machine.

"I agree. And now they can't say you went rogue." He clinked his salt-rimmed glass with hers. "I get it, sweetheart. They pay you. They're going to have to support this story, and you. And now they can't scream when you unload this little treat on them."

"Exactly. I needed their buy-in on this story." She sipped. The margarita was perfect, just sweet and salty enough, and she could feel the tequila tickle her throat. The restaurant was roomy, but packed. Part of the crowd spilled out on the street to wait for tables, some opting to wait longer for a spot on the patio, which was still steamy from the day's heat. There were a number of business-clad patrons there on this Friday evening, but some were so relaxed they had even *loosened their ties.*

"You think the power of the press will save you?" Vic asked.

"I'm counting on it. You should have heard Claudia! She could run for President. Maybe she should, come to think about it. I'd vote for her."

"I'm willing to bet that there are more people in the government who want to see the truth out there, than those who want to suppress it."

"I hope you're right. But I'm a little concerned that our main Russian source appears to be risking his life for this story."

"Don't worry, the Moscow Cowboy lives for the thrills. He's pretty tough, you know. And Lacey, we're going to chat about Pretty Boy and his wild tale of that night at the theatre, but later, in a quieter setting."

"You say the sweetest things."

They talked no more of spies for fear of being overheard, though that would be unlikely, with the Mexican music, the clatter of plates and clinking of drinks. The host showed them to a cozy table by an open window, where it was like being on the patio but better, and they ordered dinner.

"What do you want to do after this?" Vic asked.

"Besides our private chat? I know a party full of Russians we could crash. Then of course there are thousands of fireflies dancing down the river. But how about a stroll through the Bishop's Garden? It's just around the corner, and the flowers are glorious."

Later, in the rose-scented garden, they found a secluded bench in the stone gazebo, away from prying eyes, just as the sun was setting. Lacey pulled the photos out of her bag. To anyone watching, they could be any couple discussing wedding plans in a beautiful garden. Or making out.

"Photos?" Vic picked up one of the prints.

"From last Saturday. The theatre sale."

"Where this whole thing started? And you're just looking at them now?"

"It's been a busy week. Hansen only gave them to me this morning. I just enlarged this series. Besides, they were taken for Tamsin's story, and they might not tell us anything." She turned around and scoped out their surroundings.

"You're afraid Kepelov is hiding around the corner, aren't you?"

"It would be the frosting on a perfect day."

Vic laughed and hugged her. "I can think of better things to do myself. Wanna make out?"

"I'd love to." She laid her head against his shoulder. "After dark."

The shadows were long, but it would be light for another half an hour or so. Lacey spread the photos out on the stone bench, in sequence, from the first to the last. There were more than a dozen of them. The clothing rack full of costumes was in a slightly different position in each. She was puzzled. Besides the fact that she didn't know what she was looking for, she didn't know whether what was in the picture was more important than what was missing.

"What do we have?" Vic asked.

"Racks of costumes, which include the ones from Kinetic. Right after Amy Keaton left for some reason, but before LaToya and I arrived."

Lacey recognized a few actors she knew, pawing through the rack. And just before Lacey and LaToya showed up, one shot clearly showed the red dress hanging on the rack. It had suddenly appeared, as if by magic.

She backed up. In several of the previous photos, a spot of red caught her eye, progressively getting closer to the rack as people moved in and out of Hansen's frames.

"See here, Vic." She couldn't be sure, but it appeared someone had that flash of red tucked under an arm.

"That's the dress?"

"Maybe. It's the right color." The figure was indistinct and remained in the background. She flipped the photos back and forth. "It is the dress. And here. And now it's hanging on the rack. Someone deliberately hung it there after the sale started. That's why it wasn't in the inventory. It wasn't supposed to be there, just like Amy Keaton kept saying."

"But who put it there? And why?"

Lacey concentrated on the figure carrying the slash of scarlet. It looked male, but the enlargement was grainy, and in the shape-shifting theatre world, she couldn't be certain. There were also a lot of other people in the frame, partially obscuring the figure with the red dress. Lacey examined the photos one after another, tracing the figure's progress.

"I think it's a man."

She could make out a black shirt and blue jeans and a cap, pulled down to shade his eyes. There was something familiar about the shape of the shoulders. Compact, tightly wound, with an air of belligerence.

"We've seen that guy," Vic said. "I recognize that stance. At the theatre."

"Yuri Volkov."

"Volkov? The artistic director?"

Lacey checked her watch. It was the last night of previews. He'd be at the theatre, going over everything to make sure tomorrow night's opening night gala was perfect. Not expecting anything, she called the theatre and left a message for Volkov to call her. She tucked the photos away and leaned on Vic.

"What are you thinking?" he asked.

"Amy Keaton. No one loved her, but no one hated her either. Volkov complained about her, but not the way they all did about Saige Russell. Amy was efficient, hardworking, and maybe a little obsessive, the way they like it at Kinetic. Not at all like Parsnips, who looked like a star but couldn't learn her lines and infuriated everyone. Everyone but Nicky Sokolov, who loved her. The only thing the two women had in common was that red dress."

"Amy was willing to fight LaToya for that dress," Vic pointed out. "And that tells us she was more afraid of losing the dress than facing off with your intimidating coworker. I'd think twice myself about tackling LaToya."

"Did she know about the medals in the hem? Or did she just know the dress mattered to someone at the theatre? For whatever weird reason?"

"Doesn't matter," Vic said. "She knew there would be hell to pay if it went missing, or got itself sold."

"Either way, she knew who it mattered to. She knew her killer."

୦౩

They were in Vic's Jeep heading back to Virginia when Yuri Volkov returned her call. Lacey was surprised. It must be intermission. Vic turned the radio off, and she put the phone on speaker so he could hear.

"Smithsonian! Now what do you want?" Volkov sounded annoyed, yet he was curious enough to call her back. "No time for long chat. Act Two in two minutes."

In the background, people were chattering but she couldn't make out the words. It sounded like Russian. He was in the theatre lobby.

Go big, go bold. "*You* put the red dress on the sales rack, Yuri. There are photos. I know it was you."

He might dispute the fact, demand to see the photos, deny it was him. *Let him,* she thought, *whatever he says is more information.* There was a long pause. Lacey looked at her phone, afraid he might have hung up.

"So what. You want a big Pulitzer Prize for this daring revelation, Smithsonian?"

"You told me you didn't care, it was just an old dress, things happen. Why did you want it sold? And why keep it a secret?"

"Didn't I say the costume was bad luck? Like an albatross. Time to get rid of it. Why should I tell anyone? My theatre, my costume, my decision."

"Did that include getting rid of Amy?"

"Don't be stupid. Nobody kills a stage manager! Too important. Keaton was a good stage manager. I could use her now. This is a very technical show. And don't forget, it was a tragic accident, according to D.C. police."

Lacey could hear him move from the intermission crowd into another, quieter space. "Why was the dress bad luck?"

"Because of Saige Russell, of course." He said it as if she was mentally deficient not to understand the obvious. "Bad luck, curse, whatever."

"Yet the theatre lent it out every year. Helped turn it into a legend."

"I had nothing to do with that."

"Who did, then? What is the costume's secret, Yuri?"

"I don't know what you're talking about. But let me tell you this, Smithsonian. Forget this story, it will only bring you grief. And I am telling you this as a friend." He hung up.

"These Russian theatre people." Vic gave her a quick glance as he drove. "They are a friendly lot."

"If that's how he treats his friends, I'd hate to see how he treats his enemies. He knows something."

"He does, and so does Pretty Boy Pushkin."

"You heard the interview?"

"I did."

Vic swung onto the George Washington Parkway. Lacey's window was open and honeysuckle perfumed the air. The moon was tantalizingly large and gold, low on the horizon, not yet full. It would be so easy to be distracted by the beauty of this summer evening.

"What do you make of Pushkin's story?" she asked Vic. "Being on stage hiding when she died? Did he make it up to trap me into reporting something that wasn't true? Warning me off to set the hook, make me eager to run with it?"

"Either way, I don't like it. If he's lying, he's probably covering up a crime. If he's telling the truth, and most likely not the whole truth, he's a coward. He's an earwitness, he says, if not an eyewitness, but he left her lying there on the floor and went to the cast party, and he never called the cops, never told anyone. She might have still been alive, she might have been saved. If it's the truth."

"The way he warned me off made me think he does know who was there with Saige. He may be afraid of them. All that 'dangerous to know too much in this town' stuff. And to cover this up, he'd deny every word."

"He's a lawyer," Vic pointed out. "Brooke would say he's an agent in place. I can think of another possibility."

"That is?"

"Try this on. He's a killer. He killed Saige. He didn't need an alibi or a cover story at the time. It got ruled an accident, so he got away with it. But now there's a reporter poking into it. So he hands you this long-lost cover story, full of emotion. He's an actor, remember, and not just an actor: a lawyer. He tries to play you like a jury. 'Oh Lacey, I was there! I've never told anyone the awful truth! I feel so haunted by shame and regret!' Blah, blah, blah. And then he begs you to drop the story for your own safety, like he's on your side."

"Yeah, I like that one," Lacey said. "That's a really good take on Pushkin. But is he the Centipede?"

"Or maybe he was the killer's lookout, an accomplice. Same story."

"You're saying more than one of them decided to kill Saige?"

"Just a possibility."

"That's so comforting. This is a small thing, but I wish I could see the mask from *The Masque*. In a way, it should be the crowning glory of the costume. It feels incomplete without it."

"Any luck there?"

"No. Sokolov said it went missing when the theatre moved to its present location. He blamed the volunteers."

"Do you believe him?"

"Blaming the volunteers is like blaming the intern. I don't believe anybody. Somebody's got that mask."

Lacey gazed out the window at the passing lights of D.C. and the outlines of boats on the Potomac River.

"I have a totally different question for you, sweetheart. When are you going to tell your family about our engagement?"

Vic reached over and squeezed her left hand. He brought it to his lips and kissed it.

Not that question again. "It's complicated. My mother will want to be involved. She'll want to run everything. She'll want to serve pigs in a blanket and Jell-O salad at the reception." Lacey shuddered at the thought of her mother's weird food choices. "Perhaps individual meat loaf skewers. A tofu wedding cake. And your mother will want lobster."

"Nadine? No, she's more of a filet mignon gal."

"Me too. I'd prefer the filet myself."

"You really should tell Rose soon." He pulled into the exit lane for Old Town Alexandria.

"Why?"

"It's the expected thing to do before the wedding. Unless you'd like to elope? I'm down with that, lady. But you're the one who wanted a church wedding."

"Tempting. But it's the coward's way out and I do want to show you off. And if we eloped, not only would my mother be mad at me, but Brooke, and Stella too. And Nadine. I couldn't live with all of that."

"Lacey, sweetheart, I'd like to get married before I have to walk you down the aisle with a cane."

"You'd be fetching with a cane. And a top hat. That would be wonderful. Puttin' on the Ritz!"

"No top hats for me. Not after Nigel and Stella's wedding. I felt like an extra in a Gilbert and Sullivan operetta."

The men at that wedding wore morning suits with striped pants and top hats. Stella's idea. Nigel, the English ambassador's wayward son, had been game, but Vic, who wound up as Nigel's best man in spite of his best efforts, was mortified.

Lacey was laughing. "You were the handsomest man there, Vic, and you'll always be the star of my show."

"And what about all the tourists who were taking pictures of us, as if the circus had come to town?"

"Let 'em. It was a beautiful wedding, in spite of everything."

Lacey smiled at the memory. It was touch and go whether Stella would indeed go through with the nuptials after her first wedding gown was shredded by a maniac.

"You were beautiful," Vic said. "You pulled the whole thing together, as well as pulling Stella together. I'd say she owes you big time."

Ultimately, Stella's wedding became a rhapsody in pink. From the cherry blossoms in full bloom to the bridesmaids in their summer dresses, to Stella in a last-minute rose-colored wedding gown and veil. Topping it all off, Stella was chauffeured by Vic's mother Nadine, in her famous bubblegum pink Cadillac Biarritz.

"That was quite the wedding."

"Sweetheart, there's another reason you've got to tell Rose about us. Nadine wants to help with our wedding. She says time is of the essence."

Despite the steamy evening air, a chill raced down Lacey's spine. Nadine Donovan was as overpowering in her way as Rose Smithsonian.

"Nadine? Wow. That's, um, stressful."

Lacey had envisioned a wedding that was small, affordable, yet chic and elegant. The money they saved on a big, extravagant wedding they could spend on their honeymoon. In Paris. Just for example. Most of all, she wanted to develop her own vision of this wedding, hers and Vic's. Letting the families into the works would be introducing a battering ram at the castle door.

"First of all, where do you want to get married?" he asked. "Here or in Colorado?"

"Here, of course. This is my home now, not Colorado. And Washington and Virginia are so beautiful, why would I want to get married anyplace else?"

"Here, then," Vic said. "Exact location to be determined. And in church, or romping naked in a field of daisies?"

"Daisies are nice, but I want a church wedding," she said. "You've never had one, and neither have I. Maybe St. Matthew's Cathedral in the District? People who don't like it, don't have to come."

"Good, a cathedral will please Nadine. Me too. When?"

"Spring or fall. I haven't decided."

"This fall, then?"

Her eyes went wide. "Oh my God, *this* fall? That's only a couple of months away! That's too soon!"

He howled with laughter. "You should see your face. Lacey, marriage is not exactly the guillotine."

"My freedom is a big deal for me."

"As long as you're marrying me, you'll always have your freedom. And you'll have me too. As long as you don't skip town, like you did with that cowboy."

"I'm not skipping town. I love Virginia. And I love you, Vic. Always."

თ

Upstairs in Lacey's apartment, her shabby shelter in the sky, Vic swept the place for electronic bugs and double-checked all the locks before turning out the lights.

"My own resident bug exterminator. That's so romantic," Lacey said. "Makes my heart skip a beat."

He swept her into his arms.

"I'll show you romantic, lady." And he did.

When he was ready to leave early the next morning, Vic urged her to stay safe and call him if she planned on talking to anyone at Kinetic Theatre.

She promised.

FORTY-ONE

"*H*ELLO, DARLING, THIS is a courtesy call." Lacey contacted Vic late Saturday morning, as prearranged. "I'm heading over to Kinetic Theatre."

"Why? What's up?"

"It appears that the long-lost mask has resurfaced. The one from *The Masque of the Red Death.*"

"I remember." He sounded skeptical. "And why does it materialize now? Merely because Lacey Smithsonian inquires?"

"I could say because it's time and the universe wants to bring it forth, but I just got a message from DeeDee Adler. Apparently, Sokolov went searching and found it in some obscure corner of the costume shop and left it for me to examine."

More silence on the other end. "I don't like it."

"I get that. Me neither. Although he did tell me he'd look for it. You heard him say that." It was Lacey's turn to pause.

"Convenient. He's on your list, you know."

"I know. That's why I'm calling you. You can turn on the microphone, but I haven't left yet. I'll be singing along to the radio. Fair warning."

"I like your singing, Lacey."

"Flatterer. Anyway, DeeDee told me Sokolov is traveling to Richmond for something today, but he'll be back tonight for the big donor event. Opening night reception. She said he could give it to me personally tonight if I want, but I'm welcome to pick it up sooner." She mimicked a Russian accent, "and contemplate mask with my amazing EFP brain."

"What if she's lying? Isn't she on your list too?"

"Yeah, but I'm sure I could take her in a fair fight."

"She might not fight fair. Don't be a target."

"I will be on my guard, Vic. And honestly, I'd prefer to pick up the mask now, without Sokolov around."

"If there really is a mask."

"Apparently it should be quiet at the theatre until later this afternoon."

"I'll meet you at the theatre. We can run over to Kramerbooks and get some lunch in the café."

She blew out the breath she'd been holding. She didn't realize how tense she had been. The chance to peek at that mask was tempting Lacey's fatal flaw, she knew: always wanting to know how the story ended.

Careful, Lacey! Don't go into the haunted theatre! The Red Ghost will get you!

If the crimson costume had secrets, what might the scarlet mask reveal? Perhaps nothing. But it hadn't surfaced before, therefore it was still of interest. Vic was right though, the timing was too convenient and it felt like a setup. Or was that the paranoia talking?

"It's a date. Kepelov isn't going to show up, is he?"

"I make no promises where he's concerned."

"That's okay. Thanks for being my backup today."

She turned the little BMW's radio up and sang along to the Beach Boys, dreaming of being at the ocean. In Cape May, New Jersey, not California. The city seemed a little sluggish for a Saturday in June and traffic was light. Perhaps there was a ballgame somewhere, she thought. The heat was back and the humidity was on the rise. Lacey wore a vintage hand-painted Mexican skirt, black and turquoise with gold accents, and deep pockets. She paired it with a fitted turquoise sleeveless blouse.

She was surprised to spot a parking space under a sign with a lot of fine print, right by the theatre. Reading parking signs diligently was an essential skill in Washington. The fine print could yield a ticket for an unsuspecting driver. Lacey scanned the sign: It was legal to park here on the weekend, illegal every other Tuesday because of street sweeping, and illegal from four to six p.m., Mondays through Fridays, but right now she was safe.

As she walked toward Kinetic, Lacey wondered what it would be like to live in D.C., instead of across the river in Alexandria. It would require a private parking spot at the very least. Lacey transferred the little bottle of Doctor Kepelov's Spy Stopper into her right pocket. In her left pocket, she had several of the N95 respirators.

DeeDee Adler opened the theatre door for her. "Hey Lacey, you can go on upstairs." She gestured toward the staircase distractedly.

"Do you know where Sokolov left the mask for me?"

"Nope." She shook her head without glancing up. "Sorry. I'm seriously busy here. This donor thing tonight. Everyone's on edge. Anyway, Nicky said you'd find it."

It didn't feel like a trap.

"Is Yuri around?"

"No, thank God." DeeDee quickly glanced over her shoulder to make sure he wasn't behind her. "He's having coffee with some big money guys and I hope it keeps him busy and out my hair all day."

"Thanks. I'll just go on up."

"Knock yourself out."

DeeDee turned away to inventory piles of boxes of party supplies. Lacey told herself she'd be out of there in ten minutes, mask or no mask. As she walked up the stairs she could feel the little bottle knock gently against her leg.

This better not be some kind of game, she thought.

Fragrances tickled her nose, aromas of preparation, glass cleaners and floor wax, then roses and lilies, in stylish arrangements. The air conditioning was humming, chilling the lobby space for the evening's opening night gala. It made the perfumed air feel close.

The mask was not in the upstairs lobby, where she expected to see it. Lacey was certain she'd recognize it. The mannequins were still present, extravagantly attired, and in the dim light, they looked as if they might move at any moment, gliding into a minuet. Macbeth and his murderous Lady were not mannequins she wanted to see come to life. She opened the glass doors and stepped into Sokolov's costume shop, her second choice. She went from worktable to worktable, stopping at the costume designer's drafting table. No mask. The whole workroom was clean and uncluttered.

"No mask in the costume shop," she said conversationally to the empty room, knowing Vic would hear her. "I'm going to take a look in the costume closets. If I don't find it there, I'll give up."

Returning to the lobby, she saw the door to the hallway leading to what Sokolov called "the costume closet" was open.

The door down the hall was also ajar. She opened it wide and felt for the light switch. The ceiling lights were diffused through the hanging costumes, giving the room a shadowy film-noir look. It was unsettling.

There were costume-filled racks on either side of her. Above her head, to her right and her left, were additional hanging bars of clothes, all types of suits and outerwear. Lacey peered down the central aisle. At the far end, in front of a full-length mirror, she saw what looked like another figure, a white mannequin in a glittering "suit of lights," the costume of a Spanish matador. It was turned away from her. *What show could that be from,* she wondered.

She spoke quietly for Vic's benefit. "I'm in the so-called closet. DeeDee said Sokolov told her I would find it. But it's nowhere obvious. Is this supposed to be a scavenger hunt? I hate games."

From her tour with Sokolov, she knew the place was a confusing labyrinth and she tried to remember the general layout. She found the area that held bins of feather boas, costume jewelry, and other accessories. No masks. Passing baskets full of leotards and tights, she saw racks of men's and women's character dance shoes. Another aisle was full of hats. There were specific sections labeled by show, with entire costumes identified by character. *Nicky Sokolov is insanely organized,* she thought. Even so, it felt like the walls and the walls of clothes were pressing in on her.

So where did he put the mask? Was there an aisle marked "masks"? Wasn't there an open area somewhere in the middle? Were there hidden cameras? Was someone watching her? *Paranoid much?* There was only one thing to do: Go back to the beginning. Try it again.

"I'm starting over," she said softly. "One last look, then I'm out of here." She backtracked to the door, glancing uneasily down every aisle, then she took a different path, a different turn here, a different turn there. But it led in the end to the same aisle, and at the far end she saw the same mirror. It reflected the matador mannequin, silhouetted in the light of the window.

Something was different about it. Someone had moved the mirror, placing it at an angle to the matador. Now it looked as if there were *two* matadors, two suits of lights. And the missing scarlet mask from the *Red Death* covered the mannequin's face.

Oh Hell. Lacey sucked in her breath and froze.

"Found it," she announced for Vic.

The mask was even more brilliant than she had imagined. Against the dummy's white surface and its sequined suit of lights, the scarlet silk was as shocking as a splash of fresh blood. Cascading strands of faux jewels, diamonds, rubies, and pearls, sparkled among the headpiece's fountain of blood-red feathers. The crimson facepiece glittered with the seductive features of the Red Death, outlined in jewel-studded gold braid. The empty eyes and mouth revealed the dim shape of a gleaming skull, a death's head, the mask within the mask that would suddenly appear in the magic of stage lights.

As she looked at the mannequin in the mirror, she realized that someone was seeing her reflection as well. Someone who had moved the mirror into position to achieve the most dramatic effect.

"Damn it, Nikolai! What kind of game are you playing?"

"It's not a game, Lacey Smithsonian. It's a test."

It was Sokolov's voice. The matador suddenly turned, stepped away from the mirror and walked toward her.

Lacey took a step back. Her heart was slamming against her chest at the rhythm of a parade march. As the matador came to life like a living statue, he slowly removed the mask and held it high. His blue eyes were bright, the rims red, his lips curled in a smile against the dead white makeup he wore beneath the mask. Nikolai Sokolov was a ghastly figure in a costume production designed just for her.

"A test?" she managed to say. *Kepelov's secret juice had better work.*

"So far you have passed."

"I don't understand."

"You have a gift. It is your gift to understand, Lacey. You will."

Despite her rising panic, Lacey had always found *pressing on regardless* the best strategy. Well, maybe not the best, but it was all she had at the moment.

"The suit of lights?" She indicated his costume.

"From our production of *Don Juan in Hell*. Yuri envisioned Hell as a bullfighting ring."

Appropriate. I seem to be in Hell right now. "I haven't seen that show."

He smiled. "No need. I will explain everything you need to know."

"And the mask from the *Red Death.* You didn't have to look very far to find it, did you? This is your place, and everything is always in its place, isn't it, Nikolai?" She felt like a pawn in some stupid game. "It was never lost in the move."

"No, it wasn't. Are you afraid of me, Lacey?"

"Of course I am."

"An honest answer is so refreshing." He took one step toward her and she stepped back. His smile looked strange inside the white mask of his makeup. "Let me assure you, you have no reason to fear me."

"Under the circumstances that's a little hard to believe." She took another step back.

"But you were the one who sought *me* out. I am flattered." He stepped forward again.

"Just doing my job."

"I disagree. You do far more than your job requires. I suspect you have uncovered some of my secrets. Don't you want to ask me questions?"

"Is this an interview now, as well as a test?"

"If you like, Lacey, my dear." Nikolai Sokolov speaking her name felt wrong. It felt too intimate.

"You'll know what I know by the questions I ask you."

"Very good. This test is going well." His smile spread wider. Everything she said seemed to please this man.

"You don't mind if I keep my distance?" Lacey asked.

"Not at all." He took another step toward her and she stepped away again, slowly, as if they were doing some macabre dance in slow motion. Vic was on his way, she told herself. Any second. Turtledove and Gregor Kepelov too.

"Perhaps we should sit down. We'll be more comfortable. This way?" He indicated a direction past the mirror and waited until she inclined her head.

"All right." *Just keep buying time, Lacey. The cavalry is on the way.*

Sokolov let the mask hang by its red ribbons. They were knotted around his neck, its tails draped down his back. He made an exotic stage picture in the ghostly white makeup, the matador's suit of lights, and the crimson mask with its sparkling scarlet feathers spreading across his chest like a spray of blood.

Down another aisle and around a corner and then another, he had set the scene for them: a small café table and two chairs, beneath another high stained-glass window. No one could see them there. On the table, a bottle was cradled in a bucket of ice, and crystal glasses were nearby. He made a flourish with his hand.

"Sit. Please."

All this for my benefit? "How long have you been planning this?"

"I like to be a good host." He indicated a chair. She remained standing. "Would you like a drink?"

She realized her throat was dry. He uncorked the chilled bottle and handed it to her with a wine steward's gesture, as if offering it for her approval. She took it and poured some bubbling liquid into one of the glasses. She picked up the glass, but she let it hover in the air.

Polonium? Dioxin? Cyanide? What's your poison?

"You wouldn't mind taking the first sip for me, would you?" she asked.

He laughed. "You delight me, do you know that? Let me assure you, the bottle has not been tampered with. Scout's honor."

Are there boy scouts in Russia?

He took the glass from her, drank it down, and handed it back to her. "My champagne is very good. You can trust me."

"Why?"

"Why?" He smiled again. "A good question. I want to talk with you. I want to know what you have discovered."

"And in exchange, will you answer my questions honestly?"

He wrinkled his forehead. It made furrows in his white makeup. "I will try, though I must tell you, *honesty* has never been my strongest suit. How could it be, living a life in the theatre? We deal with illusion and fantasy. Now, please sit. I am way over here on my side of the table. More than an arm's length away. You are quite safe."

Maybe, maybe not. It annoyed her that he knew what she was thinking.

"Is your name really Nikolai Sokolov?"

"Oddly, yes. The name I was born with. It's easier that way."

"And Yuri Volkov is your cousin?"

"To his everlasting shame and horror, I am afraid. He is stuck with me."

"That doesn't seem to bother you."

"Not very much. People say I, and others like me, have no empathy. It is true, mostly. But every once in a while— The sensation surprises me."

"You do have feelings, though?"

"I am not a robot."

"Is that why you were drawn to the theatre? To understand human emotions, or to mimic them?"

"Very good. Both, actually. The very process of acting creates emotions, in both the audience and the actor. I like that. It's so strange. A little like magic. Do you know, I have feelings for you? I was fascinated by you even before we met."

"The Romanov diamonds?"

"And many other stories. The haunted shawl of the Kepelovs, for one. I could fall in love with you, Lacey Smithsonian."

She tried to keep her cool. It was difficult. "That sounds very dangerous for me, Nikolai."

"I understand how you might think that. We'll come back to that later. For now let's talk about the theatre. I have always enjoyed the challenge of it, to get into the psyche of it. And to learn about the emotions, the ones they say I don't have. To learn, as it were, how to be a human being." He poured champagne into both glasses and took one. Lacey let hers stand. "Most people, it seems, can't go a day or two without a big emotional scene. How do they stand it, I wonder? How does it work?"

"You mean on stage?"

"And off. Backstage is sometimes much more dramatic than on stage. Big emotions, big scenes, small emotions, quiet little deceptions. I find people very entertaining."

"Has acting human been a challenge for you?"

He laughed. "Exhausting."

"Tell me about Saige Russell. Did you love her or was it an act?"

"I did love her. A completely new feeling. A surprise. Strange and upsetting, with so many violent emotions. It was wonderful. And awful."

"Her death wasn't an accident, was it?"

He saluted her with his glass. "No, not an accident. Though no one has thought otherwise, all these years, until Lacey Smithsonian walked through the door."

"Did you kill her?"

"Your line of questioning is very direct. You are an excellent reporter, I think. Yes, I'm afraid it came to that. I must say Saige's death caused me some discomfort. Don't think it did not."

Discomfort? Lacey swallowed hard. Her throat was dry again. She eyed the bottle and her bubbling glass. "Why? What happened?"

"They say confession is good for the soul. Let's try it. You know of course I have no soul."

Exactly what Kepelov said.

"I had to do it, you see."

"It wasn't because she was a terrible actress, was it?"

"You've been talking to others from that show, I see. Saige had developed a bad reputation among the cast and crew. She wasn't very good, but even *I* don't kill an actor for a bad performance. Yuri might. Although I don't think he ever has. I know he's wanted to. Many times." Sokolov laughed at his own joke.

"Was she cheating on you?"

"Perhaps. If she wasn't, I'm sure she would have, eventually. It was her way. The truth is, I couldn't stand it. Love. The way I felt. Love, to me, it felt out of control, savage. Violent. Incomprehensible. Walking around with a stupid grin on my face. The next moment, miserable. It was as if something alien had entered my body. Yuri was happy for me, he thought love would change me into 'a real live boy,' you might say. Like Pinocchio. We've done *Pinocchio* here, did you know? I costumed a squad of dancers as a great sperm whale. It was magnificent!" He took another sip of champagne. "But Saige was not my blue fairy. I felt rage like a tiger when she wasn't on time. When she finally appeared, I floated like a feather. Things like that. Love. So very strange."

Lacey never took her eyes off Nikolai Sokolov. She let him talk, willing her heart to slow down, willing her brain to speed up, her reflexes to be ready.

"Love was an earthquake inside of me. I thought I might explode. I might change. I might die. But I was a younger man. It would be different today."

"But you were in love," she managed to say. "And yet you killed her?"

"Strange, isn't it? To most people. Not to me."

"Did you feel any remorse? What did it make you feel?"

God, I'm sounding just like a broadcast reporter! This IS Hell! And where the hell is Vic? Turtledove? Kepelov?

"I felt regret, I admit. That too was an unaccustomed emotion. But better, I felt back in control. In equilibrium. Myself, again. Don't fret, my dear Lacey. It was years ago. It would never happen again."

Don't fret?! "Why not, if I might ask?" *Love and death are the same to him.*

"I've learned so much since then. I have so much more self-control. Self-knowledge. 'Mastering others is mere strength, mastering oneself is true power.' Do you know that quote? I have that mastery now. Now I am ready once again."

She wanted to jump up and run, not walk, to the nearest exit. Instead, Lacey gripped the arms of her chair.

"You're ready? Ready for what?"

"To love again."

FORTY-TWO

"YES, I AM READY TO love again. But first I would have to find the most amazing woman." Sokolov looked directly at Lacey. "I see you are not ready to talk about this yet, Smithsonian. But you know who I mean."

"What kind of woman, Nikolai?" Lacey thought her heart stopped for a moment. Now it was racing again.

"The woman I could love has special abilities. To see who people are by the clothes they wear and the clothes they create. She would have an extra sense about these things, and she can remain calm when faced with—unexpected information. She would be very beautiful to look at. She would have an intellect I could admire. You are the only woman who captures my imagination, Lacey."

Oh my God. "Please, Nikolai."

"Very well, for now. We have much more to discuss. Amy Keaton, for one."

Lacey willed her heart to keep beating. "Yes. Amy Keaton."

"I suspected you knew about her. Quick, not painful. Everybody believed it was an accident. But for Lacey Smithsonian, it was possibly too close to the method I used for Saige. Perhaps a misstep. But what could the two women possibly have in common?"

"The red dress," she said.

"The red dress. Amy knew that gown was never to be sold."

"She was afraid of you."

"Yes, even though I was never mean to her. Never a cross word. I suppose she sensed something. Then when the costume was gone, her excuses were pathetic. She put the dress on the rack by mistake, tried to get it back, bungled that too, behaved like a crazy woman. So unlike the way she ran our shows. She was a good stage manager, but I cannot tolerate sloppiness. Or fear."

"I can see that." *What would he do if he knew it was actually Yuri who ditched the dress?*

"You have seen my creation. Saige's beautiful dress." It wasn't a question.

"I was with LaToya, when she fell in love with it."

"Then why wasn't it in her apartment?" He leveled his blue gaze at her.

"When you broke in on Sunday night?"

"Yes. Of course you knew that." Sokolov seemed amused, not angry.

"The burglary at LaToya's was very theatrical," she said. "Setting her clothes around the room, her shoes and accessories. Stuffing them so they looked alive."

"It was fun. Hard to resist. You saw them." He waved his glass like a baton and smiled. "Obviously I wanted her to know someone had been there."

"You accomplished that. And you freaked her out."

"And you?"

"Me too. I'm glad you didn't hurt her."

"She's a lovely creature. There was no reason to hurt her. However, I was annoyed that my costume wasn't there."

"LaToya said she's a light sleeper, she wakes at the slightest noise. But she didn't. How did you do that?"

He narrowed his eyes. "Insightful, Lacey. It would not do to have her wake up. I may have used something to render her unconscious for a while. I'm afraid that is a trade secret." He frowned thoughtfully. "Still, why wasn't the dress there? Let me think. If I were your friend LaToya Crawford, someone who worked with you and knew of your capabilities and your history, perhaps I would ask you to look at the dress for me and— Approve it? Or research it, or something like that?" Sokolov grinned as she broke eye contact. "Maybe she asked you to keep it for her for a while. Do you have the dress, Lacey? I won't be angry, I promise, I just want it back."

"It's not in my possession, but I've seen it."

"And it revealed itself to you. After all, clothes tell you stories. What did it tell you?"

Lying would be pointless, she decided. It might simply enrage him. The result might be unpredictable, whereas sitting calmly and telling each other stories was much more civilized. She put her hands in her lap, carefully calculating how easily she could extract the paper mask and the little bottle.

"I did examine the dress. And I found something hidden there."

"Go on."

"I found medals. Medals with Lenin's face. I didn't understand what they meant."

"You contacted Gregor Kepelov?"

"He's a friend. And he's the only one I knew who might be able to tell me about the medals. Empty medals."

Sokolov snorted. "Kepelov seems like such a comedian. But it's an act. He is no fool. He told you about the poison needles, I presume." Again it was a statement. "And yet you didn't go to the police."

"They were empty. I didn't really know what to tell them yet. How long have you known Gregor Kepelov?"

"Only recently were we formally introduced. You were there, Lacey. But he had never known me by my real name. We knew each other by reputation only. You keep dangerous company."

Lacey felt her eyes open wide. "Apparently I do. Present company included."

"Indeed, but I have tremendous respect for you."

"There were seven Lenins," Lacey said.

He nodded. "That is my count."

"Including Saige? What about Amy?"

"Unfortunately, the dress was missing. I still have the hollow medal that contained that needle. I'll show it to you, if you like."

"She was a sad little woman."

"I spared her a sad little life."

"But that's not your call."

"I disagree. In this case it was my call." He reached for the bottle and poured himself more champagne. "May I pour for you?"

She nodded. He filled her glass, but she left it untouched.

"Are you angry that I found them?" Her throat was sore from being so dry.

"Not angry. Impressed. You know some of my secrets, so now I can tell you many more things."

"There are six other Lenins. Who do they represent?"

"No one you would know. Only a few key assignments, accomplishments that are important to me in one way or another."

There really are more deaths.

"Your greatest hits? So the dress is your trophy?"

"I don't like that word. It's not like I put stuffed heads on my walls."

"A memorial then?" That's what Marie had said.

"If you like." Sokolov shifted in his seat. "Or an accounting."

"An accounting? Are you talking about the Centipede?"

He reached for her hand, but she drew it back. "Very impressive. You have been busy."

"Are you the Centipede?"

"The Centipede is dead. Would you prefer it if I were that legendary character?"

"I would prefer the truth."

"Of course you would. Ever the journalist. Where did you hear that name, I wonder? The Centipede never existed, not officially. And of course now he is dead, and I, Nikolai Sokolov, am very much alive."

"You've had other names," she said.

"Many."

"And one of them was the Centipede."

He spread his hands wide. "According to Gregor Kepelov? There are unsuspected depths to that man. But the Centipede does *not* exist. Because there is no proper accounting of him. No proper recognition. Only empty medals in a red dress. Perhaps he should exist."

"Nikolai Sokolov exists."

"He has only minor accomplishments. Costumes. Makeup. Illusions."

"Disguises," Lacey said. "A man of a thousand faces."

Which face was she seeing? She strained to listen for Vic's footsteps, anyone's footsteps, but she heard nothing.

"You flatter me. I am not only Sokolov. I am a myth. I am no man's friend. I am not recognized. There are no records of my deeds. Should we not keep a record, even of the monsters in this world?"

"Is that how you see yourself, Sokolov? A monster?"

"Not when I'm with you. I'm flattered that you sought out the secrets of the red dress. That you cared enough to explore it. And to find me."

"You still want the dress back?"

"I hate loose ends."

"Then why lend it to all those actresses?"

"My pretty little flowers, yes. Wearing my masterpiece. All innocence and hope."

"Innocence? Wearing a record of your kills?" A slight shrug. "Who were the others?"

"Not all at once, Lacey. Too much information. We have plenty of time."

"The Russian billionaire who was beaten to death in his hotel room in D.C.?"

"I believe the official cause of death was a heart attack," he said. "A condition that could have been brought on by a beating. So many heart attacks in Washington among the Russian community. Yes, he was one of my assignments, but believe me, he was an asshole. You would have thought so too. For now it's enough that I have found a woman who understands me. That is my confession."

Oh, he really doesn't know how this confession thing works, Lacey thought.

"I'm not a priest. I can't absolve you."

"You can forgive me. You understand me, and to understand is to forgive. Don't you agree?"

Vic should have been here by now. I'm on my own.

"Hold that thought. I really have to go." She stood up quickly. But Sokolov was quicker. He overturned the table and the glasses with a crash, and suddenly he was right in front of her, face to face, grabbing her arms.

"My dear Lacey, that won't be possible." She tried to step away, tried to pull free, but he was too close, too strong. He kissed her mouth. Urgently. "Don't be afraid of me, Lacey. Do you know how beautiful you are? How you move me? How you've changed me?"

She shook her head desperately. *Did he say that to Saige before he killed her?* Where did he have the next poison needle?

"That was too abrupt of me, I can see." Sokolov brushed her lips with his fingers. "I apologize, Lacey. But I cannot let you go. Not just yet. You cannot leave."

He released her and she took a step back. She needed space between them. Enough space to reach the bottle in her pocket. Enough space to use it.

"What do you think you're doing? You said you wouldn't hurt me."

"And I won't hurt you. I'm certainly not going to kill you, if that's what you think. I have a place for you here."

"A place? What are you talking about?"

"Here. In the townhouse, connected to the theatre. Upstairs there is a third floor with a private suite. Bath, bedroom, a small kitchen. A private staircase. It's mine, I live there sometimes."

The heat was becoming oppressive. Sweat was running in rivulets down her neck. Sokolov's forehead was wet, his white makeup coursing down his face in streaks.

"You are not keeping me here."

"But it's very pleasant and secure up there. Very soundproof. You can't even hear our shows from up there, and you know how loud Yuri's music can be."

"You're mad."

"Maybe. But I know what I want and I want you, Lacey."

"I'm engaged."

"Yes. To me. I will give you opals that match your eyes."

She pushed away from him and darted right through the nearest clothing rack, into another aisle of costumes. She sprinted for the door. *Where is it?!*

He called after her, laughing. "You can't run away from me, Lacey. But I admire your spirit."

She couldn't remember all the turns and twists they had taken on their way to the table. Sokolov was pursuing her, but not in a hurry. The closet was a maze of racks of clothes, she was getting dizzy, she was hot. She ducked through racks from aisle to aisle and tore clothes from their hangers.

"You will get used to my ways," she heard him calling out behind her. "You will grow to love me. In time."

"There isn't that much time in the universe," she yelled back.

Save your breath, Lacey! She wiped her face. *Keep running.* He was too close, just a yard or two away. She grabbed a heavy brocade coat from a rack and turned and threw it over him. He stopped to peel it off his face and held it up to examine it, streaked with his white makeup.

"Is that any way to treat poor Falstaff?"

"You don't want me, Nikolai."

"I do. Really. You have a great spirit. And know this, my darling, I always get what I want." He dropped the brocade coat and flicked away the feathers of the red mask. "There have always been women wanting to crowd my bed. Much too easy. You're a challenge. You are so much smarter than Saige."

Let's hope so. She stepped back, sliding her hand into her skirt pocket for the little spray bottle. He stepped toward her confidently, and with her free hand she grabbed clothes at random and threw them in his face, shirts, scarves, hats.

Where the hell is the door?!

Sokolov reached out for her. She dove right into a rack of black velvet gowns and tumbled out into the next aisle. When she stood up, she saw this aisle was right up against the wall, and she had no idea where the door was. She leaned against the wall. Nowhere else to go. Her legs were shaking and her hands were slick with sweat.

She lifted the spray bottle of Kepelov's secret juice to eye level with her finger on the button. With her left hand she slapped a paper respirator over her face, pinching the metal clip over her nose. She looped the elastic over her head and waited. Her wait was less than a second.

"Don't you know you can't hide from me? This is my kingdom!" Sokolov bellowed, only feet away. He ripped open the curtain of black clothes and thrust his head through the gap. He stared at the paper mask on her face and frowned. "Another mask?"

Lacey pressed the button hard and sprayed him right in the face. *Bull's eye.*

Sokolov's eyes registered utter astonishment, just before they rolled back in his head. He crumpled and fell to the floor. She looked down at his prone figure, holding the mask tightly to her face.

Now what, she wondered. *Do I tie him up? Spray him again?*

Finally she heard the sound she'd been waiting for.

Footsteps.

FORTY-THREE

*T*HE SIGHT OF VIC, and then Turtledove, guns drawn and paper respirators on their faces, bursting through racks of costumes and leaving silks and satins in their wake, was something Lacey would never forget.

They were a little late, but she was thrilled to see them.

Nikolai Sokolov lay senseless on the floor, a toppled white mannequin in a suit of lights. An anguished Vic grabbed her and she held on fast. It was the best thing that had happened to Lacey all day. Tears stung her eyes above her paper mask.

"I'm so sorry, sweetheart. Traffic was jammed by a freaking presidential motorcade, and all I could do was sit there and listen to that madman put the moves on you. I thought I'd lose my mind." He gazed at the fallen Sokolov. "You know, when I came through that door I was ready to beat the hell out of him, but I see you got there first."

"That was the longest and slowest damn motorcade I've ever seen," Turtledove said. He deftly stepped over a pile of costumes to contemplate the man on the floor. "I thought Vic was going to jump out of the Jeep and run. I was afraid he'd have the entire Secret Service running after him."

Kepelov showed up a moment later, pistol drawn, respirator on, and carefully treading through mounds of costumes. "Unbelievable. First, presidential motorcade. Then, no parking space. Gremlin is in a loading zone. Probably get a ticket." He considered the deflated matador on the floor and grinned happily. "I told you it would work, Lacey Smithsonian. Good stuff, my secret juice, huh?"

For Lacey, things now seemed to be moving in slow motion, and the room was spinning. She sagged against Vic and he grabbed her before she fell.

"It's the solution," Kepelov said. "She needs air. Quickly. I will take care of our sleazy friend." He whipped out a pair of handcuffs, flipped Sokolov over on his stomach, and cuffed his hands. He also took the precaution of searching him for hollow

Lenin medals or other deadly weapons. "Interesting. Nothing. Perhaps he was serious when he said he didn't plan to hurt our Smithsonian. He is unarmed. A tactical error for the famous Centipede."

Vic picked Lacey up in his arms. Turtledove hoisted the unconscious Sokolov on his shoulders. Kepelov led the way out through the maze of costume racks, down the hall and into the second floor lobby. Vic set Lacey back on her feet and fished out his phone. Turtledove dumped Sokolov on the floor and sat down on him for safekeeping.

"I have to make some calls."

"Call D.C. Homicide, Vic. Ask for Lamont." She pulled off the mask, gulped the air-conditioned air, and steadied herself against the wall. Vic found her a chair and made sure she wasn't going to fall out of it. "Seriously, Vic. Call Broadway Lamont first."

Vic stopped tapping numbers on his phone. "I was calling the FBI. You know the Metropolitan police won't get jurisdiction over this guy, sweetheart. The Feds will grab him."

"I know, Vic. But calling the D.C. cops will delay the process. Long enough until my story runs. No Feds yet."

"The Feds will not be happy about the District butting in," Kepelov said. "Feds will deny everything, take all the credit. My guess, they will shut down all information about this before it sees light of day."

"No! No way. No one is shutting my story down, or taking me into *protective* custody. Or trying to force me to reveal my sources. I'm not letting the friends of the Kremlin call this fake news. If we're lucky, the Feds don't know anything about him. If they did, they'd have already—" She stopped. "Or wait a minute. What if they've known all along that Nikolai Sokolov was the Centipede? Maybe they've been protecting him?"

"Don't jump to conclusions, Lacey," Vic said. "That's Brooke's job."

"Right. But in the meantime, the D.C. police will snarl things up nicely and give me time to break this story. After that, I don't care who gets the Centipede."

"Lacey—" Vic didn't look happy about this plan. He had friends at the Bureau. "Okay. I get your point. I'll call Broadway's cell and ask him to keep it off the radio. Last thing I need is DeadFed trying to confuse the issue."

"Smithsonian is right, guys," Kepelov said. "She must expose this scum in the sunshine so the Centipede can't run and hide again. Or be traded back to Russia. We know foreign operatives are working against us. In this case, free press is best protection. Then everyone will know the Centipede is caught. And caught by a woman."

"You heard the man, Vic," Lacey said, getting to her feet. "A free press is our only protection."

"You two sound like a recruiting poster," Vic said, but he tapped his phone. "I'm calling Broadway Lamont."

While Vic talked to Lamont, Lacey watched Turtledove cinch Sokolov's ankles securely together with a pair of plastic cuffs and then sit back down on him. At the sight of the Centipede, she felt her stomach turn over. Standing up might not have been a good idea either. She staggered to the restroom and threw up.

When she felt better, she dared a look into the mirror. *Yikes.* Her makeup had melted. Her hair was a damp mess. There was a knock on the ladies' room door. It was Kepelov. He handed over her tote bag.

"I was thinking you might need this, Smithsonian. Also I retrieved the little bottle. Is safe. Not good to leave such things laying around. Glad you found it of use."

"Thank you, Gregor."

She took remedial action: her hair, her face, foundation, blush, and mascara. She re-tucked her top into her skirt before heading back to the lobby. Nikolai Sokolov was just coming to. He stirred beneath Turtledove's considerable mass and lifted his head an inch to take in his situation.

"I am flattered by your precautions, gentlemen. Even I didn't know I was this dangerous." His eyes searched for Lacey, squinting up at her from the floor. "Lacey Smithsonian. You have redone your makeup for me. Very nice. Thank you."

"It's war paint." *War paint* was one of Aunt Mimi's favorite expressions. And Lacey was ready to do battle.

"How very appropriate," he replied. "I appreciate your spirit."

Turtledove volunteered to retrieve her laptop from her car so she could start writing. She threw him her car keys, never taking her eyes off Sokolov. White makeup streaked down his face in tracks of sweat. His eyes were bloodshot from the spray of Doctor Kepelov's secret formula. The effect was startling. He looked like a tragic-comic harlequin dressed up as a matador. The mask from *The Masque of the Red Death* still hung around his neck, its scarlet feathers now tipped with white.

Freed from Turtledove's weight, Sokolov struggled to sit up. Kepelov lifted him into a sitting position and steadied him against the wall. He locked eyes with Sokolov.

"One bad move," Kepelov said, "you're a dead man. You breathe wrong, you're a dead man. I get tired of looking at you, you're a dead man."

"I know the drill, comrade," Sokolov said.

"Call me comrade again, you're a dead man." Kepelov pulled up a chair and sat still as a snake.

"Forgive me, Lacey. I have not had a chance to make myself more presentable. My feelings for you made me— impractical." Sokolov tried to look down at the mask, still hanging around his neck. "The feathers are tickling my chin."

"You said I could see the mask."

"So I did. I want you to have it. However, I'm afraid you will have to take it from me. I am tied up at the moment." Even tied up and surrounded by enemies, Sokolov could try to be droll. Kepelov shook his head at Lacey in warning, but Sokolov gave him a look. "Not you, Kepelov. Lacey Smithsonian must do it. Or believe me, you will have to kill me."

Kepelov turned to Vic, now off the phone. "What do you think, Donovan? Trust me, there is nothing this creature can do to us now."

Vic was as tense as a panther on the prowl. "We'll take it off him, Lacey. You don't have to do this."

"Yes, I do." Lacey looked at Vic. "I've come this far."

"If you must." Vic stepped in closer and put his hand on Lacey's back. He pulled his pistol and held it down at his side. Kepelov moved in tight.

She knelt down close to Nikolai Sokolov and put her arms behind his neck to untie the mask's ribbons. Her hands were shaking.

"How close you are." He breathed in deeply. "I can smell your perfume, your distinctive scent. I will never forget it." He started to cough.

She took the mask and leaned back on her heels. Vic and Kepelov stepped back.

"Thank you. Gregor, can you get him something to drink? Like a soda? There must be a straw at the bar. And one for me, too, please."

"Sometimes, Smithsonian, your humanitarian instincts are too kind," Gregor said. "He does not deserve it." The subdued Centipede was still coughing.

Vic retrieved drinks for them. He handed one to Lacey, and one to Kepelov with a straw. "I'll cover you."

Gregor took the soda and let Sokolov drink. He sucked on the straw, swallowed, and breathed deeply.

"Much better." Sokolov coughed again, never taking his gaze off Lacey. "Thank you, Lacey. I suggest you put that artifact out of sight before the police get here. They can be grabby."

"That's evidence, you know," Vic said.

"I can turn it over later," Lacey said. "After I examine it."

"Not to worry, Donovan," Kepelov said. "Things will be busy here very soon. No one will miss one little costume item. It might even be valuable, if only for its associations with evil."

"Kepelov, your reputation precedes you," Sokolov said. "Practical and avaricious."

"And I am up here and you are down there."

"For now."

Lacey examined the mask. Vic lifted an eyebrow at the idea of concealing evidence, even something like a prop.

"I know what you're thinking, Vic, but I've earned a closer look at this thing," Lacey pointed out. "I found the Lenins in the dress, and I know we'll have to turn that over. But this may be a crucial part of the story. He loaned out the dress, but he held on to this mask. Maybe it's even more valuable to him. Why?"

"Only you, my darling Lacey, could begin to understand," Sokolov said. "After all we have shared."

"Say that again and I punch your lights out." Vic lifted a fist.

"No need. I can't fight back. You must be the fiancé."

No matter what Sokolov said, Lacey could never forget that he killed the last woman he loved. She considered the brilliant red mask. The backing was made of thin leather, and it had held its shape well for a dozen years. The front was covered with several layers of red fabric. She traced with one finger the jeweled gold braid outlining the eyes and mouth. *Did he make it in Saige's image?*

"For the longest time, I could smell Saige's scent on it," Sokolov said. "Now, forevermore, I will be reminded of you. On the side, there is a little catch. Try it."

She felt for the catch, found it, and pulled the outer mask away, revealing the inner mask, the death's head, the skull beneath the skin that shocked audiences at *The Masque of the Red Death*. She glanced up at the Centipede.

"This must have been an amazing moment on stage every night, Sokolov."

He bowed his head slightly. "I am honored."

She turned the skull mask over. On the smooth leather of the back, the side that would hug the wearer's face, she saw symbols and writing in Cyrillic.

"And on the back. A record of your kills?"

"Assignments perhaps. Perhaps other assorted achievements. Or perhaps not."

It's the key to his code, she thought. The coded marks on the backs of the Lenins. He stared at her as if reading her thoughts. He gave her the slightest nod.

"Your face gives everything away, Lacey Smithsonian. Very expressive. You would make a fine actress. And one who could learn her lines."

"It's a good thing I'm not a poker player," she said.

Footsteps pounded up the stairs and they turned at the sound. It was Turtledove, returning with her laptop and her car keys.

Lacey put the inner and outer masks back together and tucked the thing into her tote bag. She opened her laptop on one of the café tables in the lobby. While her computer booted up, Lacey called Mac's cell phone. When he answered, children were squealing in the background and there was the sound of cheering.

"Hey Mac, I'm filing that story today," she said. "The one we talked about. Things developed quickly. I suppose the weekend editor can take it, if you don't want it. How's the game going?"

"What do you mean, things developed?"

"It's a bit of a situation. But it's under control now."

"Tell him you caught the notorious Russian assassin, the Centipede!" Sokolov yelled, loud enough for Mac to hear him. "Only Smithsonian could have done it."

"Who's that?" Mac asked. "You caught him by yourself?"

"I had a little help."

"What does that mean?"

"He's tied up and we're waiting for Broadway Lamont."

"You had to do this on a Saturday? We're at the girls' soccer game."

"News never sleeps, Mac. You know that."

"I'm calling Claudia. And our attorney. Keep me apprised."

"Spread the joy. Gotta go." Lacey hung up and began to type.

Seven Deadly Lenins Hidden in a Hem: The Eye Street Observer Unmasks a Notorious Russian Spy
By Lacey Smithsonian

Just hours before Kinetic Theatre's opening night of *The Turn of the Screw* in Northwest D.C., a suspected Russian spy and assassin was apprehended in the theatre's costume shop by the Metropolitan Police Department, with help from *The Eye Street Observer*.

Many dignitaries, including the Russian Ambassador, were expected to attend an exclusive donor gala at the Russian émigré-established theatre company later Saturday evening. Russian native Nikolai Sokolov, Kinetic's resident costume designer, allegedly led a double life as a foreign agent sometimes known as "the Centipede," working undetected for years in the United States. He is thought to have breached security at the highest levels of the US government and claims credit for an unknown number of assassinations under orders from the Kremlin...

Vic stood over her shoulder as she typed. "Someone is going to have an aneurysm reading this."

"Those are the breaks, darling," she replied and kept typing. "Brooke will love it. I just don't know if she will ever forgive me. For not bringing her into this."

He squeezed her shoulders and kissed her neck. "Do what you need to do, sweetheart. She'll forgive you. Eventually. Or not."

Lacey focused on her screen.

The alleged spy confessed to *Eye Street Observer* reporter Lacey Smithsonian to two murders related to the Kinetic Theatre, and to the death of a Russian billionaire found battered to death in a hotel in the District last year. That murder was initially ruled as a death by natural causes from a heart attack.

Sokolov has been working as the master costumer for Kinetic for more than a decade, and he has won two Helen Hayes awards for his costume designs. Some might say the theatre was the perfect cover for a master of disguise...

FORTY-FOUR

"*I* LIKE WATCHING YOU work," the Centipede said.

Lacey glanced over at Sokolov, a little concerned that he might break out of his restraints. She knew she had nothing to worry about, with Vic, Turtledove and Kepelov all on guard, but *still*. Sokolov wore an enigmatic smile. He caught her eyes with his.

"Enjoy the view, Sokolov," she told him, returning to her laptop. "It's the last time you'll ever see me at work."

"Never say never," he said.

"Why have you not quoted me?" Gregor Kepelov had also come to stand behind her, peering over her other shoulder.

"You guys are worse than my editor. Back up. Do not watch me write. And Gregor, I am happy to quote you, but can I use your name?"

"Of course not," he said. "You may attribute my statements to a formerly highly placed operative of Russian intelligence services who defected to the United States."

"I'll have to finesse that."

"Not a problem. The people who need to know will know who your anonymous source is. Remember who first said to Lacey Smithsonian the word Centipede." Lacey added his comments to her story. *Nice to have experts on hand.*

Heavy steps pounding up the stairs interrupted the flow of her fingers. Everyone stopped and looked expectantly at the lobby door. Kepelov put his hand on his concealed pistol.

Like a Russian storm cloud, Yuri Volkov burst in, glaring around the room. He stopped short at the sight of his cousin trussed up on the floor. He stared at Lacey and her comrades, then back to Sokolov. He grabbed his head with both hands and opened and shut his mouth several times before speaking.

"What is going on here?!" he finally burst out. "You are making a mess in my theatre! My party begins in a few hours! Important people will be here."

"Your cousin Nikolai killed Saige Russell and Amy Keaton," Lacey said without looking up from her laptop.

"You must have suspected, Yuri," Sokolov said placidly.

"Get him out of here! Now!" Volkov's face was turning bright red.

"Did I mention, Lacey, we are not a particularly close family?" Sokolov said.

"You!" Volkov spat at him. "You have traded on our family connection ever since you came here. Don't think I will cry at your funeral. I will piss vodka on your grave!"

"As I said." Sokolov didn't bother looking at anyone but Lacey. "I anticipate your story in the newspaper with great pleasure."

"Get him out of here, please. I don't care where you take him," Volkov begged. "I will do anything you want."

Before anyone could answer, another thunderous commotion headed their way. It sounded like a rampaging bull roaring up the stairs.

It wasn't a bull. It was Detective Broadway Lamont, followed by a herd of uniformed police. Lamont was dressed casually in blue jeans and a blue polo shirt, except of course for his bulletproof vest and holstered pistol, and the badge hooked onto his belt.

"Smithsonian, what the ever-loving hell are you up to now?"

DeeDee Adler had crept up the stairs behind the mob of D.C. cops and peeked into the lobby. She stage-whispered to Volkov, "Yuri, I'll be downstairs if you need me." She backed up right into a D.C. uniformed officer, who shook his head at her.

Volkov stepped into Lamont's face and glared up at the big man.

"I don't know what's going on here, officer. We have a show tonight and our donors are coming. Opening night. Big party. I need this cleaned up."

"You mean this isn't the main event?" Lamont pointed at Nikolai Sokolov. "This white guy here on the floor, a prop in your show? Anybody want to tell me why this guy is a little *extra* white?"

"Not a prop, officer. I am the master fashion criminal himself. Ask Lacey Smithsonian."

If he wasn't enjoying himself, Sokolov was giving a good impression of it, and he clearly liked being the star of the show.

Actors, Lacey thought, typing away.

"Nice of y'all to wrap him up for me." The big detective turned to Lacey. "Speak to me, Smithsonian. This is part of the latest fashion crime? I am talking about that damn red dress."

"Yes, it's about the red dress." *And the scarlet mask.*

"How many people did you tell about us, Lacey?" Sokolov for the first time seemed pained. "What did you tell this man?"

"She told me nothing." Lamont turned his glare on Sokolov. "I know the woman who bought the damn dress and had her apartment tossed. And let me tell you, Mister Matador, it's caused me grief. A lot of grief."

"And yet Ms. LaToya Crawford is alive to complain about it." Sokolov returned his gaze to Lacey. "My feelings for you made me unforgivably human. I know you are brilliant, but still I underestimated you. You will tell my story, won't you?"

"I'm just a fashion reporter, Nikolai. But I'll try to do it justice."

"That's all I ask. The Centipede will not be anonymous anymore. He will not be a myth. I will exist, because of you."

Lamont side-eyed both of them. "Oh no, you don't. You got the hots for Smithsonian? That's a fast train to nowhere."

Sokolov gazed at Lacey longingly. "Lacey, my dear Lacey, I am tired of being a monster. I adore you. I could love you forever. But in practical terms, you know, I should have killed you."

Lacey stopped typing and looked up. She took a deep breath. "You say the weirdest things, Sokolov."

"You are not so easily rid of me. I have much more information."

The kind the government would be interested in, she thought. *Probably several governments.*

"You're not in the position to bargain for anything, Sokolov," Vic said.

"You think not? Who knows how many dresses are out there? Perhaps with additional records of my—job history?" Sokolov said. "There is a lot to learn. A lot to write."

"You're bluffing. You're no Scheherazade," Lacey said.

"But I am. Can I tell a story a day to keep myself alive? And living in comfortable circumstances here in the USA? I like my odds. And yours, Lacey. Especially if I only agree to talk to *you.*"

"I knew it," Kepelov said. "I told you so. Our Centipede does not want to go back to Mother Russia."

Broadway Lamont raised his voice.

"Enough! Everybody chill! Okay, Nikolai Sokolov, I got enough to bring you in for questioning right there. I suppose I'll get to arm wrestle with the State Department, Homeland Security, CIA, FBI, NSA, every other damn alphabet agency. In the meantime, everybody shut up until I get your statements."

Lamont motioned to his troops. Two officers took command of Sokolov and got him to his feet. Two more pulled out tablets to start taking statements. A female forensics tech pulled out a big DSLR.

"Detective, I don't care what you do with this man or where you put him." Volkov ran his fingers through his hair and tapped on his Rolex. "But please hurry! The Kinetic Theatre would be most grateful if this man's removal could be arranged with the utmost speed."

"Wouldn't we all?" Lamont said, unflustered.

"You have never liked me much, cousin," Sokolov remarked. "Understandable. Sorry to be such a problem."

"You are a tool of an evil state!" Volkov shouted at him. "I lose actors when you are around. I lose a perfectly good stage manager because of you."

Sokolov was impassive as the D.C. cops locked him in a prisoner transport body chain. Lacey's eyes went wide at this precaution.

"My suggestion," Vic said modestly.

"Good idea too," Lamont added. "Now, tell me, Smithsonian, are we expecting any more party guests at this shindig?"

Lacey didn't have to say *yes.* Her publisher Claudia Darnell arrived in the second-floor lobby, followed by staff photographer Todd Hansen, draped with cameras and his usual jaunty attitude.

"Hey, Lacey! I wasn't supposed to work this weekend, but my buddy got the flu and I got lucky." He flashed two thumbs-up and a smile.

"Claudia, this story is going to be big trouble," Lacey told her. Under her breath she added, "We have a confession.

Sokolov admits killing Saige Russell, Amy Keaton, and others. He's the Centipede."

"Well then! A hell of a story." Claudia's eyes glittered like aquamarines. She wore a white linen sheath, Lacey thought, because the good guys always wear white. And it went so well with her tan. She gazed over Lacey's shoulder at her laptop screen. "So far, so good. If we're going down, Lacey, we're going down in a blaze of glory." She winked. "And we'll take 'em all down with us."

Claudia turned her devastating smile on Broadway Lamont. She asked for a photograph and Lamont personally dragged Sokolov front and center, the big detective scowling in his fierce-yet-handsome way for Hansen's camera. Claudia pointed out other subjects for Hansen's lens, her cell phone glued to her ear.

Another loud voice was heard on the stairs, demanding access to the theatre's second floor lobby.

"Eye Street Observer! Let me in up there!" The officers at the door parted and Mac Jones burst on the scene in his jeans and sneakers and some kind of sports team shirt. Lacey didn't recognize the team. His press credentials dangled from his neck and he wore a red Washington Nationals baseball cap on his head.

"Welcome to the party. Where are the girls?" Lacey asked, still typing.

"They're waiting in the car with Kim."

She heard a high voice from the stairway. "We're here! We have to help Miss Lacey."

"I don't think they're in the car, Mac," Lacey said.

The voice belonged to Jasmine, one of Mac's soon-to-be-adopted daughters. Jasmine was thirteen and Lily Rose, now eleven, was right behind her big sister. Lacey saw a female officer trying to hold the girls back.

"Are you all right?" Jasmine shouted at Lacey. She struggled to see into the room around the cops.

"I'm fine," Lacey said.

"You don't look so good."

"Out of the mouths of babes, huh, Mac? Girls, this is how I look when I'm hard at work, writing a story for your dad."

"Are you sure you're okay, Miss Lacey?" Lily Rose asked with a frown.

"I'm so sure. I've got my whole village right here. Broadway, they're Mac's girls. Can't they sit right here with me?"

Lamont gestured to the cops at the door to let them in. The two girls slipped away from the officers and ran to Lacey's side. She grabbed them both in a group hug. The big detective warned them to be quiet and not to move a muscle, and they nodded their heads vigorously. Their heads spun in unison from Lacey to Mac to Broadway and Sokolov and back again.

Mac's wife Kim was right behind the girls. Her trim figure and immaculate outfit made Lacey feel like a mess. Lamont waved her in too, and Kim gathered her girls to her.

"Come on, girls. Now you have proof that Lacey is fine." Kim explained to everyone, "They had to see for themselves."

"You know Miss Lacey gets herself into trouble," Jasmine said to her mom.

"You know she does!" Lily Rose piped up, not to be outdone. "We have to watch her. We have to protect her." Lacey raised an eyebrow at Mac. *Was she a topic of conversation in their home?* "Now that she's okay, can we get pizza?" Lily Rose added.

"If you all don't mind," Broadway Lamont said. "I got work to do here. And Smithsonian, you've got one hell of a statement to write for me."

Wonderful. Something else to write.

Lacey Smithsonian's Fashion *Bites*

Make the Art of Illusion Your Friend

Clothing can be full of illusions—and delusions. One can enhance your look. And the other? Well, let's talk.

Illusion—the use of light and shadow, color and texture, to deceive the eye—is one of the theatre's tools of the trade. But it's not just for performers anymore. You too can employ clever illusions and a few theatrical tricks in your day-to-day wardrobe to emphasize your best points and camouflage your perceived flaws. What, you have no flaws? Right, me neither.

Consider the role you play in your life. The star? Or the understudy? I hope not the understudy! Too many people already play that part. You don't want your wardrobe to announce that you're the extra who plays that character named Forgettable Woman In An Oversized Gray Cardigan. In the theatre, your costume can tell us who you are before you even speak a line. Does yours telegraph to the world that you're the administrative assistant on the lowest rung of the ladder? A tired geography teacher who can't find a road map out of her style crisis? Or the star of your own show, whether you're on Broadway or way way *way* Off?

Hint: It's your life, so it's your show! What do you want your role to be? The sky's the limit. And your budget, of course. Nevertheless, you can make up in creativity what you lack in cash.

Remember this: In your own closet, you are the Master of Ceremonies. It is your kingdom, your production, your stage. It should reflect your choices and decisions. Your preferences, not your mother's, your sister's, or your best friend's. Do you want to be the sidekick in a kitchen-sink drama? Or the star in a sparkling Noel Coward wit-fest of a play? It's your wardrobe's casting call.

- **Think theatrically. What does a** costumer use to make a character unforgettable? Glamour. Drama. Color. Shape. The contrast of light and dark, rough and smooth, familiar and surprising.
- **Color choices on stage mean** something. Blue is the color of hope and communication. Black is the color of power and authority. Red translates as passion, sex, danger. Green is calm, serene, a deep mystery. White can be innocent—or the favorite hue of ghosts. Can you find a color theme in your clothes? Hint: In D.C., black is a given, gray is a tropical depression. Find your closet's favorite accent colors. Discard the ones that don't flatter you.
- **The shape of a garment** can hide flaws and create illusions: the suggestion of a nipped-in waist, the impression of broad, strong shoulders, that long, leggy silhouette. The right shape can work to camouflage a tummy or thighs. A well-constructed dress or suit may cost a little more, but it is invaluable. Illusion is your *almost* magical ally.
- **The contrast of light and dark** colors can also work together to enhance your appearance. Use dark colors where you want the focus to recede, light where you want pull the eye. Consider those dresses that employ colors strategically to create an hourglass frame, or simple shifts with dark side panels. Illusion can come down to accentuating the positive by illuminating your pluses, shadowing your minuses. Put the light where you want it to shine.

The Essential Full-Length Mirror

Your outfit consists of more than the three-quarter glimpse you see every morning in the bathroom mirror under those horrible fluorescent lights. That's more like a funhouse looking-glass. No wonder you don't look in that mirror for very long.

- **A full-length mirror and good light** are essential for a complete and honest appraisal. Unless you have a three-way mirror, you also need a hand mirror so you can see what you look like from behind. It may come as a complete shock. Yikes!
- **Remember, theatre dressing rooms have** wonderful mirrors outlined in lights. They have to, because they're made for people about to walk out on stage in the glare of the footlights. You need a great mirror not merely to see your flaws, but also to view your *possibilities*.

Borrow a few tricks of the theatre trade, and discover your best you!

FORTY-FIVE

*L*ACEY SAGGED AGAINST Vic and held on tight. It was the longest weekend in the world.

Saturday afternoon, on the heels of submitting her official statement to Detective Lamont, she filed her first teaser story about the Centipede, master spy and master costumer, while she was still at the theatre in the upstairs lobby.

To Yuri Volkov's immense relief, Broadway Lamont finally hustled a shackled Nikolai Sokolov out of the theatre an hour before the donor gala started. Volkov explained to his well-heeled guests, DeeDee told Lacey the next day, that the police crime scene tape that still covered the costume shop and the wardrobe closet was just a surprise sneak preview for Kinetic's next show. Lacey was sure he'd come up with something.

Perhaps *Crime and Punishment, the Musical!*

After the D.C. Metropolitan Police released the newspaper crew, Lacey met with Claudia at *The Eye* and filed her official story, with more background material. Mac worked it over on the spot and sent it to *The Eye*'s production department to remake the front page for the Sunday edition. Lacey's story ran at the top, above the fold:

SEVEN DEADLY LENINS HIDDEN IN A HEM

Trujillo had never come through, so neither did his double byline. That byline now read: LACEY SMITHSONIAN, OBSERVER STAFF WRITER. Not "Fashion Reporter." Not "Ghettoized Chick Stuff Writer." There would be more stories to come. If Sokolov had his way, they might never end. But Lacey felt sure the Feds would soon shut down his channels of communication.

Hansen had caught a picture of Nikolai Sokolov on his feet, handcuffed and shackled, gazing ardently at Lacey. In his melting makeup and battered matador costume, he looked like the saddest of sad clowns. Mac ran it with a simple cutline:

MASTER SPY NIKOLAI SOKOLOV, ALLEGEDLY "THE CENTIPEDE,"
COLLARED BY EYE STREET OBSERVER REPORTER
LACEY SMITHSONIAN

The picture wasn't so bad, she thought. *At least I wasn't on my butt this time.*

Hansen's other photos from the theatre sale, including frames of Lacey and LaToya, ran on the inside spread, as well as archive photos from the original production of *The Masque.* And to Lacey's horror, there was that alarming photo of her, the one Hansen had taken at the Baltimore HonFest. She was in Stella's full crazy-lady makeup, looking like a diva in a bad Italian film, face to face with the late Amy Keaton, Sokolov's last victim. *I hope.*

It seemed a bizarre coincidence that her front page story would run in the same edition with the feature article she'd written on Nikolai Sokolov's costumes for the LifeStyle section. Claudia added her own Publisher's Notes to both stories to link them together. She also allotted much more space for photos than usual. She promised to run everything past the paper's attorney later Saturday evening, but Lacey knew Claudia usually got her way.

The sensational news about the Centipede was online by midnight Saturday night. Claudia promised them a big celebratory dinner for the following weekend. Unless they were all in jail.

Late that same Saturday evening, Lacey and Vic rendezvoused at Vic's offices with the Troika, Gregor, Olga, and Marie. Turtledove joined them, bringing with him the Red Dress of Death from the Undisclosed Location. Lacey brought out the jeweled mask and set it on the conference table next to the dress.

She knew she didn't have much time before the first early print edition of *The Eye Street Observer* would hit the newsstands. She didn't know how much later the call would come from agents of the US government. And who? Vic's money was on the FBI. Gregor said it might be some agency they had never heard of and that officially did not even exist. Whoever they might be, they would want to scoop up the sparkling crimson items she held in her hands. She would have to turn them over eventually, she knew, but not before she had more photographs, many more. And more time to explore them, with her eyes and hands. And her EFP.

Vic, Turtledove, and Lacey took hundreds of photos of the dress, the mask, and the medals, with Olga stage managing. Backwards and forwards, upside down and inside out, in room light, floodlights, and black light. The photographs would make it very hard for anyone to deny this costume had ever existed.

Wearing white gloves, they carefully examined the remaining seven Lenin medals, the scratches and symbols, the marks on the back of each medal. Comparing them with the symbols on the mask, there were seven matches. Gregor said it was some kind of code in Cyrillic characters.

"I don't know why I didn't see it before," Gregor said.

"We didn't have the mask before," Olga sniffed. "The key. I told you the ciphertext was useless without the key." She was still irritated that she wasn't in on the takedown of Nikolai Sokolov.

Marie did not faint that evening, but she did go into a light trance. She told them afterwards she had seen the ghost in red, the spectre who had appeared to her at the theatre. This time, the crimson ghost saw Marie and she no longer seemed lost. She smiled and waved goodbye.

The team knew more than they did before. Still, they did not crack the code. Olga said there was simply not enough of it, they needed more text. Another problem was there seemed to be many more coded names on the mask than the seven medals in the dress could account for. The Kepelov siblings said they would consult a friendly cryptographer with photos of the code for further enlightenment.

Perhaps Nicky Sokolov was right about there being other trophies. Other dresses. It would have to be a puzzle for another time, as Lacey pointed out to them, because newspaper deadlines wouldn't wait.

And thank God, she thought. *Nothing would ever get written without a deadline.*

ೞ

Sunday afternoon, Lacey's story appeared to come as a complete surprise to several government agencies, including the CIA and the FBI. When reporters asked them, Lacey included, they had few comments to offer on the record. The dress and the mask and the mythical Centipede were simply "fantastical" and "a conspiracy theory" and "complete fiction," but they clearly still wanted to get their hands on them. One agent told Lacey off the record, "I don't know whether to arrest you or hire you. You got a resume?"

Late Sunday evening, Broadway Lamont informed Lacey that the Feds had finally wrangled Sokolov into their custody after he had spent twenty-four hours in dead silence in the company, and at the expense, of the Metropolitan Police.

"They showed up 'bout fifteen minutes after this Sunday morning surprise of yours hit. But it took 'em all day to get through the paperwork. I made sure they dotted every last I. And by the way, where are those damn Lenin medals, that red mask, and that red devil dress? I don't recall you coughing up those crucial items of evidence at the theatre when I rode in with my cavalry."

"Gee, Broadway, my mind just goes blank when I face a killer. Sorry. I hope they're not lost. But if the dress ever somehow made its way into your custody, how soon would the Feds get their hands on it?"

"Get something out of a D.C. police evidence locker? And me, cooperate with the Feds? You know how 'cooperative' I can be. Could be a long damn time. And you know that Centipede character, you just be glad he's locked up, wherever he is now. He's on the late-stage obsession scale where you're concerned."

"I am glad. Believe me."

She and Vic worked out an immediate delivery via the reliable Turtledove to Detective Lamont, whereby they could truthfully tell the Feds, whenever they called, that they had no idea where the dress and the mask were now, and they should probably contact the Metropolitan Police for further information. After all, the police had secured the crime scene.

A Sunday afternoon tweet from the White House said *The Eye Street Observer* was a "failing newspaper" and the story was merely "fake news."

In response, Claudia Darnell wrote a fiery online editorial that Sunday evening, defending freedom of the press. She pointed out that Smithsonian could have died unmasking the Centipede, and had certainly risked being abducted, simply while doing her job as a reporter, her job to bring the truth before the American people.

LaToya Crawford was alternately annoyed at not being included in the story and relieved to know she had been spared from putting a dress with that bloody history on her body. And she swore to Lacey that such a thing would never happen, now or in the future, because LaToya Crawford was absolutely done with "funky old clothes" that "God knows who" had worn before her.

"But it seems to me," LaToya complained, "I'm out some serious cash here. I bought that damn dress fair and square!"

"Have you still got the receipt? When they're finished with it, if they ever are, you might get it back. Maybe you could have my buddy Kepelov broker a deal for you, with the Spy Museum or someplace like that," Lacey suggested.

"You think? Or you think the damn Feds are going to squabble over it till the cows come home?"

"Maybe you could send them a bill."

"If I do, I'm going to mark it up a thousand percent. For my pain and suffering. And for yours too, Smithsonian."

Yuri Volkov continued to deny to reporters that he knew anything about Nikolai Sokolov's homicidal history. "I thought the bad things that happened were coincidence," he was quoted.

No one believed him, but no one was arresting him yet. However, because the D.C. police had waited until after Kinetic's opening night to question him, Volkov gave Broadway Lamont complimentary tickets to the show.

Volkov called Lacey that afternoon to complain about the "inconvenience" she had caused him. Following her Sunday stories in *The Eye*, his new show, *The Turn of the Screw,* would be in such demand that the run would have to be extended. They would have to find an alternate space to present their next production. He was also afraid the theatre would be put on the Washington, D.C., Spy Walking Tour.

"With busloads of people taking pictures. Of my theatre!"

Life's a bitch, isn't it?

She had the feeling he wasn't really complaining. He just wanted to talk to someone who understood what had happened.

Finally, that Sunday night in June, she and Vic were alone on her balcony. The evening was sultry, warm but comfortable. Fireworks were bursting into the air across the Potomac River at National Harbor.

"What's the occasion?" Vic asked.

"There never is an occasion with them. It seems to be random. But I feel like a celebration tonight. Unfortunately, darling, we're out of champagne."

Vic winked and stepped inside to assemble some margaritas, since the Russians had depleted the bubbly supply.

Lacey's landline rang. She stepped through the French doors, but something made her stop. She didn't want to answer one more phone call tonight. She let the machine pick up, and she listened as it recorded.

"Lacey Blaine Smithsonian, this is your mother! I called your cell phone but you didn't answer. Isn't your cell phone working? Call me. I saw the newspapers. It's even in the Denver paper."

Rose had an online subscription to *The Eye*, much to Lacey's dismay. Her mother's voice continued.

"What on earth are you up to now, Lacey? Russians? Killers? Theatre people? And you didn't call me? Your sister and I could have helped you, you know, we could have flown to Washington, we've done it before when you needed us. But no, you never call. I'm so disappointed. But that's not why I'm calling."

"You could have fooled me," Lacey said aloud to the answering machine.

"That picture of you in the newspaper: Is that an *engagement ring* on your finger?!"

ACKNOWLEDGMENTS

A SMALL THEATRE takes a large role in *The Masque of the Red Dress,* and the theatre has played a major role in my own writing journey, nearly as large as journalism. So it was a joy to revisit the stage, albeit in fiction, in this book. Many of the new characters here, even the comically self-involved playwright, come from my fond experience of being a playwright in the world of Washington, D.C., theatre.

There are so many people who inspired me when I was a budding playwright. I must acknowledge Ernie Joselovitz and the Playwrights' Forum, and Source Theatre, Pat Sheehy and the late Keith Parker for their support of my plays. I am also grateful to Lloyd Rose for her theatrical insights and her keen critic's-eye view of stagecraft and actors.

The Masque explores some of the similarities between theatre and espionage, particularly relevant with Russian foreign agents in the news. While current events have been an inspiration, my fascination with Russia probably began with the Russian history class I took in high school from Professor Reg Holmes. Reg always presented fascinating and funny stories (he made Peter the Great hilarious), and he once brought an authentic Russian (in squeaky shoes) to speak to our class. Reg has also been a wonderful sounding board for my questions and is in no way responsible for my own mistakes.

And last but never least, my husband Bob Williams, my partner, my rock, has been my constant companion, not only through this book, but in this entire publishing endeavor. You have my thanks, my gratitude, and my love.

ABOUT THE AUTHOR

ELLEN BYERRUM is a novelist, a playwright, a reporter, a former Washington, D.C., journalist, and a graduate of private investigator school in Virginia. Her Crime of Fashion mystery series features a savvy, stylish female sleuth named Lacey Smithsonian. Lacey is a reluctant fashion reporter in Washington D.C., which she lovingly refers to as "The City Fashion Forgot." Two Crime of Fashion novels, *Killer Hair* and *Hostile Makeover*, have been filmed.

The Woman in the Dollhouse is Byerrum's first suspense thriller. She anticipates exploring Tennyson's continuing odyssey in a sequel. Byerrum has also penned a middle-grade mystery, *The Children Didn't See Anything,* the first in a projected series starring the precocious twelve-year-old Bresette twins. Her plays, *A Christmas Cactus* and *Gumshoe Rendezvous*, are published by Samuel French Inc. and written under the pen name Eliot Byerrum.

Follow Ellen Byerrum on Facebook and Twitter and on her website at **ellenbyerrum.com**. Her books are available through booksellers and Amazon. Her YouTube Channel was inspired by her readers' interest in the "Fashion Bites" penned by her Crime of Fashion protagonist, Lacey Smithsonian. These short YouTube videos offer Byerrum's practical fashion advice and humorous style commentary:

https://www.youtube.com/channel/UCvnouFJdA-CTxwzY25gsncA

THE WOMAN IN THE DOLLHOUSE

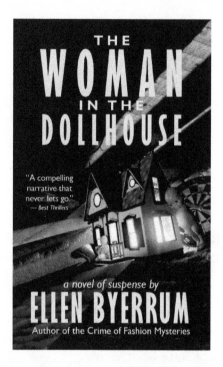

If you lost your memories,
would you lose your soul?

"In my memories, my eyes are always green."

A young woman finds herself recovering from a devastating accident in a memory research facility near Washington, D.C., in Ellen Byerrum's new psychological suspense thriller. Her eyes are brown, not green as she remembers; her memories are broken. Years of her life are blank, yet she remembers being two very different women, one called Tennyson, the other Marissa. If she can't trust her memories or her own eyes, who can she trust? To save her sanity and her life, Tennyson begins a secret journal between the lines of Homer's *Odyssey*—and her own harrowing odyssey into madness and murder. Lost among her shattered memories, can she find her true self?

Readers of Ellen Byerrum's Crime of Fashion series are sure to enjoy her first non-series novel of suspense, available now from Amazon and your favorite booksellers.